I0831643

CITY OF PROMISE AND LIGHT

MATES OF GODS AND FAE BOOK ONE

M.B. ATKINS

TRIGGER WARNINGS

Hello my friends,

Before you begin this book, please be aware that some scenes may not be suitable for some readers, and there are scenarios that could be triggering for you.

PLEASE FIND THE LIST OF TRIGGER WARNINGS IN THE BACK OF THE BOOK OR ON THE AUTHOR'S WEBSITE.

BOOK PLAYLIST

1. Grave Digger - Matt Maeson
2. IDK You Yet - Alexander 23
3. Dear Emily - Emei
4. I Found - Amber Run
5. Blow Me (One Last Kiss) - P!nk
6. Reflections - MisterWives
7. Not Today - twenty one pilots
8. Come a Little Closer - Cage the Elephant
9. Two Face (Dark Version) - Jake Daniels
10. Trouble - Cage the Elephant
11. Vagabond - MisterWives
12. This Feeling - Alabama Shakes
13. Scaredy Cat - DPR IAN
14. Dear Emily - Emei
15. Witchcraft - Vian Izak & Juniper Vale
16. Bad Side - Jake Daniels
17. Problems - Jake Daniels
18. Stranded - RudyWade & LeGrand

19. Birthday - TEN

20. Bad things - Rayland Baxter

21. God - Jake Daniels

22. Monster / I Fall Apart - Karl Michael

23. Cringe - Matt Maeson

24. I hope you know what you're doing - KiNG MALA

25. It's Alright - Mother Mother

26. Polarize - Twenty one pilots

27. Cold Little Heart - Michael Kiwanuka

28. Breaking Down - Ailee

29. Devil Like Me - Rainbow Kitten Surprise - Seven + Mary

30. Body And Mind - girl in red

31. Bilgewater - Brown Bird

32. The Otherside - Jake Daniels

33. in the darkness - mxmtoon

34. Afraid - The Neighborhood

35. You Don't Know me - Ben Folds

36. Come Here and Leave Me Alone - Alexander 23

37. Woo - Ash-B

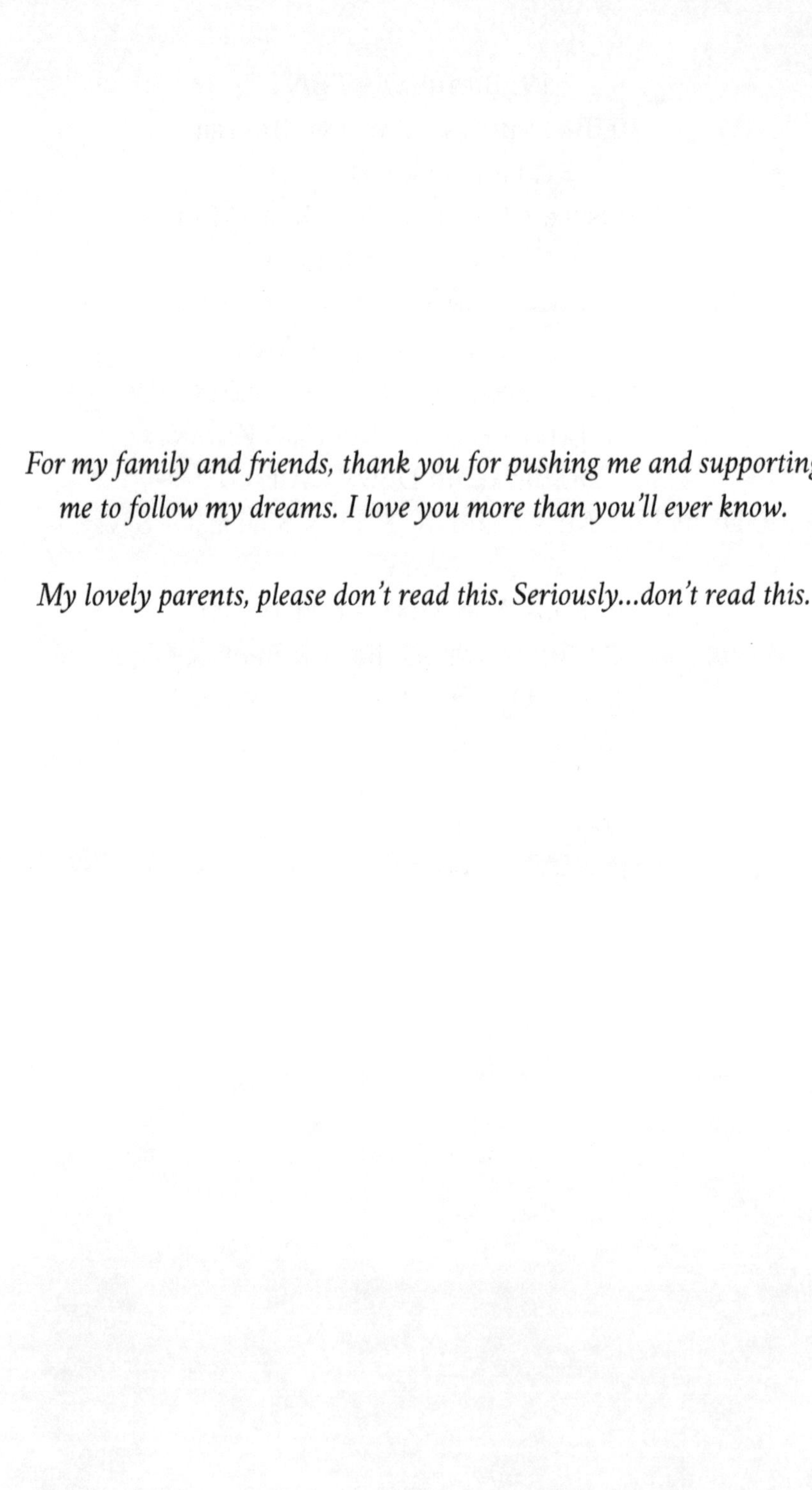

For my family and friends, thank you for pushing me and supporting me to follow my dreams. I love you more than you'll ever know.

My lovely parents, please don't read this. Seriously...don't read this.

BLURB

I knew I wasn't normal.

I was an outsider—different from my family and friends.

But I ignored it, suppressed my otherness, burying it in the depths of my mind.

They never told me I was cursed, that my tainted blood flowed stronger than the rest of my family's.

Until I met them.

Samian Olokas, a silver-haired fae with unusual eyes, and Ambrose Farra, an alluring deceiver—a master manipulator masked in charm and elegance.

They were two sides of the same coin: a guardian in disguise, a beast veiled by magic.

Was this really a promise of light—of hope?

Or was it a tragedy waiting to happen?

CHAPTER 1
SYBIL
TWENTY YEARS AGO - AGE TWELVE

The light was quickly fading; the sky was a sea of red and purple. The sun looked as if it were melting into the mountains behind us, while the moon steadily rose, and we were *completely* lost. Frustrated, I sighed as I closed my eyes, a feeble attempt to calm my nerves. I knew I shouldn't have listened to Micah when he said he knew the way back home. He had just turned eleven a week ago, and though we were cousins, he felt more like a brother, even more so than my own. My brother was eighteen years older than I, always leaving me behind to be with his friends. At least until he left for a job two years ago, which didn't help our shoddy relationship. But Micah and I did everything together, which included getting lost in the middle of a forest.

Thirty minutes had come and gone since we passed the red-leafed maple tree, which I had been using recently as our marker for the path home. However, Micah swore that the tree we needed to look for had bright orange leaves instead. Though

I knew it was bullshit, I reluctantly trailed behind him, even when everything in me warned against it.

Another five minutes passed before I stopped, refusing to make another move. Noticing my faltering steps, Micah turned to me, his sky-blue eyes flickering with anger at my defiance. Annoyed, I scoffed and rolled my eyes at his tight expression. The air had a chill to it tonight, and it seemed to grow colder every minute. It matched the growing disregard I felt toward him and his *habit* of refusing to listen to me and of constantly getting us lost. My instinct was never wrong. Even when we were so lost that we couldn't tell which way was up, I could always find my way back home. It was as if my soul somehow inherently knew the way.

"We need to turn around, Micah," I huffed, tired from our endless trek. "This is obviously not the right way, and we need to get home before the sunlight is completely gone." If we stayed out any longer, I just knew we would be grounded for days, maybe even weeks. I would *not* let that happen just because this *boy* felt the need to prove himself.

Micah narrowed his eyes, his face twisting into a sneer. "What do you know? You're just a girl."

My lips curled at the insinuation of his words. "I'm not the one who got us lost," I reminded him.

His ridiculous remark had me bristling. Micah loved playing the expert navigator when it was just the two of us, all because Uncle Tommy took him camping and hunting a few times a year. Yet, I was always the one who got us *out* of these woods and *out* of trouble.

"Fine, if you think you're so smart, lead the way, *Sybil*." His voice oozed sarcasm and contempt.

Taking a moment to gather my bearings, I pushed aside his boyish attitude. Turning my back to him, I took a deep breath, filling my lungs with the cold, refreshing air. I looked around the pasture we had somehow stumbled upon, the trees thinning out into a small field. It was mostly flat and freshly mowed with a few small trees and bushes scattered here and there, except for the steep hill a few steps away that led back into the forest.

Taking another look around the field, the encroaching darkness made the air grow heavy and charged, as if eyes were watching our every movement. The hair along the back of my neck stood at the shift in the air, the peaceful quiet of dusk forgotten as I scanned the dark woods we had left behind.

"Well, come on, Sybil. What are you waiting—"

A twig snapped in the distance, cutting off Micah's voice. I held out my hand to stop him from moving forward, alarm thrumming through my veins. "It's probably just a cow or something," Micah said, stuttering. His narrowed eyes shifted nervously along the tree line.

Our grandparents owned over fifty cows, letting them roam through the fields and woods behind our parents' homes. The cows, however, weren't the only animals that wandered through the area. Living in the quiet countryside of the North Georgia mountains meant seeing all types of animals, like deer and raccoons, but it also meant that bears and other predators prowled the area.

"The cows are usually in their stalls by this time," I whispered, my pulse quickening at the shadows that looked as if they were moving ever so slightly.

Looking behind me, I met Micah's wild gaze. He must have seen them too. Holding a finger to my lips, I prayed he would listen to my gesture to stay quiet. Though I wasn't completely positive if it was a trick of the eyes, my gut told me that something was watching us from the forest. Whatever it was, I was sure it wasn't soft or cuddly.

Not wanting to turn my back on the forest and the thing that was watching us, I gently urged Micah to trudge back to the steep hill, hoping the distance between us would be enough to make it lose interest.

We had only made it five painstakingly slow steps when more twigs snapped, this time sounding closer. The birds nesting around us flew into the sky, squawking.

Flinching at the sudden flutter of wings, Micah and I stopped, frozen by fear. I reached a shaky hand to Micah, pulling him close enough to whisper without disturbing the still air around us. "When I tell you to, run as fast as you can down the hill. Don't stop, okay?" I could only hope the panic in my voice couldn't be heard.

The pounding of my heart drowned out Micah's response. I knew our parents wanted us to stay away from these woods, always saying how dangerous they could be, especially around dusk and throughout the night. They told us tales of creatures that lurked in the forest, waiting for their next meal. We never gave it much thought, always laughing it off as over-embellished stories. The only danger our escapades led us into was the bulls or cows, protective of their calves. Never had we run into anything that we couldn't get out of, and because of that, we had let our guard down. We became reckless in our childhood, craving for adventure.

Silently cursing myself, I took another small step back, preparing to tell Micah to run, when a low growl came from behind us. Icy terror pin-pricked its way down my back, making my steps waver. The chatter of the woods fell quiet. Not daring to make another move, I stood rigid, listening closely to the sound of the deafening silence around us.

Whatever was surrounding us was large, and it was still

stalking us along the darkened treeline, refusing to make itself known.

I looked at Micah, his face blanched, his eyes wide with fear. His chest rose and fell rapidly while he was staring at the shadows along the trees. Taking a shaky breath, I looked back to the field, hoping to find a place to hide and wait until the animal moved on, but all I found was open space. Even the tall grass lay too flat against the earth for us to hide in.

I swallowed hard, and my chest tightened. This was all my fault. I should have forced Micah to follow me when we saw the red-leafed tree. I should have dragged him, kicking and screaming, down that trail instead of staying quiet. Instead, I had ignored the voice in my head urging me to turn back.

More growls filled the air, pulling me out of my thoughts, and my stomach twisted. There was more than one animal stalking closer toward us. My eyes snapped to the clearing ahead at the rustling of grass and leaves. Horror washed through me as a pack of snarling wolves padded out of the treeline, fanning out to surround us.

Circling closer, their growls and barks broke through the thick silence as they lunged at us, snapping at our feet, pushing Micah and me closer together. We stumbled back, panic making our movements careless and frantic.

Behind me, Micah quietly whimpered and grabbed hold of my shoulders, his grip tightening as he quickly pulled me closer to him. Startled, my back knocked against his chest, the abrupt movement making me feel unsteady on my feet. Feeling the rapid beating of his heart, I reached for his hand, hoping to lend him some type of strength that I wasn't sure I felt myself. Before my hand could touch his, the world around me tilted.

Using my balance against me, Micah pushed me forward, channeling all his strength to send me closer to the hungry wolves, all so *he* could make a run for it down the hill behind us. My mind blanked. Grunting, I fell hard on my knees, still unable to fully grasp what had just happened. I shook my head, my mind whirling with confusion. My body shook, and my throat tightened at the sound of a growl in front of me. Looking up, blood drained from my face when a large red wolf stalked closer, snarling and baring his yellowed teeth.

Somewhere in the distance, Micah yelped, his voice laced with pain, the sound sharp and deafening. Though the need to search for him was so strong that it almost choked me, I kept my eyes glued on the wolf in front of me, not daring to look away. Releasing a slow, shaky breath, I stood, keeping my movements unhurried, though uncontrollable trembling racked my body, making it hard to keep my knees from buckling.

I swallowed nervously as the wolf lowered his body onto his haunches, preparing to make his attack. Time seemed to slow, and my mind raced, trying—and failing—to find a way to escape. All I wanted was for this to be a terrible dream that I would soon wake up from, finding myself tucked safely in the warmth of my bed.

I inhaled sharply, my eyes widening and my muscles tensing, when the wolf leaped into the air. His mouth opened; his sharp teeth ready to rip into my flesh.

The feel of needles threaded through me, the sensation painfully running down my arms. My blood hummed from the pressure building inside of me. Squeezing my eyes shut, I lifted my hands, a small and feeble attempt to protect myself, and screamed. My hands warmed, and a light shone brightly around me. The pressure that had built erupted from me, the adrenaline making my body feel numb. This was it; I knew that there was nothing else I could do to stop the razor-sharp pain that was about to strike. Pain that was taking…a little *too* long to feel?

Slowly, I opened my eyes before widening them, surprise skittering through me as I found the wolf lying on the ground, whining and struggling to stand on his feet. Looking around me, I found the other wolves frozen in place, their ears lowered, and their hackles raised along their backs. They watched me with deadly intent, waiting for their leader's next move.

When I looked back at the wolf in front of me, he finally stood on shaking legs. I instinctively lifted my hands again, mentally preparing myself for another attack. The wolf stood still, quietly assessing me with defeated eyes, like I was the predator instead of him. As if finding his answer, the wolf's ears lowered as he turned and slowly limped back into the dark forest, his pack following close behind him, one by one.

Dazed and confused, I turned to where I had last heard Micah. Making my way down the hill, I found him sitting on the ground, rubbing his bloodied knees. He winced when his teary gaze met my icy glare. A small part of me felt relieved that he wasn't hurt, but that was a *very* small part. The rest was angry, and that anger thrummed through my body, making my hands itch with a force that felt ready to burst from me.

My lips curled into a sneer as I watched Micah quiver on the hard ground, watching how his shoulders seemed to curl inward under the weight of my scowl. Fear and guilt glimmered in his eyes when I took a slow step forward. Every thought in my mind evaporated. All except for one.

Make him pay.

I wanted to make him suffer for offering me as bait to the wolves, abandoning me to save himself. My body felt hot, outraged by how much of a coward he had become in that moment. All I could feel was a burning desire to make him face the same betrayal that clenched my heart tight within its grip.

The touch of his sweaty palms pushing me forward was burned into my memory, along with the cold from the ground seeping into my knees as he ran. My anger quickly morphed into fury and disgust. Again and again, the memory replayed in my mind, and my breath grew heavier. My body felt as if it were pulsing. It was like I was on the outside looking in, watching someone else take command of my body, moving it forward, closer to Micah's hunched form.

Lost in the memory that consumed me, I stretched my hands to him, eager to make him feel every bit of the misery he deserved, when a soft voice called to me from the darkened woods.

My hand stopped, still outstretched, while I listened to the voice, deep and calming, murmuring a plea for me to stop. Melodic and harmonious, the words wrapped around me in a language I couldn't understand but felt in my very soul. An overwhelming sense of stillness washed through me, calming the rage that had consumed my every thought. The peacefulness that followed brought me back to myself before I could do something I'd regret.

Looking to the shadowy woods, I found nothing but darkness staring back. Closing my eyes, I took a deep, calming breath, relaxing my shoulders, letting the tension drain away along with the last of the violence that purred inside me. I looked down at my hands, clenching them into tight fists as the feeling of pin-pricking needles eased.

Taking another glance at the forest, I shuddered with a breath. Cutting my gaze to Micah, my eyes must have still shown the promise of violence from moments before. His face paled as I stared at him. "Asshole," I muttered, turning my back on him, leaving him on his own. Sniffling, Micah stood and quietly followed behind, his steps timid as the trail twisted and turned, weaving us to the main road.

Retracing our steps back to the red-leafed maple tree, I paused, reaching out to the tree, letting my hand graze softly against the rough bark. The tree felt like home; the calmness it gave me was warm and welcoming. The deep burgundy leaves rustled as a cold breeze wrapped around us, as if it were celebrating our safe return.

Taking another moment to savor the peace, I pushed the anxiety I felt about returning home deep inside and continued down the path.

Reaching the street, I ignored the sound of Micah's wavering steps. The air was thick with the weight of his guilt. I almost hoped he choked on it. I would never forget tonight, or the way he pushed me toward the wolf and abandoned me. I knew he wanted my forgiveness. I knew he wanted me to turn to him, to tell him that everything was fine, and that I understood why he had done it. But I refused to give him the words that he was hoping to hear as I kept walking, leaving him standing alone in the middle of the darkened street.

My steps grew heavier when I reached the pathway to my house. The porch light was on, casting my father's menacing shadow onto the steps below. My heart pinched with guilt, knowing how disappointed and angry my father would feel after learning just how close to harm's way Micah and I had been.

Stepping into the light, I paused at the bottom of the steps, my palms clammy as I fidgeted with the hem of my shirt. Too ashamed to meet my father's glare, I stared at the ground, swallowing hard.

"Where were you?" He demanded quietly. His voice was low and unnervingly calm.

My face grew hot from the shame I felt from getting caught. "Micah and I went into the woods," I muttered softly.

The silence stretched between us; my father's stare seemed to burn right through me. Seconds passed, but it felt like an eternity until he finally said, "Do you not remember what I told you about being in those woods?" My mouth dried at the shakiness in his voice as he fought to keep his temper at bay. The heat of unshed tears stung my eyes, but I could only nod, too afraid to even whisper a response. "Did anything happen?"

I looked up at him then, his question sounding so soft that I was sure I would find relief gleaming in his gaze. I felt certain he would be overjoyed to see me home, safe and sound. But it wasn't relief or joy that I found reflected there. The same sky-blue eyes that all the men in my family shared narrowed and filled with contempt. My heart dropped when I took in the wariness carved along the lines of his jaw. His body was stiff with uncertainty and distrust as his icy glare studied me.

I swallowed down the knot in my throat, shock needling down my spine, which quickly turned to dread. I tried to find the words, any words, that would make him stop looking at me like I was a stain that he needed to remove.

"I said, did anything happen?" He bellowed, his words echoing into the darkness behind me.

Flinching, I stumbled through the events of the evening: what happened with the wolves, how they stopped their hunt, and how they returned to the woods after the bright light shone around us. With every word, my father's body shook more and more with restraint, his eyes filling with venom. My voice quivered as I tried to explain how everything was okay, that Micah and I were fine, promising him we would stay away from the woods.

Tears blurred my vision at the thought of never seeing my maple tree again, but I kept repeating my promise and my apology, though anguish tore through me. I would give it all up just so he wouldn't look at me like I was nothing. I would promise anything just for warmth and love to return to those soft blue eyes once again.

After finishing my apology, I looked back to the ground, the weight of his stare feeling too heavy, and silently waited for my punishment. His anger was so potent in the air that I could taste it, like fire and smoke, choking me with its presence.

The moments stretched until my father finally stood, his shadow towering over me, making me shrink back. Giving me one final huff of disappointment, he turned to the front door, muttering words too quiet for me to understand.

With timid steps, I followed him, walking straight to my room. Softly closing the door behind me, I flinched at the loud thud of my parents' bedroom door slamming shut, the force making the wall shake. Sliding down against the door, I sat on the floor, pulling my knees close to my chest while I listened to the angry murmurs echoing through the quiet house. Why did I ever think this was something we could get away with? Exploring the woods, following the deer trails along the streams, it all seemed so easy to do—until it wasn't. Softly, my head thumped against the door, the tears I held back finally falling free.

I wasn't sure how much time had passed when I wiped my swollen eyes and changed into my pajamas. Sliding into my soft bed, I wrapped my thick blanket around me, forming a tight cocoon. I breathed in deeply a few times and finally drifted off into a fitful sleep filled with sounds of terrible growls.

As the sun rose the next day, I opened my tired eyes. They felt puffy and full of sand as thoughts from the previous night barreled through my mind. The hungry growls still haunted me, and the fear and anger that seemed to possess me made my chest feel tight. That anger had warmed my veins; I had felt powerful, like I could do anything and everything, and the world was there, ready for the taking.

Yet, I felt sick at the same time. It was so easy for that power to morph into something else, something darker, almost deadly. A shiver shot down my spine at the memory of how I had lost all control of my body as I stalked closer to Micah, wanting nothing but revenge, or how my mind seemed to whisper three words repeatedly.

Make him pay.

A sniffling sound caught my attention, pulling my thoughts back to the present. Sitting up, I strained my ears to find where the sound was coming from. Another sniffle came from outside my door, and I recognized the sound. My mother.

I quickly pulled the covers off me, and my heart dropped. Silently, I cracked open my door enough to make out the shape of my mother hunched over the kitchen table, her ashy brown hair falling around her face. The sight broke me in two as those soft and delicate hands covered her face while she wept alone.

Afraid to move, to make any sudden noise, I rested my body against the door frame while I watched my mother's listless form, my heart tearing into pieces.

A strange silence echoed through the house as I pieced it all together. The disgust that resonated from my father, my mother crying alone, and the silence that seemed to ring throughout the house.

My father had left, abandoning us, and it was all my fault.

CHAPTER 2
SYBIL
PRESENT DAY

I was so fucking tired. I sighed heavily, leaning forward until my forehead rested against the steering wheel. Like always, the weekend had vanished too quickly, turning the already dreaded Monday into a new beast of its own.

Twisting the keys, the car's quiet rumble died, along with the cold air blasting through the vents. The humidity of summer and the tall glass buildings of downtown Charlotte made the city almost unbearable, even at eight in the morning. Within seconds, the air inside quickly warmed under the heat and sun, and goosebumps prickled down my arms at the sudden temperature change. Honestly, it was a good motivator that not-so-gently helped me muster the energy to drag myself out of the car to walk the grueling five minutes to my *lovely* job at The Metropolitan Times.

Mondays had never bothered me before. They were just another day of the week to me. At least until my company began forcing its employees back into the office five days a week, when Covid suddenly became non-existent. Though we increased our client rate by over thirty percent during the last year, while doing the work of three people. The CEO decided we weren't going "above and beyond" and stuffed everyone into an office with *very* limited space. I could still remember the irritation that burned down my spine when I read his email delivering the "good" news.

So now, every morning I sat here, forcing the heat and humidity to push me out of the car toward a job that celebrated the overworked and underpaid—not that I was bitter or anything.

I leaned back, sweat gathering along my brow. I closed my eyes, inhaling deeply, holding it as I slowly counted to ten. Just as my lungs started to burn, I quickly released my breath, letting the resentment flow out of me. Reaching over, I grabbed my bag from the passenger side seat and stepped out of the car, slamming the door shut with my hip.

Apprehension weighed me down as I leaned against my car, eyeing the empty sidewalk leading to The Metro. Excuses to skip work ran through my mind, though each one sounded worse than the last. I could always go with the tried-and-true head cold, but rescheduling my meetings far outweighed any benefit of calling out, especially with my meeting later today with my boss, Evan.

Today was our weekly check-in. Normally, our meeting was for client updates, but today I was using it to discuss my potential promotion, and I had never been more stressed.

Six months earlier, I started taking on extra work to learn the ropes for the Senior Sales Specialist role. For months, every task they gave me had been specifically for the senior role. Tired of being taken advantage of, I'd decided that enough was enough. I spent countless nights practicing my speech with my partner, Liam, to prepare for this meeting. I was ready for this, and today would be the day that I finally got promoted. Hopefully. Though I wasn't sure what would happen if my plan didn't work.

Swallowing, I pushed down the doubt that was quickly rising. I couldn't think about that now.

Pushing off my car, I started down the longest walk of my life. Fumbling with my keys, I locked the car, the sound reminding me of the past weekend. My lips curved into a small smile at the memory of Liam's silent grumblings after giving me his keys so he could carry a heavy box. I clicked the lock button repeatedly, each beep earning me an icy glare, while I conveniently looked away, unable to hide my growing smile. It thoroughly annoyed him, and to my delight, I made it a habit. I chuckled as the memory warmed my heart and put my mind at ease. I clicked the button a few more times as I left the parking lot.

Crossing the intersection, I was digging my office badge from my bag when I slammed into what felt like a stone wall. I grunted, my badge dropping to the ground, and I looked up, rubbing my nose to see what the hell I had bumped into. The crosswalk and streets had been empty seconds ago, and no cars were close by, yet standing in front of me was the tallest man I had ever seen. He must have been over six feet.

My eyes widened, and I gaped at him. His skin was sun-kissed, and his long, straight silver hair was partly tied up in a braid. Shock colored his eyes, making them so vibrant and full of mystery; one a dark cobalt and the other a deep emerald green. A faded scar just below his right eye ran along his high cheekbone, though it didn't take away from his attractiveness. If anything, the scar added to it. It was all I could do to push down my desire to reach out and run my finger over it. Shaking my head, my cheeks heated, and I moved to take a step back.

"Shit, I'm so—" I gasped, my words cutting off when he wrapped his arm around my back, pulling me into his chest as a car sped past us. Horn blaring, the driver cursed out the window, yelling for us to move out of the way.

Stunned, I blinked at him while he watched the car continue down the road, his lips dipping into a frown. Keeping his arm tight around me, my hands twitched against the soft fabric of his shirt, and I could feel the hard lines of muscle along his stomach. The heat in my cheeks grew swiftly, moving down my neck. "I'm so sorry," I breathed, bristling under his hold. "I wasn't paying attention to where I was going! Are you okay?"

His eyes cut back to me, confusion filling his expression as his gaze ran across my face. His face paled before slipping into a mask of cool indifference. "Yes," he said softly, meeting my eyes again. He quickly removed his hand and stepped back, putting space between us. He swallowed, the muscle along his jaw feathering when he nodded his goodbye and walked away. Disoriented, I turned, watching him walk along the sidewalk and disappear around a corner.

Another car honked, quickly snapping me back to reality. I silently cursed as a line of vehicles waited for me to move from the middle of the road. Picking up my badge, I jogged to the other side of the street, giving the drivers an apologetic wave. Once I was out of the way, I turned back to take another glance at the empty sidewalk behind me, an unsettling feeling gathering in the pit of my stomach.

My badge still in hand, the rest of my walk remained uneventful as I swiped in to get into the elevator. I scrolled through my phone while waiting to reach the ninth floor, pushing away any thought of the man along with the unnerving feeling that had followed our interaction. Walking to my desk, I greeted my team, unpacked my bag, and turned on my computer.

"Did you hear?"

Looking over to my teammate, Jason, I saw his wide brown eyes bright with excitement, his lips curled into a mischievous grin. My heart leapt at the buzz of some office drama and gossip. "No, what happened this time?" I asked hastily, dropping into my seat, rolling closer to him.

Looking around us, Jason leaned closer to me, his smile growing wider. "Shawn is putting in his two weeks' notice today," he whispered, amusement coloring his voice.

"You're joking!" I gasped. "Last I heard, he was only looking?" Popping my head up, I looked over to Jason's computer, disappointed to find it empty.

"He got the call last night." Jason glanced at Evan's office, making sure the door was closed. Leaning even closer, he whispered, "Apparently, a competitor got in contact with him a few days ago, offering him a lot more money and a senior-level position. He accepted it immediately."

Excitement bubbled in my chest. Shawn had been stuck in a similar situation to mine, getting senior-level assignments with the promise of promotion for months, but this could help my case when I talked to Evan later today. Shawn's leaving would create a giant hole in our group.

"Good, he deserves it!" Honestly, all of us did. "Wow, I can't wait to hear about Evan's reaction! He is going to flip." Shawn would be the third person to give their notice this month. The other teams were also going through something similar, and the petty part of me was living for it.

"Oh, Evan is going to lose his shit, I'm sure," Jason said, chuckling while turning back to his computer. "I really can't wait for my turn. I should hear back in the next couple of weeks." Jason sighed heavily. I could hear the weariness in his voice. We had all been working hard, but Jason worked the hardest out of our entire team, spending hours of overtime just to finish his assignments on time while checking over the group's work to make sure they were done properly. "Have you started looking yet?"

His question pulled me out of my thoughts. I told the team months ago that I was looking for another job, but finding the strength to even start had been difficult lately, with all my energy being spent on my latest projects. "I've been looking, but I haven't applied anywhere yet," I said, leaning back in my chair and facing my computer. "I updated my resume last week, but I don't know if I want to be in sales anymore. It's too demanding, and I just don't have the patience for it now." I paused, nervous about what Jason would say to my next words. "I'm still considering a few options, but I'm talking to Evan today about being promoted to the senior role," I muttered, hesitating on the last few words.

Even though I had been set on asking Evan for the promotion, I couldn't picture myself working in that position long-term. However, figuring out what type of job I wanted to do instead of sales had been difficult. I knew what I wanted the job to include: financial security, the freedom to set my own work schedule, and not feeling so stressed that I was like a chicken running around without a head, with the world caving in around me at every moment of the day. I wanted a job where I wouldn't feel so exhausted by the end of the week that I couldn't do anything except sleep the weekend away just to have enough energy to wake up and do it all over again. But what job listing had that in its description? It also didn't answer what type of job I wanted.

Turning back around, Jason nodded, giving me a thoughtful

look. "You'll find what you're searching for. I think the most important thing is to just find a way out. The senior role may look good on paper, but they will take everything you can give and will still ask for more. Once you're out, though, you'll be able to think more clearly and find what makes you happy."

Nodding, I considered his words, not knowing what else to say. I'd been so frustrated with myself lately. Finding a job I was interested in has been rough, and the thought of going through another interview process made me want to lie down and never get back up again. Who in their right mind would want to start a months-long process over again?

My phone vibrated, and the sound interrupted my thoughts. Looking down, I blinked at my brother's name lighting up across my screen, my face pinching with apprehension. My brother, Caleb, and I were not close. Being eighteen years older than me, he had already left the house when I was born. He loved telling me how much of a surprise I was and how much stress I had put the family through. He would stop himself from going into too much detail, but I knew the words he wanted to say. I knew how much he blamed me for our father disappearing on us when I was younger; his eyes glowed with animosity each time we spoke, especially during our mother's funeral. Stopping myself from drowning in that thought, I tapped the screen, sending Caleb to voicemail. Whatever he had to say, he could say it there.

Looking back at my computer, I waited for it to load. Guilt coiled around me, and I wondered if I had acted too hastily by sending Caleb to voicemail. The last time we had a civil conversation was at our mother's house during the holidays the year before she died. He had spent the entire time telling me stories about his son getting his first girlfriend, his latest trip, and his two promotions within the last year alone. Then he waited, eager for me to fill him in on all the gritty details of my life. Just the memory of it made me grimace.

It was easier and better that we didn't talk. Not that there had been no progress in my life. It had just been slow. Liam and I had been together for ten years, and I had just convinced him we should be engaged a year ago. Liam was kind and considerate, but he didn't like change, which was fine. Marriage had gotten too expensive anyway.

Sighing, I kept my eyes on the clock, watching the time slowly pass by. I spent the entire day feeling agitated and restless, especially after Caleb kept calling throughout the morning. Unable to focus on my work, my mind wandered to the man I ran into on the street. I thought of the way he studied my face, paling before quickly leaving. He didn't say much, but I had the sinking feeling that he knew me, though from where, I wasn't sure.

After Shawn put in his notice, the entire team quietly celebrated his new job, but apprehension gnawed its way through me as my meeting with Evan loomed closer. My body felt jittery with nervous anticipation, and my mind kept reeling on all the possible outcomes. I spent days convincing myself that the best outcome would be to get the promotion and a nice pay bump. The worst would just be Evan saying no, unless he fired me, but I doubt that would happen with everyone leaving.

Steeling myself, I straightened in my chair. I would not allow him to say no. I had made my case thousands of times in my head, each time sounding better than the last. I went over my argument with Liam every day last week, just to make sure I didn't miss anything. I *was* ready for this meeting.

CHAPTER 3

SYBIL

The morning slowly rolled into the afternoon, and my heart rate increased with every hour until two p.m. finally came. Opening his door, Evan called me into his office, and my heart jumped. Standing, I looked over to Jason, giving him a forced smile while I took a deep breath.

"Good luck!" Jason whispered, giving me a thumbs-up.

Releasing my breath, I returned the gesture and walked to Evan's office. As I crossed the hallway, my body felt heavy with those few steps, the nerves making me feel slightly sick. I questioned whether I should back out of my plan and pretend that the extra work I was receiving did not bother me.

When I walked into the room, I couldn't help but notice how tidy and unfeeling Evan's office was. Everything had its place, yet there was nothing personal about any of the items that sat along his desk or along the glaring white walls. I made my way to the chair in front of his desk and sat down, smoothing out the wrinkles on my shirt. Evan held up his finger, signaling that he needed a moment to start our meeting, and I internally rolled my eyes at the disrespect.

Two minutes passed, and I tapped the edge of the desk with my fingers, my frustration building with every second. Clearing his throat, Evan finally looked up from his computer. His short blonde hair almost looked blue from the screen's reflection. His dark brown eyes were bored and indifferent as they met mine. "Alright, let's go ahead and get started. Do you have anything you would like to discuss first?" he said, glancing back at his computer.

My heart thundered as I reached for the words to bring up the promotion, but my mind panicked and had other plans. "How was your weekend?" I said awkwardly, my clammy hands rubbing back and forth against the tops of my pants.

Evan's confusion was written all over his face when he looked back at me, his eyebrows pinching together. "What?"

"Your weekend? How was it?" I asked slowly, my inner self crying at the uncomfortable embarrassment of it all.

"It was fine. Now, do you have anything that you want to cover for today?"

Clearing my throat, I steadied myself, focusing on the clear glass paperweight that sat on Evan's desk. "I do, actually. I want to discuss the senior role I've been working toward." There, I said it. It was out, and now I could breathe and hope for the best.

With a soft sigh, Evan leaned back in his chair, letting his hands clasped together on top of his desk. "I'm not sure that this is the right moment to have this conversation, Sybil."

"I think this is the perfect time to have this conversation," I said quickly, ignoring the way Evan's words made me want to cringe. Pausing, I raised my eyebrows, waiting until Evan blew out a breath, gesturing for me to continue. I gave him a small smile. "I've been working on several senior-level projects for a few months now. Each project ran smoothly and finished ahead of schedule. The customers are extremely happy with my work and have been giving me constant positive feedback. Also, since some of the team is leaving, I know there are a few senior roles opening, and I believe—no, I *know*—that I have shown how well I can do the work." Breathless, I stopped and waited for Evan's response.

Slowly nodding his head, Evan looked down at his desk, considering my words. He leaned forward in his chair, his mahogany eyes meeting mine again. "I agree, you have done a good job with those assignments. However, I'm just not sure you're at the right level for the senior role yet," Evan said flatly.

Blinking, I sat there, confused about whether I had heard him right. I fought to process what I'd just heard. I had been doing the senior-level assignments for six months now, so surely I must have misunderstood. "I'm not sure I'm following. Haven't I been doing the work of a senior for a few months now?" I said, my throat feeling tight.

"Yes and no. You may have been doing the assignments, but there's more that goes into the senior role than what you have currently been doing. That's where I don't think you've quite reached that level for me to consider a promotion for you at this time."

"Okay," I paused, clenching my hands into fists so tight that I could feel my nails digging into my skin. "What else goes into that role, then?" I asked, my tone cold as my anger slowly began to build.

Frustration flashed across Evan's face, and he exhaled. "A senior needs to be active within the group. I don't think you have been active enough."

"I disagree with that," I shot back. "I think I have been more than active enough to prove myself. I'm constantly meeting with my teammates, helping them with all their questions or solving any client issues they run into. I'm part of several group chats to keep up with the team and how everyone is doing."

"Sybil, you have to consider—"

"No, there's nothing to consider," I interrupted with a scoff. "I have been doing this role for months now. Several of the senior staff have already left, leaving those positions open. I've been doing the work, and I've been doing it well. I *know* I deserve this promotion, and I know *you* know it too. Saying that I'm 'not active enough in the community' is just an excuse, Evan."

"Sybil, I think you need to take a moment, calm down, and really consider this," Evan said slowly, his voice steady though I could see his shoulders tensing.

My body felt hot, and my hands shook. The buzz of the fluorescent lights seemed to grow louder, the sound sharp and piercing in my head. My heart raced, and the walls were closing in on me, making it feel like there was no oxygen in the room. All I wanted to do was scream, yet the only thing I could do was swallow down the anger that was ready to explode and clench my fists even tighter, letting my nails cut into my palms.

Breathing, I calmed my shaking voice enough to speak. "My stance doesn't change. The facts of how hard I've been working does not change." I straightened, hoping to hide my nervous fidgeting.

Evan released a quick exhale. "I guess I should have led the conversation with this then." He paused, typing something on his computer, only glancing back at me after he typed the last word. "The company has decided that it is best to part ways with you."

Stunned, tension raced down my spine. "Excuse me?" I

asked, my voice sounding higher than I wanted it to. "What do you mean they have decided to part ways with me?"

"We, as a team, have considered your work, and while we do recognize that you have been an asset to the company, we don't believe that you're a good fit here culturally."

I gritted my teeth at Evan's composure, the coolness that laced his tone. "Culturally? What does that mean? I get along with the team well, and I have received no negative feedback," I said uneasily. "Why wasn't this brought up before today's meeting, and why did you wait until *after* you tried to convince me I wasn't right for the senior role?"

"We have been meaning to have a discussion with you regarding this." Evan shrugged. "But, with this conversation, it's clear that we wouldn't have been able to reach an understanding even if we had tried. I'm sorry, but my hands are tied."

"So, I'm fired? Just like that?" I asked, my stomach twisting.

"We are sorry to see you go, but yes. As of today, we are parting ways. Your account has already been deactivated. Please drop off your badge at the front desk."

I scoffed, but I couldn't move. I was dumbfounded, and my mind was blank as I sat there, trying to process what was happening. After all the work I'd put into this company, the hours of overtime, staying up through the night making sure that all my assignments were completed on time, only to be fired. Time seemed to slow as I stood and made my way out of Evan's office, letting the door slam shut behind me, the sound echoing through my mind.

Still unable to process, I made my way to my desk. Jason turned to me, opening his mouth to speak, but faltered at the last moment. I could only imagine what he saw while I slowly packed my bags.

Finally, after gathering my things, I looked up at my team

and found everyone huddled together, watching me with concerned faces, waiting for me to tell them what had happened. "I've been…I've been let go," my voice cracked on the last word.

"What!"

"Sybil!"

"Are you serious?"

My team's comments jumbled in my mind, and I could only shrug at them. I walked away then, leaving their questions unanswered, too dazed to even piece together a string of words.

Dropping off my badge, I waited for the elevator, pulling out my phone. Three more missed calls from my brother flashed across my screen. Groaning, I tucked it away and ran my hands through my hair. Releasing a shaky breath, my eyes burned with tears. I did not know how or what I was going to tell Liam. I knew he was waiting for my call, eager to hear the good news, but I couldn't even think of the words to explain that I had lost my job instead. My throat felt tight, and I fought off the wave of nausea that made my stomach turn.

My mind was in a fog when the elevator arrived, taking me to the first floor. I didn't even remember leaving the building or the walk to my car. As I entered the parking lot, I pulled my keys from my bag and looked up, finding two men waiting for me. The hair on the back of my neck rose, and goosebumps pebbled my skin. Warning bells silently rang through my mind, cautioning me to stay away.

My steps wavered when I recognized one of the men, and I went rigid. The man I ran into this morning stood leaning against my car. His tanned face was bored, like he didn't want to be there, and his head was tipped back, looking toward the sky. The other man huffed, checking his watch, irritation making his jaw clench. He was devastatingly beautiful with pale skin and short, dark auburn hair. His square jaw was sharp, and his body was tall and lean. He wore a fitted black suit, showing off his athletic frame.

Taking a step back, a loose piece of concrete crunched under my foot. Wincing, I closed my eyes, cursing myself for not paying closer attention to my surroundings. I slowly opened my eyes again, glancing between the two men. The one I ran into earlier still leaned against my car, the lines of his face hard, his lips thin. The other flashed a wide smile, his ocean blue eyes brightening as he made his way to me.

"Ah, finally! I've been waiting for you!" he said, clapping and rubbing his hands together. His voice was bright and confident. "I thought I was going to have to send Samian to drag you out," he chuckled, rumbling deep from his chest.

I glanced at the man I ran into earlier today, Samian, and gave him a small, hesitant smile while I considered my options for running and whether I could get away. The muscles in my legs flexed, readying for my escape. As if reading my thoughts, the man in front of me shifted, placing his hand on my lower back, cutting off my escape route. My body went rigid under his touch, but the man gave me a slight nudge, guiding me to my car.

"Don't worry, darling, we're not here to hurt you. Just the opposite. I'm here to offer you a job." The man's smile turned almost wolfish. "I heard you might be needing one soon."

He gave me a wink, and suspicion flooded my veins. I narrowed my eyes at him, a small, quiet laugh escaping my lips. "What makes you think I need a job?" My boldness and the confidence in my voice fell flat and unconvincing. His smile turned sharp, and he gave me another low chuckle. "I *know* you need a job, Ms. Sybil Hart, seeing how you were just fired from yours."

My gaze snapped to him, my body tensing. My stomach twisted, and those silent warning bells rang louder in my head as I tried to move away from his hand. How could he have possibly known that I was fired? It had only been minutes since it happened, and I had told no one except for the people on my team. Word couldn't have gotten out that fast. The panic must have shown on my face, because the man held my shoulder softly, the ocean in his eyes warming as he gave me a supportive smile.

"I apologize; I should have introduced myself first," he said, his voice calm and earnest. "My name is Ambrose Farra. Your brother should have told you about me?" Cocking his head slightly, he raised an eyebrow.

"He called, but I wasn't able to speak with him," I murmured, nervously shifting my shoulder away from his hand.

"Ah, I guess that explains it. My employee here, Samian, ran into you this morning. I've been looking for you for a long time, and now that I've found you, I would like to help you," Mr. Farra explained, pausing for a moment to consider his next words. "I want to offer you a job, one that I think you might enjoy."

"Right," I said slowly. The sickness in my stomach seemed to grow, and those bells grew ever louder. I wondered if it was from the men's sudden arrival or if the bells were warning me to keep my distance from *him*. "Why have you been looking for me? Have we met before?" Swallowing, I shifted back a step.

Mr. Farra's smile grew wide, his eyes gleaming with something that I couldn't quite make out. "We have, once, many years ago. Though I don't think you would remember. But," he paused, raising a finger. "We can talk about that later. Now, as for the job, financially, you'll be paid more than you were making at—what was it called? Ah, The Metropolitan Times."

He kept his voice light and whimsical, his features growing more animated with excitement. "I can also guarantee that our benefits will be better. I really believe you'll be much, *much* happier working for me." Mr. Farra paused, his eyes turning cold as they cut to Samian. "Don't you think so, Samian?"

My brows pinched together at the sudden tension that filled the air. Samian's calculating eyes met mine, studying me, though he kept his face devoid of any emotion.

"Of course," Samian said blandly. "But who's really to say?"

I felt Mr. Farra's gaze turn back to me, but mine lingered on Samian a moment longer, hoping for a clue whether I could trust this man, but Samian's hard face gave nothing away. I glanced back at Mr. Farra, and his smile sharpened. "So, what do you say, Ms. Sybil? Will you join my company and me?"

The warning bells persisted but were quickly overtaken by nervous excitement. I felt like I was stuck on a roller coaster, being fired, then almost immediately being offered another job. This would make telling Liam about today much easier, and getting paid more would be nice. However, my father's words from long ago echoed through my mind, reminding me that if something seemed too good to be true, it usually was.

"What would I be doing for this job?" I asked slowly.

"We can work out the kinks later," Mr. Farra said with a wink. "Nothing too crazy, though. Nothing illegal, if that's what you're worried about."

His playful voice felt oddly calming, soothing my nerves and silencing those warning bells. My shoulders dipped, the tension melting away. Considering his offer, I knew I should be listening more closely to the warning my instincts were screaming, but the ease that warmed my body made it hard to focus.

Shaking my head, I straightened my back, bracing myself. "I

think I'll need a little more information before agreeing to this, Mr. Farra," I said, keeping my tone flat.

Mr. Farra's smile faltered, but he nodded his head, mulling over my response. His gaze grew sharp, and I swore I could feel the air around me grow colder. "Alright, fine. Take two days to consider my offer. In the meantime, I'll put together some information on what you'll be doing in this position. How does that sound?"

Carefully, I studied Mr. Farra, taking in the deep blue of his eyes. I tried to figure out if this was really happening, to see if he was some type of scam artist, but that calming feeling rushed through me again, and the thought slipped away from my mind. Taking another moment to think over his offer, I quickly nodded my head. "Fine, I'll take the two days to consider it, and I'll let you know *after* you give me more details on what I would be doing."

"Great! I'm glad we could come to an agreement, Ms. Sybil." He smiled warmly. "I'll be seeing you soon. Oh, and please call me Ambrose." Winking, he reached out his hand.

Timidly, I shook it. I started to pull away when a sharp pain laced through my hand, traveling up my arm. Gasping, I pulled my arm back, clasping my hand against my chest. My gaze cut to Mr. Farra, but his eyes gave no indication of the pain I had just felt. Instead, he turned to Samian, who had finally moved away from my car. Looking down, I inspected my hand, unable to find anything wrong. My brows pinched, and my heart thumped hard in my chest.

"Well then," Mr. Farra said, lowering his head, his bright eyes searching to meet my gaze. "We will see you soon."

I stayed silent, only nodding to show that I acknowledged his goodbye. Seeming satisfied, Mr. Farra turned, clapping Samian on the shoulder as he walked past me. Samian's jaw clenched, but he lingered, focusing on the hand that I kept close against my chest. His face remained emotionless, but something close to concern flickered in his gaze, though it quickly vanished. Before I could say anything, Samian left me in the parking lot alone, following Mr. Farra down the street.

As soon as they were gone, I jumped in my car, locking the doors behind me. With my keys still in my hand, my arm trembled, the sharp pain still fresh in my mind. It had come and gone so fast that I almost wasn't sure if it had even happened.

I released a shaky breath and put my keys in the ignition, twisting them to turn on my car. Taking a moment to calm my racing heart, I put my car into drive and headed home to face Liam. I still wasn't sure what I was going to say, but I would figure that out when I saw him.

CHAPTER 4

SAMIAN

Reluctantly, I stood by Ambrose while he watched Sybil drive by from a small alleyway, hidden from the street. He carefully masked his irritation when she refused to accept his offer right away, but now, his face froze in a sneer. Clenching his jaw, Ambrose wiped the imaginary dirt from his suit coat. My chest swelled with pride when she rejected him and his touch. It wasn't something that happened often to Ambrose, if at all. To see it happen in real time, I had to push down the laughter that fought to escape.

However, my thoughts drifted back to Sybil, and my amusement was doused with a concern that was steadily growing. I knew as soon as she shook Ambrose's hand that he had used his power to unbind the magic flowing through her veins, releasing the constraint of the power she'd possessed since childhood. Even as a child, her magic was incredibly strong. So strong that I was exhausted by the time I finished binding it. With the strength of her power, I knew she would feel the side effects of it soon.

I had always been curious about why her magic was so strong. When her father, John, found me all those years ago, he described it as a family curse. He explained that with some generations, there were children who could do peculiar things that normal children couldn't. It had caused a lot of strife for those children and their families. The people of that time believed magic to be the work of the devil or demons, and most of the time, it ended with the child's early death. However, no matter how hard they tried to wipe the bloodline clean, the magic never left the family.

When I worked with John and studied his blood, the magic was barely noticeable, so small that I almost missed it. But Sybil's magic? I could never forget how I stood, blinking at the screen, shocked by the strength of her power and how it grew each time we tested her. She was still too young to be aware of what we were doing, only being a year old when we first tested the strength of her magic. We continued until she was three, when her family started noticing how different she was. That's when John begged me to bind her magic, to hide what she was becoming.

During those two years, I slowly realized just how much her magic resembled the queen's magic, the way it warmed and shone so bright as it hummed like a melody of hope. When I told Queen Cassia about Sybil, she merely shrugged it off, muttering that her magic wasn't unique to Nemos, the upper world. But the hard glint in her sky-blue eyes told me there was more to Sybil's story and that I should stop asking questions.

After Sybil turned the corner, Ambrose's lips thinned. He rolled his shoulders and cracked his neck. "Well, that didn't go as well as I had hoped," he said with a sigh, wiping the hand that touched Sybil on his vest. "Go and make yourself useful, Samian. We need to make sure she accepts my offer."

"Right," I murmured with a sigh. "We wouldn't want my talents to go to waste."

Ambrose whipped his head toward me, but I gave him a passive wave of acknowledgment, accepted my dismissal with a quiet glee, and turned to walk away. My part in his plan was making sure John heard of Sybil's offer if she didn't outright accept it. Ambrose was counting on John's inability to stay away from Sybil, to 'randomly' show his shameless face after disappearing twenty years ago. It would be the perfect little push Sybil needed to accept the offer. Tension slowly crept up my neck; Ambrose had something else up his sleeve, something that he wasn't—

"Oh, and Samian?" Ambrose interrupted my thoughts. I turned back, keeping my face bored as Ambrose gave me a half smile, his head tilting to the side with a promise of violence flashing in his eyes. "Try not to mess this one up, yes?" His gaze was sharp, and his tone was flat. Even in the form of a question, it was hard not to miss the threat hiding beneath his unbothered facade.

The past few assignments I'd been a part of all ended in failure. At least, in Ambrose's view. Not so much in mine. It was my life's goal to bring him down, to make him suffer the way he deserved.

I bowed dramatically, making him growl, and slowly backed away. Straightening, I turned my back on him, earning another deep grumble. I let my magic loose, letting it gather around me. The world momentarily fell away before snapping back into place, transporting me directly to John's front door. Exhaling, I rolled my shoulders, preparing myself to knock. My last interaction with John wasn't a pleasant one.

It had been several years ago, right after John had met a few members from a group of heretics called The Harbingers of the

Divine. The heretics believed magic was the source of all evil in the world, a blight spread by the demons and devils of the land and, potentially, other worlds. The humans of this realm mostly shunned them for being too fanatical in their purpose. When magic had been forgotten, the Harbingers acted in secret, silently hoping that one day they would finally rid the Earth of magic. Nothing but empty hopes filled their heads. I even told John as much, but amid his desperation, he became foolish, to say the least. Though that was a problem for another day.

Today's problem was that I now must knock on this pathetic iron door, the Heretics swore kept beings like me away, and face the man who had abandoned his wife and children instead of cherishing and protecting them, all without killing him. I could only imagine what Ambrose would do if I ended John's miserable life before he could talk to Sybil. The thought of it slightly amused me, but I had promises to keep. Killing John would only interfere with that.

Studying the iron door, my blood warmed, and I clenched my fists so tight my knuckles turned white. Taking another moment to convince myself not to break it down, I knocked and waited for John to answer.

The door swung open. John's eyes widened, stunned to see me standing on his porch. Scrutinizing him from head to toe, a jolt of pleasure calmed my growing temper as I saw how haggard he looked. Before his time with the Heretics, John was a man who stood tall and proud, his frame lean but strong. However, it seemed that time had not been kind to him. His once chestnut hair was now faded to a peppery gray, and his pale skin seemed to sag. His cold sky-blue eyes were sunken, with deep, dark circles beneath them. A smirk threatened to form, but I composed myself, keeping my face neutral.

"What are you doing here?" John grumbled, a sneer curling his cracked lips.

"Is this how you greet an old friend?" I asked innocently, cocking my head to the side.

John hissed, then opened the door wider and stood aside so I could enter his home.

"Nice place," I mused, taking in the mess around me. Stepping into the living room, I noticed piles of clothes strewn across the chairs and floor. Looking into the kitchen, I saw containers stacked on the table and counters, still filled with stale food. The house was older and run-down. The brown-paneled walls made the home feel dark and unpleasant. My nose crinkled in disgust.

Coming up behind me, John clipped my shoulder as he walked past, settling into a chair at the kitchen table. "What do you want?"

Pushing down my growl, I took in his bloodshot eyes. It looked like he hadn't slept for days. "Research not going well?" I asked calmly.

Narrowing his gaze, John's lips curled into a snarl. "What do you want?" he repeated, quickly losing patience.

Turning to the desk beside me, I studied the books and notes littered across it. "I'm here to tell you that our good friend, Ambrose, has found her and offered her a job to work for his," I paused, trying to think of a better term for what we were, "company."

Picking up a book that was flipped open, I skimmed the page, recognizing John's handwriting. The page detailed his recent bloodwork, and I took a quick note of the results. The percentage of magic in his veins hadn't changed, but something else was new about their findings.

John quickly jumped from his chair and snatched the book

out of my hands, slamming it to the table beside us before I could figure out what he had found. I shifted my focus to him, my anger rippling through me when John bared his teeth at me.

"What do you mean he found her?" he growled, his breathing becoming uneven. "Weren't you supposed to keep her existence a secret?"

Sniffing, I looked away, taking a moment to calm myself and remember my purpose for being here. I noticed a wooden frame on the wall; a picture of John and Sybil when she was a child, sitting beside a fire. His arm rested on Sybil's shoulder, pulling her closer for the camera. She held a stick, her attention focused on the marshmallow at the end that had just burst into flames at the exact moment the shutter clicked. Her face was filled with delighted shock, widening her eyes, and her smile was so broad it took over most of her face. Guilt hung heavy on my shoulders, and I forced myself to look away.

Cutting my gaze back to John, my face hardened. "I don't know how he found her," I said, glowering, my voice filling with contempt. "I have kept my word on remaining silent regarding her existence. But it seems that someone gave away our little secret."

Taking a slow, deep breath, I released it, pushing that anger further down so I could keep up my mask of indifference. Still, it made my blood boil to hear the accusation in his voice. I had been investigating how Ambrose managed to find her for years now; however, my search remained fruitless. But when I found out who told Ambrose about Sybil, I swore I would tear them apart, limb by fucking limb.

Returning my focus to John, he stood in front of me, as still as a statue except for his chest, which started swiftly rising and falling. His composure shattered as he turned, picking up the book and throwing it against the wall while roaring a curse. Raising an eyebrow, I glanced at the book that now lay flat on the floor, but returned my stony gaze to John. Bringing his palms to his eyes, John fell into his chair, resting his elbows on his knees while he fought for air, gulping down steadying breaths. Keeping a close eye on him, I gathered my magic, transferring myself to the book. Reaching down and wrapping my fingers around the beat-up leather, I stuffed the book into the hidden pocket of my jacket and quietly returned to my spot.

Clearing my throat, I found a bottle of water and handed it to John. He gingerly took the bottle, draining it in one go. Leaning back in his chair, John's head fell back, and he closed his eyes. "Did she take his offer?" He asked, his voice rough.

"No, not yet," I sighed, looking back at the picture of John and Sybil. My chest tightened with regret for the part I was playing in Sybil's fate. "She asked for a few days to think about it."

Keeping his eyes closed, John swallowed thickly. "Will she do it?" His voice trembled slightly, almost as if he cared for her.

Pausing, I ran a hand through my hair, not knowing how to answer. I wasn't sure what she would decide. I'd been observing her throughout the years, but she remained a puzzle to me. I wished I could confidently say that her suspicions would convince her to decline Ambrose's offer, but I knew all too well the power Ambrose held over those around him. An offer from Ambrose was near impossible to refuse.

Clearing my throat, I looked back at John, his tired blue eyes meeting mine. Keeping my face blank, I shrugged. "Well, now you know," I said, heading to the door. Before I stepped through the doorway, I stopped. "Sybil lives not far from here. About an hour away. Do what you want with that information."

With that seed of knowledge dispensed, I closed the door

behind me. My magic danced around me, letting the world fall away as I transferred myself to Ambrose's office. Standing in front of his desk, I watched his hand move across the paper as he finished writing a letter. Keeping my emotions hidden, I waited for his permission to speak, my fingers drumming impatiently against his desk.

"Well?" Ambrose asked, his eyes narrowing on my hands, his voice thick with resentment.

"It's done," I said calmly, though my anger was on the rise.

AFTER MY BRIEF meeting with Ambrose, I had meant to return to my room and sort through who could have given away her location. I didn't mean to return to Mide, didn't mean to find myself waiting in front of Sybil's house to check on her. But I couldn't help myself. It was like a force that wouldn't stop urging me to make sure she was okay.

She hadn't returned home yet; her cherry-red car was still missing from the driveway. Worry gnawed through me as I sat in the tree branches, hidden from the view of neighbors passing along the sidewalks with their small children clinging to their legs.

I tapped my fingers nervously against my thighs, waiting for the red glint of her car. However, after an hour had passed, I couldn't wait any longer. I was due to meet with the war general to discuss Sybil joining our *team,* though calling ourselves such was a stretch.

Forcing myself to stand, I looked to the street one last time, willing for Sybil's car to appear. Relief coiled through me, and I released a breath when I saw the red gleam of her car shining in the sun. I lingered while Sybil quickly pulled into the driveway before stepping off the thick branch. I let the world slip away until I found myself in the middle of a sea of grass and flowers in Nemos, the upper realm.

Finding a hidden door along the rolling hills of the meadow, I opened it, heading for the darkened passage that would lead me back to the palace and court rivalries. The queen had told me long ago that a time of chaos and turmoil was coming, but being the young male I was, I had laughed it off, believing it was just another one of her rambles. And now, I couldn't stop thinking of what she foretold, of the warnings she murmured in secret.

I glanced behind me, back to the grass billowing in the wind as if Sybil was already here, as if she lingered in that field, taking in the new world around her. My gut twisted at the thought of her saying yes to Ambrose's offer, of her coming here to this infectious court.

Rolling my shoulders, I gathered my strength, bracing myself for what was to come, and then stepped through.

CHAPTER 5
SYBIL

The drive back home was worse than I could have ever imagined. Usually, it was a breeze with traffic only backing up every now and then. However, today was an absolute nightmare. Soon after I drove out of the parking lot, a small headache crept up from the base of my neck, quickly turning into a massive migraine. The sensitivity of my eyes made the sunlight pure agony, and every smell made me sick to my stomach. Multiple accidents had the roads so clogged that car horns blared nonstop as they slowly merged in and out of lanes, making the congestion worse. All I wanted to do was scream.

After two hours of torture, I finally pulled into my driveway, rushing to the bathroom to empty my stomach. When I was done, I sat with my back flat against the cool tiles of the wall, letting the refreshing cold seep into my body. I took a few deep breaths to relax, hoping it would help ease my pounding head, but it only made it worse. My head swam, and the nausea made my stomach roil again.

A gentle knock on the door pulled my focus away from the pain enough to look up, finding Liam slowly opening the door. "Hey, I thought I heard you come in," he murmured, his warm hazel eyes filled with concern as he lowered himself to the floor beside me. "Are you okay?"

I opened my mouth to speak, but quickly lurched toward the toilet instead, heaving and coughing.

"Shit, I'll be right back." Leaving my side momentarily, Liam returned with two white pills and some water. His brows pinched with worry when he handed me the medicine, watching me swallow it before I gulped down some water. "Let's get you upstairs." Bending down, his caramel-colored hair fell into his eyes as he carefully pulled me to my feet.

Leading me up the stairs to our bedroom, Liam helped me change into shorts and a tee and tucked me into bed, covering me with a plush blanket. I wanted to thank him for helping me, but my eyes drifted shut before I could even form the words.

OPENING my eyes to the dark room around me, I rubbed the sleep from them. My migraine had lessened during my sleep, but a small, dull ache remained. The sound of steady breathing caught my attention, and I found Liam on the other side of the bed, his breath slow and even as he slept. Grabbing my phone from the table beside me, I turned on the screen to check the time. I groaned. It was 3:05 am, which not only meant I had slept the whole day away but also that I now had only one more day to decide whether to accept Mr. Farra's job offer. My chest tightened, and I rubbed my hand against it, hoping to ease the anxiety that bloomed there.

Not wanting to disturb Liam, I slowly sat up, set my phone

back on the table, and made my way to the bathroom. My body felt sticky with sweat from the fever I must have had. I quickly showered and returned to bed.

Relaxing my body, I stared at the ceiling, thinking back to Mr. Farra's offer. The more I thought about it, the more I couldn't shake the feeling that something was off about him and Samian. *We have, once, many years ago,* was what he said, but I had no memory of him. He also said as much, but his face wasn't one that was easily forgettable. His ivory skin, the deep ocean blue of his eyes, highlighted by his dark auburn hair—he looked like a god chiseled out of marble. No, he wasn't someone you could easily forget. Neither was Samian, for that matter. It wasn't every day that you met someone with heterochromia, especially one who looked so carelessly ethereal with his silvery moonlight hair.

However, if this new job paid more than the Metro, then it might be worth whatever I'd be doing. Sighing, I turned over to watch Liam sleep. My chest tightened again at the thought of telling him I'd lost my job, but that was a problem for tomorrow. Closing my eyes, I drifted back into a deep rest.

Morning soon came, the sunlight seeping through the blinds and waking me. I opened my groggy eyes, giving myself a small mental check. The headache was still there, though it was more of an inconvenience than the painful throb it had been the previous day. Liam was still fast asleep, and a small smile formed when I thought back to how he had taken care of me yesterday. At times, his thoughtfulness surprised me, especially because he was usually so reserved. Taking another moment to watch him, a warmth spread through my chest, easing its tightness. I gave him a small smile before I grabbed my phone and headed downstairs.

Walking to the kitchen, a shadow in the hallway caught my

eye, making my steps falter. I narrowed my eyes, focusing on the door, on the dark object attached to the window. Apprehension prickled down my back, though curiosity got the best of me, and I padded over, finding a thick envelope taped there. Pulling it off the window, I checked the street, hoping to find the person who left the envelope, but found it empty. My brows pinched together, and I quickly closed the door behind me.

Opening the envelope, a small note from Mr. Farra slid out, his sleek handwriting explaining how much he looked forward to hearing my answer tomorrow. I pulled out the rest of the documents, a mix of excitement and anxiety knotting in my stomach.

I still didn't know what I was going to tell Liam. As I flipped through the documents, a lump formed in my throat. Liam hated change, even when it was positive for everyone.

Pushing that thought aside, I focused on the documents once more, skimming through the job description. The position itself seemed simple enough. I would start as an intern and learn about the various roles at Mr. Farra's company. His note explained that most of his employees went through the same process, making it easier to identify their strengths and to place them where they would be most useful.

It still seemed off; those warning bells kept ringing in my head. But it made sense to have me shadow different positions. There wasn't a formal interview, so Mr. Farra was unfamiliar with my skills. However, that unsettling feeling kept worming its way through me, settling deep in my chest. All my attempts to look at this in a positive light fell short. Nothing about Mr. Farra finding me and offering me a job made sense. Though I would feel less guilty starting as an intern if I took the job.

Going back to the kitchen, my headache started to grow again, and nausea had my stomach flipping. I dropped the envelope on the counter, deciding to make some cinnamon tea so the spicy aroma would clear my mind and tamp down the sickness threatening to return. I pulled open the drawer to take more Tylenol when I heard Liam's footsteps coming down the stairs. Reaching the bottom, Liam looked up and gave me a soft smile, the corners of his eyes crinkling with warmth.

"Good morning," I said, returning his smile. "Sorry, I slept all day. I didn't even hear you come to bed."

"Good morning," he said, walking over and giving me a soft kiss on my forehead. "That's alright, I figured you needed it. Are you feeling better now?"

Liam put his hand against my forehead, checking whether my fever had gone down. "I still have a slight headache that's getting worse, but I took more medicine. We need to talk, though."

Liam's brows pinched together, confusion flickering in his hazel eyes.

Rubbing my chest, my heart rate sped up as I cleared my throat. "It's nothing bad. Well, I guess it could be, depending on how you see it, but I don't think it's bad," I rambled, trying to summon the courage to tell him about yesterday. I knew it shouldn't affect me so much, but no one had ever fired me before. I didn't react well to it, and it made me feel a touch ashamed.

I swallowed and looked down at the floor, unable to meet Liam's eyes. "My boss fired me yesterday," I murmured, my face heating.

The silence that followed grew heavier with each moment I waited for Liam to respond. Looking up, I could see his anxious thoughts forming on his face. His shoulders were tight, and his throat bobbed, his eyes growing distant, and I knew he was panicking.

"But," I quickly added, hoping to calm him. "I got another job offer while I was leaving."

Liam's gaze cut to mine, his face pinching. "What do you mean you got another job while you were leaving?" he asked, his tone skeptical.

I told him everything that happened yesterday, from running into Samian to finding him and Mr. Farra waiting for me by my car. Finally, I ended with Mr. Farra offering me a job, though I left out the parts where I felt uneasy. By the time I was finished, my body was so tight that it ached.

"And you think that it's a good idea to take this offer?" Liam asked, his voice thick with doubt.

Rubbing my aching head, I closed my eyes, frustration building at Liam's tone. "I think that yes, it's a bit odd, but it might be a great opportunity for me," I breathed. "You know how much I hated the Metro, and you know I wanted to get out of sales. With this position, I'll be starting as an intern. I'll be able to learn about different jobs and find something that fits what I'm looking for. I'll also be paid more. Doesn't that sound like an amazing opportunity for me? For us?"

"It sounds too good to be true, Sybil," he laughed roughly. The ridicule in his voice made my face flush, especially at the reminder of my father's saying. I could hear his voice now, telling me with a pointed look: *if it sounds too good to be true, then it probably is.*

"I know it sounds too good to be true, Liam," I snapped. "But that doesn't change the fact that I would get a pay raise *and* find something that I actually enjoy instead of wasting my time complaining about being somewhere I don't want to be."

Liam's eyes narrowed at the accusation in my tone. Wincing, guilt hung heavy on my heart. We both hated our jobs, but when it came time for him to look, Liam listed reason after reason why it wouldn't be a good idea. It would be too hard, too complicated, he would say. He would have to start back at the bottom and work his way up again. So instead of finding something new, he settled for staying miserable, content to complain about it but doing nothing to change it.

Rolling his eyes, Liam huffed and shook his head. "And on that note," he sneered, "I'm going to work."

I watched Liam walk away, disappearing up the stairs to his office. Letting out a groan, I tipped my head back, closing my eyes. I didn't mean to take out my frustration on him, but I'd hoped for him to take the news better than he had, and it didn't help that this damn headache was getting worse again.

Sitting down at the table, I rubbed my aching temples when pain sliced through my chest like a knife. I sucked in a breath, my hand pressing against the throb, which was growing sharper with every breath. My stomach churned, and the world seemed to tilt around me as black spots danced across my vision. I leaned forward, resting my head against the table just as another shot of agony ripped through me, reverberating through my bones.

I slowly stood, my legs feeling like lead. Propping myself against the wall, I wearily made my way to the couch. My chest heaved from another jolt of pain that seized my body, and I collapsed onto the thick cushions, falling into complete darkness.

SEVERAL HOURS LATER, I woke to Liam scoffing as he came down the stairs from his office. Ever since Covid, he worked from home, and unlike the Metro, his company steadily allowed employees to work remotely. I opened my eyes, my mind feeling foggy. Liam remained silent, giving me an icy glare when he walked past the couch. Irritation snaked through me, and my jaw clenched, knowing how he believed I was lazing around and sleeping the day away without a care in the world. He acted oblivious to the pain I was in—or he just didn't care.

While Liam made his lunch, I moved to my own office so we could both stew in our frustration alone. As I sat at my desk, my headache eased, and I rubbed at the memory of the slicing ache in my chest. Like when Mr. Farra shook my hand, the pain quickly disappeared, but this time, it left behind an echo of discomfort, which was concerning.

Exhaling, I opened my laptop to find information on Mr. Farra. He left out his company name in the job description, and I hoped learning more about him would help me make my decision. I also figured that if I was considering taking his offer, I should at least confirm whether his company was real. However, after thirty minutes of searching, I couldn't find anything on Ambrose Farra or Samian, though I had expected little from Samian, since I didn't know his last name. Still, the lack of information on Mr. Farra made my instincts scream for me to refuse his offer and keep far away from him.

After a few more attempts at searching for him, I sighed, frustrated with the lack of results, and closed my laptop. I looked out the window, my brows furrowing at an old beat-up Honda, its color a faded blue, parked in front of my house. I couldn't make out who was inside the car as they leaned forward, letting their head rest on the steering wheel. I watched closely to make sure they were okay, my mind flashing back to a fuzzy childhood memory of a shiny light blue car, similar to the one outside my window.

My face paled when the man stepped out of the car. He had aged quite a bit since the last time I saw him. He looked thin and shorter than I remembered, but his face and narrowed eyes were burned into my memory, still haunting my dreams.

My father made his way to my front door. I watched as he hesitated, looking back to his car as if he were rethinking this moment, wanting nothing more than to drive away. Slowly turning back to the door, he lifted his hand and knocked.

My body froze, unable to move. My strength evaporated. I hadn't seen or heard from him since he left my family twenty years ago. It had been twenty long years without a letter or phone call explaining why he'd disappeared. But here he was, standing at my door, not noticing me while I stared at him through the window of my office.

The ache in my head immediately returned, though this time, it was from tension climbing up my body. My breath quickened, my vision blurring as icy panic set in.

I heard Liam's footsteps coming down the hall. Looking into my office, Liam stopped, his eyes widening when he noticed my swirling anxiety. Whipping his head toward the door, he started, "Is that—"

"Yes," I blurted, my body shaking.

Liam looked back at me, uncertainty filling his eyes as he waited for me to decide whether to open the door or let my father walk away. Meeting his gaze, I nodded, telling him to open the door.

Taking a deep, unsteady breath, I stood and walked to Liam's side, coming face to face with the man who abandoned me as a child. "John," I said slowly, taking in the haggard figure in front of me.

"Sybil," John paused. "It's been a while." His voice was timid, his bright blue eyes misty as he studied me.

A cold, mocking laugh escaped my lips. "What are you doing here? How did you even find me?"

Clearing his throat, my father shifted his eyes between Liam and me. "I heard you were considering a job from a man named Ambrose Farra. I wanted to talk to you about it before you decide to accept it." His voice quivered, but at least he had the decency to look ashamed.

Stunned, I could only stare at him with wide eyes. Luckily, Liam answered for me. "How do you know about her offer?" he asked, his voice flat.

Straightening, John looked at Liam, fixing him with a rigid glare. "I have my ways, son." He looked back at me, his voice softening. "I know I don't deserve to be given a chance, but please hear me out. I wouldn't have come if it wasn't important."

I winced at his words, my heart breaking slightly. The job offer was important, but I wasn't. He abandoned me all those years ago, yet I had always hoped that one day he would find me again and apologize for what he did. Now, even though he had found me, it wasn't to apologize or explain why, and that realization left a gaping hole in my heart.

Dazed, I looked up at Liam, hoping he could tell me what to do. Liam grimaced slightly and exhaled. "I think you should listen to what he has to say," he whispered.

Slowly, I nodded, standing aside to allow John to come inside. Making our way to the kitchen, I offered him a drink, though he refused. John sat at the table as Liam came up behind me, his hand meeting my lower back. The warmth of it felt reassuring.

"This might be hard to hear, but you can't take that job with Ambrose Farra," John said without a hint of remorse or hesitancy.

A laugh crawled up my throat at the audacity of this man. Of course, he would come here after twenty years just to dish out commands. "How did you even hear about this?" I asked flatly.

"As I said, I have my ways," John stated, his lips thinning.

"No, that's not enough," I hissed. "You don't get to disappear for twenty years of my life and then randomly show up one day demanding that I say no to a job. That's not how this situation is going to play out."

"Look," John hesitated, his eyes flashing with guilt. "I can't go into details, but you *cannot* take this job, Sybil. Terrible things will happen if you do. I won't let you do this."

I huffed another cruel laugh at the severity of his tone. "I'm not twelve anymore, John, and I'm sure as hell not going to listen to you." I could feel my temper fraying, the heat climbing up my neck. "Your opinion has no standing here, and I'm going to take this job whether you like it or not."

"Sybil, I know my words will mean nothing to you, but please reconsider this," John begged, his breath becoming uneven. His gaze wavered, though I couldn't tell if it was anger that caused his face to flush or panic.

My body felt like it was vibrating, as if the adrenaline running through my veins sparked an emotion I had buried deep inside. I had never been good enough in his eyes, never worthy of his love, and this was just a reminder of that. My head dropped, and I squeezed my eyes shut as my body shook.

"Get out," I whispered quietly, so quietly that I could hardly hear it over the sound of my blood ringing in my ears. Twenty years. Twenty fucking years had passed, and he came here as if none of it had ever happened. My heart rate spiked, and my breathing felt erratic. My body felt like needles were pricking me all over.

Looking back at my father, he was still sitting, but his fingers were nervously tapping the table. A muscle in his jaw feathered and tension grew in his shoulders. There was a hard glint in his eyes, as if it were an inconvenience that he had to come out of hiding just to see me. Seeing him there, watching the way his eyes were narrowing like the last night I saw him, made my patience finally snap.

"*Get out,*" I roared, my chest tightening painfully at the shame I'd pushed down all these years now bubbling up. My body felt like it was throbbing, and the prickly feeling grew as it crawled down my arms and into my hands. My blood hummed with a rage I hadn't felt in years, not since that night in the forest with Micah.

Slowly, John stood from the table, his body rigid, his face muddled. He walked to the hallway, brushing past me without even a glance. Stopping at the door, my father paused for a moment, his hands clenched in tight fists, before walking out, slamming the door shut behind him.

CHAPTER 6
SYBIL

The rest of the day was quiet. Seeing my father only worsened my bad mood, along with my headache. But now it wasn't just a migraine. My whole body ached, leaving me feeling like I had been hit by a bus.

Liam gave me space after my father left. Though I couldn't tell whether it was because he was still upset about our earlier conversation, or because my father had shown up out of the blue and he wanted to give me time to process. Either way, I decided to take the job, no matter what he or my father thought. Something in my gut still warned me about Mr. Farra and his offer, but being able to test out different jobs until I found one that I enjoyed *while* getting a pay raise was an opportunity that wouldn't come often, if at all.

By the end of the day, I felt so sick that I had to take more Tylenol. Hobbling up the stairs to the bedroom, the sun was still up, so I pulled down the blinds, turned off the light, and pulled the blanket over my head, praying the pain would go away soon. This wasn't like any cold or flu I had ever experienced, and my anxiety was steadily growing. The intense pain had become more constant, making the world feel too bright and loud. Everything I touched felt like it grated against my skin. Tucking the blanket tightly around me, I took a few slow, deep breaths, relaxing my body enough that I eventually drifted off to sleep.

The next morning came fast, but I woke up feeling refreshed. My body felt strong and light, especially compared to yesterday. I wrote off that thought, telling myself it was because I was no longer in pain. Looking around my room, my brows furrowed as I noticed that the soft blue-green walls looked more vivid. There was also a crack in the ceiling that I had never noticed. Sitting up, I glanced to the other side of the bed, finding it empty. I sighed and reached over to my nightstand to check the time. It was 9:30 a.m. My heart thumped heavily in my chest, my stomach flipping. Today was the day, and I had a feeling Mr. Farra wouldn't wait long to contact me.

Stepping out of the bedroom, I quietly made my way downstairs, trying not to disturb Liam while he worked. My vision was oddly sharper, but my perception felt off, causing me to stumble down the stairs. By the time I reached the bottom of the steps, my vision had adjusted enough for me to find my footing as I walked into the sun-soaked living room.

After going through my usual morning routine, I walked to my office with a hot cup of tea, the spicy aroma tickling my nose. I sat down and started preparing questions for Mr. Farra. He didn't specify how much money I would make or what benefits he would offer, so I wanted to fully prepare for our talk, though I wasn't sure how I'd even contact him.

I had been so preoccupied with being fired and with him and Samian bombarding me that I hadn't thought about giving Mr. Farra my number before I drove home on Monday. Yet, he made it sound like he already knew how to get hold of me. He even knew where to send the envelope. He mentioned my brother, but the thought of Caleb giving him my number and address made me bristle.

After a few hours of prepping what I could, Liam finally came down for lunch. The air was thick with an awkward tension from yesterday's unresolved conversation. My father's sudden appearance hadn't helped matters either. Running a hand through his hair, Liam cleared his throat when he saw me. His eyes shifted nervously. "How are you feeling?" Liam asked slowly.

"Better," I murmured. "No headache or anything."

The conversation stalled for a moment as Liam rubbed the back of his neck. "I'm sorry about yesterday," he said softly, his hand falling to his side. "I know you are trying your best, and it couldn't have been easy to tell me about being fired. I also know that seeing your father yesterday was hard." Pausing, Liam shifted and avoided looking my way. "You might not like what I'm going to say next, but I think you should at least listen to John."

The air felt heavy from the weight of his words. I narrowed my eyes and listened to Liam, though anger slowly crept up my throat.

"You don't know this Ambrose guy, but it seems like John does. And by the way your father acted, I think Ambrose is someone you should stay away from."

"You mean, the man who abandoned his daughter and family thinks someone is bad news?" I mocked. "That's the person you're really going to listen to—the side you're going to take?"

"I'm not taking anyone's side," he said quickly, putting his hands up in front of him. "I just think that you should take a moment to think this through. John hasn't spoken to anyone in the family for years, but after hearing about this job offer, he came to talk to *you*, to warn you."

Ignoring his last point, I scoffed. "Not taking anyone's side? Liam, you should be taking *my* side," I said, my frustration quickly building. "You should be listening to *my* opinion and *my* thoughts. Not the opinion of some random sperm donor."

"Sybil, stop for a moment to think here," Liam said, exasperated. "It just doesn't make sense! Why would a random dude come to *you* with a job offer from a company that you never even applied to?"

His words struck deep, making my cheeks flush and heat creep down my neck. The tingling feeling from yesterday returned and crawled down my arms as my breath grew sharp and my muscles tensed. My father never thought I was good enough or even worth staying for, but with Liam taking his side about Mr. Farra's offer, it felt like Liam shared those same thoughts about me. My chest ached as if it were being torn in two.

I was about to respond when an odd, melodic knock sounded at our front door. Exhaling, I walked down the hall, finding Mr. Farra and Samian waiting outside. Spotting me through the window, Mr. Farra gave me a wide smile, wiggling his fingers in a small wave.

Suspicion wormed through me, making my shoulders stiffen. Hesitating, I slowly opened the door, greeting the two men with forced politeness. Mr. Farra's smile grew while Samian gave me a slight nod, his face still carrying that reserved, bored look from yesterday. Opening the door wider, I gestured for them to come inside.

Acting like he owned the place, Mr. Farra made his way to the kitchen, Samian silently following behind, his hands in his pockets. Closing the door, I cringed at Liam's low, mumbled hello when I heard Mr. Farra's deep voice eagerly introduce himself.

When I entered the kitchen, Mr. Farra quickly turned to face me, the sudden movement making me stagger back a step. "Well? Have you thought about my offer?" he asked. His eyes were bright, excitement coloring every word.

Swallowing, I glanced at Liam. His face was hard and cold, refusing to meet my gaze while he picked at something on the counter. I opened my mouth to answer, but before I could, the front door slammed open, hitting the wall behind it.

I jumped, turning to the hallway. I quickly shuffled out of the way as my father stormed into the kitchen, his face mottled and red. Grabbing Mr. Farra's shirt, my father pulled him in close and bared his teeth. "I don't know how you found her, but you need to leave. Right *now*," he growled, shoving Mr. Farra back toward the hallway. My father was shorter than Mr. Farra by a foot, and his haggard frame looked so brittle compared to Mr. Farra's athletic one.

I stood there, stunned, when Mr. Farra laughed loudly while straightening his shirt. "Ah, John! It's so great to see you. It's been so long, my dear friend. Tell me, how is your research going?" Mr. Farra raised an eyebrow, taunting my father.

My father's face paled. He stepped closer to Mr. Farra, his rage radiating from his body. "My *research* is none of your concern," my father seethed. "Leave my daughter out of whatever plot you're planning." His voice trembled with venom.

My heart jumped, my throat growing tight. "So, you do know each other?" I whispered, mostly to myself.

My father grimaced, quietly looking away, while Mr. Farra gave me a wicked grin. "We do indeed, Ms. Sybil. We met, what was it now, ten years ago?" Smirking, he eyed my father, who looked away, his face etched with the memory that haunted him. "He was working on a little project when we met, and I graciously offered my help."

"What project?" I asked, my voice trembling. What was so important that my father searched out strangers instead of turning to his family?

My question only made Mr. Farra's smile grow wider. "Hmm, I wonder. What was it again, John?" he asked, his voice mocking and wry. "If I remember correctly, it was something about you, actually, my dear Sybil."

My eyes whipped to my father's, disbelief surging through my veins. The man who wanted nothing to do with me was working on some kind of project about me? It didn't make sense. If it were about me, he should have stayed and worked on it *with* me. I would have gladly helped him with anything that he asked of me. I would have done anything to make him stay.

I waited for my father to answer, but all he could do was shake his head, shame flickering in his eyes. Done with my father's inability to answer a question, I turned back to Mr. Farra. "Mr. Fa—"

"Ambrose," he interrupted, giving me a warm smile. "Please, darling, call me Ambrose."

"Fine," I sighed, exhausted by the entire exchange. "Ambrose, I accept your offer."

"Sybil," my father breathed, his voice filled with alarm.

"I accept your offer," I said more firmly, glaring at my father. "However, I would like to discuss the specifics," I continued, glancing back at Ambrose.

Hastily walking up to me, anger etched across every part of my father's face. My pulse jumped, and my breath caught in my throat when he grabbed both of my arms, holding them tight, trapping me. "You will not take this job," he growled. "I may not have been in your life, but you will listen to me." His grip tightened.

Fear morphed swiftly to anger at his attempt to intimidate me. The corner of my lip curled as I narrowed my eyes. "Get off me," I hissed, bristling against his hold. Shaking him away, I shoved him back, and his eyes widened in shock. "You do not get to come here after abandoning me to tell me what to do. I'm a grown ass woman, and I don't need your permission to live my life."

My father lunged at me, his eyes dark, his face blotchy and red. Gasping, I stumbled back against the wall as he was suddenly pulled backward.

"Let's not do something we will regret," Samian said calmly, his deep voice protective as he held my father by his shirt. His eyes flicked to mine, my heart fluttering as I caught in the heat burning in his gaze.

Samian let go of my father, who stumbled. Liam reached out to break his fall. My father pushed Liam aside, pointing at Ambrose. "She is my daughter, and I will not allow her to work for you," he bellowed.

"It's not your fucking choice," I yelled. Everyone turned to look at me. Flustered, I could feel my cheeks turning red. "It's not your *choice*," I repeated, my voice softening.

"It may not be his choice, Sybil, but my opinion should be taken into account," Liam said quietly, as though he was trying to defuse the rising tension. "I agree with John. I don't think you should take this job."

Too stunned to talk, I could only stand there watching Liam gaze at me with a coldness I had never felt from him before. Your partner was the one person who should always take your side, yet mine so easily disregarded me, siding with the man who deserted his family—that deserted me. My heart squeezed at Liam's cold and empty eyes, looking at me as if I were no longer the person he knew and loved.

The tingling sensation returned, creeping its way down my arms. My heart raced, and I felt like I couldn't breathe, like my lungs were seizing. My body trembled, a pressure coiling through me, tightening my muscles. So many emotions swirled within me—heartbreak, rage, confusion—and their bickering quickly became too much. My skin felt too thin and my body too small.

Ambrose said something, laughing at Liam's response, but his words drowned beneath the roaring in my ears. Liam's face flushed, and he lunged at Ambrose, pulling back his arm, ready to strike. My eyes widened, and I cried out, throwing up my hands to stop him.

My hands stung as a bright light burst from my body like a powerful rush of water breaking through a dam. The light blinded me, but I could hear Ambrose's deep laughter over the shocked yells of Liam and my father.

The light faded, leaving me breathless. Terror rushed through me as I stared at my hands while the throbbing eased. The sounds of groans snapped me out of my shock. Taking in the kitchen, my breath caught in my throat. The cabinets hung shattered, some barely hanging by the hinges. The chairs lay scattered, some knocked over. Then I spotted Liam on the floor, clutching his stomach in pain.

A cry left my lips as I rushed toward him. Liam's eyes widened, fear flashing across his face at my approach as he stumbled away from me. He was afraid of me—afraid of what I just did. Stopping, I caught sight of my father crouched against the wall, holding a hand to his head while blood dripped down his neck.

Groaning, my father stood. His eyes were empty as he held

my stare. "This is what I was trying to stop. Evil runs through our veins, Sybil. Through *his* veins," he said, pointing at Ambrose. "You need to listen to me and stay away from him."

Ambrose's lips slowly curved into a devilish smile. Watching my father closely, I saw his eyes gleam with exhilaration. "Aw, come now, John," he said with a cruel laugh. "Don't be like that. Am I different? Yes, but that doesn't make me evil. If that were the case, that would mean our darling Sybil is evil as well."

Sickness consumed me, my chest heaving. I looked back at my father, my face paling when I caught the disgust reflecting in his eyes. Was this why he left me? Because I was something evil, something monstrous, a thing to be feared? I looked at my hands, hot tears streaming down my face. I could feel the hum of power inside me, could feel the wild, unrestrained force begging to be released. Choking back a sob, I slowly began to back away. Being here, seeing that fear burn in Liam's eyes, it was all too much. My chest began to rise and fall rapidly, but it felt like there was no oxygen left in the room.

Taking another step back, soft hands gently gripped my face, keeping me in place. Slowly, my eyes lifted to Ambrose's deep, warm blue gaze.

"It's okay, Sybil," he said softly, his thumbs gently wiping away my tears. "You're not what they think you are. But if it helps, I can offer you a bargain so that if you lose control again, I can stop it—stop you—before you hurt anyone else." Giving me a soft smile, Ambrose carefully pulled me into his chest, his arms tightening around me. "I can protect you and make sure that you don't hurt anyone else. Will you allow me to give you that?" he whispered against my ear.

CHAPTER 7

SYBIL

I closed my eyes, my tears flowing harder from the warmth of Ambrose's embrace. I never meant to hurt anyone. I only wanted to stop Liam from doing something he would regret. But now, seeing the terror shining in his eyes, my heart crumbled, knowing I was the one who caused it.

"Ambrose," Samian warned, "now isn't the time to make bargains. She doesn't know what that entails."

"Hush now, Samian," Ambrose cooed. "Can't you see how frightened the poor girl is? Or," he paused, his voice accusatory, "would you rather bind her powers again?"

The silence deepened, and his words echoed in my mind. My head felt scattered and chaotic. Logically, I knew what being bound meant: to be confined, restricted. But I struggled to understand how it related to this moment, to my magic, and to the power thrumming inside me.

Blinking away my tears, I looked at Samian, though it wasn't me he watched. I took in the hard edge of Samian's jaw, his narrowed eyes at Ambrose. I studied his ashen face and the scar running along his cheek. His eyes, each one so different from the other, were resentful, and his usual passive mask was gone, replaced by bitterness. His jaw clenched, as though he were contemplating his next move.

"What does that mean?" I breathed, wariness seeping into my tone.

Samian's eyes shifted to mine, softening with regret. Samian hesitated, opening his mouth to answer, when Ambrose pulled my face to his, forcing me to meet his gaze.

"It means, my darling, that this gift you were given was ripped away from you by those who claimed to have loved you. But they were afraid of you, frightened by your potential. They sought Samian to snuff out your light. Isn't that right, John?" Ambrose murmured. His hand tightened around my face, though not enough to hurt.

My father sneered, flicking his gaze to Ambrose. His bright blue eyes hardened, his lips thinning. "You know as well as I do that her *power* isn't normal," he spat, his face contorting with ire as he cut his gaze to me. "The power that runs through your veins, through my veins, only knows how to hurt and destroy. Nothing good can come from it."

"I-I don't understand," I breathed, my stomach twisting as I tried to grasp his meaning.

"Our family was cursed long ago," he said, his lips curling with disgust. "Every now and then, a generation is born with this *ability*. And every time a child showed this power, nothing but destruction came. Everything around them was ravaged, and people were hurt. Our family tried to rid ourselves of this curse by killing off those who showed these traits, but it always found its way back into a different generation."

I swallowed hard, my chest tightening as I followed my father's gaze to the destruction around us.

"I didn't want to hurt you," he confessed with a soft sigh. "I loved you, but I knew I couldn't allow you to remain as you were. After months of searching, I found Samian. Though I knew he had abilities like yours, he agreed to bind your magic so that you wouldn't be able to access them and hurt someone."

"But why couldn't he just teach me how to control it? If he were like me, he could have taught me not to hurt anyone," I stammered.

"Look around you," John roared, slamming his fist against the wall behind him. "Look at what you have done. Think of what might have happened if I had allowed you to continue as you were."

Flinching, I held onto Ambrose's shirt, hoping to hide my trembling. "But I didn't mean to hurt anyone," I cried, my voice quivering with every word. "It was an accident."

"Is that the excuse you'll use when you kill the next person you lose control around?" John asked, revulsion lacing his voice. "That you didn't mean to do it? Do you really think that this," he said, pointing around the kitchen, ending on Liam, "is something you can control?"

I looked at Liam, and my heart dropped. I saw him leaning against the wall, bewildered and shocked. When our eyes met, Liam pressed himself further against the wall.

Nausea rolled through me, and my mind blanked. My heart raced as my brain fought to convince me that this magic was something that I could control, that I wouldn't harm anyone else. But apprehension smothered any hope that formed in my mind and heart when I watched Liam's terrified gaze dart wildly between my father and me. My father was right. How could I ever hope to control something like this?

"Let Samian bind you again," my father urged, catching my hesitation. "Let him bind you and forget that any of this happened. I'll take you with me, and we can pretend none of this ever happened."

I slowly shook my head, unsure of what to say. Did I want my magic to be bound again, to pretend as if nothing had happened? To act as if this moment were nothing but a terrible nightmare? I didn't want to hurt anyone else, but to reject this part of myself felt wrong, almost unnatural. I could never forget this moment or pretend—

"No," Samian growled, interrupting my thoughts. "I told you before that her magic should never have been bound, but I did it for her own safety. It is something I will not do again."

I looked toward Samian, our eyes meeting. His stare was severe, yet beneath it flickered something protective, almost warm. A spark of some unnamed emotion heated my blood, and my breath caught in my throat. Before I could respond, Ambrose tilted my face back to him, wiping away the last of my tears from my cheeks. The tightness in my chest eased under the gentleness of his touch.

"I agree with Samian," Ambrose said, his eyes refusing to leave mine. "I will not allow your magic to be bound again, and if anyone tries, they will come to regret it."

Liam's voice shook as he finally found the courage to speak. "Sybil," he said softly. "Sybil, tell them to bind your magic again." He stumbled over the word as if he still couldn't believe this was real.

When I glanced at Ambrose, then Samian, I found both of their eyes narrowed on Liam, filled with malice.

"I—I…no," I breathed. Even though I had caused so much destruction, I hadn't known what I was or what I could do. But now I understood, and I knew I could do better. If given the chance to prove it, I was sure I wouldn't hurt anyone else. I was sure of it. "I can learn to control it. I promise you, I'll learn to control it. You can teach me, right?" I asked, looking between Samian and Ambrose, hope swelling in my chest.

Ambrose stepped back, resting his hands on my shoulders with a comforting smile. "Of course, my darling Sybil. That's what my job offer is for, hence the lack of specifics in the documents I sent you. I was waiting for you to discover your magic, about what you truly are, before I told you *everything*. However, you will learn to control your wonderfully *beautiful* magic, along with discovering what you are."

I looked back at Liam, the corners of my lips curving into a small smile, but it quickly fell when Liam's jaw clenched and his nose wrinkled.

"Then you need to leave," Liam said, his voice hard and cold.

"Liam," I muttered, taking a small step forward, my stomach dropping at the way he balled his hands into tight fists.

Liam snarled through gritted teeth, each word clipped, "*Get. Out.*"

Hot tears burned my eyes as I stepped closer to Ambrose, Liam's rejection slicing through me. I knew I could learn to control whatever this was inside of me. No one would get hurt. I could prove that I was more than just some monster, cursed with an evil that couldn't be erased. But he ripped away my chance to prove that I was still the woman he loved.

My eyes moved to my father, but he refused to look at me, his gaze remaining fixed on the floor in front of him. His body was rigid, his face tight.

Disbelief hollowed out my chest at their rejection. As my heart fractured, the hum of my magic grew stronger. Looking down at my hands, I clenched them into fists, my knuckles turning white. A pair of smooth, reassuring hands covered my own, giving them a small squeeze. My skin seemed to buzz from his touch. When I looked up, Samian stood in front of me, his eyes soft and encouraging. Finding solace in his touch, I took a deep breath, holding it for a few counts before letting it go. My heartbeat slowed, and the ripple of my magic settled beneath my skin.

"Well, I guess that's our cue to leave," Ambrose said coolly, his grip tightening on my shoulders as he led me toward the front door.

Numbness spread through me as we stepped out the door. Samian followed in silence, pulling the door shut behind him. I paused, glancing back at the house Liam and I bought together. The memories of us creating our home flashed through my mind. I saw us standing in front of the door, excitedly holding our keys as Liam's father snapped our picture. I remembered the time we replaced the bright white walls with warm colors, laughing at a stupid joke one of us made or arguing over how to hang the pictures along the walls.

Bittersweet pain tightened my chest at the thought of never being able to return to the home I had carefully crafted with Liam. Silently saying goodbye, I turned to Ambrose, taking the hand he held out.

His fingers curled around mine, and he tugged me into his chest. Putting his knuckles under my chin, he lifted my face so I could meet his bright gaze. He gave me a soft smile as he started gently rearranging my hair. Heat rushed to my cheeks, and I took a step back, quickly using my fingers to flatten any flyaways. I'm sure that after everything, I looked like a mess.

Ambrose chuckled, glancing at Samian, their eyes locking as if they were having a silent conversation. My brows furrowed at their silence, so I looked away, checking the street for a car. The street was empty. My brows furrowed further when I looked back to Ambrose, finding him watching me, his eyes gleaming with amusement, a hint that I was in over my head. His lips curled into a wolfish grin, and for a moment, I forgot where I was.

Behind me, Samian cleared his throat, bringing me back to the moment. Flustered, I looked back at the empty street, and Ambrose laughed softly to himself.

"Now that you know we're different, I suppose I should explain what exactly we are. But first, I believe it's best we leave here before we continue our conversation. I expect that our dear John will soon be calling his friends for help," Ambrose said, wrinkling his nose. "Now, this may be a tad uncomfortable, but just close your eyes and take a deep breath. It will all be over with momentarily."

He held out his hand again, and I hesitated, casting one more glance up and down the street. Fumbling with the hem of my shirt, I bit my bottom lip softly before finally taking his hand. Steeling myself for whatever was about to come, I closed my eyes and breathed deeply, shuddering as Ambrose slowly wrapped his arm around me, drawing me closer to him. As I breathed him in, he smelled of patchouli with a hint of citrus. Comfort washed through me as I exhaled, my body relaxing into his. However, the feeling didn't last long when Ambrose leaned in close to my ear, making me tense from the intimacy of his nearness.

"Ready?" he whispered, his breath tickling my ear.

Nodding, I tried not to think of the heat that gathered in the pit of my stomach from the low rumble of his voice. Liam was only a door away, still bleeding and repulsed by what I was, and Samian was so close, yet the heat of Ambrose's hand pressing on my lower back had me wanting to lean in closer. I felt like I was a traitor, and I never hated myself more.

I nodded and took another deep breath to clear my mind. Suddenly, Ambrose moved us forward a step, and the world felt like it fell away as if we were plummeting to the earth. My stomach flipped, my grip on Ambrose tightening as a scream lodged in my throat. Then, as quickly as it vanished, the world snapped back into place.

CHAPTER 8
SYBIL

Opening my eyes, I pushed away from Ambrose, collapsing to my knees as I vomited onto the ground. My hands gripped the soft grass beneath me, my muscles tensing when I heard quick steps rush closer. Gentle hands gathered my hair back and rubbed slow circles along my spine. Closing my eyes, my shaking body relaxed at the comforting warmth. Finally, I sat back, wiping the tears from my face.

Samian knelt beside me, his worried eyes keeping a close watch on me. "The first time is always the hardest," he said softly, giving me a reassuring smile. I couldn't help the blush warming my cheeks or the small smile that rose on my lips.

Samian gently pulled me up to my feet. When I looked at Ambrose, his face quickly shifted from a grimace to a tight smile that didn't quite reach his eyes. Taking a step away from me, Ambrose motioned to the field around us. My gaze lingered a moment longer, not missing the distance he placed between us, confusion clouding my mind.

"Welcome to Nemos, the upper realm," Ambrose said, the lines of his face relaxing slightly.

Following his gaze, I gaped at the breathtaking beauty of the rolling hills stretching before me. We stood in the middle of a field of tall green grass that danced from the balmy wind, the breeze brushing my skin, feeling light and soothing. Flowers of all different species and sizes grew wild and free, scattered across the field, transforming it into a sea of color.

Looking up, I saw the sun setting, painting the sky and clouds as if they were on fire. My heart pounded with wonder as I spun around, taking it all in, only stopping when I spotted a dense forest that ran along the field's edge. Its peaceful darkness called to me like a song, luring me to walk along its winding paths.

Placing a hand on my shoulder, Samian pulled me closer to him while keeping a wary eye on the forest. "Be careful with the call of the woods, Sybil. There are many creatures here that prey on beings like you. Until you're strong enough to resist its call, never come here alone. Understood?"

Swallowing the lump in my throat, I nodded slowly. His warning twisted my stomach, reminding me of my father's cautions during my childhood and of the wolves that lurked in the darkened trees. Samian led me away, ushering me closer to Ambrose, but I looked back to the shadowy forest, longing to learn more. Even as a child, part of me yearned to get lost in the flora of the woods, and this place was no different. Something about that cool darkness called to me, beckoning me to explore its secrets.

Ambrose led us through the field until we reached a long, cobbled road, stretching into the distance. We walked along it for some time, Ambrose and Samian chatted quietly as we went, though I caught Samian's wary eyes watching me more than once. Our eyes locked again, and I blushed, twisting my head away to take in as much as I could before the night fell upon us. This place was achingly beautiful. The colors of this world seemed more vivid and alive. But the more I lost myself in the awe of this magical place, the more a deep sadness inched its way into my heart.

For so long, I knew what each day would look like. But here, with everything so wild and beautiful and free, I couldn't even begin to fathom what the coming days would bring. I rubbed at the tightness in my chest. Everything felt so overwhelmingly strange and unfamiliar. Excitement bubbled within me, but it was mixed with apprehension at not knowing where I would go next. I knew I would learn about my magic and how to control it, but after that, who knew what the future would bring?

The cobbled path eventually led us to a road with a massive gate that gleamed like polished pearls. My eyes widened, and I blinked at the stark contrast between the iridescent gate and the wild nature we'd left behind. As we drew closer, the gates swung open, revealing the bustling city beyond as Samian slowed down to walk behind me. I could feel Samian's gaze on my back while a pressure in my ribs tugged, wanting me to slow my steps, but the splendor of the city stole all my focus.

The buildings were a mix of historic and modern, as townhomes and shops lined the streets. The lampposts were a work of art; the metal looping and weaving around the shining orbs that gave the street a soft, warm glow. Horse-drawn carriages dashed along the streets while people hurried along their way. We passed restaurants overflowing with patrons as Ambrose and Samian pointed out parts of the city, telling me about the different shops on the street. My mouth watered, my stomach grumbling at the scent of the savory meat and herbs that filled the air. We continued along the cobbled sidewalk, and I took in as much as I could, mesmerized by the splendor of the city.

Eventually, we stopped in front of an opulent building made of white stone. My mouth gaped open, my mind spinning. Ambrose turned his head to me, flashing me a wide grin before leading down a path toward the building. We passed through a smaller gate and crossed a manicured lawn lined with a variety of white flowers. It was beautiful, but it felt too clean, too unblemished. Walking up to two oversized doors, I carefully took in the carved design of two birds on either side, their wings opened as if in flight, like guardians protecting what lay inside. This place looked like it was built for royalty, and the thought made my stomach drop.

As if reading my mind, Ambrose moved to stand behind me, leaning in close. "Welcome to the Marble Palace—my home for the time being," he said, gesturing to the doors.

The doors opened into a stunning foyer. The walls were a pristine white marble that gleamed brilliantly in the light. Gold-trimmed moldings lined the tops of the walls, their antique designs laced and woven together to create intricate flowers. The floors were laid with a similar white marble but were ingrained with golden veins. Toward the back of the foyer, a grand staircase split into two sweeping curves along the walls.

I swallowed, feeling out of place, unused to such pristine elegance. Not allowing myself to get lost in that thought, I followed Ambrose up the magnificent golden stairs until we reached a private study. Ambrose opened the door, allowing me to walk in first. I fought the urge to bristle as I glanced around the room. The study matched the marble-and-gold theme of the palace, but it was accented with a dark wooden desk and leather chairs. It was simple in design, but it didn't diminish the room's luxurious feel. It seemed to match Ambrose, at least from what I'd learned from him in our short time together.

Ambrose motioned for me to sit on the dark brown leather couch as he went to a small cart stocked with different drinks and spirits. He poured me some water, walking back to place it on the table beside me, and settled into the chair across from me. Samian stood close to the door, leaning against the marbled wall, idly picking at his nails with an air of boredom.

"Welcome to my study," Ambrose said with a wave of his hand while leaning back into his chair. "I know you must be confused and probably a bit shocked by the events of today, but let me start off by saying one thing: this is where you belong. Although you are human, the blood of this realm runs through your veins."

My heart raced. I had always felt different from my family and friends, but I just thought it was because I was more aloof and reserved than they were. But now, listening to Ambrose, my mind felt jumbled with the weight of his words. *The blood of this realm runs through your veins.* My back straightened as I braced myself and nodded for Ambrose to continue.

"Now with that out of the way, let's start our little story," he sighed, pausing while I nervously took a sip of the cold water. "Long ago, there was a time when only one realm existed. In this realm, all types of beings roamed the Earth together. It was a time of great chaos, to say the least.

Wars often broke out across the realm, famine ran rampant, and creatures and humans alike lived in terror of one another. Eventually, the rulers of the realm came together and decided to combine their magic and divide the Earth into three realms: the lower, the middle, and the upper. You were born into Mide —the middle realm, which consists mostly of humans and little magic, though there are cases of beings like me that make Mide their home. Dubnos, the lower realm, was created for the creatures born of the dark and shadows. Demons, dark fae, the unseelie, and creatures of shadow rule in the lower realm. Here in Nemos, the light fae, the seelie, seraphim, and creatures of light rule. With me so far?"

My mind blanked, and I swallowed hard. I had never thought there would be worlds beyond the one I came from. It was hard to process it all, to believe it was true, but here I was, in a different world, so I stayed silent and nodded.

"Great," Ambrose continued. "When the rulers separated the realms, there were some creatures that stayed in Mide. They integrated with humans to keep an eye on human progress. However, some stayed so they could continue terrorizing the humans. That is why humans like you exist. Guessing by your magic, a faerie or someone from the Seelie Court came together with one of your ancestors."

"A faerie?" I interrupted, leaning forward with wide eyes. My throat bobbed as I thought back to the fairy tales and myths I had read as a child. Depending on the stories, faeries weren't supposed to look like the men who brought me here. No, the stories showed them as brutal and wild. I fought against the shudder that threatened to rack my body.

"Yes, a high fae," Ambrose stated with a wicked smile. He flicked his hand, and the air around him rippled, revealing ears that were arched and slightly pointed. Blinking, I kept my focus on his ears as he continued. "Pointed ears, long lifespans, *devilishly* handsome, and all with magical abilities. Samian and I are both high fae, as are most of those you will soon meet. Our magic is elemental-based, each of us controlling a different element. Take Samian here. He can control the earth, while I control water and ice. However, there are fae that have unique abilities along with their elemental magic."

"Like what?" I asked, looking at my hands, wondering which element I might show. I remembered a bright light, but after that, the only thing I could remember was the terrified eyes watching me closely. I pushed away the thought before the nausea could creep up my throat.

"You'll learn that at a later point in time," he said with a wave of his hand. "As for your magic, I believe you have the power of light, though we still need to confirm this. In the coming days, you'll go through some tests. We will also have you do some blood work to find out if you are a descendant of fae or the Seelie Court, and how much of their blood runs through your veins. You'll spend your time with mentors who will train your magic, teach you more about our history and the types of creatures and magic you'll eventually run into, as well as combat training."

"I'll have mentors?" I asked, perking up. I could learn. I could really learn to control this power. This could be my chance, my shot to prove to Liam—to my father—that I was more than the monster they saw me as.

"Of course," Ambrose said with a laugh. "How else are you going to learn, my darling Sybil? Samian will be your main mentor. He will oversee your studies and will accompany you everywhere you go. Your other mentors should—"

A quiet knock interrupted Ambrose. A woman with beautiful, slightly curled golden hair and a faint smile on her rosy lips was standing at the door. Her piercing light blue eyes latched onto Ambrose as she moved gracefully into the room. She wore a fitted rosy silk dress that delicately flared at her waist with a wide split to show off her long, slender legs. She glided toward Ambrose, her dress whispering softly behind her. Following her, an enormous bear of a man entered. My jaw nearly dropped at the sight of him. He had a rugged appearance, yet with his chiseled jaw, dark ash brown hair, and eyes that looked almost black, he was surprisingly handsome.

"Ah, right on time," Ambrose mused, standing from his chair and offering it to the lovely woman. "This is Arianna. She will help you with your combat training, as well as court etiquette. Over here, we have Ezra. Ezra is our war general in the palace. He will oversee your combat and weapons training." Moving behind me, Ambrose began twirling my hair before letting it fall down my back. I fought against the electricity that zipped through me at his touch, my eyes flicking to Samian, whose gaze narrowed on Ambrose's hand. "Arianna, Ezra, meet the newest member of our team, my darling Sybil."

Heat rose in my cheeks, but I smiled, giving Ezra a small wave. My smile faltered when I glanced at Arianna. Her cold eyes darkened, and her lips formed a thin line as her gaze flicked over me, from head to toe and back up again.

"Do we really need a new member, Ambrose?" she asked flatly, her eyes cutting to him.

"Samian," Ambrose sighed, still not breaking eye contact with Arianna. "Show Sybil around the palace." Finally breaking away from Arianna's gaze, Ambrose looked down at me, giving me a warm smile, though his eyes were sharp. "I have meetings for the rest of the day and during the morning tomorrow. However, I'll find you once I am finished."

I glanced back at Arianna's impassive face, the tension in the air growing thick. Her eyes cut back to mine, her icy stare making me shiver. Giving her a tight smile, I found Samian waiting for me by the door. I quickly moved to Samian, following him into the hallway, hoping to find comfort in his presence.

"Don't take Arianna's words to heart," Samian said gently,

leading us away from Ambrose's study. "She's rude to everyone except Ambrose."

I let out a weak laugh as I followed him through the twists and turns of the palace, but kept quiet from the nerves curling inside of me. Samian had stayed mostly silent during all our interactions. I wasn't sure how to act or what to say. Plus, being here in this new world—in Nemos—it still didn't feel real. I felt like I was drifting in a dream—or nightmare—that I would hopefully soon wake from. My stomach twisted, my nausea returning as I stole a glance at Samian. His hair was now tucked into the arched ear of a faerie—a real faerie. I flinched, my face paling when he caught me staring. Heat crawled up my neck, and I glanced away.

"I figured you might be tired after everything that happened today," Samian finally said, breaking the awkward silence. "Plus, with your magic returning, you'll find yourself more exhausted over the next few days, at least until you can control it a bit better. I'll take you to your room so you can rest. Tomorrow, I'll show you around the palace."

"That would be great, thank you," I said quietly, already feeling the fatigue he mentioned.

The palace felt like a maze, each hallway looking the same, with windows and sconces lining the walls. The only difference was the gardens or parts of the palace you could see through the windows.

After turning into yet another hallway, Samian stopped and leaned against a doorframe. "This is it. My room is right across from yours, so if you need me for anything, I'm only a knock or a yell away."

Samian opened my door, allowing me to enter the room first. My eyes widened at the sheer size of it. It wasn't just a bedroom as I had imagined; it was more like its own apartment.

The front door opened into the living area, and to the right was a small dining space. A short hallway led further into the suite, bringing me to a small study lined with bookcases and a beautiful mahogany desk. Further down the hall was a French door leading into the bedroom.

"Is every room in the palace made with the same marble and gold trimmings?" I asked. I cringed, not meaning for my voice to sound so disturbed. The palace and the rooms were beautiful, but it all felt too bright for what I was.

Samian gave a small laugh as he came up beside me. "Unfortunately, yes. It's called the Marble Palace for a reason," he shrugged.

"Will I ever be able to go back home?" My voice sounded meek, small, almost a whisper. But I had to know. I needed to know if I would ever see my friends' bright, smiling faces again. If I would ever get to see Liam, though, after today…

"I'll let you look around on your own. The servants brought dinner in case you were hungry. I'll be in my room across the hall, so just knock if you need anything."

Not looking to see if he waited for a response, I heard the door close softly behind me, leaving me to myself. I went to my new bedroom, my body feeling heavy. Samian hadn't exaggerated when he said my magic would leave me exhausted. I felt ready to topple to the floor, but curiosity got the best of me.

Opening the bedroom door, I took in the white-and-golden room, my mind still overwhelmed by the grandness of it all. This was a room fit for a queen, not for some cursed thing like me.

A plush bed sat in the middle between two tall windows overlooking a small garden, layered with soft, cream-colored blankets and piles of fluffed pillows. The room was filled with cozy rugs, soft velvet chaises, and silk curtains hung above the bed, making the room seem like something out of a fairytale. Another set of French doors opened, revealing the most glorious bathroom I had ever laid eyes on, with a large ivory tub with golden legs in the middle. Floor-length mirrors hung on most of the walls, leading to a closet with a bay window. Leaning against the doorframe, fatigue hit me hard.

Deciding to explore more tomorrow, I found some toiletries and brushed my teeth. Searching the closet, I spotted a silky set of pants and a matching shirt to change into. After braiding my hair, I padded back into the bedroom, slipping under the heavy covers. Settling in, I let the darkness take over, pulling me into a deep sleep.

CHAPTER 9

AMBROSE

I watched Sybil follow Samian out the door, waiting until it fully closed before returning my focus to Arianna. Ezra still stood by the door, his gaze lingering after Sybil, keeping his thoughts hidden. Arianna, however, picked invisible dirt from underneath her manicured nails.

Ezra, while irritatingly honorable, was a male of ambition. He knew that with my rise to power, he would quickly ascend through the ranks if he stayed by my side. He had been faithful to that promise of power throughout the years, and I had no doubt that he would continue to fight by my side.

Arianna, on the other hand, was vindictive, spiteful, and volatile. Her emotions were constantly shifting and could turn against another in a heartbeat. She was like the ever-changing flame that flowed through her veins, and was someone that I needed to keep a close eye on. Luckily, her emotions were simple enough to read and even easier to mold. Ever since our younger school years, I could simply grab hold of her emotions, crafting them into a weapon of my choosing. I just needed to give her the right motivation. Fortunately, her lithe body curved in just the right ways, making that motivation pleasant enough to endure.

"Is it really necessary to bring her onto the team?" Arianna asked pointedly.

My gaze drifted to Arianna's hands, my irritation flaring while she continued to pick at her nails. Rolling my shoulders, I moved around the couch, stopping in front of her chair. I leaned over, grabbing her face, my hands tight enough to bruise. A gasp escaped from those full lips, and I pulled her face close, forcing her to look at me. Fear flickered in her eyes when my lips curled in a snarl.

"Yes, Arianna," I growled, pushing her back into the chair, but I remained close. "She is the answer to us gaining complete power over that bitch of a queen. She may not know how to control her magic yet, but she's powerful; I could feel the hum of it. If I can get her to agree to my bargain, we can use her as a weapon to wipe out the queen and those infernal rebels for good."

Walking over to my desk, I sank into my chair and leaned back, picking up a picture of Sybil that lay there. It was taken unknowingly as she crossed a street in the city I found her in two weeks ago. The picture captured the sunburst of green surrounding the golden-brown of her eyes as she looked almost directly at the person taking it.

"She's vulnerable right now, having been rejected by her father and fiancé. We can use that against her, make her feel as if she cannot control that power. We need to make her so afraid of it that her only option is to come running to me. Only then will she agree to my bargain, and she *will* agree to my bargain, Arianna. Have I made myself clear?"

Scoffing, Arianna looked toward the window, her body

tight, but eventually nodded her head in agreement. Cutting my gaze to Ezra, his indifference gave away nothing of his emotions, but his curt nod was all the assurance I needed. My plan would not fail.

"Good," I said, glancing back at Arianna. She still looked out the window, though her eyes were misty. "Ezra, leave us."

Ezra bowed as I continued watching Arianna, then made his way to the door, closing it softly behind him. Tilting my head, I inhaled deeply, letting the air fill my tight lungs to calm my frustration. As much as Arianna grated my nerves, I needed her for my plan to work.

"Arianna, my love, come to me," I said, softening my voice. Arianna stayed seated, though I could see the bobbing of her throat. "I won't ask you again, Arianna." My voice deepened, and I grabbed hold of her emotions, pushing a small amount of longing through her.

Arianna sucked in a breath before finally cutting her heated gaze to me. I arched an eyebrow, a silent command to not keep me waiting.

Arianna stood, her tight dress clinging to her supple body, showing off her delicate curves. Her back straightened, and she boldly strode to me until she stood between my legs. Sweeping my gaze along her body, my blood sang. "Kneel for me," I muttered softly, the corner of my mouth rising.

Arianna's breath caught, her eyes burning as I watched her slowly drop to her knees, tilting her face up to hold my heated gaze. I rested an elbow on the arm of my chair, reaching out and grasping Arianna by the chin. Gently drawing her closer, I leaned down, running my lips along her jaw and breathing in her sweet lavender scent. Arianna leaned her head to the side, giving me easier access. Reaching her ear, I nipped at it softly before licking the pain away. Arianna's gasp turned into a quiet whimper. I could feel her shifting on her knees, my nostrils flaring at the scent of her arousal filling the air.

"I know it will be hard, my love, but I need you for this task. Will I be able to count on you to take care of this for me?" I whispered softly into her ear.

"Yes," Arianna breathed, slightly arching her back, giving me a delightful view of her full breasts.

Humming my approval, I placed a tender kiss on the nape of her neck, and Arianna's breath quivered. I slowly left a trail of kisses down her shoulder, giving her another soft bite. Arianna's soft cry made my blood heat. Catching the strap of her dress between my teeth, I drifted it off her shoulder, while my hand moved the other strap down her arm.

As I leaned back into my chair, Arianna's face warmed, giving her a soft glow. Her eyes were glazed as the top of her dress fell to her waist, revealing her full and heavy breasts. Her nipples pebbled from the chill of the air, her chest quickly rising and falling. She dropped her gaze, her lips curving into a sensuous smile at the tightness of my trousers.

Her hands moved to the tops of my thighs, slowly winding their way up to my belt. Before she could fumble with the buckle, I grabbed her wrists, using my strength to pull her hands above us, lifting her off her knees so her face was a hair's breadth from mine. "Not so fast, my love. What do you say?"

"Please," she breathed, her voice thick.

Chuckling softly, I caught her lips with mine, kissing her slow and deep. Capturing her moan in my mouth, I released her hands to grab her waist. I broke our kiss, pushing her back down to her knees, allowing her to continue what she'd begun.

Arianna whipped off my belt in one steady motion, undoing my trousers and freeing my hard length. Licking her lips, she eyed me hungrily before meeting my gaze, her eyes eagerly asking for permission. My cock twitched at her pleading look. With a nod of my head, her smile grew before leaning down, taking me deep into the warmth of her silky mouth.

Groaning, I twisted a hand into her hair, pushing her to take me deeper. Her moans reverberated through me and my other hand tightly gripped the arm of my chair. Tipping my head back, the swirl of her tongue had me fighting for air.

Before I lost all control, I tightened my grip on her hair, pulling her head back. Arianna whimpered in protest as I pulled her to her feet and moved her back against my desk. I stood, my mouth crashing into hers, my tongue forcing her lips to part so I could deepen our kiss. Running my hands down her back, I stopped at the curve of her ass, gripping hard and drawing her closer to feel my hardness against her. Arianna moaned, loving the roughness.

I lifted her, and Arianna gasped when I dropped her on top of my desk. Before she could react, I closed the distance between us, deeply breathing in her lust and letting it consume me. It felt like fire burned through my veins as it fueled my magic, and my control shattered.

Roughly dragging the silky fabric of her dress to her waist, I used my knees to spread her legs further apart. Arianna's hands craftily pushed down my trousers before working on the buttons of my shirt. I pulled her hands away, and my lips met hers in a bruising kiss. One hand firmly held onto her hip while the other snaked up her arm and continued across her chest, only stopping when I reached her neck. My grip tightened around her throat as I shoved her down against the desk.

Arianna cried out, but her whimper quickly turned into a moan when I pushed my magic into her, intensifying her desire. The sudden rush of hunger had her wrapping her legs around me, clawing and begging for my touch. Her skin was flushed;

the sight of her half-naked and quivering for me made my cock throb.

With an uneven breath, I gripped my cock, giving myself a quick pump before lining myself against her slick center. "Please, Ambrose, I need you," Arianna panted, as if the heat at her entrance would drive her mad.

Giving her a wicked smile, I slammed into her in one quick motion. Her moans echoed through my study, her silky cunt clenching tightly around me. Groaning, I pulled out slowly, then slammed back into her before setting a hard and unforgiving pace. A deep rumble sounded low in my chest at how well she was taking me.

"I know what I'm asking of you will be difficult, my love," I repeated, growling as her cunt clenched tighter around me, "But once this is over and her magic belongs to me, you will be the one standing by me. You will be my queen." Arianna's breathless mewling grew louder, and my pace quickened. "You will be the one they all bow down to, and you will be the one who rules by my side."

"Yes," Arianna breathed, her face fixed with pleasure, her back arching off the desk.

"Now tell me," I grunted, "what are you going to do for me?"

"I'll bring her down," Arianna whimpered when my lips clamped around her peaked nipple. "I will make her magic yours, and you will become my king."

My lips found hers again before my hand tightened around her throat, constricting her breathing. I pushed more of my magic into her, heightening her pleasure, making her feel so sensitive that even a soft breeze could make her scream. My thrusts deepened; her cunt clenched around me as ecstasy ripped through her. Continuing my unforgiving pace, I rode out the waves of her pleasure until I yelled out, finding my own release.

Arianna wrapped her legs tighter around me, pulling herself up from the desk. Her lips met mine in a slow but passionate kiss, and she sighed deeply, still unknowingly relishing in the remnants of my magic.

Giving her one last kiss, I walked to the washroom to clean myself. When I returned, Arianna had fixed her dress and hair, though her complexion was still flushed, gleaming in the soft light. Leaning against my desk, she held out my trousers, giving me a wicked smile.

After I dressed myself, I leaned into her, inhaling her soft lavender scent. "Now, are you ready, my queen?" I purred, low and deep.

Arianna placed a finger at the center of my chest, pushing me away. "I'm ready, my king." Her lips curled into a slanted smile before stepping away, her finger sliding across my chest as she headed toward the door. "I will rule by your side, Ambrose. There will be no one else but me."

Opening the door, Arianna left before I could say anything. Exhaling, I dropped into my chair, rolling my neck. Glancing down, Sybil's picture stared back at me, glaring in the light. Seeing her magic on display today told me everything I needed to know. If I were to be a king, she was the key to getting me there. She would be the one who could eliminate those who opposed me. She would make me into a fearsome king, but I needed her to fall for that to happen.

CHAPTER 10
SAMIAN

A knock at my door pulled me from the books I'd been gathering for Sybil's first lessons. Without thinking, I strode to the door, swinging it open. My throat tightened when Ezra's hard face emerged from the shadows, his lips set in a thin line. Frowning, I gestured for him to enter, widening the door enough to allow him through. Peering out, I searched the darkened hallway, making sure no one had followed him before silently closing the door.

Ezra walked through my room, pulling on a discrete handle at one of the bookcases that lined my wall. The bookcase opened, the hinges groaning as he pushed his way into the hidden room behind it. Securing the bookcase behind me, I followed Ezra to the table in the middle of the room, sliding into the wooden chair.

"Did you find out anything?"

"No, I'm just here so you can teach me whatever insufferable thing you've learned about lately." Ezra's tone was thick with sarcasm, but his eyes were hard as stone.

Snarling, I cut him an icy glare.

Rolling his eyes, Ezra continued, "He is planning on using Arianna and me to make Sybil afraid of her magic. He wants her to agree to his bargain so that he can control her powers."

"Shit." I leaned back into my chair, running a hand down my face. "Anything else?"

"He dismissed me but asked Arianna to stay, so I didn't get everything. But whatever he has Arianna in charge of, it's not going to be good, Samian. Arianna is not someone to mess with."

I studied him for a moment, waiting to see if he knew more than what he was telling me, but Ezra's tone was tight, and his body was rigid. He didn't like Ambrose's plan any more than I did. And with Arianna receiving a task on her own, whatever she intended to do would be vile.

Arianna was the worst type of fae imaginable, always playing dirty or using people's secrets and fears against them. She was always so willing to do Ambrose's foul deeds since the damned bastard was too afraid to defile his own hands. But she would do it. She would do anything to make him love her and that made them a dangerous pair.

Leaning back into my chair, I released a tight breath, considering our options. Sybil was new to this world, so I had to be careful with what I shared with her. Outright telling her not to trust Ambrose would just make her shut down and be more cautious around me, which meant I would need to leave hints wherever I could and pray to Morgiana that she would understand well enough to be wary of him.

Keeping my eyes glued to the table, I restlessly twirled the ring on my middle finger, letting the warm metal soothe my anxious thoughts. "I'll discuss bargains with her during our first lesson. I'll make it imperative that she never agrees to one, but especially one with Ambrose. We won't know where her allegiance lies until she learns more about this realm, so be careful what you share with her."

Ezra shifted in his chair, his throat bobbing. "Let's just hope she listens," he sighed. "I'll see if I can schedule our training during the times Arianna has meetings, or at least have one-on-one training with Sybil far enough away from Arianna to where she won't be able to butt in."

The tightness in my chest eased slightly. "Thank you, Ezra. Let me know if you see or hear anything else."

Nodding, Ezra pushed on the stone wall behind him, which opened into a passageway that lined the inner palace. The passage system had been long forgotten after the new palace was built around the original. Ezra only knew about this section of the passage that led to the courtyard. There were more stone openings hidden along the way, but they were a secret that I kept close to my heart. A secret that only one other knew of, besides the queen.

Exhaling, I gripped the edge of the table and stood from my chair. Whatever Ambrose was planning for Sybil, I knew he was going to start by manipulating her emotions, and with his magic, it wouldn't be hard to do. Until she learned how to use her own magic, she would be vulnerable to him and his whims.

Leaving the hidden room, I pushed the bookcase back into place and searched the books along the shelves, finding ones on bargains and the various types of magic. If she was going to have any chance of resisting Ambrose's powers, learning how to recognize the magic of others was imperative and something she would need to learn quickly.

My hand paused on a worn book, my mind flashing back to earlier in the day. Ever since I ran into Sybil in the middle of the street, it was a continual fight to shut down the urge to see her, to be near her. Even now, I could feel my soul begging to cross the short distance to her room and hold her close. My hand tightened around the book, and I pushed back the need to be with her.

She's too new to this world, to her magic.

I repeated that to myself over and over, hoping that it would calm the force pushing me to her. It would be too dangerous for us both if I acted on my wants, if I lost control of myself and followed my heart's demands.

I knew she could feel it too, this link between us. I could see it in the way her eyes always found mine, in the way her body reacted to my touch. She could feel this pull as much as I did, though I knew she didn't understand it, couldn't comprehend why or what it implied. Which meant that I would need to keep a firm hold on myself, possibly even a barrier to stop Sybil from acting on her emotions.

Letting my hand fall from the book, an idea popped into my head, though not a very good one. I cringed, knowing the lashing I was about to receive, but I pulled on my magic, transferring myself to a brightly lit office.

Standing behind the female, hunched over, lost in her thoughts while reading her research, I braced myself and cleared my throat.

Aster leapt from her chair, gasping, launching a thick book toward my face with a curse. I caught it before it could do any damage and gave her a sheepish grin. "Sorry, I didn't mean to scare you."

"Are you insane?" Aster hissed, her face pinching in anger.

"I need a favor, and I didn't want anyone to know I was here," I shrugged. "It was the only thing I could think of."

Aster glared at me, her gray eyes piercing and cold. "And you think I'm the one that would help you with this favor?"

My smile widened, but before I could laugh, Aster flung her sharpened pen in my direction. I stepped to the side, the edged point lodging itself into the wall behind me. "It's just a small favor, I promise. You wouldn't have to do anything really."

Aster's brows pinched, her lips thinning. She stared at me with such cool regard that I could have sworn she was the one with ice magic instead of Ambrose. Finally, Aster let out a quick breath. "Tell me your favor and *then* I will decide whether to help you or not," she grounded out.

Drumming my fingers against my leg, I considered my words carefully. "I need you to pretend that we're together," I said slowly.

"Excuse me?" Aster balked, appalled by the words that escaped my lips.

"You don't have to do anything," I said quickly, holding my hands out in front of me. "And you just need to pretend in front of one person in particular."

"And *why* do you want me to do that?"

"The woman I would check on in Mide? She's here." I forced out the words, my stomach twisting in the process.

Aster raised a brow, her nose lifting in the air. "And?"

"And," I breathed. "I need her to believe that I am unavailable."

"You're not giving me much to go on, Samian," Aster pointed out, annoyance making her words sharp.

I let out a shaky breath and found a chair to settle in. Running a hand over my face, I leaned back, letting my head fall back against the wall behind me. "I can barely control myself around her. I need her to think I'm inaccessible because if she makes a move toward me, I don't know if I would have the strength to stop myself. I need *her* to be the one who holds back."

An unreadable emotion flickered across Aster's face as she studied me, though it doesn't take long for realization to dawn. "She's your—"

"Don't say it," I hissed, straightening in my chair.

"I don't understand. Why are you avoiding it? This is a good thing, Samian." Confusion filled those steely eyes of hers but quickly shifted into alarm.

"Exactly," I pressed. "If Ambrose finds out, I don't even want to think what he would do to her." I swallowed, memories of Aster's detached eyes finding mine when I found her lying so still in the middle of a dark room flitting across my mind. I pushed the thoughts away, not wanting to relive those moments of me holding her brutalized body to mine as I rushed her to the closest healer I could find.

Aster's eyes remained distant for a moment, until she blinked away the flashbacks of Ambrose.

"Sybil is new to this world, to her magic. She just lost her fiancé. I don't want to push this onto her, and I can't allow Ambrose to find out. He already has some plan ready for her. I can't allow him to have that too." My stomach dropped at the thought of Ambrose hurting Sybil, of doing the things he did to Aster just because he saw how close we became. I wouldn't allow another person I cared for to become his plaything.

"Fine," Aster sighed, her sharp eyes finally meeting mine. "I'll play along. *However,* I will not lie if she asks me any questions. Understood?"

Relief flooded through me, my body relaxing into the chair. "Understood."

Aster rolled her eyes and returned to her desk. "Go away, I'm busy."

Standing from the chair, I snorted and walked up behind

Aster. "I appreciate you," I said, giving her a quick pat on her head.

Aster twisted in her chair, cursing, throwing another pen my way and I laughed. It was the first real laugh I felt in days since Ambrose found Sybil. Picking the pen from the floor, I waved it at her. "Thanks for this," I grinned before pulling my magic to me, transferring myself back to my room.

CHAPTER II
SYBIL

A knock sounded at my door, waking me from a deep sleep. Groaning, I turned over, pulling a pillow over my head, hoping to drown out the sound. The knocking paused for a moment before starting again, this time growing louder and more persistent. Grumbling, I sat up, blinking so my eyes could adjust to the bright light coming in from the windows.

Stretching over to my bedside table, I reached for my phone but stopped short. I wasn't at home—I no longer *had* a home. The chaos of yesterday quickly came rushing back, and I frowned at the glaring luster of the room glimmering from the beams of light. Through all the mayhem of yesterday, I had forgotten to grab my phone on the way out. Not that it would have worked here, anyway. I rubbed at the tightness in my chest, feeling oddly numb without it.

The knock sounded again, and I grimaced, crawling out of the warm, plush bed and making my way to the door. As I swung it open, my frown deepened into a scowl at the sight of

Samian's smile widening. His gaze moved from my face to my feet and back; amusement glittered in his eyes at the sight before him. Gone was his mask of iciness.

"Looks like someone had a good sleep," he laughed, a small dimple forming as he grinned. My heart fluttered in my chest at the sight, but I pushed it as far out of mind as I could.

Rolling my eyes, I turned back to my room and padded to the bathroom, leaving the door open for Samian to saunter in. Hearing the door close behind me, I glanced back, making sure Samian stayed in the living area before rushing to the mirror.

Swearing, I leaned in close to my reflection. I had slept well last night, and it showed. Cringing, I quickly brushed out my knotted hair and rinsed away the drool that had crusted on the side of my mouth before moving to the closet.

I didn't pack any clothes when I left. I didn't even think about it when Ambrose pushed me out of the house. I wasn't even sure Liam would have *let* me pack my things before leaving. His fear had been too strong to allow me that. My heart squeezed at the reminder.

It felt strange to think of Nemos as my new home. My friends and family were so far away, but maybe it was a blessing that they weren't closer. With this curse running through my veins, I wouldn't have to worry about hurting them or further tainting any of the warm memories I cherished of them. Shoving that thought aside, I focused on looking for clothes.

Opening an armoire, I found a pair of black leggings that fit well enough and a beautiful burgundy tunic. I quickly slipped them on and studied myself in the mirror. Lifting my arms, the sleeves of the tunic flowed wider toward my elbows, making me scrunch my nose. I looked like a character straight out of a "Lord of the Rings" movie. Running my hands down the front, I noticed the pretty golden designs sewn along the top and bottom of the tunic, reminding me of leaves blowing in the wind.

Sighing, I took in the view in front of me again. I couldn't decide what to make of my reflection. While I was on the shorter, curvier side, the tunic was flattering, beautifully outlining my body. The color was nice as well, softening the curves of my face and making my hazel eyes appear greener, but I still felt out of place. It was like my reflection was an imposter of some kind, as if *I* were in a strange new body that felt lighter and stronger.

Biting my bottom lip, I ran my hands over the tunic again before slipping on the sneakers I'd worn yesterday. I made my way back to the living area, finding Samian perusing through the different trinkets on the shelves and tables.

Clearing my throat, Samian twisted, quickly inspecting me, and hummed his approval. "The clothes look like they fit well. I hope the color is okay."

"It is," I said, smoothing out the lines of the tunic, trying to fight off the heat building in my face. "I like burgundy and gold, though I feel a bit weird. I'm not used to clothes like this."

Samian laughed softly. "It will take some time, but I'm sure you'll get used to life here," he said, smiling warmly. "I noticed you didn't eat last night. Would you like to come with me for some breakfast?"

As if on cue, my stomach growled. Samian laughed again as my face burned.

"Come, let's get you something to eat."

We made our way through the endless hallways of marble and gold. I tried making mental notes of all the turns so I wouldn't get lost in the future, but quickly gave up. This place felt like a labyrinth. How anyone knew their way around here was astounding.

We finally arrived at the dining hall, the tall wooden doors opening to a large room with walls of massive arched windows. A glittering glass chandelier hung in the middle. There were multiple long wooden tables spread throughout the room with cream-colored velvet chairs. Each table had plates of assorted meats and pastries, coffee, and tea.

The room was bustling with women in shiny silk and gossamer dresses, their hair finely pinned, and well-dressed men chatting happily away. Their voices filled the room, but a wave of silence rippled through the crowd when they saw me enter beside Samian.

Judging by their looks, everyone in the dining hall was a high fae like Ambrose and Samian. Each one of them was as breathtakingly beautiful as the next, yet their pretty faces were carved with arrogance while they leaned toward each other, whispering insults about me, and about Samian.

I clenched my hands into tight fists, my knuckles turning white as the whispers about my wild, ashy hair, my short stature, and my too-thick curves grew louder. I paused when laughter from a familiar voice came from a table close by. Glancing over, Arianna and Ezra sat with a group of delicately dressed fae. Their brightly colored dresses put my plain tunic to shame. Rolling the hem of my tunic, unease crept up my spine. Noticing my stare, Arianna stood and gracefully made her way to me, her delicate golden hair glistening in the light, looking like woven gold.

My back straightened when Arianna stopped in front of me, her viper's smile laced with venom. "Well, well, look who finally decided to grace us with her presence," she said, her voice sweet and colorful.

The table behind her erupted with soft giggles, but quickly quieted when Samian snarled at them viciously. "Is there something you need, Arianna?" The sharpness in his voice made me want to curl up and hide.

"Oh no, Samian. What could you do for me? Or her, for that matter?" Arianna laughed, her eyes glinting with conceit. Slowly raking her gaze down and back up again, her lips curled in disgust. "You obviously don't belong here, girl. Why don't you go back to where you came from?" Arianna laughed cruelly and snapped her fingers. "Oh, yes, from what I've heard, you can't."

Her songlike laughter echoed through the dining room, the other high fae joining in. Heat crawled up my chest to my face, and I glanced around the room. Thankfully, Ezra didn't join the laughter; his body rigid, his hard gaze fixed on Arianna, tracking her every move. Behind me, Samian growled, grabbing my arm to pull me behind him. But the thought of needing him to protect me made me sick.

Jerking my arm from Samian's grip, I stepped up to Arianna, my heart pounding. "What the hell do you know?" I sneered, unable to contain the shame masked in anger.

"I know that your little boyfriend and father rejected you," Arianna said, taking a step closer. "I know you were fired from your job," Arianna paused, giving me a cruel smirk. "I also know that you can't even control your magic. Tell me, how is little Liam and your poor father doing?" Puffing out her bottom lip, Arianna made a teasingly sad face before twisting to her table and laughing.

My nails dug into my palms, and heat flooded my veins as I watched them laugh, but their voices didn't reach my ears. Swearing, my chest heaved, and I lunged. I lunged at Arianna, ready to do something, anything that I could. Rip out her perfect hair, tackle her to the ground, fight, kick, scratch—anything to take her down. But Samian's hands gripped tight around my arms, stopping me before I could even move a step forward.

As if in response, my power started coiling underneath my skin, preparing to strike. Pulling me away from Arianna, Samian pushed me toward the entrance of the dining hall, not stopping until the door closed behind us, cutting off the laughter that followed.

I stood there, silently staring at the floor, my eyes burning. Glancing back to the dining hall, Samian exhaled, swearing softly under his breath. "Sybil, look at me," he said, turning me to face him. "Arianna is mean and vindictive. She's a bully, and her words mean nothing. Don't listen to her and don't give them any part of you, do you understand?"

His voice was severe, but there was a tone hidden in his words that seemed to beg me not to lose myself. Looking down at my feet, I swallowed thickly. Unable to say a word, I gave him a small nod.

Arianna's words were sharp, and they cut me to my core. Liam rejected me without giving me a chance to prove that I could control my magic, and that hurt settled deep inside me. I couldn't even do anything about it. I couldn't change his mind, and I couldn't defend myself against Arianna. She was right about me not belonging here, but I didn't belong in Mide with Liam either.

My breath grew tight, and my chest ached. There was a gaping hole in my heart where Liam's love had lived, and I missed him. I missed the comfort of knowing he was by my side, that I could go to him with the good and the bad, and that he would stand by me through it all. Except when it came to this blight running through my veins.

Clearing my throat, I blinked away the burning in my eyes and looked back at Samian. Giving him another quick nod,

Samian reached out, giving my shoulder a warming squeeze. "Come, let's go to the medical ward. I'll have the servants send food to the library for us while we run your blood tests. We can eat while we go over our study plans."

WE ENTERED THE MEDICAL WING, the smell of sanitized rooms burning my nose, reminding me of the hospitals back home. Except this place was a large, open space with shelves lining the walls filled with herbs and different concoctions. There were three hallways with doors leading to separate rooms. Chairs and chaises lined the middle for people to sit while they waited to be seen.

A small, slender woman with a long braid of chocolate-colored hair made her way to us. Her ivory skin was accented with a hint of rose on her high cheekbones. Her cold grey eyes met Samian's, narrowing when he gave her a low, playful bow. I blinked, shock coloring my face as I stared at Willow, my closest friend from college, or at least her twin.

"Nice to see you, Aster," Samian smiled, only straightening when Aster was a step away. "Ambrose wanted Sybil to get some blood work done. Do you have time?"

Aster lifted her pert nose in the air, studying me. "So, this is the new girl?" She clucked. "She doesn't seem like much. Come," she said as she twisted, already walking to the furthest door in the center hallway, "follow me."

I rolled my eyes, cutting my sharp gaze to Samian, who laughed, his eyes twinkling in the bright light, though he kept them glued to Aster. Motioning for me to follow, Samian led the way to the room Aster had entered.

"Sit there," Aster demanded, gesturing to a chair in the corner of the room as soon as I stepped into the room.

"So, how is everything going?" Samian purred, leaning against Aster's desk.

Ignoring him, Aster turned to me with a small cloth that smelled strongly of alcohol. Samian laughed softly, his smile growing wider at Aster's aloofness toward him. Aster's lips thinned while she pulled my arm to her, checking for veins. Samian glided across the room, sliding into the chair beside me.

I glanced at him, raising an eyebrow when Samian gave me a quick wink. "I heard today was going to be a beautiful day. Sunshine, warm breezes, little white flowers in full bloom," he grinned at Aster, eagerly waiting for her next move.

With a click of her tongue, Aster turned away, pulling a cart beside her. A thick silence blanketed the room, which only seemed to egg Samian on.

Aster pulled out a needle and some vials while Samian continued his one-sided small talk. "One *could* say that today is the perfect weather for a walk or a picnic. Don't you agree, Sybil?"

Flicking my eyes between the two, I fought off a smile. "Sure," I huffed, earning me an icy glare from Aster, and I cringed.

Aster stabbed the needle in my arm, and I sucked in a sharp breath, watching the snide smile that graced those rosy lips. I paled, the pain radiating down my arm. Samian coughed, trying to hide his laughter. This woman was not someone to trifle with.

After taking two vials of blood, Aster walked back to her desk, clearing her throat. "It should take an hour or two for the results to come back," she said, not looking up while she labeled the vials. Pausing, she put them down, giving Samian a sidelong glance. "Should I inform you or Ambrose when they are ready?"

"Me. Inform me first when the results are ready," he said, his voice suddenly tight.

An awkward silence wrapped around us as they held each other's stare. I eyed them suspiciously as the silence stretched between them. Another moment passed before Aster nodded and turned back to her desk. Samian took a sharp breath and opened the door, gesturing for me to wait outside while he talked with Aster. Alone.

I narrowed my eyes on him, but hopped up from the chair and made my way out of the medical wing, leaning against the cold marbled wall in the hall.

Minutes slowly passed by until Samian walked out, his hands running through his hair. "Sorry about that," he said, taking a quick glance back to the medical wing. His face wore that cold mask of indifference he had when we first met, and I couldn't help the disappointment that squeezed my heart. "We can head to the library now."

Pushing that discontent away, I followed Samian and thought of his interaction with Aster, the playfulness that glimmered in his eyes. Forcing down the touch of envy I felt, a grin slowly crept up. "So, you and Aster, huh?" I asked, hiding my smile.

Samian whipped his head to me, a hint of pink touching his cheeks. "What makes you think that?"

"I know I've only known you for a day, but I don't see you as the playful kind of guy with just anyone."

Frowning, Samian looked ahead, his growing pinching together. "I wouldn't say I'm not the playful type. I do edge on the side of seriousness, especially the past few years." His tone dipped, making me wonder what had caused the solemnity in his voice. "However, there are some people who bring me out of my thoughts long enough that I can be the playful male I once was." His words were thoughtful, though a bit distant.

"And Aster is part of that few?"

"Yes, though she would never admit it." The corners of his eyes crinkled with fondness as he continued. "Aster and I have known each other since our school days. We met during my weapons training class. We had around twenty faeries in the class, and one of them slipped during a drill and landed on the pointy side of his sword," he laughed softly, shaking his head at the memory. "Someone sent for a professor, but Aster was passing by when it happened. She immediately ran up to him, tearing the bottom of her uniform, and kneeled beside him, wrapping the cloth around the wound while giving out commands to anyone close by. She wasn't allowed to use her magic since we were still training. We were all so stunned that no one seemed to question the young, bright-eyed female barking orders. We all followed her instructions until the professor came to take him away. She left me stunned, and I have never been able to forget her since."

His face softened at the memory, and I smiled, picturing the frosty woman dishing out commands to unsuspecting men. She was a force to be reckoned with, but a force that I wanted to be friends with, reminding me so much of Willow. They even looked similar, though Willow's hair had a hint of red.

"But if you tell anyone, I'll deny it until my dying breath," Samian added, pulling me out of my thoughts.

Chuckling at his boyish request, we turned the corner to a pair of large wooden doors. My mouth gaped open as we walked into the royal library; it was vast and magnificent. It had three floors, two of which had bookcases that rose from floor to ceiling, with marble columns in front that supported the second-floor balconies. The ceiling was made of multiple skylights that gave the library a soft, natural light. Wooden desks filled the middle of the room as people sat, studying or taking notes.

"A fan of libraries, huh?" Samian smirked, noticing the awe that lit my face.

"Who wouldn't be with a library like this?" I said breathlessly.

"Oh, I could think of a few." His tone was passive, if not a bit detached. I dared a glance in his direction, noticing how his lips pressed together. "Come, we're going to the third floor."

Taking in the breathtaking scene around me, we made our way to the stairs. The bookcases were sectioned by subject, with ladders attached for easy access to the higher shelves. Walking up the stairs, the second floor was like the first. Tables filled the overhang of the second floor while more bookcases lined the walls. Golden sconces lit up the bookcases, and each desk had small, delicate lamps for every seat.

Finally reaching the third floor, Samian walked us to a table near the back wall. The tables on this floor weren't in any order; it was like people regularly moved them around. Bookcases behind our table lined the middle, creating a makeshift hallway that led to secluded rooms in the back. I made a mental note to explore more of the third floor during my free time.

When we reached our table, there was already a stack of books waiting for us, along with two plates of food filled with a mix of savory and sweet pastries. There was also a coffee carafe and a teapot with small cups on a cart beside the table. My mouth watered at the delicious smell.

Making a quick move to the cart, I poured the steaming coffee into a cute porcelain cup with dusty-pink roses painted on the sides. Bringing it to my nose, I inhaled the amazing, robust smell. I took a small sip, letting the salted caramel and hazelnut warm me.

Sitting down, I sighed and relaxed in my seat, eyeing the plate of pastries and finding it hard to choose which to taste first. Samian chuckled, helping himself to some tea and a savory pastry filled with ham and cheese. Finding one with jam and cream cheese, I moaned at the burst of tart raspberry sweetness filling my mouth. Samian stifled a laugh, but we ate in peaceful silence until both plates were almost gone.

CHAPTER 12
SYBIL

After finishing the last of the coffee, Samian stood, grabbing a few books from the top of the closest stack. As he handed them to me, I quickly looked over each one. The books seemed to be beginner guides to understanding magic and the various magic found in Nemos, the history of the realms, and the creatures that lived in each of the realms.

"Today, we will go over any questions you might have and some information about Nemos. It's important that you have a good understanding of how this realm is ruled. Before we start, do you have any questions?"

"I do, actually," I said hesitantly. "Since this is a palace and Ambrose mentioned you work for him, does that mean Ambrose is the king?"

Samian scoffed, his eyes darkening, leaving me unsettled. "No, though he may like to act as if he is, Ambrose is not the king. We are ruled by a kind and compassionate queen. Her name is Queen Cassia Aberra, and she has been this realm's queen since before the realms were split into three. Her brother, Dryden, was king before her; however, he abdicated to remain in Mide. He cared for the humans and wanted to make sure they stayed safe."

"Wow," I blinked, stunned. The stories said that faeries were long-lived, but encountering someone who had lived before the realms became three felt daunting. "Am I going to meet her? Is Dryden still in the middle realm?"

Samian's face tightened, his lips forming a thin line. "No. To both," he mumbled. "Queen Cassia is indisposed at the moment, though this is something we can discuss later. As for Dryden, no one seems to know where he is or if he is still alive. Now, like you learned last night, this is the Marble Palace," he said, quickly changing the subject when I opened my mouth to ask another question. Confused, I sat back, my brows knitting together. However, I stayed silent, letting him continue.

"We are currently in the city of Volmire, which is made up of a mix of nobility and commoners who oversee the restaurants and stores around the city. Outside of Volmire, there are smaller villages where the rest of the general population lives. A different lord governs each village and city. At the moment, the lords and ladies closest to Ambrose all live in the palace." Samian grimaced as he said the last sentence, his lips dipping with distaste. "Any questions so far?"

"If Ambrose isn't the king, why is he able to choose which families are allowed to reside in the palace? Shouldn't that be up to the queen?"

"Yes, it should," was all Samian said. Leaning back in his chair, his brows furrowed as if he were testing the words he really wanted to say. Finally, his gaze flicked to mine. "Sybil, I don't know how to word this delicately, so I'll just say it. Be careful around Ambrose. He may seem kind and caring on the surface, but that's where it ends. Underneath, he is not someone you should consider a friend, and he is not someone that you should ever rely on *or* enter into a bargain with."

Frowning, I thought back to yesterday after losing control of my magic. My stomach twisted as Liam's wide, terror-filled eyes flashed across my memory. Ambrose had offered me a bargain then, one he said would protect those around me from being injured if I ever lost control again. I had forgotten about it in the chaos, but something that felt a lot like unease crawled up my spine, warning me to listen and pay attention to what Samian was trying to say.

"Why should I be careful about making a bargain with him?" I asked, hoping he would tell me more about Ambrose.

"Bargains are not something you can easily get out of. Once you are in a bargain, it is bound by death. Meaning, if you don't keep up your end of the bargain, the magic of it will take your life instead. The only way to get out of one is if one of you dies or whoever offered the bargain releases you from it. That's why it's essential that you listen to me when I say this. Never, and I mean *never*, enter a bargain with anyone, especially Ambrose."

My blood chilled at the warning in Samian's tone. His eyes were dark and severe while he waited for me to respond. "I'll try not to," I laughed, hoping to break the heavy tension in the air.

"No, there is no try in this, Sybil. I mean it. I need you to tell me you understand that."

"I understand," I stammered, blinking at the severity of his tone. The weight of his stare felt like it was pressing down on me, and I fought against the shiver that threatened to rise.

Samian exhaled, the tightness in his shoulders relaxing. "Good. Now, on to the lighter topics of the day. These are the books we will cover first. We'll focus on learning how to feel for your magic first, then how to recognize the magic of another, especially when someone tries to use it against you." Opening the book, Samian turned to the first page and slid it to me. "Having a magical ability depends on the user's strength. The stronger you are, the more likely you are to have a magical ability. Like Ambrose mentioned yesterday, I can use earth magic."

Pausing, Samian put a gentle hand on the wooden table. I stared in awe when a soft green glow formed a halo around his hand. Slowly lifting it, a small pink flower bloomed underneath. My eyes widened at the ripple along the table as Samian plucked the flower from the wooden surface and handed it to me. Hesitantly, I took the flower, studying the soft petals as a small smile rose on my lips.

"So, does that mean there are people who don't have magical abilities?" I asked, my eyes still focused on the flower twisting between my fingers.

"Correct. They still have an immortal life, but it is a life without magic."

Setting the flower aside, I rubbed my thumb along the palm of my other hand, my brows knitting. "How do you know what type of magic you'll have?"

"We don't. In some cases, families breed specific powers into their lineage; however, like eye or hair color, a child can be born with a different magical ability. There are also a few creatures that have abilities outside of their elemental magic. Take me as an example; I have another ability called soul bonding. Once I form a bond with someone, I have access to their memories, emotions, their physical pain, and even their thoughts. However, I don't have access to them for long. The bond always remains, but I must shield myself from it, or it could cause serious issues for me and those I am bonded with. Does that make sense?"

As he was describing his soul bonding, I thought back to earlier with him and Aster, remembering how odd it felt when they watched each other, their eyes conveying emotions as if in an unspoken language. Was he using that bond to have silent conversations with her?

I must have asked the question aloud because Samian nodded, saying, "Yes, that's right."

"So, you have a bond with Ambrose, too." I blurted, thinking of when we were outside of my ho—Liam's house. He had done the same with Ambrose before we left. But if he had a bond with Ambrose, why was he so keen to warn me away?

Pausing at my statement, Samian twisted the ring on his finger. "Unfortunately, I do. But it is not because I wanted to. I was forced into creating one with him to show my loyalty. However, there are others that I have bonded with where the bond wasn't forced, like Aster."

Nodding, I leafed through one of the books, considering his words—and warning. Samian had known Ambrose for a long time. He had a better idea of who Ambrose was than I did. But my instincts told me that Samian wasn't telling me everything. It was also hard picturing Ambrose as someone other than the kind and considerate man from yesterday, shielding me from my father's scorn—and Liam's. Not to mention, he gave me a place of my own, even if the room was too grand for someone like me. He didn't have to go through all that trouble.

"I think we should get started with our lesson," Samian sighed, snapping me from my thoughts. "The first thing you need to learn is how to feel for your magic. Feeling your own magic and another's magic will each have a unique sensation. Your magic will feel welcoming and safe, while others' magic will feel foreign, like it doesn't belong. I want you to close your eyes and clear your mind."

Exhaling, I shifted in my seat to get comfortable and closed my eyes. Taking another deep breath, I pushed away all the questions and restlessness of my magic to focus on my breath.

Once my breathing became steady, Samian continued in a calming tone. "Good, now breathe toward your center. Tune into the sounds around you. What do you feel? What do you hear?"

Focusing on the smooth feeling of air expanding my lungs, I felt the feathery-soft smoke of power curling and twisting under my skin. I felt it dance within me, ready to be known. I concentrated harder on that feeling, and my body seemed to hum in response. Before I knew it, warmth spread through me, relaxing my body until I was sitting in the middle of a vast field with nothing but sky around me. Tall grass lay out before me, mixed with flowers of pink, purple, yellow, and blue. The warmth of the sun seeped into my skin, the brightness melting away all my anxiety and loneliness—my fears. Birds flew overhead, playing in the gentle breeze, their chittering sounding like music in my ears. A quiet peace overcame me, and I felt a tear slide down my face. I had never felt such stillness before.

I heard a distant murmur calling my name, but it felt like a world away, and I wasn't ready to leave this place. The voice called my name again, and I opened my eyes, finding Samian watching me closely. Something flickered in his eyes, but it was gone before I could tell what it was.

"That was your magic," he murmured softly, as if the quiet calm of the room was something fragile and frail, something that could be easily broken with words louder than a whisper.

Opening my mouth to answer, I closed it when a blond, slender man walked up to Samian, handing him two notes. He kept his brown eyes averted, focusing on the papers Samian held.

Samian went rigid as he read the first note. "Seems like Ambrose is ready for you," he said, his voice tight. Crumpling the note, he read the other. "It's just as well. Your tests have come back," Standing, Samian pocketed the second note that I assumed was from Aster, tucking it deep within his vest. "We can leave the books here for now. Follow Hale to Ambrose's office. I'll find you afterward."

Unease filled my veins at Samian's dismissiveness, and I looked over to Hale, who gave me a slight bow and hurried to the stairs. I followed, but glanced back at Samian as I went, catching him frowning at the note crumpled on the table before I rushed to catch up with Hale.

CHAPTER 13
SAMIAN

The results are ready—come as soon as possible.

-A.

Restless, I rushed down the steps of the library. The urgency of her note, the sense of secrecy, the phoenix drawing at the bottom—it all worried me—and I knew that whatever she found wasn't good. We created the drawing years ago in case there was something important—and secret—we needed to discuss. Sybil's blood work was just supposed to tell us how much of her was fae and how potentially strong she could be. Ambrose assumed that her ability to use her magic while still mostly human meant she could be incredibly powerful. Part of me feared just how right he was.

Leaving the library, I checked the hallway, making sure it was empty before summoning up my magic, transferring me to the doors of the medical wing. As I opened those doors, I was greeted by one of the healers, just as Aster turned the corner.

"Ah, right on time," Aster said, looking at a folder filled with documents. "I was beginning to think you were going to miss your appointment, Samian." The sharpness of her voice was enough to send the healer running into another room.

I laughed softly, tracking the healer's movements. "My apologies, Aster. I lost track of the time."

Aster walked past me, huffing as she led us to a room down the furthest hallway. She opened the room wide enough for me to enter before closing it softly behind her. Peering through the small window in the door, she quickly locked it and moved a tall cabinet to block it. Raising an eyebrow, my jaw clenched tightly as I studied the tightness in her features.

"Aster," I breathed, taking a step toward her.

She put her hands in front of her, stopping me from getting closer. Taking a step back, she leaned against the shelf; her face was pale and worn. "I don't know what you've gotten me into this time, Samian, but whatever it is, you have to promise me that Ambrose will never find out what I'm about to tell you." Aster took a shaky breath, swallowing hard. "He will kill me if he finds out that I've kept something like this from him."

"Aster, I don't understand," I murmured, my chest tightening with alarm at the shadows flickering in her eyes.

"Promise me, Samian," Aster demanded out.

"Fine, I promise. Aster, what's going on?"

Grabbing my arm, Aster pulled me to a table with a microscope, throwing Sybil's folder on the desk. "Look into the microscope and tell me what you see." Her voice was tight, trembling slightly.

My brow furrowed, but I leaned over, carefully peering into the microscope, finding Sybil's blood on the plate. I could see the mix of blood cells, both fae and human. Taking a closer look, a human cell slowly morphed into a cell that looked remarkably identical to that of a fae. Whipping my head to Aster, she pointed to a computer on the table behind us, showing a more detailed view of Sybil's DNA.

"What is this?" I asked, my voice hard while my heart started to race.

"I had assumed Sybil's fae blood was on the lower end. I thought that she probably had a distant relative who was fae or mixed. But there are three abnormalities that I noticed when I studied her blood closely." Pausing, Aster took a deep breath as we watched another blood cell change. "The first and most concerning is that she's not exactly fae. She belongs to the Seelie Court."

As I watched another cell morph, my stomach dropped. She was part of the Seelie Court, the court of the gods, the children of the first faeries and elves who created our realm. Ambrose would kill her if he knew. He would kill *anyone* who knew. "What are the other two?"

"Her human blood is changing rapidly. Those cells look similar enough to fae cells that anyone untrained wouldn't be able to tell the difference. However, they're morphing into seelie cells."

Shaking my head, I tried to piece together what Aster was saying, but I couldn't understand. I could see them changing, but this… this was unheard of.

Aster exhaled sharply at my ineptitude and pulled a closer image of Sybil's blood work. "You bound her when she was a child, correct?" she asked, annoyance coloring her words.

"I did, but I don't see what that has to do with her blood changing," I confessed, slightly cringing when Aster's frown deepened.

"Because she was bound, her seelie blood was put to sleep, so to speak. However, when the bind was broken, her newly awakened magic kick-started her seelie blood." Cutting her gaze to me, Aster leaned forward, whispering so softly that I could hardly understand her words. "She's turning less human with every second, Samian. It seems like it has slowed down for the time being, but at the moment, she's around twenty-five percent seelie."

I blinked. "What?" My stomach twisted further as unease gathered in the pit of my stomach. "That can't be. Her father mentioned that this had existed in her family for centuries. His own blood work showed less than half a percent. I can understand how her percentage could be higher than that, but not to that degree."

"I don't know what to tell you, Samian," Aster shrugged. "The results are showing twenty-five percent and growing. You saw it yourself. Her human blood is changing."

Frowning, I looked back at the screen, my throat tightening as another cell changed. "You said there was a third abnormality."

Aster exhaled through her nose, pulling up another image of a cluster of seelie blood cells. "Do you see that cell?" she said, pointing to a cell on the right.

I leaned in closer, focusing on the cell when it suddenly pulsed before returning to normal. "What was that?" I asked quietly, unable to look away from the screen.

Aster hesitated, rolling her hand into a tight fist. "I don't know."

We continued watching as the cell pulse again, others joining it. The thick silence stretched between us.

"Have you seen that before?"

Shaking her head, Aster stood, turned to me, and leaned

against the desk, crossing her arms. She eyed the microscope, her finger tapping against her arm. Her lips thinned as she bit the inside of her cheek. Shaking her head again, she exhaled sharply, picked up the folder, and shoved it against my chest. Taking the folder, I opened it, running my eyes over Sybil's results.

"I've never seen anything like this before, but my gut is telling me that this," Aster said, pointing to the computer screen, "is something that Ambrose shouldn't know about." I opened my mouth, ready to ask a question, but she put her hand up, silencing me before I could even speak. "I can't explain why. However, my intuition is warning me against it. I-I changed the numbers on the results I sent to Ambrose to show that she's ten percent fae and left out the abnormalities. Those," she said, pointing to the folder in my hands, "are the results that show the correct numbers. I suggest you either keep this to yourself or keep it within our group. I would even suggest not telling Sybil until you know if she can be trusted with this information."

"Shit," I breathed, trying to calm my racing thoughts. "I'll do some research to see if anything similar has happened before."

Eyeing the folder, I opened it and skimmed through the results again.

The Seelie Court.

Sybil belonged to that dangerous group. I fought against the shudder that threatened to surge through me. Taking out the papers, I released a quick breath while I folded them, placing them in the hidden pocket of my vest. Glancing over to Aster, her eyes were hard as they stared at the floor. I studied the rigidity of her stance, the fear in her eyes from the moment I entered the medical wing, and my heart clenched at the sight of it.

Without thinking, I moved, closing the distance between us. Putting my hands on either side of her, I leaned in, giving her a soft kiss on her cheek, lingering for a brief moment before I straightened. Aster swallowed thickly, looking away, but my smile grew when I noticed how she was holding her breath. Chuckling, I put my finger under her chin, pulling her head back to me. The pink in her cheeks grew, her eyes narrowing at me, giving me a steely glare.

Of all the years I'd known her, she was reclusive, always preferring the quiet over the presence of people. She could be cold and hard to those around her, but for anyone she allowed close, she cared for them deeply. It was a wonder people couldn't see that.

"Thank you," I murmured, and meant it.

Aster just rolled her eyes, and I knew she was fighting the urge to elbow me in the gut. Reaching for the end of her rich brown hair, I gave it a slight tug. "Goodbye, Aster," I said, moving the shelf and leaving the room, her quiet tsk following me out the door.

Before leaving the medical ward, I sent Sybil a note, letting her know that the rest of today's lesson was canceled and asking her to read the books I had given her earlier. I made my way back to the library, found the biology section, and pulled any book I could find in hopes of uncovering answers about the pulsing cells or her blood changing. After gathering a good selection of books, I let my magic free, transferring myself to my quarters and making my way to the hidden room, grabbing John's journal along the way. I needed to do this research away from the eyes of Ambrose's spies. The last thing I needed was for Ambrose to get suspicious.

THREE HOURS PASSED, and I still hadn't found a single thing about Sybil's abnormalities. Looking through John's journal didn't provide much help either. His thoughts were scattered and erratic, like a man slowly losing his grip on reality. I couldn't make sense of most of what was written. However, there was one section that caught my attention. John and The Harbingers had noticed the abnormal pulsing cells in his blood. According to their research, it was further proof that John's lineage came from a demon, but their explanations were too short-sighted, limited to believing only in angels and demons. They had no idea of the hidden creatures that roamed Mide and beyond.

However, this told me it wasn't an anomaly that started with Sybil, nor did it seem like some odd mutation. This was proof that Sybil's lineage came not only from the Seelie Court. There was something else hidden in her bloodline, something that I needed to find before Ambrose learned of this.

Leaning back in my chair, I closed my tired, bloodshot eyes, letting them rest. I still hadn't decided whether I should tell Sybil about the results of her bloodwork. She was still too unaware of the danger Ambrose posed to her, still too naive about his character.

Exhaling, I opened my eyes, scanning through her results. We confirmed during her lesson that her magic is the element of light. The glow surrounding her was bright and warm as she settled into herself, and the power radiating from her was strong. She could be powerful if trained well. She could be the weapon the rebels had been searching for if she would stop letting the fear of her magic consume her.

Setting the results aside, I flipped to the next page in an ancient journal I had stumbled on. Oddly enough, though the tome was in the biology section, it turned out to be a journal of medical logs for those of the royal bloodline.

Scanning the page, my heart stopped before thumping hard against my chest. I straightened in my chair, feeling blindsided by what the page showed. A lump rose in my throat, and I skimmed the rest of the long-forgotten passage of a high fae named Lux. Slamming the book shut, I called my magic to me, preparing to transfer myself. I stood, letting the world tilt around me until I stepped in front of a quiet cell.

The dungeon was dark, wet, and cold. The musty smell of fear and piss filled the air. However, the cell before me was clean and warm. There was a small window near the ceiling, letting in a small amount of light, while lamps illuminated the room, which was decorated with velvet furniture. Silk curtains hung along the stone walls; a small, warm bed with fur pelts lay on top, and plush rugs covered the floor, giving the cell a surprisingly cozy feel, considering the circumstances.

I grabbed the bars, the icy cold biting at my hands. My heart thrashed in my chest. Formality long forgotten by a burning need for answers, my eyes narrowed on the female inside. "She's your descendant," I breathed, a sickening shock rolling through me.

Releasing a sharp breath, Queen Cassia closed her book with a thud before slowly making her way to the iron bars that had kept her imprisoned for over fifty years.

CHAPTER 14
SYBIL

The next morning dawned brightly. Samian's persistent knocking on my door grew louder as I groaned, not wanting to move from the warmth of my bed.

"For fuck's sake, enough already," I yelled, crawling out of bed. I made my way to the bathroom to get ready.

Today felt better. After Samian bailed on me yesterday, I spent the rest of the day exploring the palace. I even brought a notepad with me so I could draw a makeshift map for myself. It ended up coming in handy more than once, especially when Hale, the pale blond servant, conveniently disappeared and I had to make my way back to the library after my meeting with Ambrose. A lingering annoyance crawled down my back at the memory.

The meeting went as well as it could have after Samian's warnings. The air felt awkward and uncomfortable while sitting with Ambrose. My body felt tense as I sat there answering all his questions. I tried my best to hide my unease, but Ambrose still somehow noticed the tension and decided that after his meetings today, he would take me out to show me the city.

Anxiety twisted through me all night, making my mind spin. I ran through our meeting over and over, picking at his words or the way his body moved to figure out the real reason he was being so generous. I barely got any sleep because of it. My mind created so many different stories and outcomes of our meeting today that I felt jittery. Especially when I tried to study the books Samian gave me. It was a very long and restless night of rereading passages until my eyes felt like they were bleeding.

Tugging on a white buttoned shirt and a navy tunic with silver threading, I pulled my shoes on and grabbed my books on the way out of my room. When I opened the door, a troubled Samian was leaning against the marbled wall opposite of my door. His elegant face seemed dulled. He looked tired. His eyes were drawn and hollow, his face paler than usual, and the warmth he had greeted me with yesterday was missing. Frowning, I stepped closer, putting my hand against his forehead to check if he had a fever.

He swatted my hand, his brows knitting and forming a wrinkle in the middle. "What are you doing?" he asked, taking a step away.

I blinked, fighting the cringe I felt welling inside. It was a habit learned from my mother that followed me into adulthood, and to do it to Samian felt oddly natural, though I doubted he felt that way. "I'm checking to see if you're sick," I shrugged, pretending that it wasn't weird how comfortable I felt in his presence after only knowing him for one day. "You don't look well, like something is bothering you."

"Nothing is bothering me," he sighed, though his eyes darkened for a moment before returning to normal. "And I'm not sick, so you don't have to do that. Faeries aren't prone to sickness like humans are."

I raised a brow and gave him a knowing look, but nodded, not wanting to pry. Samian returned my look before walking away. I rolled my eyes, shooting glares into his back, but followed him, bristling at the uncomfortable silence between us. Something must have happened yesterday to make him act so detached.

As if he could feel the weight of my gaze, Samian stopped short, making me gasp when I almost ran into his back. Hesitating for a moment, Samian clenched and unclenched his hands before turning to me. He opened his mouth to speak, but closed it, glancing at the wall beside us. I could feel him wrestling with the words he wanted to say, and my heart squeezed at seeing him look so uneasy.

I watched him closely, my nerves eating away at me as I noticed the muscle in his jaw feather over and over.

"I apologize," he said a moment later, his face tight with apprehension. "I received some troubling news last night, so my mood for today is not the best. However, I will try not to let that get in the way of our day."

"Did something bad happen?" I asked, wondering whether it had anything to do with my meeting with Ambrose and the plans we discussed yesterday.

Pausing, Samian held out his elbow, waiting for me to take it so we could walk together. Sliding my arm into his, he gave me a warm smile, and the tightness in my chest eased, filling with warmth, though it didn't last long.

He's with Aster, I reminded myself, feeling guilty for how it felt so easy to be around him, to find comfort in his touch.

"No," Samian sighed. "Fortunately, nothing has happened yet. But I would also like to apologize for canceling our lesson.

How was the rest of your day? Did you read the books I gave you?"

Plastering a smile on my face, I laughed nervously. "It was nice. I had a chance to explore the palace while expertly avoiding Arianna and her crew of unhinged busybodies," I said, hoping he wouldn't notice how I avoided his second question. "I also found my way back to my room *without* getting lost."

"However did you manage that one?" Samian laughed, the corners of his eyes crinkling.

The change in his voice and the lightness of his laugh made my heart swell. I pulled my arm away and opened the top book, pulling out my map. Handing it to Samian, his smile grew wide as he studied it.

He handed me my map, and we continued our walk. "I guess I should let you lead us to the library, then. But," he paused, tapping on a section of the page that had a lousy drawing of a dragon statue, "you should probably keep away from that area as much as possible if you're trying to avoid Arianna and her band of followers."

Nodding, I thanked him while I took out a pen to jot that down.

The rest of our walk felt relaxed. I described everything I saw yesterday, Samian oohing and aahing as if he had never been around the palace before. It was silly, but my heart felt light for the first time in days. Samian's stiffness had eased by the time we made our way up the stairs, but when we turned toward our study area, Samian quietly let out a curse. His body went rigid beside me. Surprised, I looked to our table, only to find Ambrose leaning against it. The books that were piled in neat stacks yesterday were thrown about the table while Ambrose thumbed through one of them, his face set in a mask of casual boredom.

Hearing us step closer to the table, Ambrose lifted his head, a wide smile brightening his face. His hair was styled back, and those dark blue eyes twinkled.

"Ah," Ambrose said, closing the book with a soft thud. "Right on time. Are you ready, my dear Sybil?"

I sucked in a breath, my face blanching. He said that he had appointments this morning, which would have given me enough time to tell Samian about our meeting and today's plans. However, here he was, bright and early. Mortification bled through my entire being.

Samian took a sharp breath, pulling me closer to his side. "Ready for what?" he asked flatly.

Ambrose tilted his head and studied Samian for a moment, as if he were questioning whether to answer him or not. "Sybil and I have a date today," Ambrose finally answered, smiling wickedly as if to taunt him.

Samian whipped his head toward me, my cheeks flushing when I met his gaze. Anger flashed across his face; his eyes filled with something close to suspicion. Tightness crept its way up my throat, and I swallowed thickly, not understanding the meaning of that heated look.

"Ambrose thought it would be a good idea to show me around the city today," I said, my voice soft and timid. "It would give us a chance to get to know each other better." Even though I was just repeating the words Ambrose had said to me yesterday, they felt thick as I said them.

Samian searched my face, slipping into his mask of indifference. My stomach twisted at the cold dimness in his eyes before he turned back to Ambrose, disregarding me entirely. "We have a very busy day today. Sybil cannot afford to miss her lessons."

Waving a dismissive hand, Ambrose chuckled while he sauntered over to us, his body tense as if ready for a fight. "I believe, Samian, that our sweet Sybil will be fine missing one lesson. And it's not like you had that same sentiment yesterday, when you missed the rest of her lesson to laze around in your room, right?"

Samian's jaw clenched, a low, threatening growl rumbling from his chest, and I couldn't help the fear that skirted down my back. Ambrose stepped closer, his hand grabbing onto Samian's shoulder and tightening. "Sybil and I will be leaving now. You're dismissed for the rest of the day. Why don't you go back to your room to continue whatever you were doing yesterday? Understood?"

A tense moment passed before Samian looked away, his jaw clenching. Ambrose smiled, tapping his hand on Samian's cheek and laughing as if the strained bubble surrounding them had never existed.

"Great," Ambrose said, turning his attention to me. Sweeping his gaze over me, his face softened, though his eyes still resembled those of a predator hungrily eyeing its prey. I shivered at the thought. "I've been looking forward to this all morning, my dear. So much, in fact, that I canceled all my meetings so we could spend more time together."

Ambrose offered me his hand, but I glanced at Samian, unease making my chest tight. Samian stood unnaturally still; the line of his jaw was hard, and his hands were balled into tight fists. Ambrose cleared his throat, a hint to not keep him waiting any longer. Samian gave me a sidelong glance, tipped his head in a slight nod, and took my books. Taking a deep breath, I warily took Ambrose's hand, trying not to let the disappointment I felt show on my face.

Tightening his grip, Ambrose swung me around, twirling me as if we were in the middle of a dance, making me gasp. Tension made my movements awkward, and another deep laugh rumbled through Ambrose's chest as he turned back to Samian, giving him a wink before guiding us to the stairs. I fought against the urge to look back, too afraid of what I would find if I did, so I kept my eyes forward and swallowed down the acid that rose in my throat.

Taking my arm and looping it through his, Ambrose led us through the palace, waving and smiling to all the women who passed us. My body felt heavy with an irritation that grew with every long sigh that escaped from their lips. Ambrose seemed to enjoy the attention, though. He softly chuckled to himself before shifting his focus to the next set of ladies, their gazes sharpening on where my hand rested on his arm.

After passing the fifth group of women, my patience had begun to wane when Ambrose finally turned his attention to me. "So, I heard you had quite the day yesterday. Going to the medical wing, seeing the library, and exploring all the nooks and crannies of the palace. Tell me, did you find anything interesting?"

His tone was light and playful, like he was prodding me to spill all my secrets. But my mind could only focus on one thing —how did he know? "Are you having me followed?" I asked, narrowing my eyes. I tried to keep my tone just as light, but I couldn't stop the hint of suspicion that wove through my words.

"Gods, no," Ambrose laughed, his dazzling smile growing wide. "Though there are a few busybodies who love to fill me in on anything I might have missed. Speaking of those busybodies, I would like to apologize on Arianna's behalf. After our meeting yesterday, I heard about your time with her in the dining hall. I know she can be a bit difficult; however, with time, I'm sure you'll become fast friends."

Ambrose kept his face solemn, but there was a lightness in

his tone that made my jaw clench. He made it sound like our *time* in the dining hall was just a little argument. Like a childish antic. But the memory of how adamant Arianna had been in her abuse crossed through my mind. Her cold blue eyes gleamed with joy while her wretched laugh rang through the dining hall. She knew all about how I lost my job and how Liam kicked me out. I bristled at the flashback. I felt like I was just a joke between her and Ambrose. Did they laugh about how incapable I was? The thought set me on edge.

Ambrose's eyebrow rose, and I realized he was still waiting for me to respond. Pushing aside my uneasiness, I shook my head. "I'm not sure about that."

Ambrose watched me thoughtfully for a moment before saying, "I know it may be difficult to see, but she does mean well. She is fiercely protective of those she cares for. I hope you can understand that and give her the benefit of the doubt."

Something in Ambrose's eyes made me hesitant to disagree with him, joking or not. A cool feeling prickled through me, but quickly soothed into a quiet understanding as I thought about how I could have reacted. My temper had always gotten the best of me, especially in moments like the dining hall. That hot rage took over so easily that I would often react before I knew what I was doing or even saying.

"I'll try to get along with her," I mumbled, looking away.

"Good girl," Ambrose hummed, gently patting my arm. For a moment, his approval had me fighting a smile, and I cursed myself for letting his words have that effect on me. "Now tell me, what did you learn about the palace yesterday?"

The tightness in my shoulders eased, and I flashed him a quick grin. "I learned every hallway looks almost the same." I laughed shyly. "But I was able to find enough small differences to help me learn my way around. Like the hall that leads to the library from my room has a small crack in the marble near the entrance of the hall."

Frowning, Ambrose hummed a low tone of disapproval, but kept his face masked with an earnest interest. I knew his disapproval wasn't toward me, but it didn't stop me from wanting to apologize.

The rest of the walk through the palace was silent. Ambrose's mind seemed to be elsewhere, and I kept my breathing as steady as I could, tension wracking my body at the thought of upsetting him. However, when we stepped onto the street outside the palace gates, Ambrose's body relaxed as he breathed in the fresh air and took in the street around us.

"I noticed when you came to the library that you carried your books. I think the first thing we should do is find a bag for you to carry your things." His eyes brightened as if another idea came to mind. "Ah, I've got it," he purred, moving back a step and slowly sliding his gaze down my body and back up again, making my face feel warm. "We will go on a little shopping spree, and then we shall get something to eat and re-energize ourselves before seeing the sights of the city. How does that sound?"

"I think it sounds like too much," I laughed. His excitement melted away any strain that had been there before. "I don't have any money, and I have clothes that fit well enough."

"Nonsense," Ambrose exclaimed, stepping close enough to me that I could feel the heat from his powerful body. "Though that tunic does fit you well," he drawled, his smile turning wicked, "you need something worthy of your new status within the palace. Something that not only shows off those delicious curves of yours, but also lets others know that you're not just a *commoner*."

My cheeks flushed at his deep, sensuous voice, and I shifted, trying to put some distance between us. The way he had said commoner, as if it was a disgraceful thing to be seen as one, didn't sit right with me. It was easy to lose myself in the pleasing timbre of his voice, easy to let that sound slide across my skin like velvet, but his saying commoner as an insult made me feel wary. "According to everyone in the palace, that's exactly what I am," I muttered, my stomach twisting. "A commoner."

"Not anymore." Ambrose smiled sinfully.

CHAPTER 15
SYBIL

Not anymore? My brows knitted together, waiting for Ambrose to explain.

"As of today, you were added to my court, which makes you one of us and in need of attire worthy of that."

I blinked, unable to think of words—any words—to say. Ambrose laughed at the shock that took over my face. That wariness doubled when Ambrose's pleasant smile widened as if he had done me some incredible favor. Those warning bells screamed for me to go back to the palace, to the safety of Samian's presence. Noticing my discomfort, Ambrose pulled me closer until my body rested against his, and I could feel every hard muscle beneath his shirt.

I swallowed a gasp as a surge of warming comfort rushed through me, traveling low in my stomach as he tucked a lock of hair behind my ear. The unease I had felt quickly vanished, and my brows furrowed, but Ambrose grinned, and my apprehension melted away. Ambrose turned to the street, his eyes searching for where we should start first. Once he found the store, he tugged me along while my mind swam at how quickly I had relaxed from his touch.

Ambrose didn't stop pulling me along until we reached a little shop that smelled of musk and leather. Opening the door, Ambrose gestured for me to enter. Beautiful leather bags, boots, and other leather goods lined the walls and tables. My eyes widened as I walked to a dark brown bag. My fingers ran over the floral designs etched into the soft leather. I had seen nothing like it.

"Do you like that one?" Ambrose murmured, leaning in close enough that his breath brushed against my neck.

My body trembled, my face heating at his nearness. Nodding, I looked away, not wanting him to see the flush creeping up my neck.

Ambrose called over the attendant, handing him the bag while we walked around the shop. I found a smaller bag matching the one I found earlier, along with a pair of black leather boots I could wear during training or when I traveled outside the palace. As the attendant boxed my items, Ambrose made me wait by the door while he paid the owner.

Once he was finished, Ambrose took my hand, holding it tight in his as we made our way across the street to the next shop. Ambrose held the door open for me again, giving me a gentle smile. The shop turned out to be a boutique, and my eyes widened at the variety of colors and fabric types that filled it. Mannequins lined the far left wall, displaying different dresses —some with full skirts, while others were fitted to show off the lines of the person who wore them. Each one was beautiful and splendid.

A female attendant excitedly rushed toward us, her eyes wide and eager, ready to help Ambrose with all his needs while ignoring me completely. Rolling my eyes, I exhaled and walked to the fabrics closest to us while Ambrose discussed what he was looking for in hushed tones. I glanced over to them when the attendant giggled, finding Ambrose sliding a finger gently down her arm. Swallowing, my stomach twisted, and I walked in further, hoping the yards of fabric would block the view. Spotting a reel of beautiful dark green silk, I rubbed my thumb across the smooth top before letting it glide across my hand, falling back into place.

"That color would look amazing on you," Ambrose murmured softly behind me, his voice deep and luxurious.

Gasping, I turned around, meeting his gaze, my heart beating wildly against my chest. My eyes narrowed, and my lips rose in a small, playful smile. "Do you do this with all the ladies of your court?" I teased, though I secretly hoped he would say no.

Ambrose laughed and stepped closer, his face bright. "No, I don't do this with all the ladies of my court. Just the ones that interest me," he purred.

I lifted my chin and studied him—the lines of his jaw, his lips, the way his eyes shone in the light, looking like the deepest ocean. "Do I interest you?" It sounded like a challenge, I realized, but I refused to back down, especially when his smile turned downright lethal.

"I find you incredibly interesting."

Heat curled low in my stomach, and I could hardly breathe. The fire that glowed in his eyes felt so intense that I had to look away. Turning back to the fabric, I slid my hand across it. "I love colors like this," I said, changing the subject, trying to ignore the weight of his stare. "Darker colors feel comforting, like they match who I am, if that makes sense."

"They pair well with certain nighttime activities, as well,"

Ambrose drawled, sliding his heavy hand down the side of my waist.

My breath hitched, heat pooling low in my stomach. How long had it been since I'd felt this warmth? With Liam, it was nothing more than a comfort, a way to pass the time. It was something I just went along with because I knew how much he wanted it. But Ambrose's touch made me feel awake. It made me want to feel more. I opened my mouth—to say what, I wasn't sure—just as the attendant appeared, telling us a room was ready to take my measurements. Any heat I felt was quickly doused.

Following the attendant to the room, I paused, looking back at Ambrose, who lingered at the deep green silk. His hand ran over the delicate fabric, lost in thought. The woman cleared her throat again, annoyed at my dawdling. With one last look at Ambrose, I pushed any emotions I felt for him down and quickly made my way to the room.

AFTER BEING POKED AND PRODDED, I felt exhausted when the attendants finally finished clearing their things. They sent me out to the main floor in a dark lavender floor-length skirt with a fitted cream top that formed a deep V down the middle and showed off the swell of my breasts. The skirt wasn't cotton or silk; it was soft and smooth, and I had been too afraid to ask the tight-lipped woman what it was made from. The attendant had braided the top of my ashy brown hair, letting the rest fall down my back in waves. I felt odd, like I was playing dress-up. The outfit was beautiful, though. I looked soft and feminine.

I found Ambrose waiting patiently on a chaise with a glass of wine. Spotting me, he raised an eyebrow, the corner of his lips rising as he swept his gaze over me. Ambrose stood and quickly closed the distance between us, extending his hand for me to take. My cheeks flushed, and I took his hand, letting him spin me around before pulling me into him.

"You are absolutely breathtaking, my dear Sybil," Ambrose said gently, pressing a kiss to my cheek.

I blushed and put the back of my hand against my face. "You're exaggerating," I breathed.

"Oh, I assure you, there is no exaggerating how lovely you look." His voice darkened as he took me in, his eyes lingering on the deep cut of my shirt. My body felt too hot, too thin under the intensity of his stare.

Taking a steadying breath, I faced the door, the blush on my cheeks deepening. Ambrose laughed softly, then led me to the chaise to sit while he settled our account. Embarrassment coiled inside of me. I was too old to be acting like a schoolgirl with a crush. But those eyes, that touch, I couldn't help but want more.

We left the boutique, and Ambrose took my hand, pressing a soft kiss to it as we walked down the cobbled street. "I was thinking we could stop by a little tea shop that I think you would love. We can rest and talk before we return to the palace. Does that sound okay?"

"I think that sounds amazing," I said, placing a hand on my empty stomach. Like yesterday, Samian and I had planned to have our breakfast in the library to avoid Arianna and the dining hall. Because of that, and this *date* as Ambrose called it, I hadn't been able to eat, and my stomach cramped as if it were devouring itself.

We walked to a quaint tea shop with a small section set up for tables. The shop was busy, but the owners found us a table right away. The inside was light blue, with a floral wallpaper that gave it a whimsical feel. Ambrose ordered for us while I studied the fae around us. They were all so beautiful that their elegance and grace never ceased to amaze me.

Given Ambrose's status, many of those in the shop eyed us, curious about who I was and, I'm sure, my relationship with Ambrose. The constant stares made me want to slip further into my chair and hide. Ambrose acted oblivious to the constant attention, like he was used to it all, but the pleasant smile plastered on his face looked forced.

"So," he purred, "what questions could our dear Sybil have for me?"

I paused, thinking back to the question that had been nagging me all day. "Why did you add me to your court?"

"Hmm," he murmured, considering his answer. "To reside in the palace, you must be a noble or linked to one with noble blood in some way. I wanted to keep you close; therefore, I made you a part of my court." He shrugged, simple as that.

Thinking of Samian and his warnings, I hesitated with my next question, but the need to know ate away at me, so I forced myself to ask. "Is Samian a part of your court as well?"

"No," Ambrose said, his forced smile twitching. "He is not part of my court, nor will he ever be. He is not officially a noble, though he lives in the palace under special circumstances."

I shifted in my seat at the sharpness in his voice, but continued my questions. "Samian told me about Queen Cassia. Wouldn't she need to approve of me being added to your court?"

Any pretense of pleasantry, fake or not, was abandoned with my question. Ambrose's smile faltered; his face hardened, and his eyes glinted with warning. Tapping his finger against the table, Ambrose leaned back, staring, unblinking, at me before taking a deep breath. Slipping his fake smile back into place, he let out a small laugh. I shrank at how easily he slid back into that charming pretense of his.

"No, I do not need her approval. As the queen's advisor, I take her place in palace decisions when she is not available to do so. What exactly has Samian said about the queen?"

"Not much, just that she was kind, and that she's traveling, I think."

Ambrose hummed and picked at the table. Our conversation halted with the arrival of our tea and plates of pastries and petits fours. The silence grew thick as the servers arranged the plates and poured our tea. After they left, Ambrose flashed a smile, but his eyes remained distant as he gestured for me to try the tea. I took a sip; the floral taste felt warm and relaxing. Ambrose filled my plate with an assortment of sweets and watched me try each one. Each tiny cake looked perfect and delicately soft, but they tasted like ash in my mouth.

I had just taken a bite of my third petit four when Ambrose set down his cup with a sigh. "I apologize," he said softly. "I fear I may have made you uncomfortable with your last question. It wasn't my intention. Being the queen's advisor comes with certain difficulties, such as accusations of overreaching. That is why I tend to shut down when asked such questions. However," he said, reaching out and gently wrapping his hand around mine, "I should have realized that you were just asking to learn how our world works here. For that, I am sorry."

Tightening his hand around mine, Ambrose rubbed his thumb in tiny circles along the top of my hand, and I gave him a weak smile. It was true that I was curious about how the palace operated and his role within it, but I also couldn't deny my lingering suspicion after Samian's warnings. However, after spending time with Ambrose, my perception of him was quickly changing. He was charismatic and enchanting. It was easy to fall for his sweet murmurings and warm touches. He had acted as if we were close companions from the moment we met, which made me feel comfortable and safe. It was getting harder to believe Samian's cautioning.

"It's okay," I said, placing my other hand on top of his. "I get it. It's hard not to react when you've constantly had to deal with issues like that. I'm the same way."

"It seems like we have something in common," he said, giving me a soft smile before pulling my hand to him and placing a tender kiss on top.

My mind zeroed in on where his lips met my hand. His lips were soft and pleasant, and my body seemed to hum at his touch. My heart jumped when he placed another kiss a little higher on my hand. I swallowed thickly, a rush of heat sweeping through me and pooling low. I let out a nervous laugh, and he gave my hand a soft squeeze before letting it slide away. Images of him kissing other places flashed across my mind. I quickly reached for my tea, taking a sip to wash away those thoughts before they morphed into something else. Ambrose was a flirtatious man; I needed to remind myself of that. He was just being nice to me. None of it meant anything to him. But even as I repeated that silently to myself, I knew he was someone I needed to be very careful around.

CHAPTER 16

SAMIAN

Keeping my eyes on the table in front of me, I ground my teeth, recalling the moment that Ambrose led Sybil down the stairs, away from me. My breathing came in quick bursts, the sound of my blood roaring in my ears. I couldn't move, knowing that if I took one step, I would hunt them down and remind Ambrose just how I was able to find my place in the court.

My jaw clenched so tightly it ached. I fisted my hands, taking a deep breath, letting the air expand my too-tight lungs. My heart was racing, but I needed to calm myself before I did something I would regret. Ambrose was trying to goad me, hoping that I would slip and make a mistake that allowed him to get rid of me, as he had done with Queen Cassia.

Taking another few deep breaths, I finally walked to the table, reordering the books Ambrose had scattered. I could feel the eyes of Ambrose's spies on me, waiting for me to do something damning they could report back to him. Shifting through the books, I schooled my face into indifference as I carefully—

casually—took in my surroundings. Unable to pinpoint the spies' locations, I fought the urge to snarl and grabbed Sybil's notebooks before making my way back to my room.

Though Sybil being with Ambrose ate away at me, his dismissal came at an opportune time. After I visited with Queen Cassia, I left a signal requesting a meeting with the rebels. The information I learned yesterday was too significant to ignore. A meeting with them was imperative and could not be put off, even if all I wanted was to find Sybil and separate her from Ambrose's scheming. All I could do now was hope that my warnings sufficed to keep her safe from his poisoned, honeyed words.

When I reached the door to my room, I paused, my hand tightly gripping the handle. Ambrose's spies were still watching me, hiding in corners and dark spaces. Ever since last night, I had felt more eyes on me than usual. It made me wonder if Ambrose knew what I had learned after my visit with the queen. Stepping into my room, I let the door shut softly behind me, my shoulders relaxing from the heavy weight of their watchful eyes. With a wave of my hand, the lights flickered on. My eyes narrowed on a missive lying on my desk, marked with the symbol of a phoenix in flight—the answer to my request.

Swallowing, I stared at the missive, pushing down the dread that had been consuming me since last night. My visit with the queen left me unsettled and restless about Sybil's safety. When I confronted her, Queen Cassia didn't deny that Sybil was her descendant. Instead, she let out a disappointed sigh and slowly made her way back to her velvet chaise. She stared blankly at a lamp in the corner of her cell before straightening herself and finally meeting my gaze, tapping a delicate finger against her temple—a signal for me to use our bond.

Closing my eyes, I cleared my mind, finding the invisible

string tethering my soul to hers. I breathed in deeply, opening myself to the magic as a memory formed, though it was blurry at first. When the memory cleared, I realized it was one from long ago.

Turning the corner, the hall was dark, but I could see the light from the room at the end. My breath grew tight as I—in Queen Cassia's body—entered the room. The figure of a male with long, pale blond hair emerged. His cool sky-blue eyes were distant as three other males surrounded him, pleading for him to change his mind. Exhaling, he closed his tired eyes and lifted a hand to silence them. Opening his eyes again, he looked to me as I lingered silently in the doorway. His eyes softened, and a gentle smile spread across his face. I stretched out my hands toward him, returning that smile, though my heart swelled with a deep sadness.

"Sister," Dryden said, rushing to me and taking my hands into his. "I must do this. Please understand that I must do this," he pleaded, his voice cracking on the last word. "I can't leave her behind. She is my mate, and to leave this world without her would shatter me. Please, please try to understand."

My heart squeezed so tight I could hardly breathe. "I understand, brother," I said, his face blurring through the tears that threatened to fall. "Stay here with your mate, watch over the humans with her, and protect them. I will take your place and rule in your stead until you can return."

The vision faltered, morphing into another memory.

My hands clenched tightly around a low oak branch as I watched a beautiful woman with flowing black hair walk into a courtyard filled with wild, colorful flowers, toward a crying child. Picking up the small child, the woman smiled softly, gently cooing to calm him.

"My love," Dryden called out, his voice filled with such tenderness.

The woman looked back at the doors as Dryden entered the court-

yard; her smile spreading across her face. Hugging her child closer to her chest, Dryden gave her a tender kiss before hugging her and the child from behind.

The memory faded, and I swallowed back my shock. My heart raced as the queen held my wild gaze.

"Sybil isn't your descendant...She's Dryden's," I said through our bond, my stomach twisting, bile threatening to rise in my throat.

"Yes, that's correct. I had hoped this secret would be kept as such," Queen Cassia said, looking back at the lamp. *"However, it seems as though fate has other plans."*

A curse left me, and the queen clucked her tongue in disapproval, giving me a reprimanding glare. Those same sky-blue eyes, the same as Dryden's and Sybil's father's, were bright. In different circumstances, I would have laughed, giving her a soft kiss on the cheek while she swatted me away.

"Has he figured it out yet?" she asked hesitantly. Worry filled those kind eyes, making her face seem hollow and pale.

"No, not yet," I sighed. *"Aster changed the information on Sybil's tests before giving them to Ambrose."*

"Smart girl," Queen Cassia chuckled. *"So, what shall you do next?"*

Shaking off the memory of last night, I focused back on the missive on my desk. There were no words, just the symbol of a phoenix—a request received and accepted. I ran a hand down my face, tipping my head against my door. Other than showing me those memories, Queen Cassia confirmed nothing else. She left most of my questions unanswered, refusing to even listen to them, only asking what my next move would be. But I stood there, unable to say a word.

I wasn't sure what I was going to do. Sybil wasn't supposed

to be here. She was supposed to be living her life with the other humans, oblivious to what she was and what she could do. More than anything, I wanted to ask the queen for advice as I did as a boy, but I knew she would just give me that motherly smile of hers before telling me how I needed to make my own decisions—my own path. So, for now, all I could do was meet with the rebels and make a plan.

Pushing off the door, I went to the closet and changed into plainclothes so I could blend in with those who lived in the city. Pulling my hair back, I slipped into a coat and drew the hood up to hide my hair and face. With my hair concealed, I could easily roam around unnoticed, at least until I got close enough to people for them to see my eyes.

Leaving through the hidden passage, I made my way into the city, weaving through the crowded streets. Observing the buildings around me, I looked for signs placed by my informant. I passed a stone tavern and caught a glimpse of something from the corner of my eye. Looking across the street at a shop, I found a small paper with a phoenix drawn in red nailed to the side. Slipping through the busy street, I ripped the paper from the wall, shoving it into my coat as I glanced at the crowd behind me.

The fae rushing through the streets and walkways disregarded me as they passed by, without a care in the world, unaware of who I was or what I was doing. Glancing at the tops of the buildings, I watched for any spies in the area before slipping into the alley, following the paper trail left by the informant as my only guide.

Coming to the end of an alley, a door to a tavern with a small phoenix carved in the upper right corner slammed open as a cook came out for a smoke break. He nodded to me, and I slipped in through the door that opened to the kitchens before making my way to the bar up front. The tavern was small and discreet, known only to those who had been told its location, but the worn tables and chairs gave the place a homey, welcoming feel.

I searched through the crowd, my eyes narrowing when they landed on the large male sitting near a window, watching the crowd pass by. I knocked on the bar, and the barkeep made his way to me. I set down some coins, sliding them over, and asked for two beers.

While I waited, I observed the fae in the tavern, my jaw clenching when I noticed that every single one of them wore a pin of a phoenix in flames. Although they made themselves look busy, they were here to watch me, to make sure I did nothing unsavory, like bringing uninvited guests. I fought the urge to roll my eyes and lost.

The barkeep slid the pints of beer to me, and my gaze cut to his. His eyes widened, recognition blooming across his face before he jerked his chin to the male near the window. Grabbing the pints, I walked to his table, scowling at the overcoat he wore to hide his body and face. He wasn't the one I was supposed to meet today, and he certainly wasn't supposed to be in the city.

I sat opposite of him, passing one of the pints over to him, and looked out the window toward a patisserie across the street. Inhaling sharply, I watched as Ambrose took Sybil's hand, her face turning pink from a soft blush.

"She's new," the male said coolly, his eyes never leaving Sybil. My hand tightened around my drink at the darkened tone of his voice. I watched his crimson eyes narrow in the window's reflection when Sybil smiled sweetly at Ambrose. I snarled, looking away.

"Ambrose and I brought her here a few days ago," I grumbled, shifting my focus to the foam of my beer, watching it slowly dissolve. I couldn't bear to watch her give *him* her smiles.

"And?" he grunted, quickly annoyed by my hesitance.

"And her name is Sybil," I shared warily. "She's the child I watched over after I bound her magic years ago in Mide."

His head whipped to me, our eyes meeting. Those dark crimson eyes bored into mine, and I slightly winced. He knew how protective I was of her. Though he never understood why, he never questioned it—never questioned *me* when I would slip into Mide to make sure she was okay. I glanced back at Sybil, snarling quietly when I caught Ambrose kissing her hand.

My throat tightened when her blush grew darker. "Ambrose found her, somehow, without my knowledge. He is planning something regarding her, though I do not know what that is. My informant is keeping a close eye on it, but I have a feeling he is going to trick her into a bargain. He already tried it once, when she lost control of her magic in front of her fiancé and father."

My eyes never left Ambrose as he pulled Sybil from her seat into his chest. I watched her linger in his arms before they made their way out of the patisserie. A silent growl left me, hot anger lacing through my veins. Vines curled from the table, making the male raise an eyebrow. When Ambrose and Sybil cut around the corner, I finally looked away, exhaling. I felt his eyes on me, and when I met them, they were filled with an amused interest, which only grew when I noticed the vines blooming along the table. Cursing, I flattened my hand against the table, making the vines disappear back into the worn wood.

Running a hand down my face, I leaned back into the chair before I quietly explained everything that had happened since finding Sybil. From her loss of control, the odd blood cells that pulsed or morphed, the raw power of her magic, to the queen's memories that she shared. By the end of my telling, the glint in his eyes had turned dangerous.

"Is she going to be a threat?" he asked flatly. His eyes were sharp, almost lethal, tracking every move I made, every expression.

Not wanting to answer, I took a long pull of beer, letting the taste of bitter hops soothe my nerves. "Yes and no," I finally answered, my stomach twisting with the words. "As I said, she doesn't know how to use her magic, and she can be a bit hot-headed, which will make her dangerous to anyone who provokes her. But watching her over the years, I know she will be on our side once she understands more about this world—about Ambrose. She's kind and has a good head on her shoulders; she just needs to learn how to control her magic. My informant and I will do our best to protect her from whatever Ambrose is planning. However, you should prepare yourself in case his plan succeeds."

Grunting, the male looked to the rebel closest to us. Her short black hair bobbed when she jumped from her seat, quickly leaving the tavern through the kitchen. "Thanks for the information," he said gruffly, pulling out a coin and tossing it to me. "Have another one on me," he said teasingly before leaving through the kitchen.

I scoffed, watching the rest of the rebels drain their cups before they stood and walked through those doors, following him out of the tavern. Waving to the barkeep for another pint, I relaxed into the chair, watching as the fae of Volmire made their way to different shops. The barkeep placed another pint on the table, picking up the coin that I had left at the edge. Feeling him linger, I gave him a sidelong glance, noticing a folded paper in his hand. My eyes narrowed at him, and I hesitantly took the note, watching as he walked back to the bar.

Opening the note, I barked a laugh at the messy handwriting telling me to get my sorry ass home before anyone noticed my absence and to visit the camp later this week. Tucking the note in my jacket, I quickly finished my beer and made my way back to the palace.

CHAPTER 17

KIERAN

The tavern door slammed shut behind me when amber eyes found mine, blocking the way toward the alley. Groaning, I closed my eyes, pinching the bridge of my nose. This girl was going to be the death of me. "Didn't I order you to help Vivi around the camp?" My voice had more bite to it than I intended, but this female seriously needed to learn to listen to orders.

"You needed someone to make sure the alleyways stayed cleared," Amara shrugged. "I figured I could help."

Opening my eyes, I narrowed them at her, ignoring the ridiculous grin she wore. "And are they?" I sighed, fighting the urge to strangle her. The city was dangerous for those of us *not* invited. If the guards had caught her without Volmire identification, they would have dragged her back to the palace for questioning.

"Are they what?" Amara blinked up at me.

This fucking girl.

"Are they clear?" I growled, quickly losing the battle to keep my hands to myself.

"Oh," she giggled. She fucking giggled. "All clear and ready for us to head back to camp!" Her voice rang out, echoing down the stone walls.

Amara's head whipped toward the empty back street, grimacing. Cautiously turning back to me, she shyly looked up, whispering an apology. A dark hand reached out, playfully hitting her on the back of the head. Orin stepped beside her as she rubbed the pain away, putting his hands on her shoulders and leading her down the walkway, scolding her. My lips twitched, wanting to curve into a smile when her shoulders dipped, but I pushed back on the impulse.

We left the side street in small groups, dispersing to conceal ourselves within the crowded streets, steering clear of the guards posted along the sidewalks. We timed our movements, allowing each group enough space to find the hidden passageway that led out into the city without being noticed, courtesy of Samian.

As their leader, I lingered in the alley's entrance, waiting until the last of the group filtered away and counted the minutes as they passed by until it was finally my turn to leave. Once it was time, I gave the passageway one last glance, thinking of the woman in the sweet shop with that bastard.

The moment I saw her, I couldn't look away. Those hazel eyes entranced me in a way that I had never felt before. I was completely powerless against her pull. It was all I could do to keep myself planted on that bench, to stop myself from marching into the cafe and stealing her away from Ambrose. It was a struggle that I was losing until Samian entered the tavern, until I saw him eyeing her with the same intensity I felt when he saw the kiss Ambrose had pressed against her delicate hand.

Shaking my head, I focused back on the busy street in front of me. Time was up, and I needed to move, to slip unseen along the horses, carts, and faeries of Volmire until I reached the hidden passage.

Stepping into the crowd, I crept along the streets, following the waves of people until I reached the door of the passageway. Entering the dark corridor, I silently continued along the path until the light of the exit blinded my eyes. Blinking, I let my vision clear while scanning the vast green surrounding me.

Luckily for us, the guards didn't roam the fields outside of Volmire's city gates, which gave us free rein to travel back and forth from the forest. I walked along the small hills of the meadow until I found the worn path along the shadows of the forest.

Before stepping between the trees, I paused at the threshold and closed my eyes, listening to the sounds of the woods. There were creatures here that were dangerous even to me. With the large group heading back to the camp, it was a sure way to attract unwanted attention. It was another reason we separated into small groups. While some rebels traveled along the treetops, those who could used their magic to transfer themselves to the gates of the camp.

The forest remained silent, though I could feel the scrutiny of hidden eyes wrapping around me. Sighing, I stepped into the dark shroud of the trees, carefully heeding every crunch of leaves, the creaking of wood, and the sharp calls of the birds.

It didn't take long to find my way out of the forest, to find myself standing in front of the rusted gate blocking the entrance to the estate once used by the royal family. The gates groaned open, revealing Amara and Orin waiting for me on the other side. The latter had his face tilted toward the sky, irritation rippling across his features.

"What happened?" I asked gruffly, stepping past the gates, letting them shut behind me.

"Amara believes she should be allowed to join our mission tonight," Orin said, putting his hand up to silence Amara before she could even say a word.

"No," I growled, walking past them both.

"But if you would just—"

I stopped short, my eyes rolling when Amara ran into my back. Facing her, I blew out a quick breath when I noticed her rubbing her nose. "My answer is no, Amara. You couldn't even follow my orders to *stay* in the camp. If I can't trust you with that, I cannot trust you in a potentially dangerous mission."

"But—" The pitch of her voice rose into a whine, her pleading eyes wide.

"Enough, Amara. My answer is no. I'll be putting you in Bryony's charge while we are gone. Understood?"

Tears welled up in her eyes as she looked to the ground. Sniffing, she whispered out a *fine* before running off through the camp.

Orin stepped up beside me, exasperation brightening the gold in his eyes. "She's going to be the death of us one day," he lamented.

"Let's just hope it will be later rather than sooner," I chuckled.

Clapping him on the shoulder, Orin trailed behind me as we made our way into the estate to the chamber we had commandeered as our strategy room. Viv already stood at the round table, along with the other members who would join today's mission. There would be twelve of us total sneaking into Lord Lowell's grounds tonight to help Lady Lowell and her son escape his lunacy.

For too many years, this male had taken to killing his

servants and past wives, hiding their bodies throughout the realm. Lady Lowell feared her time was coming to an end at the Thanlyl estate, not to mention the constant letters sent by Lord Astaroth requesting us to help her. Viv finally convinced me to get her out, saying her visions from Edris showed Lady Lowell would be useful to the rebellion's future. Not that the bastard of a god would give us anything concrete enough to form a plan effectively.

Moving into the room, I came up beside Viv, helping her fill her pack. "Everyone ready?" I asked, eyeing the rest of the rebels.

"As ready as we can be," she muttered. "What did Samian need?"

"To tell me that his charge is now in Nemos."

Viv slid her eyes to mine, her lips thinning. "So, Edris' vision was true then?" I nodded, handing her a canteen of water. "I guess this means war is right around the corner. We'll need to inform the leaders, let them prepare the villages and cities."

"We will," I murmured. "Once we return, we will." I held Viv's stare a moment longer before turning to the rest of the rebels. "Remember, this mission is to get in and get out. Once we have Lady Lowell and her son, do not dawdle. Meet back at the post and return with your group. Only three of our group can transfer us back to camp, so stay as close to your team as you can. Is everyone ready?" The room broke out in agreement, the rebels splitting into pairs and transferring one at a time to the Thanlyl estate, starting with my team.

Viv's magic swirled around me, Orin, and Halyn; the world whirled by before finally snapping into place under a large oak tree. My stomach churned, queasiness crawling up my throat, but I swallowed back the bile and focused on our surroundings. Landing at the edge of the courtyard, hidden by bushes and smaller trees, I watched as each group arrived and moved into their positions. I was just about to look back at the estate when short brown hair caught my eye.

I cursed, catching the attention of Amara as she positioned herself between two rebels in the furthest group. She cringed, giving me a weak wave.

"I guess we jinxed ourselves," Orin sighed, his hand rubbing the back of his neck.

"Try to keep an eye on her if you can," I growled. Viv snorted, and I threw a glare her way, though she ignored it.

We stayed in our positions until the moon shone high in the sky, the silver beams casting a soft glow around the trees. Rolling the stiffness from my shoulders, I froze when movement along the front of the estate made the hair on my neck stand on alert. Signaling to the group, I heard a sharp gasp to my right. Before I could look at Viv, Lady Lowell ran out of the estate, her son in her arms, with a wild, frantic look on her face and guards hot on her trail.

I swore as I counted the guards pursuing them, more than what was originally expected. I hesitated, weighing our options between fighting the thirty guards chasing her or retreating to camp. Viv hissed out my name, snapping me out of my wavering. Stepping out of my position, I commanded my team to move.

The rebels lurched forward while I rushed to Amara, catching her by the arm. "I told you to stay at the camp," I hissed. "Stand by that tree and do. Not. Move. If I catch you out there, I will lock you up and throw away the key. Do you understand?"

Amara nodded, her eyes wide with fear. Pushing her toward the tree, I followed the rest of the rebels, slipping my sword free from its sheath. Lady Lowell yelled out as a guard yanked her by her long, fiery hair. Another guard held her son, grunting as the kid fought like a hellcat to get to his mother.

The guard turned, raising his fist to strike the boy, and I lunged. Raising my sword, I swiped it across his back. Blood gushed, and the guard cried out, dropping the boy and falling to his knees.

Snatching the boy into my arms, I passed him to a rebel, commanding him to run toward the trees before I turned toward Lady Lowell. The guard still held her by the hair, dragging her back to the estate.

Chaos and the cries of my soldiers enveloped the courtyard as I fought my way through, cutting down guard after guard, ignoring the hot blood spraying across my face. The guard was edging toward the doors of the estate, and I roared. Calling my magic to me, I let the pressure around me build until the air was so thick I could hardly breathe. Releasing my hold on my power, lightning rained down on the guards around me, burning their flesh in an instant.

Panting, I searched the grounds for Lady Lowell, my feet moving toward the sound of her screams. I spotted them just as I turned the corner of the estate; the guard pulling Lady Lowell up to her feet when Viv flickered into sight behind the male. The guard didn't even have a chance to react before her sword lodged into his back. The guard's eyes widened, his mouth gaping as he looked down at the silver, blood-coated blade sticking out of his chest.

Viv pulled the sword back, letting the guard fall to the ground. She grabbed Lady Lowell, her eyes clashing with mine, and nodded.

"Retreat," I bellowed, twisting to my soldiers. "Retreat to your positions!"

Running past the bodies of dead guards and rebels, I only

spotted six remaining of my team, each vanishing as they transferred back to camp. Cursing, I picked up my speed as more guards filed out of the estate. Amara was waiting with Viv and Lady Lowell when I spotted Orin limping toward them. Sheathing my sword, I pulled Orin's arm over my shoulder, wrapping my arm around his waist as we raced to Viv. The guards were closing in fast when Viv stretched out her hand, her fingers wrapping around mine, just as a sharp edge of a blade cut across my back.

The world fell away, pain radiating down my spine, and when we landed in the middle of a mountain village, I collapsed to my knees, taking Orin down with me.

CHAPTER 18

SYBIL

The day started off great. It really did.

After returning from my outing—not date—with Ambrose, I tried to practice my magic and failed completely. It had taken me just an hour of either nothing happening or me blasting my books across the room to feel completely exhausted, my mind reduced to mush. I finally gave up any attempt at control and slept so soundly that nothing had woken me until the sunlight brightened my room. I woke up refreshed, hopeful that my struggle to get my magic under control and *not* go haywire was just from first-day jitters.

I could feel the power writhing under my skin, stronger than yesterday. I couldn't help the nerves that gathered in the pit of my stomach, but I felt optimistic about my training today.

Half of the new clothes Ambrose bought for me arrived late last night, which meant I would be able to look and feel like I belonged here today. Sliding out of my bed, I took a quick bath before slipping into a burnt orange floor-length skirt and a black buttoned corset-like shirt with flowing sleeves that cuffed at my wrists. Looking in the mirror, I braided my ashy hair, which looked richer today, almost browner. I pushed the thought aside, assuming it was a trick from the light.

Tying off my hair, I stared at my reflection, surprised and a little awed by what I saw staring back. I looked soft, but powerful. I fisted my hands, rolling my shoulders back to stand tall and proud. I would go to the library today, and everything would go right. My magic *would* be stable and not go wild within seconds.

Unfortunately, that hope was doused within the first thirty minutes of my lesson.

Samian and I had our breakfast in the library again. Even after my talk with Ambrose, I still wasn't ready to have another run-in with Arianna and her haughty attitude or deal with everyone's stares and not-so-quiet whispers. We ate our breakfast while I told Samian about my day with Ambrose, not missing the way his mouth tightened every now and then.

After we finished our pastries, we immediately started working on my lesson for the day. A lesson, Samian said, would be simple. I was tasked with forming a small ball of light, but at first, it was barely a pinprick of *something*. It wasn't quite a ball. It was hard to tell what form it had taken. There were ridges and sharp edges that would start to smooth into a curve, only to suddenly morph back into sharp edges before completely winking out or exploding in my face.

I shook out my hands, grinding my teeth together. "I just don't understand," I moaned, my body tight with frustration. It had been hours of creating either an explosion of light or nothing at all, and this task was starting to feel next to impossible.

"You're thinking about this too hard. Your body is too tense, and your mind is unsettled. Calm your mind and let your body lead you," Samian said calmly, his voice barely above a whisper. "It knows what to do; you just have to allow it to guide you."

Letting out a loud groan, I threw my hands in the air, letting them fall on my face. I knew he meant well, as he kept his voice calm and collected. But hearing it just pissed me off more. It felt like he didn't understand the importance of my getting this under control quickly.

"It's not that simple, Samian," I muttered through my hands.

Laughing, Samian walked over, gently pulling my hands from my face. The bastard looked serene, his eyes gleaming with amusement. I think he was enjoying watching my magic blow up in my face every few minutes. "Take a deep breath and relax. Why do you think it's not that simple?"

"I don't know! I just—I just… " I trailed off, my throat growing tight, and I looked to the window, my vision blurring with hot tears. Back home, I was known to be a perfectionist. Everything I touched had to be exactly right. There could be no faults, no mistakes. Every year, I had it on my list of goals to work on, but it was always pushed aside to make room for other goals that seemed more important at the time. Plus, what job has ever complained about having a perfectionist on their team?

Samian sighed, taking my hands in his, giving them a gentle squeeze. An unreadable emotion flickered in his eyes, but before he could say anything—probably some grand but vague saying—someone behind me cleared their throat. I turned further toward the window to hide my heated face as I fought to make my tears stop falling. Samian walked over to whoever lingered by the bookcases, their soft murmurings echoing around me.

Samian returned to the table, shuffling through the stacks

of books he had pulled earlier. Landing on the book he was looking for, he knelt in front of me, angling his face so that I would look at him. His eyes, each so different from the other, were gentle as he spoke his next words. "Take a deep breath and try to relax, Sybil. Empires aren't built in a day. The same goes for your magic. It takes time, practice, and patience." Pausing, he glanced at the person still waiting for him. "I have something I need to take care of. Take some time to calm yourself and start reading this book. I promise I'll return soon."

Nodding, I ran my fingers over the cobalt cover, which complemented the silver lattice edging. Placing his hand over mine, he gave my fingers another gentle squeeze, lingering for a moment before following the person out of the library.

Sighing, I tossed the book on the table beside me. Closing my eyes, I took a few deep breaths, and my tears finally slowed. I knew I was being hard on myself, but I could feel the magic whirling inside me, ready to burst, hurting anyone who dared to get close enough.

Swallowing, I shook my head. I couldn't let that happen again. I needed to learn how to control it, and I needed to learn soon. Every time I ran into Arianna or the other nobles, hearing their whispers and gossip made that clearer than ever. Just practicing with Samian made me uneasy, so afraid of what might happen. If I didn't master my power soon, someone was going to get hurt, and who knew if it would be just as bad or worse. Pushing down my panic, I wiped my eyes, opened the book, and started reading.

A few minutes passed, and my thoughts still haunted me. After rereading the same sentence repeatedly, I finally slammed the book shut, huffing at the ridiculousness of my sudden lack of ability to understand words. If Liam were here—if he weren't disgusted by what I was—he would have laughed at my restlessness, telling me to do some stretches or take a quick break.

A sad smile formed, and a quiet laugh escaped my lips. I looked out the window, watching the wind blow through the trees. I thought back to the last time I saw Liam, seeing the fear shining in those hazel eyes.

"If only I had a camera."

Gasping, my head whipped toward the stairs, where the deep voice called me out of my thoughts. Ambrose stood, leaning against the rail, giving me a devilish grin. I stared at him, my eyes wide while the warning bells silently rang in my head. I'm not sure how long he had been there, watching me, and my throat bobbed.

"What would you do with the camera?" I asked, giving him a careful smile, hoping he couldn't hear how fast my heart pounded against my chest.

Ambrose quickly closed the distance between us, pulling me from my chair and spinning me around like the day before. I laughed softly when he pulled me back to him, my hand landing on his firm chest. "I would capture a scene of pure beauty, entranced by the world, my dearest Sybil."

I quivered, his voice—his words—feeling like velvet against my skin. Shaking my head, I swatted his chest and backed out of his arms. He was a notorious flirt, I reminded myself silently. His rakish smiles and sweet mutterings were directed at everyone, not just me. While it did feel nice to be on the receiving end of his attention, letting it pull me out of my misery, I would be an idiot if I thought it meant anything more.

Grabbing my hand, Ambrose tugged me back to his chest, holding me close to his body. "What, my darling, are we learning today?"

"You mean, what am I failing at today?" I scoffed. But when

Ambrose angled his face, silently waiting for my answer, I sighed and finally answered. "My goal for today is to create—and hold on to—a *luminous,* glowing orb of light." My throat felt tight, though I tried to hide it behind exaggerated words.

"And I take it's not going well, my love?" His voice was soft and gentle, and I hated it. I hated that he kept seeing how incapable I really was.

I slowly shook my head, my face heating as I looked down at my hands still against his chest. "It either implodes in my face or barely forms at all. There's no in-between," I sighed. "Samian says I'm thinking too much, and my body is too tense, but I can't help it. I need to learn how to control it. I need to get this right. I just don't know what else to do." My panic was rising again, my heart beating wildly as Ambrose let me move out of his arms to lean against the table.

Ambrose hummed thoughtfully, a finger tapping against his chin while considering my words. Then, a slow grin formed, his deep blue eyes shining with a plan. Apprehension crawled up my spine at the sight. "I think I know just the thing that could help," he purred, taking my hand and pulling me behind him.

We walked further into the library, weaving through the bookcases until he found a room toward the back. Opening the door, he gestured for me to walk inside. My eyes widened, and I gasped, taking in the stunning dark navy room. There were two levels, with a spiral metal staircase in the left corner leading up to the upper level. The bottom level had wall sconces set in between wooden bookshelves. A beautifully crafted desk sat near the far wall, midway between two large windows overlooking the courtyard. Looking up, bronze accented the dark navy ceiling, making it look like stars shone above us.

I beamed, looking back at Ambrose, who still waited near the door, tracking my every move, his face unreadable in the dim light. "Well, what do you think?" he asked, his voice low and deep.

"I…it's beautiful," I breathed, trying to ignore how alluring he seemed, how good the muscles in his arms looked with his rolled-up sleeves. "But I don't understand how this is going to help me relax."

Ambrose laughed as I turned back to the room. Stepping up behind me, I could feel the heat from his body seeping into mine. His powerful frame towered over me before he leaned close to my ear, breathing me in. Shivers danced along my skin, my stomach tightening from his presence.

"The room, dear Sybil, is supposed to help you relax," he whispered, the rasp of his voice making my heart flutter. "This room will give us some privacy. You don't have to worry about anyone walking around, watching your every move. You don't have to worry about hurting anyone here. This room frees you from their judgment and your fears." Wrapping one hand around my stomach, his other hand ran softly across my chest, making my skin pebble from his touch.

Gasping, I tried to step out of his hold, but his arm tightened around me, not allowing me to move. "Ambrose," I warned, making another move to get out of his arms. With Samian returning shortly, I didn't even want to think about what would happen if he caught us here like this.

"Shh," Ambrose murmured. "I'm only here to help you relax, that's all." Moving his arms away from my stomach and chest, he pulled me into him, his body becoming flush against mine. "Cup your hands like you are holding water," he said, moving my hands in front of me, positioning them side by side. "Good, now close your eyes and breathe in nice and slow."

Scoffing, I looked up over my shoulder, giving him an unamused frown at his less-than-helpful advice. If taking deep breaths was going to help me, I wouldn't be here with him, struggling with my magic.

Tutting, Ambrose tapped the side of my face and leaned back down to my ear, his breath warm against my neck. "Now, now, my love. That's not closing your eyes."

"I'm glad you're enjoying this," I said flatly, looking back to my hands.

"You'll enjoy it too once you start listening to me," Ambrose reprimanded lightly. "Now, close your eyes and take a deep breath."

Snorting, I rolled my eyes before closing them. Ambrose hummed his approval, the timbre vibrating against my back, and my traitorous heart leaped at the praise. I breathed in deep, then slowly breathed out, pushing away that part of me that basked in his favor.

"Good, again."

Taking another breath, I let the air fill me, and a sense of calm washed over me, soothing me and making me feel warm and safe. The tension in my muscles softened against his touch. I could feel his smile against my ear.

"Good girl," he hummed, gliding his hands up my arms and down the sides of my waist. My body felt feverish from his touch as I tried to stay focused. "Now," he whispered, keeping a firm grip on my waist with one hand, letting his other hand drift up my stomach toward my chest, "I want you to search within yourself until you find the warmth of your light."

Heat pooled low in my stomach at his soft touch. My breath caught when his hand slowly moved back down to my stomach. My thoughts were scattered between focusing on my magic and the desire for his hand to drift lower.

"Focus, my dear Sybil," he murmured softly, his words feeling like a caress against my ear.

A soft moan escaped me as his lips grazed the shell of my ear, and I cursed myself. My face heated when I felt his lips curl into a wicked smile.

"That's not focusing, Sybil," he whispered, nipping at my ear, making me tremble against his touch. "Where's the warmth of your light?"

Shaking my head, I focused, pushing all thoughts of how good his touch felt down deep inside—another day. I would think about this moment another day, when I didn't feel so lost with my magic and who I was.

Centering myself, I focused on Ambrose's hand slowly making its way back up, my muscles quivering at his touch until his hand moved between my breasts. There. I felt it then, a heat that felt like a piece of me, my essence, curling at my center.

When I nodded, Ambrose stopped his movement. "It's there," I gasped.

"Good, now focus on that feeling and breathe into it," he said, putting more pressure against my chest. "As you breathe out, imagine that light flowing through you to your hands, letting it gather. Form the shape that you want in your mind."

My eyes squeezed tighter, and I imagined the shape of a ball, letting my mind dwell on its smooth, curved edges. Ambrose kept his hand still, but another wave of calmness swelled through me, and I leaned against him, my body feeling relaxed. I imagined my light flowing like smoke through my veins as my hands began to tingle.

"Open your eyes, Sybil."

CHAPTER 19
SYBIL

I slowly opened my eyes, gasping at the soft light that hummed above my hands. The warm glow illuminated the area around us, and tears of joy blurred my sight. I did it. I finally had enough control to create something. I had been so close to giving up, so lost in feeling like this was an impossible task. But now, with such exhilaration swelling through me, I held something so beautiful, so magnificent.

Looking over my shoulder, the deep blue of Ambrose's eyes glowed from the soft light, taking my breath away. His heated gaze swept to mine, making my legs feel weak. His grip loosened on me, allowing me to twist in his arms, the shining orb now between us. A wide smile spread across my face, and I couldn't keep my excitement hidden as I gazed at the light, letting its warmth sink into my skin.

My eyes burned from the joy and relief that flooded my heart. I looked back at Ambrose, his eyes widened slightly as he searched my face, and I couldn't look away. The moment stretched between us, the air turning taut. His hands moved slowly, hesitantly at first, until he cupped my face. I blinked at him, my lungs feeling tight.

It started off as a flicker, a spark of heat pooling low in my stomach that quickly turned into a firestorm. Goosebumps pebbled down my skin, need skirting through me at a single touch of his hand. My heart raced, my light flickering in my hands. My breath quivered when I took in the longing reflected in his eyes.

Another wave of heat pooled low when Ambrose pulled me into him, his lips crashing into mine. He swallowed my gasp, his hands threading through my hair, tilting my head up for better access, deepening our kiss. My light winked out, and I grabbed hold of his shirt, pulling him closer against me. He groaned, his tongue sweeping across my lips, and I opened for him. Electricity shot through me, all the way to my core.

Ambrose moved, stepping us further into the room until my legs pressed against the wooden desk. His hands slid slowly, tauntingly, down my body until they were behind my thighs. Lifting me up onto the flat surface, he stepped between my legs, our kiss becoming more fervent, more wild.

I leaned into him, feeling his hand slide down my leg and lazily inch my skirt up. But something in my chest ached, the feeling dull. My eyes squeezed tighter at the pang, and suddenly it wasn't Ambrose in the room with me, it wasn't his lips on mine. All I could think of was silver hair brushing against my face, smooth hands pulling me closer.

Ice cooled the heat in my veins, and I sucked in a breath, pulling away from Ambrose. I swallowed, willing my breathing to even out as I put my hand flat against Ambrose's chest, pushing him away.

"Did I do something?" Ambrose asked, his voice low.

Guilt laced through me, and I stared at the space between

us, unable to meet his gaze. "No, I just…it just feels too soon," I whispered.

It was a lie and probably not a good one, but it was the best thing I could think of at the moment. I wasn't even sure if the truth would have been something I could have spoken out loud. That it was another's hands on my body, another's lips against mine, kindling the fire inside me.

A shiver shot down my body, and I sucked in a breath. Need pulsed along my skin, and my breath became heavy. Ambrose's hands came to my arms, the touch so sensitive that I bit back a moan. I shook my head, pushing him further away so I could move off the desk and out of his reach.

"Darling, I—"

"Sybil?" Samian's voice echoed from the rows of bookcases outside the room.

My head whipped toward the door, and Ambrose silently growled. When I glanced back at him, he had turned and leaned against the desk. His face was hard, like it was set in stone, and his eyes were filled with annoyance. Alarm prickled at the edges of my mind, but was engulfed by the lust still clinging to my body, making my skin flush.

"Sybil, are you in—?"

"I'm here," I said, a little too loudly. Grimacing, I ran my hand over my hair, hoping—praying—I didn't look as strung out as I felt.

Samian walked into the room, his gaze bouncing between Ambrose and me, his mouth tightening. Ambrose grumbled something, too silent for my ears but not silent enough for Samian to miss. The wood along the walls groaned when Samian focused on Ambrose. His features were tight with icy rage.

Samian looked back at me, noting my tousled hair and

flushed face. Embarrassment scorched through me, quick and abrupt, and I stammered. "I—He—A-Ambrose and I were just training with my magic. He was guiding me through it."

"Is that right?" Samian asked flatly. His voice was a cold calm that made my stomach drop.

Wincing, my body—my lungs—felt tight as a heavy tension thickened the air of the room, making it hard to breathe. I dared to glance at Ambrose, who leaned against the desk, picking at an invisible string on his tunic, and I paled. Samian's lips curled, the wood along the desk rippling from his anger.

A small noise escaped my lips when Samian started toward Ambrose, making him pause. His infuriated gaze flicked to me, and I swallowed, everything in my mind emptying. I did the only rational thing I could think of.

I ran.

I ran out of the library, leaving my books and bag.

I ran down the hallways, almost knocking into several servants.

I ran all the way to my room, slamming the door shut behind me.

Leaning against the cool wood, I gulped down air, my lungs burning. Cursing, I let my head thump against the door. All I wanted to do was curl underneath a rock and disappear. My mind replayed the moment that Samian realized I was alone with Ambrose, seeing me so tousled, knowing *why* I looked that way. I was a complete mess. Mortified.

I walked mindlessly to my bathroom, turning on the bath and letting the water run very, very cold.

Sitting in the freezing water, I hoped it would rinse away my humiliation and the lingering feel of Ambrose's hands. But when my teeth started chattering, I gave up and dried myself off. Turning off the lights, I slipped into bed, my mind still remembering the feel of his touch. It meant nothing—couldn't mean anything—I repeated to myself again. I forced myself to repeat that he was a flirt and nothing more, but his touch felt like a fire scorching every part of me. It still had my body burning.

Of all the times Liam and I were intimate, nothing—*nothing*—compared to this flame inside of me. A flame that Ambrose ignited. I shivered, my breathing still unsteady at the memory of his rough hands moving along my body.

The soft sheets teased my sensitive skin, and need pulsed through me. I felt wired; my body throbbing with an endless ache that would not disappear. Rolling to my side, I squeezed my eyes shut, trying to forget that moment, but Ambrose's kiss along my neck fluttered through my mind. Groaning, I shifted onto my back, pushing the blanket down to let the cold air cool my skin. I clenched the sheets, letting out a sharp exhale, unable to take any more of this throbbing ache.

Replaying our time in the library, I moved my hands up and down my body, following Ambrose's touch. My breath quickened, and I squeezed my thighs together, reveling in the feel as my hands massaged my breasts. Moving my fingers along my nipple, pinching and twisting, I imagined Ambrose biting at my ear—my neck.

I quietly moaned, moving a hand down to my slick center, pushing a finger inside. Whimpering, I focused on the silky warmth, picturing a rougher, larger finger slowly pumping inside me. I moved my hips, meeting every thrust of my finger. Giving my nipple another twist, I added a second finger, pumping faster, mewling as my pleasure started building. Kneading my breast, I imagined Ambrose spinning me around, but it wasn't him in front of me. Silver hair, blue and green eyes stared back, dark and full of longing, before his mouth met mine in a frenzied kiss.

My body grew taut as I pictured Samian deepening that kiss while picking me up, placing me on the desk. His lips moved then, slowly down to my breast, licking and sucking until he continued lower, taking his time until he reached my clit and feasted like he was starved for me and only me. My fingers curled, matching the speed of his movements. My breathing was nothing more than rasping as my fingers hit that sensitive spot, making my stomach wind tighter and tighter.

Giving my nipple another painful twist, I cried out, my pleasure exploding through me, like lightning zipping through my veins. My fingers slowed as I rode out wave after wave of pleasure. Removing my fingers, I closed my eyes, letting my heart calm and my breathing slow.

After getting up to clean myself, I slipped back into my plush bed, the ache finally fading. Feeling satisfied and exhausted from my magic, I tried not to think of Samian as I quickly drifted off into a dreamless sleep.

CHAPTER 20

SAMIAN

I waited until Sybil left the library, my eyes never leaving Ambrose. Icy hot rage sliced through me, filling my veins with a fury so potent that it threatened to consume me whole. The air, thick with tension, stretched around us, building every second it took for Sybil to run through those doors, leaving us behind.

Ambrose, still leaning against the desk, refused to meet my glare while he spun a pen between his fingers. Boredom carved along his face, as if this moment were nothing but an inconvenience to him, something that wasn't worth his time or energy. The thought prickled through me, making my blood boil.

The moment the doors closed behind Sybil, Ambrose finally deigned to look up, his lips curling into a smug smile. "Did you have to come back so soon, Samian?" he drawled. "The lesson was just getting to the good part."

I let loose a snarl, low and vicious. "Stay away from her," I growled. "She has just started to learn who and what she is. She doesn't need *you* messing with her head."

Scoffing, Ambrose stalked toward me, not stopping until we stood merely an inch apart. Ambrose lifted his nose, his eyes narrowing, glowing with ire. "Now what do you mean by that?"

"You know exactly what I mean," I said, my voice lowering to a dangerous tone. Shoving him away from me, I continued. "I know you, Ambrose. I've watched you plot and scheme your entire life. I've seen all that you have done and who you have hurt in the process. *She* will not be one of them."

A mirthless laugh escaped him, his face tightening into a predator-like calm. "You've seen all I have done? My, my, aren't you the ever-watchful *dog*?" Ambrose spat as he grabbed my shirt and slammed me against the wall. I grunted from the force of his strength and locked my hands tight around his wrists, baring my teeth. "You think I don't know how you like to hide behind corners and closed doors? How you follow everyone around, scraping for a morsel of information?" Snarling, Ambrose moved closer, his voice lowering as he said, "You think I don't know how you, the great and mighty Samian, have been following our lovely Sybil since she was a child? And all without her knowledge. I wonder what she would think about that. Would she see you as her great protector, or would she be disgusted, horrified even, by your lurking in the shadows?"

Pushing away, Ambrose turned his back on me, releasing a soft, cruel laugh. My blood turned to ice. How long had he known? I had made sure I slipped out of the realm without any of his spies following me. My stomach dropped as realization slowly dawned. I was the one who led him to Sybil. My fixation on keeping her safe brought her here. My chest, my body, my veins filled with a loathing so strong I heaved. Whether it was for myself or for him, using me to get to her, I wasn't sure. The lights flickered, the wood of the walls groaned from the power that hummed inside me.

Picking up on the shift in the air, Ambrose slowly turned, facing me. The temperature quickly dropped, and frost climbed along the walls and windows. "What secrets are you trying to keep, Samian? Why would you be following her around? What is so important about a human girl that you would seek her out?" Ambrose goaded, his eyes bright with the promise of violence.

"Stay away from her," I repeated, moving my hand to the hilt of my dagger hidden beneath my jacket.

He threw a shard of ice in my direction, my blade slicing through it when I realized too late that it was merely a distraction. Ambrose lunged at the same time, a dagger in hand, pushing me back against the wall, the blade resting against my throat.

Blood trickled down my neck when Ambrose opened his mouth, only to be cut off by a startled gasp and the sound of books falling. Whipping our heads toward the sound, a pale-faced female stood by the door frame, her eyes wide. She lifted a hand to her chest, her eyes shifting between us, not knowing if she should run or stay frozen while the books she had been carrying lay on the floor around her. Coming to her senses, the female blinked and dashed to the safety of the bookcases.

Ambrose straightened, taking a step back, his lips forming a thin line as he sheathed his dagger. Closing his eyes, Ambrose breathed deeply, rolling his neck and shoulders before opening his eyes again. His haughty stare met mine as his hand stretched out, straightening my disheveled shirt. Once satisfied, he smirked, lightly tapping my face before leaning in close, his voice barely above a whisper. "Last time I checked, Samian, *I* give the orders around here. You will do well to remember that. Do I make myself clear?" Pulling his head back, his face was dangerously calm.

"Yes," I said, swallowing my rage.

"Good," he said, finally turning to the female, giving her a lazy smile. "Oh, before I forget, Sybil will join Arianna and Ezra during their rounds to the outer villages this week—without you."

My lips curled, and I pushed down the curse that fought to escape me. My hands fisted, resisting the urge to swing at him. But with an audience, I knew it would be dangerous and foolish to do so, and I had to keep my promise. Shoving my anger down, I responded with a tight, "*Fine.*"

Keeping his eyes on the bashful female, Ambrose waved his hand to the door. "That will be all, Samian," he said, his voice nothing more than a purr.

Sneering, I left the room, the sounds of the female's giggles filling the air.

Passing through the lounge on the third floor, I sighed when I found Sybil's books still lying on the table. My anger and disgust were quickly extinguished, leaving nothing but a resounding emptiness in their wake. Stopping to gather her things, I looked out the window. The sun was setting, casting shadows around the trees in the gardens. My throat tightened as I made up my mind. I would not allow Sybil to fall for his tricks. I needed a plan. A plan that would require me to meet with the rebels tonight instead of the agreed-upon time.

Leaving the library, I rounded the corner, grunting when the lithe body of a female ran into me. Looking down, Arianna glared at me, rubbing her nose. Arching a brow, I swallowed my growl, ready to excuse myself when an amusing thought formed. "If you're looking for Ambrose, I just left him in the library," I said coolly, fighting a smile.

"I have better things to do than look for Ambrose," Arianna sneered. "Get out of my way, dog."

My jaw clenched, but I shoved that insult aside when her eyes flicked to the library door. Smirking, I moved, letting her pass, giving her a dramatic bow as she went. I swallowed my laugh and continued walking down the hall. Ambrose was about to have an interesting night, and I hoped Arianna would burn him alive.

When I stopped in front of Sybil's door, a part of me begged to knock, to check if she was okay. But I was still furious with her, furious about how she let Ambrose get so close to her. I was torn between wanting to throttle her, spending every moment warning her against him, and letting fate play her little games. But I knew, even if I spent every waking minute urging her to see reason, Sybil would not take those warnings to heart, not when *he* toyed with her emotions. Deciding not to knock, I set her things by the door.

Leaving the hallway behind, I entered my room, walking to the bookcase that blocked the hidden room and passageway. I pulled on the book that opened the bookcase and slipped through. My meeting with the rebels wasn't for another two days, but given the timing of the soldier's visit to Lowbrook, two days wouldn't give them enough time to prepare, so I needed to meet with *him* as soon as possible.

The meeting that pulled me away from Sybil earlier today did not go well. Ezra was on edge when we met to discuss Sybil's training. According to him, Ambrose decided they would make a trip to Lowbrook, a village outside Volmire. Seeing as Ezra had just returned from Lowbrook on his latest round, he figured—as I did—that the trip was just a disguise. Officially, it was a search for rebels who may be camped nearby. But we knew that some type of plan was being put into place.

With him ordering Sybil to join their search, every part of me itched to take her away—to take her someplace where

Ambrose would never find her again. But I knew that if I did, Sybil wouldn't see it as me trying to help her, to protect her. I swallowed down the bile that rose in my throat. Sybil was smart; however, she was still too wary of this world and her magic. She needed more training, and Ambrose knew that, *counted* on that.

Breathing in the stale air of the passageway, I bristled, thinking back to yesterday, seeing *him* sitting by the window. The clod knew being in the city was reckless, yet he showed up anyway, pretending his scarf was enough to hide him from the guards that patrolled the city.

I walked along the dark passage that led into an empty field near the back of the palace, annoyance from his foolishness trickling down my spine as I went. Pulling my hood up, I hastily made my way through the field into the dark, haunting forest I had warned Sybil of when we came, and eventually found myself in front of a once beautiful but now rusted gate.

Knocking once, then twice, and finally knocking once more, the gate slowly groaned open. Standing there, in the middle of the path, a brute of a man blocked my way, his arms crossed over his chest. Daggers adorned his belt, ready to be used, and the hilt of a sword rose behind him. His hair was black as night, but those crimson eyes glowed bright in the moonlight.

"You're early. Our meeting isn't until two days from now," he grunted. My shoulders tensed at the deep rumbling of his voice.

"Yes, but there have been some developments that couldn't wait that long," I said, keeping my tone calm. Casual.

The silence stretched between us, neither of us making a move as I unblinkingly held his stare. A moment passed, followed by another, when he suddenly barked a laugh, crossed the gate, and pulled me into a hug, his large hand clapping against my back. I grinned, returning the action.

"It's been a while, Kieran," I teased before I frowned at him. "You shouldn't have been in the city. He could have caught you." My frown turned into a scowl when he waved me off, his face tight. Worry tugged at my heart for him. Last I heard, he was visiting the outer villages, giving out food and medicine while finding more faeries to join our cause. "I hope your mission went well," I asked softly.

"As well as it could have gone, I suppose," he said, sniffing, avoiding any eye contact. "Made it back in one piece, that's all that counts."

I stayed quiet, nodding thoughtfully, and followed Kieran into the camp toward the abandoned manor the rebels camped in, waving to those who knew me as we passed by. Studying the tightness in Kieran's back, my jaw clenched. I knew better than to ask what had happened in the villages that made him act so reserved. Kieran and I had been close friends since our teenage years. As a boy, I had accompanied the queen during her visits to the villages. I was young and restless in those days, which drove her crazy. Exasperated, the queen would eventually throw me out of her meetings, telling me to make myself useful elsewhere.

During one of those trips, a farmer found me eating from one of his apple trees. After a good scolding, he made me help his son, Kieran, pick the rest of the ripened fruit. Ever since then, Kieran and I had been thick as thieves. I even convinced Queen Cassia to allow him to attend the school with me at the palace, against the advice of her former advisor and Ambrose's father, Alister.

Finally reaching a dimly lit room inside the manor, we came to a table covered in maps of the outer villages. "So," Kieran said, straightening the papers thrown about the table, "what important news do you have for us that couldn't wait two more days?"

Sighing, I took a seat across from him. The room was empty except for Kieran and me. Looking to the door, I huffed a laugh when a shadow crouching low to the ground moved.

Kieran's eyes followed mine and frowned. "Amara," Kieran grumbled, rolling his eyes, though his tone was soft.

Giggling, a short, willowy girl burst through the door, followed by two others, Vivi and Orin. "Sit and be quiet," Kieran gently ordered Amara.

As they took their seats, I cut to Kieran's, my expression darkening as I swallowed. "He's sending a group to Lowbrook in three days. From what my informant has said, he will send Arianna and Ezra, along with a few of their soldiers."

Kieran cursed, and the others paled. Packing and moving the rebels away from Lowbrook would be difficult to do in just three days.

"That's not all," I said hesitantly. "Sybil will be joining them." My jaw clenched tight. The rage I had pushed down surged through me, and the table splintered down the middle. Kieran's mouth tightened, giving me a look of warning.

"Is that bad?" Amara asked quietly, her eyes nervously shifting between Kieran and me.

Shoving that rage back down, I gave her a small, apologetic smile. "I don't know," I offered truthfully. "He is going out of his way to get close to her, and she's not listening to my warnings. He has something planned for her, though I'm not sure what. Neither does my informant. All I know is that she's having trouble controlling her magic. Her emotions are all over the place, which makes her dangerous. I have a feeling that he will use that against her. He has already offered her a bargain once, which she refused. I doubt he will let that slide. I believe he *wants* her to feel unstable, to be afraid of her magic and what she can do."

Kieran nodded, his features stiff while quickly thinking of a plan. "Viv, tell the camp to pack up. Have them leave by tomorrow night and move them to the other side of the mountain until the soldiers leave. Don't let them dawdle. Orin, get to Lowbrook as quickly as you can. Remain unseen and warn Silas about the soldiers' visit, including the fact that they are bringing a newcomer. Tell him she is potentially dangerous and to tread lightly around her. Tell any rebels in the village to hide or lie low."

Standing quickly, Vivi and Orin bowed and left the room.

"What can I do?" Amara's voice was soft, uncertain.

Sighing, Kieran tapped a finger on the table, his face softening. Amara was the youngest of the rebels, having joined their group a few years ago as an orphan after an uprising in one of the villages. She became fast friends with Orin and Vivi and promptly wormed her way into Kieran's heart. He didn't stand a chance against her bubbly personality, reminding him too much of better days. She was quick and stealthy and often got into trouble in the camp, but Kieran didn't like her running around with the other rebels.

"I want you to help Bryony prepare food for the villagers after the soldiers leave. There's never a visit where something doesn't happen."

Smiling, Amara jumped up from her seat and rushed to the door. Pausing at the doorway, she spun around, giving Kieran a half-hearted bow before running out of the room. Kieran shook his head, a soft laugh escaping him. He didn't say it, but I knew Amara reminded him of his younger sister, Elaine. Sadness wormed its way through me as I watched the door, remembering the last time we saw Elaine standing by a gnarled tree, her long black hair fluttering from a light breeze. Clearing my throat, I pushed away the memories, focusing on the maps in front of me.

As Amara left the room, Kieran straightened, shifting back into the mask of a leader. "After our talk yesterday, I sent a few of my group out to search for answers regarding Sybil's abnormal blood cells. We should hear back from them soon, though I don't know if it will be before her visit to Lowbrook." Kieran looked down, reluctant to say what we both knew. "I believe we should prepare for a worst-case scenario with her getting closer to that bastard."

Nodding, I looked back to the door, my shoulders dipping as I exhaled. "She wasn't supposed to be here, Kieran," I said softly, finally letting the regret I felt show. "She was supposed to live her life with the rest of the humans. Supposed to have kids, grow old. She wasn't supposed to be put in this type of danger."

"I mean, she can still do the kids thing and potentially grow old, though it will take a little longer now," Kieran teased, his tone light.

Giving him a sharp glare, I watched as Kieran laughed softly and apologized. "Look, I may not know her as you do, but she will be okay. We'll make sure of it."

The softness of his tone clashed with the severity of his features. His crimson eyes gleamed with a promise that death would come to anyone who got in our way. I let out a weak laugh before running my hand through my hair, composing myself.

"I'll hold you to that," I murmured.

Kieran answered with an arrogant smirk before we spent the rest of our night planning out our next move.

CHAPTER 21
AMBROSE

My eyes flicked to Samian, watching him leave before returning to the female in front of me, annoyance flooding my veins. He was becoming a stain that would not disappear, no matter how hard I sought to remove him. Taking a deep breath, I angled my head, sliding my gaze along every part of the female's body as she shifted, showing off every curve, her eyes hungry for attention. She was one of Arianna's inbred followers, always wanting everything that Arianna had, though never daring to cross her for it. If I remembered correctly, her name was Ciera. Or Cyra? Or maybe it was Cressa, though it didn't really matter to me.

Ciera's face flushed into a beautiful pink as I gave her a wicked smile, gesturing for her to come closer. Giggling, she quickly made her way to me, forgetting all about the angry outburst she had just witnessed. Stupid girl, this Cyra. It was a wonder that Arianna put up with her all these years.

Deciding to stick with Cyra, I slowly took her in from head to toe. Her muted auburn hair was styled so that half of her long hair cascaded down her back, gently curling at the end—a not-so-subtle attempt at mirroring Arianna's style. The other half was braided and pinned, forming a crown. Her olive eyes gleamed at my perusal as she shifted ever so slightly, the low-cut of her dress leaving nothing to the imagination. Her breasts weren't as full as I liked, but that wasn't my focus for tonight.

My tryst with Sybil left my cock so hard and stiff that even my clash with Samian didn't douse the heat she had ignited within me. I didn't expect it—the pleasure I felt when I wrangled those soft moans from her lips. I could just imagine that pretty mouth of hers wrapped around me as I slammed into the back of her throat. My cock twitched at the thought. Oh, how I looked forward to more *lessons* with her.

Cutting my gaze back to Cyra's wide, innocent eyes, my smile sharpened, and I pushed my magic into her, making her breath hitch at the desire that threaded through her. Stepping close to her, I ran a finger across her chest, moving her hair behind her. Cyra quietly moaned, arching her back at my touch. I pushed more magic into her, and her breath quickened as I hummed my approval. It was all too easy—taking hold of her emotions, twisting them to my needs.

I walked her backward out of the study, and she gasped when her back hit the wooden shelves. Stuck between me and the bookcase, I pressed my cock into her stomach, letting her feel its hard length. She giggled again, but that laugh soon turned into a whimper when I ground against her. Bracing herself on her toes, Cyra leaned forward, attempting a kiss, but I would not allow that to happen.

Roughly grabbing her by her hair, I pulled her head back, making her hiss in pain. Her hands tightly gripped my shirt, and I tutted in a reprimanding tone. "None of that, sweet girl," I murmured.

Tonight was not for affection or fondness, at least not with her. No, this dalliance was to stop the ache that was consuming me.

Quickly spinning her around, I pushed Cyra against the bookcase, letting her hands settle on the shelf. Books fell to the floor as I undid my pants, groaning in relief as my cock sprang free. Leaning over, Cyra gasped as I grabbed the edge of her tight, silky dress, ripping it so that I could spread her legs further apart. I laughed, low and deep, when I breathed in the lust that dripped from her. She liked the roughness. Probably dreamed about it.

Wrapping my hand around my cock, I fisted myself before grasping Cyra's hip, dragging the tip along her pussy, reveling in the feel of her slickness. Wasting no time, Cyra cried out as I seated myself in one quick thrust, only pausing for a moment to let her adjust to the fullness. I moaned at the silky warmth that clenched tightly around me.

Still holding her hip against me, I twisted her hair around my other hand, pulling it, forcing her back to arch. Cyra moaned at the new angle, and I slowly pulled out to my tip, letting her squirm beneath me before roughly thrusting back into her. This time, I did not pause. Setting a brutal pace, I pumped into her as she cried, wailed, and moaned. Her voice echoed through the library. Pushing my magic into her, I amplified that pleasure, making her so sensitive that goosebumps pebbled along her skin as she pushed back into me, meeting my every move.

Thrusting deeper and faster, a movement from the corner of my eye caught my attention. Without stopping—not even slowing—I looked at the feminine figure standing in the hall. Arianna stood there as still as a statue, horror and grief paling her beautiful face. The sight of it loosened a wild, primal urge in me. My eyes darkened as I pumped in and out, my balls tightening, my breathing becoming rough and unsteady. Holding her stare, I saw tears begin to fall down that elegant face as Cyra's cries and moans grew louder and more fervent. Just the sight of Arianna so crestfallen seemed to electrify me, my blood heating, making my movements feral.

Cyra screamed out, her cunt clenching my cock as she came. I pulled her against me, going deeper when pleasure erupted from me. Yelling out, I closed my eyes, finally breaking eye contact with Arianna while I rode out wave after wave of pleasure. Spilling the last of my seed, I slowly pulled out, grabbing Cyra's torn dress to clean myself.

"You *bitch*," Arianna roared, her face a teary mess.

Gasping, Cyra whipped her head around to Arianna, her face paling when she saw Arianna standing there, seething. A crimson glow snaked along Arianna's veins as she fought to keep her flame under control.

"I think you'd better run along, sweetheart," I whispered, a hint of amusement coloring my tone as I fixed myself.

Looking up at me like a frightened little doe, Cyra grabbed the torn part of her dress, quickly departing, giving Arianna a wide berth as she went, leaving Arianna and me alone in the library.

A quiet laugh rumbled through me when I looked back at Arianna, and I casually made my way to her. That crimson glow still made its way down her arms and into her hands. Stopping in front of her, I twisted my lips up in a casual, lazy smirk.

Arianna trembled, her eyes blazing with rage and heartbreak. The sight was so resplendent. Raising her hand, she swiftly brought it down, striking my face. My cheek burned, and my amusement instantly morphed into something more dangerous.

"You fucking bastard," she snarled, her ivory skin burning from the flame inside struggling to break free.

When she reached up to slap me again, I gripped her wrist with one hand and her throat with the other, pulling her forward. Baring my teeth, I growled, "For your well-being, you will not do that again."

"Fuck you, Ambrose," she hissed, attempting to wrestle out of my grip.

My hand tightened on her wrist, twisting it, causing her to suck in a painful breath. Her icy glare cut through me, and my cock twitched at the sight. I loved seeing her so…breakable. So delicate. So *fragile*. Leaning down, I captured her lips with mine. Arianna struggled to push me away, but my tongue forced her lips to open, parting them so I could deepen our kiss.

Arianna grunted before biting down on my tongue. A harsh breath left me, my mouth filling with a metallic taste. Snarling, I tightened my hold on her throat, cutting off her air.

"You fucking bitch," I spat. "Do that again, and it will be the last thing you ever do." Incensed, I pulled her in close as she struggled for air, her soft, pale skin beginning to purple. "Do I make myself clear?" I asked, low and vicious.

Arianna nodded, gagging a mumbled response, tears flowing freely down her face. Squeezing her throat slightly tighter, I pushed her away from me, letting her fall to the floor. I watched her then, gasping and coughing, my lips curling back in disgust at her petulance.

Cocking my head to the side, I crouched down and roughly caught her cheeks, forcing her face to meet mine. She whimpered at the awkward angle, and I breathed in her fear—her desperation. "Once you've composed yourself, let's take this lovely chat to my office. There are things we need to discuss."

I let go of her face, letting it fall to the floor. Standing, I stepped over her trembling body, leaving her to cry softly to herself.

I SAT IN MY OFFICE, flipping through one desperate request after another for food and medicine from the outer villages, each sounding more wretched than the last. With my patience beginning to fray, I looked at the time. Thirty minutes had passed while I waited for Arianna, and my tolerance was growing thin. My plans for Sybil were not progressing as quickly as I'd like, and that cursed, inbred, Samian was trying his damnedest to make Sybil wary of me. That little chit, Arianna, and her dramatics weren't helping matters either.

I slammed the documents on my desk just as a timid knock sounded at my door. "Enter," I growled, annoyance seeping through my calm exterior.

This day was quickly growing troublesome for me. I should be relishing in Sybil's desperate need for love. I should be making her succumb to my every desire, making her writhe beneath my touch, leaving her begging for more. I should be with her now, twisting that desperation, making it grow so strong that she would easily give in to me, grateful for any morsel of affection I'd grant her, until I had her so lost and desolate that she would willingly grant me control of her power. Instead, I was here, having to deal with a little frightened twit while I tried to put a restraint on my ever-growing contempt.

Opening the door, Arianna crept inside, her eyes red and swollen, refusing to meet my glare. Her slender neck had already started to bruise from our little tête-à-tête.

"Have we composed ourselves, Arianna dear?" I asked, my voice laced with venom.

Arianna still stood by the door and nodded, fear wafting off her in giant waves. Gesturing to the chair in front of my desk, Arianna quickly sat down, clasping her hands together on her lap, attempting to hide how they trembled. Once settled, she dared a glance in my direction, catching how I still watched her before looking down again and curling into herself.

"Good," I said, leaning back into my chair. "We need to talk about our plan for Sybil. It's not progressing as fast as I would like it to."

Arianna paled, her body going rigid. "I haven't seen much of her lately. Samian has been taking her straight to the library for her studies," she explained, her voice wavering.

Raising my hand to silence her, Arianna swallowed thickly, her throat bobbing as her chest began rising and falling quickly. I could feel the panic growing in her. "I don't care for excuses, Arianna," I said flatly. "I have decided that she will accompany you and Ezra on your next excursion at the end of the week. She will also join you tomorrow afternoon for your training. I want you to use that time to pressure her, to make her feel defeated and unable to control her magic by the time she visits Lowbrook. I need her to be *terrified* of it. Once she is at Lowbrook, you will make her lose control by any means necessary. She must be broken by the time she returns to the palace. Do I make myself clear?"

"Yes," Arianna stammered. "What would you like me to do?"

Releasing a quick exhale, I slowly stood and made my way to Arianna. Sitting on the arm of the chair, Arianna flinched as I gently ran my hand through her hair before gripping it, pulling her head back so our eyes could meet. Arianna shuddered a breath, her eyes glistening with fear. "Are you incapable of making a plan, Arianna?" I lowered my voice to a deadly tone. "Do I need to find someone else who can get the job done? Someone more capable of being my queen?"

"I can do it," Arianna pleaded. "I'm sorry. I can do it, I swear. When we return from Lowbrook, Sybil will be yours. I promise. She will be yours."

I studied her, her breath becoming unsteady. I leaned down, softly placing my lips against her head before letting go of her hair. Arianna took a quivering breath while I stood and made my way back to my desk. Sitting, I waved her off, her presence grating on my nerves. Arianna shot up from her chair, rushing toward the door, blinking back her tears.

"Arianna?" I asked calmly before she could open the door. "Make sure you fulfill your promise, or don't bother coming back. Understood?"

Arianna inhaled sharply as I picked up a document from my desk to read through. Softly confirming that she understood, she opened the door, letting it gently close behind her as she left.

CHAPTER 22

SYBIL

Waking up before the sun, I quickly washed my face and dressed myself in a simple aqua tunic with tights, completely skipping over the skirts Ambrose had bought for me. Humiliation heated my blood as the memory of soft fabric gliding across my skin, only to be interrupted by Samian's face crossing my mind. I wasn't sure how I was going to face him again without wondering what would have happened if he were the one in the library with me instead of Ambrose, if it were his hands that roamed my body, lifting the silky fabric—

"No," I whispered to myself. I couldn't think about that; I shouldn't even allow the thought to finish.

Although last night eased some of my craving for closeness, there was still an undeniable ache to fill the emptiness. It was hard not to feel lonely here. I missed Liam. I missed how comfortable and normal he felt. And how comfortable and normal *I* felt with him. And though Ambrose and Samian had been with me, making sure I had help integrating myself here, it didn't change how much I missed being home. No, not home. That place was now too far out of my reach. *Liam* was too far out of my reach. I felt like a rat after caving to Ambrose's heated touch, even worse when Samian replaced his image even though he was with someone else.

Wincing, I left the bathroom, pausing at the door of my bedroom. I looked back at the empty bed, a somber feeling squeezing my heart. Shaking my head, I stopped my thoughts there. I couldn't allow myself to continue down that path, so I forced myself not to think of long, silver hair and those deep blue and green eyes.

Steeling myself, I left my bedroom, quietly shutting the door behind me. Last night still felt too fresh for me, too raw to have the courage to face Samian this morning. To see the disappointment in his eyes, knowing what happened between Ambrose and me, my stomach dropped at the thought. I still wasn't sure if it was from embarrassment or shame.

Turning to leave, something brown on the floor caught my attention. I silently cursed when I found my bag lying by my door. I had hoped Samian would have left it in the library, and now my mind was swiftly edging toward a downward spiral. Mortified, my throat tightened. If he had heard me last night, if he knew what I had done after the library, I would never recover. My blood felt cold and hot at once, and my dread of seeing him tripled.

Picking up my bag, I slung it across my body and headed to the library. The hallways were quiet, the sconces dim, giving the palace a peaceful stillness. Traversing the stairs, I set my bag on our regular table and lit the small lamp, casting a soft orange glow around me.

A sigh of relief left me when two servants brought up coffee, tea, and pastries. I had skipped dinner last night, and my mouth watered at the smell. Waiting for them to finish setting up the cart, I emptied my bag when an envelope fell to the table. My brow knitted when I saw my name written neatly across the front.

Picking up the envelope, I turned it over, noticing a phoenix in flames was stamped across the flap. Confused, I hesitantly opened the envelope, pulling out a letter from Samian. My face heated, and I shoved the letter back into my bag, hoping the servants didn't see.

Later.

I would read it later, when they were gone.

With the coffee set up and Samian's usual teapot and cup readied, one of the servants poured some coffee for me, adding some cream and sugar. Thanking her, I watched as she walked to the stairs where the other servant stood waiting. My heart galloped in my chest, and as their heads disappeared from my sight, I ripped the letter out of my bag. Swallowing, I opened the letter, my hands slightly shaking, terrified of what he had written. But after reading the first few lines, a small smile formed, and my chest loosened a bit.

He apologized for pushing his opinions about Ambrose on me and for not allowing me to form my own opinion. He wrote that he knew I could make my own decisions and that he would always remain by my side, no matter what. Though he still believed I should be careful around Ambrose, it was up to me to decide Ambrose's character and who he was to me.

Sudden and instant relief filled my chest, pushing out the nervous bundle of tension that had lodged itself in my heart.

I smiled softly, letting that wall of dread I had built through the night fall. I still felt a tiny bit awkward about what he had interrupted last night—and what he might have heard after—

but I felt more assured about facing him today, and I felt more confident with my magic.

Leaning back in my chair, I closed my eyes, searching for the warmth of my magic that was settled deep in my chest, and let it radiate through me. My body sang, and when I opened my eyes, a small orb of light glowed above my hand, pulsing as satisfaction swelled inside me. Holding it for a moment longer, I let the light fade away before opening my book on the creatures of Nemos.

AN HOUR PASSED before I heard footsteps making their way to me. The steps sounded slow and hesitant, which made my shoulders tense. While his letter made me feel slightly less embarrassed, I still felt a sting of awkwardness when Samian approached the table, our eyes meeting.

Samian flashed me a tight smile before reaching for the teapot and a cup. "How was the rest of your night?" His voice was wary, his eyes glued to the tea pouring from the porcelain pot.

I blinked, fighting my cringe. "It was fine," I murmured, closing my book.

The silence grew thick and uncomfortable. Samian still kept his eyes on his cup, not daring to look at me. I stared at the table, tapping my fingers against the smooth wood.

Eventually, Samian cleared his throat, and I looked at him. Both of us winced, and we let out a nervous laugh. "Ah, did you get my note?" he asked quietly, looking back to his tea.

"I—um, did," I breathed. "Thank you, you know, for what you said. It meant a lot. I did want to show you something, though."

Samian perked up at the change of subject, the stiffness between us finally easing. Moving the chair back, I stood and put my hands together. Taking a deep breath, I felt for the hum of my magic, letting it flow down my arms and into my hands. My eyes flicked to Samian; his face lit with excitement. Standing, he walked to me, examining the ball of light that floated between my hands.

He grabbed my shoulders, giving me a small shake, a laugh escaping his lips. A laugh that skittered across my skin, heating my blood. "You did it," he uttered, pride filling his eyes. "This is amazing, Sybil. I knew you could do it once you had enough time to calm yourself."

Giving my shoulders a gentle squeeze, I pushed back the thoughts of his hand in other places. But when Samian's smile curved slyly, something told me that whatever was coming out of his mouth next wouldn't be good.

"Since you have enough control to create the ball of light *and* keep it steady, let's move on to the next step. I want you to turn that ball into an object. Let's say," Samian paused, his eyes roaming around the library, "a dagger. Lengthen and sharpen your light to form a dagger."

"Samian," I breathed, my heart lodging in my throat. "I literally just grasped how to make this light."

"And now you'll turn it into a dagger," Samian smiled sweetly.

Too stunned for words, I watched him walk back to his chair, my mouth ajar. My mind reeled; I couldn't think of what to say or do.

A dagger.

This man really thought I could make a dagger. A hard thump on the table pulled me out of my spiraling head. A sharpened dagger lay there, the steel glinting in the light.

"In case you didn't know what one looked like," he smirked, giving me a quick wink.

Bastard. What a damn bastard.

I could feel my cheeks turning red. "I know what they look like," I grumbled, more to myself, but Samian's chuckle made me hiss. Slumping into my chair, I exhaled sharply. It was already hard enough figuring out how to control my magic and *not* have it explode in my face, and now he wanted me to make sharp and pointy objects with it? This was a disaster in the making.

And that's what it was.

A complete and total disaster. A dumpster fire that never stopped burning.

Two hours passed; sweat dripped down the side of my face as I grunted with exertion before a blast of light abruptly expanded, piercing Samian's cup. Panting, I cried out in frustration while a puddle of tea dripped from the table to the floor. I groaned, walking over to the mess and picking up the shards of porcelain.

Samian sighed, and I faltered when he crouched down to help me clean the mess. His brow furrowed as if he were lost in thought. I couldn't tell whether he was as frustrated as I was or disappointed. I'm sure he was thinking both, though. I could hear it now, a voice that sounded so similar to my father's, telling him—telling me—that this was all pointless. Telling him I would never be able to do this.

A sharp edge of a broken piece of his teacup cut into my finger, and I hissed. Breaking his concentration, Samian gently took my hand, his smooth skin softly caressing mine, sending a twinge of electricity up my arm. Swallowing, Aster's face flitted across my mind as I watched Samian set aside the pieces of broken porcelain before taking a cloth napkin, ripping it into a smaller piece, and wrapping it around my finger. My chest ached when he put a touch of pressure on the cut.

I have never hated feeling so useless as I do now. "Why am I not able to do this?" I asked bitterly, my voice cracking.

Exhaling, Samian stopped cleaning, his lips dipping in a frown. "What makes you think that you're not able to do this?" he asked, his tone was soft and steady.

"I'm sorry, have you not seen what has been happening the past few hours?" Frustration dripped from my tone. My heart pounded hard against my chest. "I completely shattered that cup. That bookcase?" I said, pointing behind me. "It's destroyed. I am destroying everything around me." Shame twisted my stomach, and my voice trembled. Every breath I took felt empty. All I wanted to do was scream and shout. I wanted to throw something and let it shatter against the wall. I wanted to bang my fists against the floor or the table. I wanted to do *something* that would make this room feel less suffocating.

"Sybil," Samian sighed, his eyes turning sharp, and I tensed, waiting for him to agree with me. To tell me that maybe it was time for me to give up. But the words that came were not what I expected. "The fact that you are 'destroying' the things around you tells me you *can* do this. If you couldn't, there would be no magic. My cup would still be intact. That bookcase," he jerked his chin to the splintered wood, "would still be standing in one piece. You are learning faster than you think you are. It takes children months to learn how to hold on to their magic without it going haywire. You learned it in a day."

My eyes burned, and Samian tucked a piece of hair behind my ear. His gaze felt endless, and I couldn't look away, couldn't even breathe under the fire that lingered in his eyes. "You are doing so much better than you think you are, Sybil. Let go of this *fixation* that you have on needing to control your magic.

Accept that your magic is something beautiful, warm, and completely you. It is a part of you. If you want to control it, you need to feel it. Become it. You need to create a love for its beauty and the warmth it can provide." Pulling his hand away, he looked down at the shards of his cup, swallowing. "You fear your magic too much. You're afraid of what will happen when you use it, afraid of hurting someone like you did with Liam and your father. If you can let go of that fear, you will be amazed by what you can do, Sybil. I promise you that."

Breaking away from Samian, I stood, taking a deep, unsteady breath. There it was, my fear laid out, stripped and bare. I felt sick. Sick and exposed.

"It's not that simple."

How could it be? My power hurt Liam and my father. Who knew what else would happen if I just let that go? Yes, it was amazing to feel—to see—that magic pouring out of me. But that power could be a terrible, dangerous thing.

Samian's lips thinned, and he opened his mouth, but before he could say whatever he was going to say, he closed it again. Closing his eyes, he shook his head, wincing before opening them again. Wariness filled his eyes and face as his back straightened. "Last night, what did Ambrose do to help you?"

Cringing, I looked to the floor, fumbling with the edge of my tunic. "I thought we weren't going to talk about that," I murmured, my throat feeling tight.

"When did we agree on that?"

I blinked once. Twice. Samian tilted his head, waiting for me to respond, but his question—the brazenness of it—left me stunned. My heart felt like it leapt into my throat, and my stomach dropped. "The letter you gave me?" I finally said. "Wasn't that a 'hey, let's not discuss this ever again?' kind of thing?"

"I don't remember writing or agreeing to that in my letter," Samian teased with a smirk.

"Are you serious?" I sputtered. "This isn't funny."

"Yes, I'm serious, Sybil," he said, all amusement gone from his voice. "Obviously, he was able to do something that helped you focus enough for you to keep your magic steady. So, what did he do?"

"I'm not going to tell you that," I scoffed, my blasted, traitorous face heating before I could stop it.

Samian narrowed his eyes as we stood at a standstill, watching the redness creeping up my neck. Frustration mixed with a bit of shame further twisted my stomach while I refused to meet his stare. "Did he do something to you against your will?" he said a moment later, his voice deepening to a threatening tone.

"No!" I cried. "He didn't do anything against my will. I asked him to—for—he did nothing that I didn't ask him to do." I stammered, turning away from the violence in his eyes.

Samian took a step toward me when a knock interrupted us. Our heads whipped toward the sound, and I blanched. Arianna stood near the stairs, her lips curling with anger and disgust. Her jaw clenched, telling me she had heard everything we just said. My heart stood still, my blood turning to ice.

"Ambrose ordered me to tell you that you will join Ezra and me for combat training today," Arianna sneered, those blue eyes of hers like chips of ice. "Meet us in the training yard after lunch. Samian can guide you there."

Arianna's sharp gaze sliced through me as it slid down my body and back up again, her face pinching with disdain. As if finding me worthless, she scoffed and turned to leave the library. Anger rose, lodging in my throat while I watched her lithe form saunter down the steps.

Samian cursed, slamming his fist on the table. The wood groaned, and I flinched at the sudden burst of anger. Paling, my heart squeezed tight in my chest, making it hard to breathe. He'd had enough of me. This was too much for him. *I* was too much. Closing his eyes, Samian pinched the bridge of his nose and breathed, calming himself. Blinking his eyes open, he looked away, refusing to meet my stare.

"Let's take a break. You've used too much magic already, and you need to recover before your combat training. I'll grab us some lunch and return shortly. In the meantime," Samian paused, opening one of the books and turning to a page in the middle. "Read this chapter on the ability for emotional manipulation."

I nodded silently, but waited until I heard his steps disappear before returning to my chair. Plopping into my seat, I rubbed the back of my neck, blinking back the burn in my eyes. I couldn't remember a time when I fucked things up this much. Resting my chin in my hand, I stared at the page of the book, though it might as well have been empty. I mindlessly grazed the edge of the book binding with my thumbnail, moving up and down, finding comfort in the sensation.

Maybe Samian was right. Maybe I am holding on too tight to my promise to Liam. But just letting go was harder than it seemed. This life—this magic—it was all so new to me. I remembered how my father had looked at me when I lost control. I remembered how cold his eyes were. I saw how much he hated what I was, and it had left me so unsettled. It was worse than that, though. Liam, crying out in pain, had haunted me every night since I came here. No matter how hard I tried to hide that from Samian, the volatility of my magic was just a mirror to how I felt inside. My mind—my emotions—they were so muddled. So chaotic. Like I was one moment, one step away from everything falling apart.

My heart started to race, and I clutched my chest as anxiety wrapped its claws tight around my heart. Taking a few slow, deep breaths, I pulled the book closer, focusing on the words written on the page before my mind could spiral out of control.

"Emotion manipulation is a magic ability that allows a user to influence the emotional states of others, evoking or suppressing feelings such as joy, fear, calm, or sorrow. Usually found in those who are part of the Seelie Court, this power can be used for a range of purposes, such as calming anxiety, inspiring happiness, or inducing fear for control. However, the magic carries significant risks. Overuse can cause emotional detachment, where the user loses touch with their own emotions or emotional overload, leading to confusion or burnout. There is also the danger of emotional backlash, where manipulated emotions backfire on the user, causing unwanted feelings as the user feeds on others' emotions to strengthen their own magic. Additionally, prolonged use may lead to a destabilization of the user's sense of self. Ethically, while the power can be used for healing or peace, it also has the potential for manipulation, coercion, and exploitation, as it is highly unlikely that the influenced will know it is happening at the time of influence, making it important for users to exercise caution and moral integrity with its application."

My brows furrowed as I skimmed the rest of the section, further explaining the mechanics and dangers of the ability. Warning bells rang in my mind when I thought back to Samian's questions about my time with Ambrose and whether he had forced me to do anything. I leaned back in my seat, thinking of all the times Ambrose had helped me calm down when I was lost in my thoughts or my feelings. Even when I felt cautious and tense around him, I remembered a strange warmth flooding through me, melting away my worries and helping me feel comfortable and safe around him, as if I were blanketed in a sense of ease that settled deep inside me.

But Ambrose couldn't have this ability, could he? The book said that the ability was a part of the Seelie Court, and Ambrose was a faerie. Plus, Samian would have told me when we were discussing unique magic outside of the faerie elemental magic, wouldn't he?

After my father left us, I had to learn how to regulate my emotions. I learned how to file them away for another day so that I could take care of my mother, especially when she became sick. It became second nature to me. I may have been letting those emotions get the best of me recently, but I would know if Ambrose was using magic to manipulate me, right?

After our first lesson was interrupted, we never returned to learning how to feel for another's magic influence, but Samian said that it felt different—foreign.

Samian's footsteps rang out, and the scent of ham and fresh bread filled the air. My mouth watered as I eyed the toasted sandwich, thick cheese melting over the sides. As if on cue, my stomach growled, making Samian laugh and breaking any remaining tension between us; my heart felt lighter at the sound. I'm sure Samian would have said something if Ambrose had that power.

CHAPTER 23
SYBIL

Samian and I ate the rest of our lunch in silence before he led me back to my room to change into my uniform. It had arrived with the clothes Ambrose had bought for me. The pants and jacket were made of a black, stretchy leather, which was lucky for me—and my curves—since the fit was a bit tighter than the usual clothes I wore. Black leather boots had arrived as well, matching the uniform perfectly.

Testing the leather's feel, I did a few stretches and lunges around the closet. The leather felt a tad stiff, and I prayed to whoever would listen that it would break in soon.

Giving myself another look in the mirror, my shoulders sagged. This morning had been a complete failure. I didn't feel ready enough for combat training. I took a martial arts class as a child, but that was years ago. Since then, my workout regimen has been inconsistent. There was never enough time or energy in the day to stick to a routine.

I feared this moment was going to come, but I had secretly hoped that Ambrose would either forget or give me enough time to get comfortable with my magic before sending me out to train.

My stomach churned, and I swallowed hard, the sounds of Liam's yell echoing through my mind. I wasn't ready for this. It was too soon. One wrong move could cause someone to get hurt. I could already feel my light whirling inside, itching to be released.

And Arianna…

This was going to be a shit show.

Not daring to look in the mirror again, I sighed and walked out of my room, meeting Samian in the hallway. His eyes were hard and refused to meet mine as they swept over me. He adjusted my jacket before spinning me around, and I fought against my cringe. When I turned back to him, he nodded, the muscle in his jaw feathering. An approval, though reluctant. But his silence only confirmed that I was right to worry about what would happen today, not only with my magic but with Arianna too.

Wariness crept up my back, my body stiffening. Ambrose said he had spoken to her, but after today, I knew the hostility between us had grown because she had overheard Samian and me in the library. Part of me wondered if I would survive my first training. I could only hope that Ezra would lead the training and that he would be kinder to me. He hadn't laughed that day in the dining hall, only watched Arianna with enough quiet precision that made me wonder if he had disapproved of her actions.

My chest tightened. This was going to be an unpleasant afternoon.

Not speaking a word, Samian turned, guiding us through the area of the palace I hadn't explored to the training grounds.

I pulled out my small notebook and pen from the pocket of my jacket, taking notes to add to my map later.

Leaving the main palace, we walked through an open corridor that was lined with a mix of white roses, dahlias, and camellias. White wisteria hung from the ceiling, while benches sat underneath. It was beautiful. Slowing my walk, my brows furrowed at the natural stone used for the column of the corridor. It was so different from the marble used for the rest of the palace.

Sensing that I had stopped, Samian turned, following my gaze to the stone column. "Before the palace became the Marble Palace, it was built with these stones. This is the oldest wing. You'll find sections further in where they kept the original stone." Nostalgia with a hint of sadness filled his eyes, as if he were reminiscing about distant memories.

"It's amazing," I breathed.

Samian hummed in agreement, his face hardening, and we continued to the training ground in silence. The corridor ended at great wooden doors, which were open, revealing a large oval pit in the middle. The pit was surrounded by a covered passageway where other uniformed faeries stood watching people inside. They all looked like soldiers, with weapons at their hips, ready for use.

Samian led me further into the passageway, but I stopped, wanting to see what was happening. Arianna stood in position, ready for an attack. Her black uniform matched mine, except for a golden cuff on her left upper arm with tiny letters on it. Opposite of her, a soldier stood holding a sword before him. The glint of silver felt menacing as he shifted his hold on the weapon.

As he attacked, the soldier lifted his sword and brought it down in a slicing motion. Arianna stood still, waiting, biding her time until she met his blade head-on in a loud clash. She arched her blade, letting the soldier fall to the side before turning and striking him in the head with her elbow. Grunting, he fell to the ground and froze when she held the tip of her blade against his throat. I watched her closely, my heart heavy, as her lips curled into an arrogant smile.

"Glad to see you could finally make it," a raspy and commanding voice said from behind.

I turned, my eyes widening when I saw only a muscled chest. Swallowing, I looked up, finding large chocolate-colored eyes staring back. Ezra's eyes crinkled at the shock rippling across my face. I remembered meeting him on my first day here, remembered how he towered over Samian, and the surprise I felt when they stood side by side. But I had forgotten about his size in the days after our meeting. And now? Now I felt like nothing more than a child compared to him. I laughed nervously as he walked up to Samian, clapping him on the back in greeting.

Those rich brown eyes slid to me then, and I blurted, "How tall are you?" Immediate regret hit as soon as I said it, and my face burned hot.

Ezra barked a laugh, the sound so loud and deep that nearby soldiers looked our way, their eyes wide, stunned by the sound erupting from their war general. "Welcome," he said, grinning from ear to ear. His eyes were bright with amusement. "Arianna and I are in charge of this unit, so we will guide you through the training." Moving closer to me, Ezra took out the same golden cuff Arianna wore from his pocket. "This cuff marks those in our unit. It will have their rank written along the middle. Those without one are still in training." Tapping my shoulder, he moved past me, Samian following behind.

As we walked through the passage, the soldiers eyed me

suspiciously, their bodies rigid. Keeping my eyes forward, I tried not to notice when they bent their heads close to one another, whispering something, probably about my appearance or some other quality I lacked. At the end of the passage, we entered a massive room that was filled with different types of weapons. Swords, daggers, and spears lined the walls. Barrels of arrows were gathered in a far corner with bows stacked on the tables beside them.

"This is our weapons room. Most of us carry our own weapons; however, soldiers still in training use the weapons here. They are blunted to avoid any serious injuries while they are learning. You may carry a dagger if you wish, but leave it when you come to the training grounds." Stepping beside me, Ezra leaned down close to my ear, my pulse spiking. "I'm almost eight feet, by the way," he whispered before laughing and clapping me on the shoulder with his giant hand.

Grunting, pain laced through my arm, and I fell forward a step, Samian's chuckle following me. Catching myself before I face-planted, I winced, massaging the pain away. Frowning at Samian, Ezra moved away, studying the wall of weapons before finding one he deemed suitable. Plucking it off the wall, he strode back to me, dropping it into my hands. My eyes widened when my hands dipped at the weight of the small sword, which was heavier than I expected.

"I think this one will suit you well enough," Ezra said. "It's shorter and lighter than the other blades, so it will be a good starter weapon for you, especially since humans stopped using swords—from what I've heard."

Snorting, I gave the sword a slight wave toward Samian. He shook his head and rolled his eyes, but I caught the faint curve on his lips when he looked away, a fleeting expression that made my own lips twitch as I fought against a grin. Catching the moment, Ezra gave me a weak smile before murmuring something too soft for me to hear, to Samian.

Samian's mouth tightened, his eyes cutting to mine when Ezra straightened. Ezra patted Samian on the shoulder before moving to the back of the room, making himself look busy.

I watched Ezra sift through the bows with narrowed eyes. When I glanced at Samian, his face was tight with worry. He hesitated, his thumb stroking the ring on his other hand before coming to my side, his eyes still on Ezra.

"It seems I have been called away," Samian finally said, his voice hard.

"What?" I rasped. "You're leaving me here alone?" My chest twisted, my uneasiness morphing into dread.

Guilt shone in his eyes. "I'm sorry I won't be able to keep an eye on you during your training. But Ezra will be here to help you. He will make sure nothing happens while I'm away. But I will try my best to join tomorrow's training, okay?"

I stood there silent, not knowing what to say, when Ezra stepped up beside me. He placed his large hand on top of my head, giving it a small pat, like I was a child in need of consoling. I scowled, swatting his hand away. This man, so teasingly comfortable in my presence, felt different compared to the first day, when he looked so surly and unwelcoming. I didn't know what to make of it.

"I'll be sure she makes it back in one piece," Ezra grinned.

Samian narrowed his eyes at the poor attempt at reassurance, but gave Ezra a slight nod before leaving us alone in the weapons room. We stood there, the silence making my chest tight, and I fought the urge to rub at the ache. Instead, I clenched my hands. They felt clammy, and the prickling feeling started making its way down my arm, warning me that my power was threatening to lash out. As if he could feel my magic building, Ezra cleared his throat and asked me to follow him to the training area.

The sandy pit was large enough that we didn't interfere with those training on the other side. Their calls and whoops filled the air as two soldiers fought, their swords clashing loudly together. I looked at Ezra, my eyes wide. I had never been in an actual fight. Even as kids, Micah and I would pick up sticks, treating them as swords. We choreographed pretend fight scenes from movies or shows we had watched. There was never any authenticity in it, not in the way these soldiers moved now, with a quickness my eyes could barely keep up with.

Ezra's eyes softened, and he released a small laugh. "It's not as scary as it seems. You won't be starting off in that type of training just yet. First, we will go over the correct way to hold a sword and your positioning. Though you look sturdy enough, you'll be using muscles you're not used to using, so we will take time to build up your strength before I throw you in the ring with someone."

Releasing a shaky breath, I nodded, my hands tightening on the hilt of my sword. I glanced back at the others, swallowing when someone lost their weapon, losing the fight. I flinched when Ezra put his hand on my back, urging me to the spot he cleared for us.

"Lift your sword in front of you like you are preparing for a fight," he said, slipping into the mask of a war general. All the teasing and smiles forgotten. He circled me then, adjusting my hands and my feet until my positioning looked correct before he unsheathed his sword and stood beside me. "We are going to keep it simple. I just want you to raise your sword, then drop it in a slashing motion as you take a step forward."

Ezra demonstrated, and I copied his movements while he watched. His eyes tracked every move in my arms, legs, and even my feet, adjusting them as I went. Easing into a nice flow, Ezra nodded his approval before telling me to repeat that motion fifty more times.

I gaped at him, half expecting to hear his booming laugh like it was a joke. It wasn't. His face remained serious while he waited with an arched brow for me to start. Blinking, I exhaled, my shoulders dipping when I looked back at my sword. Groaning, I repositioned myself and got to work.

At first, the task seemed easy enough, but after the thirteenth swing, my arms and shoulders screamed at me, trembling while sweat dripped from my face, falling to the sand. Ezra wasn't lying when he said I would be using muscles I wasn't used to using. I was so exhausted that by the time I reached fifty, I dropped to the ground, panting. My body felt heavy as I set the sword aside to massage my shoulders and catch my breath.

Kneeling beside me, Ezra handed me some water as he frowned. "I was worried about your strength. It seems my worries were right." He eyed the trembling in my fingers when I took the water, his mouth tight.

"I mean, there's not much happening in Mide that would call for me to be battle-ready," I huffed, rolling my eyes.

Ezra took a breath, about to say something, when his eyes moved to someone behind me and scowled. Turning to see what he was looking at, I fought a groan when I spotted Arianna walking toward us. Her bright golden hair was tied up; her eyes burned like an icy fire, and one side of those full lips of hers rose in her usual snide, arrogant smirk.

"Tired already, little girl?" Arianna laughed, twisting to the soldiers behind her.

Their laughs mirrored Arianna's, sounding cold and cruel as Arianna turned back to me. She looked as if she had just finished getting ready for the day, not like she was in the middle of a training session. Her face was soft, her cheeks were tinged with pink, and her hair looked so smooth and flattering. My face heated when a bead of sweat dripped down my temple into the sand below. I must have looked almost feral compared to her.

Pushing the loose strands of hair from my eyes, I picked up my sword and stood. My muscles screamed, begging for more rest, but I pushed the feeling down, not wanting to show Arianna just how weak I felt. Disregarding her, I turned my back on her, moving to stand closer to Ezra.

Ezra grimaced while a few soldiers gasped, whispering excitedly to each other. Understanding that I had somehow made a mistake dawned too late when Arianna gripped the end of my braid and pulled me back. Tripping over my feet, my breath caught in my throat when I landed on the ground hard, my bones aching from the impact. Hissing, my gaze jerked to Arianna, narrowing on her face, which was pinched with anger.

"Never turn your back on me, *girl*," Arianna seethed, her veins glowing a crimson red that webbed down her neck and arms. "You may be new here, but I am still your commander."

"You're not my anything," I scoffed, standing and brushing the sand from my leathers. "I'm here to learn how to protect myself, not to join some army." Hurting someone wasn't something I could do, at least not with intention, and I sure as hell wasn't going to let *her* force me into joining an army.

Arianna stalked closer to me, those graceful steps taking their time until she was a mere inch away. Unmoving, I looked up at her, meeting her fiery glare with one of my own. "As long as you are on these grounds, you belong to me." Her voice was unnaturally calm, and she continued to hold my stare, daring me to respond.

My grip tightened around my sword while my pulse picked up, beating hard against my chest. "I belong to no one but myself," I said, my voice tight.

The soldiers around us laughed, but I couldn't hear them over the roar of blood in my ears. My power thrummed just below my skin, pulsing, matching the beat of my heart. I shivered, and the feeling of needles prickled down my arms, preparing to protect me. Ezra called out Arianna's name, but she ignored him, refusing to break eye contact with me.

Arianna smirked. "We'll see about that." Turning to a soldier close to her, she whispered something to him before looking back at me. A wicked smile slowly curved across her face. "I heard the humans in Mide are weak, that they've grown fat and lazy." Pausing, Arianna's eyes swept over my body before lifting her sword, pointing it at my chest as the heat in my cheeks grew hotter. "I think we should have a little fun and just see how *weak* the humans have become."

Ezra let out a curse while cheers and laughter erupted around us. "Arianna, she's not ready for this," Ezra growled, his voice low and filled with warning. "She needs more time to learn before being thrown into the middle of a fight. Especially one with you."

"If you think she is too weak, Ezra, just say so," Arianna taunted. "Every single one of my soldiers was thrown into duels on their first day—why shouldn't she?"

"You know as well as I do, our soldiers grew up learning how to fight before they joined our unit. She hasn't had that privilege." Ezra's voice grew louder and more threatening as he stepped between us, his sword glinting in the light.

"Well, I guess now is as good a time as any to learn, don't you think?" Arianna jibed, the crowd snickering along with her.

Ezra opened his mouth, ready to defend me again, when

Arianna sidestepped Ezra and lunged at me. Ezra cursed and quickly cut her off, blocking her path to me. "Don't do this," he said, raising his sword.

Arianna cocked her head, studying him with narrowed eyes. In one quick movement, faster than a blink, she closed in on Ezra, her sword in the air. Panic gripped its claws tightly around my chest, and my body felt glued to the spot, unable to move or look away. Time felt slowed as Ezra met all of Arianna's blows with ones of his own, their swords clashing, the sound ringing in my ears.

Arianna's attacks against Ezra were ruthless, aiming to kill, while his were entirely defensive. The jeers around me continued as the commander and war general fought, Ezra's powerful body keeping up with Arianna's nimble movements until she suddenly feigned going left. I yelled out in warning, but Ezra heard me too late, letting her slip past him.

Arianna was circling him when two rough hands shoved me into Arianna's path. Gasping, my blood rushed, and I lifted my sword just in time as Arianna swiftly brought hers down, colliding with mine. The vibrations jarred the muscles in my shoulder and arm. Crying out, my hand felt weak, and I almost dropped my sword.

Pushing away from her, I swiftly moved when her sword swiped at me again. Tripping over my feet, I felt the hum in my body grow more intense as I ducked, narrowly missing her next strike.

My heart beat wildly in my chest, and we circled each other. Arianna studied me, calculating her next move while I carefully searched the crowd for Ezra's massive form, making sure to keep an eye on Arianna as well. Stepping too close to the crowd behind me, someone pushed me back into the pit just as Arianna launched her attack, swinging her sword. My knees buckled, and I fell to the ground, my bones aching from the impact. I raised my sword in time to clash against hers; another painful jolt laced up my arm, and this time, my sword flew from my hands, landing several feet away.

Clutching my hand to my chest, a painful ache seeped into my bones. I panted heavily, desperately searching for Ezra in the endless crowd of soldiers, praying that he would help me. A cold panic set in, and it felt like I couldn't breathe, like I couldn't get enough oxygen to fill my lungs. Somewhere in the crowd, I heard a faint call of my name, but the pounding in my ears drowned it out. My power grew more intense, amplifying the needle-like sensation to something nearly excruciating. My body shook, and my panting turned into painful gasps, my lungs burning and feeling too tight.

Movement from the corner of my eye caught my attention when Arianna hurtled toward me. Fear flooded my veins, and my body felt paralyzed. I couldn't even scream; my voice was gone. Time slowed, and everything in me hollowed out before I heard a panicked but familiar voice screaming my name from deep within, like an echo in my head.

Time snapped back into place, and my breath caught in my throat. I had nothing to protect me, nothing to stop that sword from slicing my skin. Lifting my hands in front of me, a blinding light exploded. The pressure that had built up whooshed out of me like water breaking from a dam. Yelps and shouts filled the air around me, and the light continued to shine intensely while I waited for the sharp sting of Arianna's sword.

But it never came. The brightness began to fade around me, painful groans filling the training grounds. My body trembled uncontrollably when I finally lifted my head, taking in the turmoil and confusion. My stomach roiled at the sight of blood in the sand, and I turned, heaving the contents of my stomach into the dirt beside me. Tears streamed down my face, my eyes burning and my vision blurring.

It happened again. I couldn't stop myself again, and it was worse. This time was so much worse. People were hurt, moaning from the pain that I had caused.

I did this—I hurt them.

The words repeated themselves.

My vision tunneled, my breath growing too short and quick as the awareness of what had just happened hit hard. It was just as my father had said would happen. I lost control, and it wasn't just two people this time. There were more, and from the sounds of their groans, the injuries were worse. I covered my ears with my hands, letting my head fall against the ground. I screamed into the dirt, unable to stop the feel of needles from renewing its downward crawl to my hands.

I couldn't stop it. Inescapable pressure welled up inside my chest, preparing to let loose.

Somewhere beside me, a pained moan caught my attention, and Ezra called out my name. His voice sounded weak—so different from its usual richness. Choking out a breath, I slowly looked up, finding Ezra stumbling toward me, his wide eyes flashing with wariness while blood poured down the side of his face. My eyes narrowed on the drops that fell to the sand below.

I swallowed my whimper as a soldier yelled out Arianna's name, and I turned. Arianna lay motionless, blood seeping into the ground beside her. My heart and my mind froze while I watched several soldiers run to her, lifting her head off the ground, attempting to wake her. I felt empty and hollow while I watched them call out orders for someone to bring a healer, as if I were no longer a part of my body.

Ezra called my name again, and my gaze slid back to his, still fighting against the power that threatened to burst from me.

My body trembled violently as I watched him survey the chaos around us, silently counting the number of injured soldiers. I watched as his eyes found mine again; he whispered my name too quietly for me to hear, but terror filled every line of his too-pale face. Horror and agony ripped through me. Taking a shaky breath, a sob broke free from me when I stood on weak legs, taking a step away from him—away from Arianna, still lying motionless on the ground.

Before Ezra could get close, I staggered back a few more steps, then turned and ran as fast as I could from the training grounds, letting Ezra's pleas for me to stop echo behind me.

CHAPTER 24
AMBROSE

A heavy knock pounded against my door before suddenly swinging open. I growled at the disturbance as Arianna entered the study, her nose in the air, dripping with arrogant pride. I raised an eyebrow, studying her. Her leathers were covered in dirt; her hair was clumped together from blood. A large gash, slowly stitching back together, streaked along the side of her head where her ivory skin was tainted red. Confusion with a touch of excitement sparked in me, and I couldn't help the smile forming on my lips.

She strode to my desk, those icy blue eyes bright. Her hand clenched her side, and she had a small limp in her step, but the smile that curled along her face was breathtaking.

"Training went well, I take it?" I asked.

"It went more than well, my love," Arianna breathed excitedly. "She didn't even make it the full session before running off, so upset from all the injuries she caused."

Her soft song-like laughter danced along my skin, her excitement burning through me. This is more like it. This is exactly what I was waiting for. "Is she ready to accept my bargain?" I asked quickly, my heart beating faster and faster.

"No, not yet," Arianna murmured, slightly paling at the twitch in my smile. Arianna moved around the desk, kneeling in front of me, taking my hands into hers. "I have more planned for her. Once we visit Lowbrook, she will be yours for the taking. I promise you that, my king."

Arianna rose quickly, her lips meeting mine in a passionate kiss as she straddled me, my hands snaking up her back. Arianna winced when my hand moved over the wound hidden by her leather jacket.

Recovering quickly, she pulled her head back, her glossy eyes meeting mine. "Go to her," she breathed. "Go and offer her the bargain again, but do not push it. Murmur sweet nothings in her ear and let her think about it." Arianna paused, bringing her lips back to mine, moaning as she moved her hands slowly up and down my chest. Breaking the kiss, she rested her forehead against mine. "I will bring her down to her knees before you, begging and pleading for the bargain you offer by week's end."

A laugh, low and deep, rumbled through my chest, and I gripped the back of her neck, letting our lips crash together once again. My plan was finally coming together, and all I could think about was Sybil on her knees, her beautiful, tear-stained face, overcome by grief, begging me to take control of her magic. Need pulsed through me at the thought, and my cock twitched.

Before letting that need consume me, I broke our kiss, our breaths mixing. Arianna slid off my lap, letting me stand. Fixing my crumpled shirt, my heated gaze met Arianna's. "I guess I should make my way to see our darling little Sybil."

I STOOD in front of Sybil's door, inhaling slow and deep, feeling her terror and shame seeping from her room. If I could feel them from here, I could only imagine how heavy her emotions would be once I was inside. I rolled my neck, the thought of it almost making me moan. Exhaling, I calmed myself before I could get too excited. I was so close to reaching my goal; it would be a shame to give it all up by tossing myself in the waves of such powerful emotions.

Reaching for the door, I found it unlocked and slowly opened it, letting myself inside. Once the door clicked shut, I softly called out Sybil's name and waited, letting my eyes adjust to the darkness of the room, but no answer came.

I followed the muffled cries echoing from her bedroom and stopped at the doorway of her room. Sybil lay curled in a ball on her side, so lost in her despair that she didn't notice me as I watched her. The darkness hid my smile, and I breathed in the anguish that wafted off her, the feel of it sending a bolt of electricity through me.

Breathing out, I slipped into my role of worried friend, gasping Sybil's name before rushing to her bed. "Sybil," I breathed. "Sybil, look at me. Are you okay? Are you hurt?"

Sybil blinked, wiping the tears from her eyes. But then her eyes widened, recognition finally hitting as wild, frantic fear consumed her. Pushing onto her knees, she swallowed, gripping my shirt tight in her hands. "It was an accident. Please believe me, I didn't mean to hurt anyone. I didn't mean to hurt Arianna. Please, Ambrose, I'm sorry. I'm so sorry."

"Shh," I whispered, sliding into the bed beside her. I wrapped my arms around her, and she shook against me. "It's okay, Sybil. I know you didn't mean to do it. It's okay, I promise. Aster said that Arianna should wake up by tomorrow and, after some rest, she will make a full recovery."

Sybil cried harder into my chest, the feel of her wet tears soaking through my shirt making my lips curl in disgust. Gently patting her back, I repeated that everything was okay until her cries lessened, and she could hold herself up on her own.

Once her sobs were nothing more than her sniffling, I brushed her hair away from her face. "May I turn on the light?" I asked softly, keeping my tone light and encouraging. "It's easier to lose yourself in the darkness, but I find that the light always brings hope, even during our darkest moments."

Nodding, Sybil whimpered as I stood, as if the loss of my warmth was too much to bear. Turning on a lamp beside her bed, a soft, warm glow illuminated the room. Sybil winced at the brightness. She kept her eyes on the blanket in front of her, shame and disgust apparent. She was still in her leathers, which, like Arianna's, were covered in grime. Her tears made the dirt streak down in wet lines, and her hair looked wild—matted and unruly.

Inwardly, seeing her so downtrodden caused a thrill from deep within to bubble up so fiercely that I had to remind myself why I was here. I needed her to be hopeless to convince her that only *I* could help her control her power.

Pushing down that excitement, I forced myself to give her a soft and tender smile, brushing my knuckle along her damp cheek before heading into her washroom.

Grabbing a cloth, I soaked it under warm water and headed back to Sybil. She was still sitting in the same spot, messing with the edge of the blanket, lost within her thoughts. I sat in front of her, putting my hand on top of hers. She flinched but slowly raised her head, her eyes so dull and weak, meeting mine. I gave her another soft smile and wiped the dirt from her face. Her eyes fell, and I could feel the guilt and regret whirling inside of her, begging for me to latch onto.

So I did.

I gripped her emotions tightly, feeding into them, making them grow stronger. Shame, grief, remorse, disgust, they all settled deep in her heart.

Sybil choked on a sob, and I pulled her into a tight hug, refusing to let go until she relaxed into my arms. "I know you might not want to hear this, my sweet girl," I murmured, keeping my tone gentle. "But my offer still stands." I pulled her back then, letting her see the sincerity I forced into my eyes. "You don't have to decide right now, but just know that I am here to protect you in any way I can. You didn't ask for this life or this beautiful and amazing power that flows through your veins. I care for you so much, my darling. I care for you so deeply that it pains me to see you this way. I just wanted you to know that it still stands, should you ever want it."

Sybil loosened a shaky breath, her shoulders dipping. Even as she searched my gaze, hoping to find the answer to make her pain disappear, tears welled up in her eyes once again, and she opened her mouth to reply.

I held a finger to her soft pink lips, stopping her before she spoke. "I don't want you to answer now," I whispered. "I want you to take some time and think about it. Bargains are not something to take lightly, my love, and I don't want you to do something you might regret later. I just want you to know that if you ever decide you want it, I will always, *always*, help you."

Sybil sat, lost in thought, so lost that I half-wondered if she even heard me, but eventually she nodded while more tears fell.

"How about we get some rest?" I asked, gently wiping away her tears. "Would you like me to stay here with you tonight?"

Sybil nodded, still unable to speak under the weight of her despair, while I smoothed the hair away from her face. Cupping her cheeks in my hands, I let my mouth curl into a small, soothing smile. Leaning in, I pressed my lips to hers in a delicate kiss, lingering only until Sybil pulled away, gasping. Those wide hazel eyes looked greener after all her tears as they searched mine, and I felt a flicker of arousal inside her. It was such a small amount, but it was enough to send need pulsing through me.

I was so close to having her right where I wanted her. So close to having her agree to my bargain. Arianna's words rang silently in my head, telling me to wait—to be patient, but that didn't mean I couldn't have some fun.

I gathered her into my arms and fed into her emotions. I felt for her sorrow—her shame—and I threw my magic into them, letting them take hold of her. I filled her heart with so much despair that she wept until exhaustion overtook her, pulling her into a deep and fitful sleep.

CHAPTER 25

SYBIL

Waking up, the sun burned my swollen eyes. Wincing, I looked over, finding the place where Ambrose had slept now empty. On the pillow, a note with my name written across in delicate handwriting lay waiting for me. I breathed, pulling my hand against my too-tight chest. After what happened yesterday with Arianna and Ambrose, I felt sick. No matter how upset I was about losing control of my magic, I shouldn't have let Ambrose stay.

I turned on my back, looking up at the ceiling.

Later.

I would read his note later.

Swallowing, I squeezed my eyes shut, my stomach turning with a sudden wave of panic. Fresh tears burned my aching eyes, and I thought back to Arianna lying unconscious on the ground, blood pouring from her body. And Ezra, the look on his face, so much like Liam's. He was afraid of me—of what I could do.

I pressed the palms of my hands against my eyes, choking

back a sob. I failed. I failed Liam. I broke my promise and proved my father right. I was only going to hurt more people if I continued this way.

I turned over to my side, bringing my knees to my chest, curling myself into a ball. My chest heaved, and I gulped down air between my cries, making myself as small as I felt. Pulling the blanket over my head, I wrapped it tight around me, making a tiny cocoon as I did as a child when the world felt like it was going to hell around me, except this time, it really was. In the safe confines of my shroud, my tears finally slowed but still fell. I spiraled deeper into the despair that gripped me tight before exhaustion pulled me into a fitful slumber.

THE SOUND of my door swinging open startled me from my sleep. Gasping, I jerked up, pushing myself back into the headboard, my magic prickling in my hands, ready to erupt.

I blinked when Samian rushed into my bedroom, freezing at the door. His face was pale, and his eyes filled with concern. My heart pounded when he cursed and rushed over to me. I wasn't ready for this. I wasn't ready to face him—to hear how much I had disappointed him, how I failed again.

Stretching his arms toward me, I strangled out a breath, icy panic taking over, and I jerked away from him. Samian paused, his face falling. His arms dropped, unsure of what to do. His throat bobbed, and he looked away from me, but a too-calm silence fell over the room when his eyes narrowed on the note I had forgotten about on my pillow. My stomach twisted, and my heart raced when he picked up the note, opening it to read what was inside.

His face was blank—utterly unreadable. His body went

rigid; his eyes locked on the note. The only way I could sense his fury was through his magic. The ground, even the walls, seemed to shake as that quiet rage slowly took over him.

Crumpling the note, Samian cut his sharp gaze to mine and released a furious breath. "He offered you the bargain again." It wasn't a question. His voice trembled in an effort to hold back his outrage.

I couldn't answer him. I wasn't *able* to answer him. My body shuddered, and I couldn't tell if it was from my fear of Samian's wrath or the fear of what my answer would be if he asked me what I chose to do.

"Answer me," Samian said too quietly.

I shivered, blinking back the burn in my eyes. I swallowed and watched the way Samian tracked the bob of my throat. I nodded then, too afraid to speak the words out loud.

"You will not take that bargain," Samian growled through clenched teeth, his eyes glinting with rage. "Do you understand me? You will *not* agree to it. Tell me you will not agree to it, Sybil."

The picture of Arianna's body and Ezra's terror flashed through my mind, and I winced. "What choice do I have?" I cried, my hands curling into tight fists. "You heard what happened. You know what I did! How can you say that when you know it will happen again?" My voice cracked.

"You have every choice," he roared, making me shrink into myself as he stepped closer to me. "You have every choice, Sybil," he said once more, his voice softening. "Please don't agree to this."

His eyes bore into mine, pleading with me—begging me—to agree. "What about Arianna?" I whispered, my chest tightening.

Samian snarled, low and vicious. "She's fine. I saw her last night happily *prancing* around the palace. She's no more hurt than you are. In fact, I'd say she's feeling a lot better than you are now."

No, that—that couldn't be. She was badly hurt. She was…

"You're wrong," I whispered. "Ambrose told me last night. She's still unconscious and wouldn't wake for another day or so."

"He lied to you," Samian said flatly. "He's *been* lying to you. Arianna is just fine, I promise you that."

"No, that can't be true. That's not true. He wouldn't lie to me. He just wants to help me." Whether that was through the bargain or helping me with my magic, he had done nothing but help me—encourage me.

"Help you?" Samian's laugh was cruel as he stepped away from me, roughly running a hand through his hair. "Ambrose doesn't want to help you," he spat, turning back to face me. There was a dangerous gleam in his eyes that sparked a storm in me that I hadn't felt since coming to this realm. "I'm the one trying to help you, Sybil. Ambrose just wants to use you—use your power. Open your eyes before it is too late."

I scoffed. "You? Helping me?" I hissed, every word laced with venom. "How have you helped me, Samian? The last time I checked, Ambrose was the one who helped me with my magic—my control. He was the one who showed me around the palace and the city, helping me feel more comfortable in my new *home*. All you've done is just tell me to fucking breathe." My words grew louder, my heart pounded, and my hands started prickling from my power begging to be released.

Samian glowered at me, his eyes bright. The muscle in his jaw feathered, his hands clenched into tight fists, his breathing quickening. We glared at each other; the room seemed to quake from our ire. Finally, Samian let out a sharp breath and turned away, the fight in him vanishing.

He walked to the bedroom door, pausing once he reached the threshold. "Rest today," he said, his voice tight, refusing to look my way. "Tomorrow you will go with Arianna and Ezra to Lowbrook, a village on the outskirts of the city. Ambrose wants you there on their patrol to learn more about our realm."

"And you?" I murmured, my voice empty.

Samian hesitated, the muscles in his back tightening. "I will be away."

With that, Samian left, letting the door slam shut behind him.

I crumpled into the headboard, my control finally shattering as I covered my eyes with my hands and screamed. Whether in shame or anger, I wasn't sure which. Maybe it was both—for letting things get this far, for how I treated Samian, for questioning Ambrose even though he has been so kind to me.

The lights around me brightened, the sound ringing in my ears before the glass of the lights—the windows—shattered, flying across the room. I panted; the use of my magic so soon after yesterday made me feel tired and empty, like a shell of myself. Pulling the soft plush blanket over my head, I slid down into the bed, letting misery and darkness take over.

I DIDN'T WAKE until the next morning when a soft knock gently pulled me from my sleep. My eyes were puffy, and I felt tired. So tired and weak. The knock sounded again, and I huffed, sliding out of my warm cocoon to pad across my room to the door, ignoring the shards of broken glass on the floor as I went. When I cracked it open, Ezra's warm brown eyes greeted me. Worry quickly flashed through them before disappearing, and he gave me a soft but timid smile. I swallowed the lump in my throat, considering whether I should close the door and return to my bed, but the concern that flashed in his eyes…

I widened the door and moved aside for him to enter.

Stepping into the living area, Ezra wasted no time hurling me into a tight hug, making it hard for me to breathe. Sputtering, I patted him on the arm. Ezra let me go, his laugh booming across the room as I gulped down air. But his laugh grew silent when my eyes met his. We shyly looked away, shame tightening my throat while Ezra rubbed the back of his neck, considering his next words.

"I just wanted to say I'm sorry," he finally said softly. "I should have been more forceful with Arianna. I should have stopped her and protected you better than that."

I breathed, mustering up the courage to look at him, and when I did, his eyes looked so meek—so dejected. This giant bear of a man looked as if he was about to crumble—to be blown away by the slightest gust of wind.

It was genuine. His apology was genuine.

I swallowed, blinking back my tears, and looked at the floor, trying to find the words I wanted to ask but was too afraid to speak out loud.

Steeling myself, I wrapped my arms around me, my nails digging into my skin. My voice sounded so quiet—so hollow—as I asked, "Are you afraid of me now?"

Ezra sighed and gripped my shoulder tightly, but not enough to hurt. "No. I'm not afraid of you. It was—I was more afraid *for* you than of you, if that makes sense. Samian told me about how you're afraid of your magic—of not being able to control it. I was afraid of how the incident was going to affect you."

"You're not afraid of me?" I breathed, more to myself as shock rippled through me.

Ezra's deep laugh rumbled through me, easing the tension in my chest. "You'd be surprised how often something like this happens. I mean, don't get me wrong, it's not every day that someone brings two of the strongest fae in Volmire to their knees," Ezra teased, lightening the mood, "but it does happen. If anything, you should be proud of yourself. No one will be looking at you like you're fresh meat," he winked.

"What about Arianna?" I sputtered, my mind whirling too fast at how carefree Ezra was acting.

"Eh, she's fine," Ezra waved, moving further into the living area. "She needed someone to knock her on her ass, if you ask me. I would have done it eventually, but you beat me to it." Another deep laugh reverberated from his chest. "Now," he said, his voice turning stern, "Samian had to run off somewhere, but he asked me to help you get ready for your first patrol. Luckily, we're not staying overnight, so you don't need much. I've already packed a bag for you with some essentials, but I think you should refresh yourself. You—ah—smell." Ezra pinched his nose as he glanced at my rumpled nightclothes.

I looked down, casually lifting my arms to sniff. My cheeks flushed as I grimaced and rushed to the bathroom, leaving Ezra sitting in a chaise that looked almost too small for his powerful body.

I quickly bathed and changed into a new uniform, feeling more refreshed and ready for the trip. I still felt sick about what happened during training, but I swallowed that guilt and focused on the excitement of going to Lowbrook. After only seeing the palace and Volmire, I was ready to see more of Nemos—to learn more.

Braiding my damp hair, I ignored the glass thrown about the room and walked back into the living area while Ezra was plating a warm, savory pastry filled with ham and cheese. My mouth watered, and my stomach grumbled. Too weak and lost in my despair after the incident, I didn't have much of an appetite. But now, I felt like that hunger was going to eat me alive.

"I saw the plates of food on a cart by your door. I figured you might be hungry," Ezra said, handing me a plate.

My eyes widened. "There was food by the door?"

"Samian was worried about you yesterday. He said this was one of your favorites."

I frowned, looking at the door as if Samian would stroll right in while Ezra ate his food. "He'd be right." Taking a bite of the pastry, it tasted like ash on my tongue.

My heart squeezed. I couldn't get our conversation out of my head. I was awful to him, yet he still made sure I was taken care of. He didn't deserve me lashing out at him the way I did. The truth was that Samian *had* been helping me. If it weren't for him, I would have probably stayed hidden in my room, too afraid to face this new world. He had given me hope and friendship when I felt worthless. He had stayed with me, patiently teaching me about what I could do.

Exhaling, I popped the last bite into my mouth, feeling more determined to make it up to Samian when I returned later today.

CHAPTER 26
SYBIL

After clearing the plates and returning them to the cart outside my door, Ezra led me out of the palace, where a unit of soldiers stood, waiting by their horses. At the front, there was a large white and golden carriage that felt too pristine for travel outside of the city. Stepping out of the carriage, Arianna scanned the soldiers, her eyes narrowing when she caught sight of Ezra and me weaving between the crowd. I studied her, searching for the injuries Ambrose had hinted at, but found none. She looked as she always had—beautiful and polished.

Wariness rippled through me, but I pushed aside the questions that were churning inside when I noticed how the soldiers were eyeing me, like I was an explosive ready to blow. I silently thanked whoever would listen for Ezra's comforting presence.

Ezra led us to a beautiful black horse that stood tall and proud beside the carriage. Snorting, the horse pawed at the ground, waiting for Ezra to give him a small pat on his thick neck.

"I didn't know if you knew how to ride a horse or not. I also figured you wouldn't want to ride with Arianna," he said, stealing a glance at Arianna walking to a soldier near the carriage. "If you're okay with it, you can ride with Midnight and me," he added, giving the horse another pat on the neck. Midnight stepped closer to him, leaning his head on Ezra's shoulder.

"I haven't really been on a horse since one bucked me off when I was a kid," I laughed nervously, eyeing Midnight cautiously. "Riding with you works."

Ezra chuckled while he helped me into the saddle before climbing on behind me. Putting my hands on the pommel, Ezra quickly explained how I should grip Midnight with my legs before he took the reins, making Midnight turn toward the soldiers. Whistling, he called for the soldiers' attention, telling them to prepare to leave. The soldiers settled themselves on their horses while Arianna made her way to her carriage, sneering when she caught me watching her.

Ezra commanded the unit to move, and we left the palace grounds, riding through the city. The faeries in the streets stopped, letting us through, but their faces were grim as we passed by. An odd feeling wormed its way through me when a hooded figure caught my eye. His powerful body and face were hidden beneath his cloak. I could only see his mouth, tight and dipped in a frown, but I could feel his eyes narrowing in on me. I swallowed hard, looking away and focusing on the cobbled streets in front of us, leading to the pearly gates of the city.

We kept a steady pace as I watched the fields of tall grass and the distant mountains with wide eyes. We were in the foothills, Ezra had told me. The mountains were a day's ride to the east and were the central point in Nemos. He pointed out unique rock formations, or specific fields, telling me the history of the land, where some battle was held long ago, never speaking of the mountains or what was past them.

After an hour of riding, my muscles screamed for a break when a small town came into view. "This is the village of Lowbrook," Ezra explained, his voice oddly tight.

I looked around the village, noticing how the buildings looked small and almost run-down. They were made of a mix of stone and wood, with sections falling apart. But I could see that they used to be beautiful and tall; that time had been brutal to them. We went further into the village, passing by several homes. Children ran to their houses, while their mothers quickly closed the doors and windows behind them, their faces hard and wary.

"Why does everyone look so scared?" I asked quietly. The air had a strange pressure, as if it were heavy and charged.

Ezra exhaled, as if he were buying time to consider his words carefully. "It's complicated," he finally said, swallowing hard. "What have you been told about the villages outside Volmire?"

"Not much, just that an aristocratic family is in charge of specific villages and that some of the family members only stay in Volmire."

Ezra stayed silent while we watched a man bow, not straightening until the unit passed him. Only the top of his dark brown hair showed. "Volmire is unique," Ezra continued. "Certain families that are not part of the nobility are invited to set up shop in the city. Those families make a good amount of money. Others, however, are not so lucky. Most of the villages are poorly maintained." Ezra paused, contemplating his next words, his face pinching like he wasn't sure how much he was allowed to tell me. "The taxes in the villages are fairly high. It's costly to keep up with those living in Volmire. The families here survive by growing their own crops or by receiving help from others."

"Help from whom? By people in Volmire?" I interrupted, my brows knitting as we passed a home with the roof caved in.

"No, not anyone in Volmire," Ezra sighed. "The fae here in Lowbrook, and in the other villages, are made of strong will and grit. Their kindness runs deep, as does their love for each other. That alone motivates them to fill any gaps or needs in the communities."

I thought back to the grim faces we passed in Volmire, to the children and fae here who looked at us with fear shining in their eyes. "Why are we patrolling this village?" I asked hesitantly.

I couldn't see his face, but I felt his body tense against my back. "We are looking for members of the rebellion," Ezra said. His voice was guarded, his words careful.

"Rebellion?" I winced, my voice sounding louder than I intended. I glanced around to see if I had caught anyone's attention, but the soldiers kept looking forward, or at the bare homes we passed.

"There's a large group that is steadily growing in numbers. They want to change how the lands are ruled." Ezra's hands gripped the reins, the white of his knuckles showing. "There was a time when the villages were just as beautiful and prosperous as Volmire, if not more so. The trade and culture were vibrant. Each village was essential to the other. The rebels want to return to that time."

"That doesn't sound like a bad thing," I confessed softly.

"No, no, it doesn't. But you should keep that thought to

yourself," Ezra warned. "Times are dangerous, especially when you say things like that."

I swallowed hard. "How long has it been like this?"

Ezra didn't answer, not when the carriage with Arianna rolled past us. But when he pulled on Midnight's reins, bringing him to a stop, he whispered, "For too long."

Chills ran down my spine. I wanted to ask more, but the soldiers filed in around us, dismounting their horses. Ezra hopped out of the saddle, moving aside and helping me as I slid out. The soldiers moved into a formation while Arianna stepped out of her carriage, looking prim and proper, though she was in her uniform, like a queen ready for battle. My stomach felt queasy when she stood beside us, the memories of her on the ground, her blood pooling around her, flashing across my mind.

The crunch of rocks sounded, and we turned to the group approaching us on steady feet. I blinked while trying to calm my racing heart. Some of them looked almost human, aside from the unnatural beauty of the high fae. But the others, some had gray skin, others were blue with long, sinewy arms. One was short with wild red hair, his clothes entirely made of moss.

Once they drew near, they stopped, allowing an older man, who looked as if he were in his sixties, to move to the front. He was tall and lean, and his face looked weathered, tanned from long hours in the sun, but kind. His eyes were the color of honey, and his hair was golden brown. The man bowed low, and the faeries behind him followed suit, waiting until Arianna and Ezra were in front of them to straighten. Not knowing what to do, I crept along behind Ezra.

Ezra greeted the man by returning his bow, while Arianna rolled her eyes, scoffing. The villagers behind the man refused to meet our gaze, their lips curling into sneers as Ezra spoke quietly, and the man nodded patiently.

Finally, Ezra turned to me, calling me over. I swallowed, pushing back the strands of hair that fell loose from the ride. Seeing me walk to Ezra, the villagers lifted their heads, eyeing me warily as Ezra introduced me to Silas Tuluin, the village elder. I gave him a weak smile and a small wave. Silas returned my hello, smiling warmly, placing his hand over his heart, and giving me a slight bow.

Ezra continued talking to Silas, explaining that I was accompanying them to learn more about the outer villages and how today would be a quick visit. I tuned out their conversation to eye the other villagers peeking through windows. Few ventured outside, safely watching from the confines of their homes, far enough away to not catch the attention of the soldiers. All of them, even the children, kept their expressions tight, seemingly troubled by our presence. I shifted nervously on my feet from the unease charging the air.

Finishing their discussion, Ezra shook Silas's weathered hand, their greeting lingering a beat as Ezra discreetly passed a note between them before stepping away, returning to the unit of soldiers. I narrowed my eyes, glancing between Silas and Ezra, unsure of what to think about what I had just witnessed. But I kept my mouth shut, pushing that nagging suspicion aside to follow Ezra back to the soldiers. I would ask him about it later, when we were away from listening ears and wandering eyes.

"Thank you for your patience." Ezra's voice rang out, grabbing everyone's attention, including the villagers. "Tie up your horses and start searching the area. The villagers have been told to help in any way possible and, as always, remember to be respectful. You know my rules on how to treat those in the outer villages."

The soldiers bowed, then tied their horses to a nearby fence and split into groups to search the village. Ezra kept an eye on them for a long moment before focusing on me. "You'll come with me while I search further in the village."

I nodded, taking a step toward him when Arianna grasped my arm, pulling me to her. "Actually, she will be coming with me," she said coolly. "Apparently," she paused, looking me up and down, "we have some *issues* to resolve." She gave me a tight smile, then looked at Ezra, blinking innocently.

Ezra grimaced. "Fine, but I will join you. I refuse to leave her alone with you after the last time."

Arianna shrugged and walked to the nearest building, her hips swaying as she went. Exhaling, Ezra followed her. I groaned, tilting my head back to look at the cloudless blue sky. This was going to be fun.

FORTY MINUTES PASSED as we searched homes and alleyways, with no one finding any trace of rebels in the area. Ezra leaned against a nearby tree, impatiently tapping against the hilt of the sword that hung at his waist.

"I think it's safe to say that there's nothing suspicious here," he growled to no one in particular, but I had a feeling he meant for Arianna to hear. His eyes narrowed on her while she shuffled through empty pots that lay broken in front of a building that had been boarded up.

"I know we are supposed to be looking for rebels, but *what* exactly are we supposed to be looking for?" I whispered to Ezra.

The search had felt aimless with Arianna rummaging through a few of the homes in our section of the town. Each home seemed to be chosen randomly. At some point, she just opened the door, only to turn back around and choose an entirely different house. Ezra just eyed the villagers that passed us, never speaking to them.

Arianna scoffed, overhearing my question, leveling me with an icy glare until movement caught our attention. A younger faerie with dark ebony skin and eyes that looked like bright gold was eyeing us, pulling two children along behind him. Arianna's glare flickered with delight, her lips curling into a sharp smile that sent chills down my arms.

Arianna yelled at the man to stop as she marched to him. He froze, the muscles in his arms flexing, his wide eyes glancing around, looking—hoping—for someone to help. But when she drew near, he snapped out of his panic, pushing the children behind him. They looked like twins, with the same golden-brown hair and honey-colored eyes as Silas. They held onto his legs, trembling under Arianna's cold gaze.

"This is exactly the type of thing we are looking for," Arianna said to me, circling the man, eyeing him hungrily. "I don't think I've seen you here before," she said to him with an unsettling interest.

The man straightened his back, steeling himself. "I came here a few months ago with my siblings from the mountains. Our parents died, and we couldn't stay, so we moved here," he said, his voice slightly trembling.

"And these are your siblings?" Arianna said, studying the children.

The man hesitated, his gaze flicking to Ezra and me. "No, my siblings are at home. These are Silas's grandchildren."

"Right. And what made you come here, of all places?

Certainly, there are other villages closer to the mountains than this one, yes?"

The man hesitated, like he didn't know how to answer without further condemning himself, and before I knew it, I said, "I know I'm new here, so correct me if I'm wrong, but there's no law that says he must go to one of those villages, right? He is free to move wherever?"

The man's gaze cut to me, gratitude flickering in his eyes.

"No, there isn't a law," Arianna hissed. "But these rebel scum like to travel between villages to convince people to join their cause."

"Right," I interrupted, keeping my face as calm as I could. "But we haven't found any rebels, and he is here because his parents died. Shouldn't we give him some slack?"

Whirling, Arianna marched toward me; the fierce expression in her eyes had Ezra carefully monitoring me, a hand on the hilt of his sword. I steeled myself, holding my breath even as she loomed over me with fire in her eyes. "You don't get to dictate that, girl," she said, her voice low and edged.

I didn't give up my ground, meeting her glare with one of my own. "He isn't here to harm anyone or start some rebellion. He is trying to take care of his family."

"You are nothing but a child who knows nothing of this world. You do not know how *they* operate—how they think."

A beat of silence followed, and Arianna turned her back on me, marching over to the man, but her words echoed in my mind. I recognized that rhetoric, that hate, that line between them and us. "You're wrong. What you're doing is wrong. He has done nothing to warrant this type of treatment." It started off with a whisper, my voice barely audible, but it grew louder and stronger with every word.

Arianna turned to me, snarling. She took a step, just one, before shadows whirled around her, and then she was in front of me. So close that I could feel her breath on my face. A powerful hand gripped my shoulder, pulling me back as Ezra stepped between us, his eyes narrowed on Arianna.

"You need to calm down," Ezra demanded, his voice tight. "Sybil is right, the boy was just getting the children out of the way so the soldiers could search the area, as we told them to do. You cannot fault him for listening to our orders."

"Look at that boy and tell me he doesn't look suspicious, Ezra," Arianna insisted, the veins around her eyes starting to glow crimson. "He doesn't belong to this village."

"He told you why he's here," I argued, unable to keep quiet at her words and lack of empathy. I knew she was a part of the aristocracy, but her lack of understanding and her blatant disregard of the people outside her circle made my blood boil. My gaze cut to the man and the children, who stood frozen, watching us with careful calculation. "Go, take the children and get somewhere safe."

Giving me a quick thanks, he turned, pushing them toward the villagers who had gathered around us. Silent agitation rippled through the crowd; the tension stretched so much it was on the brink of snapping.

Arianna growled and started toward the family. I followed, not really knowing how I was going to stop her, but I needed to before she could reach them. Ezra grabbed my arm to keep me from going further, but I jerked my arm out of his hand to run in front of Arianna, blocking her from the villagers.

"Let them go, Arianna," I warned, my voice trembling slightly. "They have done nothing wrong. You said earlier that it's not a crime for them to come here. He's allowed to be here."

"Get out of my way," she seethed, the crimson glow now snaking down her neck. My own magic was humming inside me. "You are getting in the way of an investigation. I command you to step aside."

"I'm not part of your army, and I don't take orders from you," I reminded her. My knees felt unsteady. I wasn't even sure I was breathing. "There is no investigation here, just you creating a problem out of nothing."

"If you don't get out of my way," Arianna said severely, sliding her sword from its sheath, "then I will cut you down."

I swallowed, the scrape of her sword against its sheath sending an icy chill down my spine. I fought against a tremor, begging my heart—my magic—to calm its frantic beating.

Ezra cursed, moving between us again, his body strained and restless, tightly gripping the hilt of his sword. "You both need to calm down," he ground out. "The kid did nothing wrong by coming here. He is trying to protect his family. We aren't here to interrogate anyone. We are here to see if there were any signs of rebel activity. There is none, so put your sword away and return to the palace."

"No signs of rebel activity?" Arianna scoffed. "*He* is a sign of rebel activity, and you're letting him walk away."

"You don't understand what life is like in the mountains. Life is hard and unforgiving. He is doing his family a favor by bringing them here. Cut him some slack."

"If we gave everyone with a sob story some slack, we would be overrun by rebels," Arianna snarled, her eyes narrowing on Ezra. "Stand aside, or else."

Movement caught my eye, and I glanced around us. A thick silence blanketed the villagers. Though it was subtle, they had surrounded us, ready to defend their town from Arianna and the soldiers. Even from me, I realized, the thought was making me sick.

Sensing the growing agitation in the air, Ezra swore and shifted in front of me to guard and protect. "I didn't bring any weapons for you," he said, handing me a small dagger. His voice was steady but edged. His eyes were unreadable as he watched Arianna, tracking the veins glowing as they slithered down her arms. "Try not to hurt yourself with it and don't be afraid to use it if you need to, even if it's against Arianna. We need to—"

A pebble rolled away from a tree close by, our heads snapping at the sound, where a small child was trembling behind it. I wasn't sure how she got there—or when—but Ezra's sharp inhale told me everything I needed to know. Arianna saw her, and when a serpentine smile curled up her face, fear, cold and swift, shot through me.

The air in the town turned deadly, the villagers waiting for us to make our move, each of them palming knives and farming tools as makeshift weapons.

Arianna's eyes were still on the girl, her head now tilting like she was forming a wicked plan. A group of villagers on the left shifted, their movements catching Ezra's and the soldiers' attention. But my eyes focused on what they were trying to hide.

A man, short and stocky, eased through the crowd, weaving to get closer to the girl. I pulled on Ezra's sleeve, getting his attention. "On the right," I whispered, my heart pounding frantically. "She will see it as an attack if she catches him."

Ezra nodded, pushing us back. Arianna slid her gaze to us, narrowing her eyes at Ezra as if she could see him working up a plan to de-escalate the growing tension. She smiled at him then, and my blood went cold. She wanted this to happen, wanted there to be conflict, a fight.

"Fuck," Ezra growled, the muscle in his jaw flexing. "There's no other way out of this. Get to the girl while I distract Arianna. Do *not* engage with any of the villagers. They won't take it as anything other than an affront."

I nodded as Ezra drew his sword, stepping up to Arianna to block her path to the girl.

"You're making the wrong choice here, Ezra," Arianna hissed, the fire in her veins spidering along her hands.

"No, I don't think I am," Ezra said, more to himself than to her, as he lifted his sword in front of him.

I breathed, slow and steady, before inching my way to the girl, keeping an eye on the man as he edged closer to her. Ezra continued his demands for Arianna to back off when he grunted. He yelled my name, and I whirled, finding Arianna charging me.

Cursing, I jumped out of the way, pain lacing down my arm. Too afraid to take my eyes off Arianna, I brought my hand over the pain, feeling the slick wetness of blood from where her sword nicked my arm. The smell of iron stung my nose as my heart hammered against my chest.

The sounds of swords clashing made me flinch, and I stole a glance at the sound where Ezra was now fighting against a few of Arianna's lackeys. The rest of the soldiers joined the villagers, watching with wide eyes, not knowing which leader to follow.

Noticing my distraction, Arianna lunged at me, her sword raised high. My legs felt heavy, but I stumbled out of the way, her sword narrowly missing me.

"Stop this, Arianna," I yelled. The pain in my arm grew hot, and my chest heaved from the magic pulsing through my veins. I could feel it, the panic setting in. This was different from our fight in the training ground. There were innocent people—children—around us now. Their angry shouts and their unrest reeling around me. It grated on my ears, screeching in my head. It was too loud—everything was too loud.

If I lost control now, how many people would get hurt from this? Would their injuries be the same? Would it be worse? My magic felt like sharp talons clawing through my skin into my mind, begging for release, but I couldn't give in to it. I needed to push it down. I needed the world to stop moving so fast.

Arianna rushed at me, but I couldn't move. My body felt disconnected, unwilling to listen to my mind's commands. As if on instinct, I raised my dagger just in time, meeting Arianna's blow. I cried out, pain radiating through me from the force of her attack. Using all her strength, Arianna pushed down on her sword, forcing me to my knees. I grunted, my arms barking under the weight. Angling my blade, Arianna's sword slid off, making her stumble. I gasped, pushing off the ground to run when Arianna tackled me into the dirt.

She twisted me, forcing me onto my back before straddling me. I struggled against her, bucking my hips to push her off when a fist met my cheek, pain lacing across my face, giving her the time she needed to wrap her slender hands around my throat, cutting off my air. Choking, I fought like a wild cat, thrashing against her hold, blindly hitting her where I could while my vision grew dark around the edges. My mind spiraled into chaos, and I lifted my hips into the air before kicking out my legs, finally making Arianna lose her grip on me.

I crawled away, but my movements were slow as I tried to gulp down the dusty air. Someone called out my name, but the voice sounded far away, and the world around me spun. I looked up, finding another soldier running to me, his sword lifted, ready to strike me. My magic pulsed against my skin painfully, ignoring my attempts to temper its wrath. I screamed into the ground, my body feeling like it was being ripped apart as a bright light erupted from me. Screams of pain, of fear, of panic swelled, joining my own as my body burned like a raging fire.

CHAPTER 27
KIERAN

My fingers drummed against the round, wooden table. I've been sitting in the council room for hours now, recalling memory after memory of our previous mission. About what tipped off the guards regarding Lady Lowell's escape, of how Lord Astaroth ran out with Lord Pasian and a healer following him to stitch mine and Orin's wounds, of the strange look in Lord Pasian's eyes as he waited for the healer to look over Lady Lowell. I lost more soldiers than I thought I would, and not knowing the reason behind it ate away at me.

"Am I interrupting?" Viv's soft voice snapped me out of my thoughts, my gaze slamming to hers.

"Lord Pasian and Lady Lowell," I murmured. "Are they close?" Viv opened her mouth, ready to answer, when I lifted my hand, silencing her. "No, never mind. It's not important." Flattening my hand against the table, I let out a heavy sigh. Lady Lowell agreed to help with the rebellion, which was the most important matter. "Is there something to report?"

"Yes, actually." Viv straightened, her shoulders tense. "I've received word that Arbus didn't show up for his weekly check-in." The silence stretched taut between us, the pressure in the room growing. "Kieran," Viv warned.

Pulling my magic back to me, my hands curled into fists. "I heard you. Has Samian sent word?"

Sybil was being sent to Lowbrook today with General Darktree and Commander Fenleth. We knew that there was a plan against Sybil, but for now, it was just a waiting game.

"No, still no word," Viv exhaled, falling into a seat. "Nothing from Edris either. It's like he is still unsure of how the future is going to turn out."

A weak laugh escaped my lips. "I wouldn't say that too loudly. The bastard isn't one quick to forgive."

"I guess out of anyone, you would know," Viv mused, biting back her laugh.

I hummed, thinking back to the last time I was in the god's presence, how it ended with him in the middle of Zarina's treasure hoard and the water dragon's hostile *welcoming*. It took three days of hiding and battling the fierce dragon to escape Zarina's clutches, and he hasn't forgiven me since.

"It was just a harmless prank," I grumbled. Edris had not been amused after almost losing an arm, but it was the least I could do after his prank of sending me to Dubnos, the lower realm.

"So," Viv said hesitantly. "Arbus?"

My fingers started their drumming against the table's surface again. "I'll sneak into the palace and see what I can find out. It's not like him to miss a check-in."

Viv nodded, her expression darkening. "Will you be okay going in alone?"

I shot her a glare, my magic stirring beneath my skin. "They haven't noticed me yet, nor will they this time. I know how to get around the palace unseen. Just keep Bryony occupied while I am gone. We don't need her to overhear some idiot before we know more."

VIV WOULD KILL me if she knew where I was right now. Not even I thought I would end up on the streets of Volmire, watching the parade of palace soldiers riding through the streets to Lowbrook. However, each passage exit was blocked by guards and servants running through the halls, helping the soldiers prepare for their trip.

They started later than I expected, but there she was, riding on the proud black horse with General Darktree. My chest ached at the sight of her, feeling that strange pull toward her. I couldn't help but stop to watch her leave the city, anxiety gnawing on my soul for her.

She scanned the crowd, taking in their wary faces until her gaze landed on mine. I saw her eyes widen as they lingered on me, though she couldn't see my face underneath the hood covering me. She couldn't see the fire taking over me, pushing me closer to her. Her throat bobbing, Sybil quickly turned away, focusing on the cobbled road in front of her, cutting off the strange feeling overtaking my body.

Rolling my neck, I shook Sybil from my thoughts and stepped through the crowd to find the hidden tunnel we used to leave the city. Luckily, the guards left the area to control the mass of citizens watching the soldiers leave the city.

Dipping into the passageway unseen, I followed the darkened path to the route leading into the dungeons. Usually empty, save for the few guards going on their rounds, I easily climbed out of the small opening, dropping quietly to the floor, careful not to disturb the heavy silence hanging in the air.

I quietly followed the hall that would take me to the next entrance, which would lead me to Samian's room. Blood, piss, and death stung my nose, and I pulled the scarf around my face tighter, hoping to block the smell. I walked carefully along the cells, eyeing the prisoners sleeping on lumps of hay. The occupied cells were becoming more dispersed, as if they wanted to keep this area clear of unwanted attention, until finally every cell was empty. A pained scream tore through the silence, and I put my hand on the hilt of the dagger strapped to my side, stopping to listen to the groans sounding from three cells ahead.

I crept up to the cell, peering around the corner. I swallowed my curse; my eyes went wide when I saw Ambrose standing in front of Arbus's limp form, tied to a chair.

Ambrose's muffled voice hissed out a question, the muscles in his arms flexing when Arbus refused to answer. Ambrose raised his hand, his dagger glinting harshly in the cold light, and slammed it into Arbus's leg.

I swallowed down my repulsion, making sure my mental shields were up, keeping my emotions locked inside my head, as I watched Ambrose lean close, whispering into his ear. Arbus shook his head, tears mixed with blood pouring down his face in a crimson streak. My hand tightened around my dagger so tightly that my fingers ached. I needed to do something—to stop Ambrose from his interrogation. But there were too many guards around, too many for me to handle on my own.

Instead, I backed into the next cell, my jaw clenching tight. I hid within the shadows, waiting until Ambrose roared out a curse, throwing his dagger against the wall. Ambrose briskly left the cell, his guards warily trailing after him, giving me the chance to help Arbus escape.

Rushing into the room, I didn't stop until I was kneeling in front of him, inspecting the severity of his wounds. His eyes were blackened and swollen, with an ugly gash along his brow. His body was littered with cuts, slashes, splitting his skin. Blood poured from the stab wounds on his thighs. He panted, his chest heaving with every raspy breath.

My throat tightened, and my hand found his. Arbus moaned, his eyes slowly opening to slits. He blinked the haze away, focusing his gaze on me. His pupils flared when he recognized who was kneeling before him.

"You're okay," I murmured, turning my focus on the chains tying him to the chair. "How long have you been here?"

"He caught me three days ago," Arbus croaked, a tremor wracking through his body. "I didn't realize Ambrose was close by until it was too late."

"It's okay," I breathed, trying to break the metal links. "We're going to get you out of here so you can get back to Bryony."

Arbus coughed, blood flowing out of his mouth and down his chin. "He is going to be back any moment."

"Then I will—"

Voices cut off my words before I could even finish my thought. Two guards grumbled about the heaviness of the table they carried, the sound of metal scraping across the stone floor bouncing off the walls. I swore, working faster to break the chains before they could get to the cell. I could fight them off, then carry Arbus out of here.

"Leave," Arbus begged, his voice a raspy whisper. "Leave before he catches you."

"I almost have it," I whispered. "I'm not leaving without you."

"Kieran, tell her," Arbus paused, taking a gravelly breath, "Please tell her I love her and that I'm sorry."

"I'm not—"

"Hey," a guard roared, the sound of the table dropping cutting me off.

I whirled toward them, drawing my dagger. With this confined space, my sword would be useless. The guards charged me, and I braced myself, letting one of them barrel into me, shoving me against the stone wall. Grunting, I lifted my arm, crashing my elbow against his back. The guard cried out, his arms loosening as he fell to his knees. Catching his face, I rammed my knee straight into his nose. The crunch of bone breaking sent a thrill up my spine when Arbus yelled out my name.

Looking up, more guards ran into the cell. I released a sharp breath and moved, sending my fists toward the closest guard. My hand connected with his jaw, his head snapping back from my blow. Another guard lunged toward me, and I caught him, sending my knee into his gut. He coughed, the breath leaving his lungs as I hurled him into the guard behind me.

The rest of the guards surrounded me, blindly throwing hits in my direction as footsteps echoed down the hall. If I waited any longer, they would overrun me, and I would end up sitting next to Arbus, awaiting my own interrogation.

Blocking their throws, I glanced at Arbus, his wide eyes frozen in fear. His eyes whipped to the entrance before meeting mine again. "Go!" he cried out. "You need to go now!"

My heart broke at the sound of his voice, begging me to leave. He was a friend and loyal soldier, a guide when I needed someone to talk to. I squeezed my eyes shut, taking a sharp breath. My magic was useless in closed spaces. It needed the open air to be effective.

I opened my eyes, resolve settling deep in my bones. I threw Arbus one last glance before bellowing, attacking any guard close enough for me to strike. Chaos circled me as I fought my way through the horde of soldiers until I made it out of the cell and ran like hell. Reaching the hidden passage door, I wrenched it open, throwing myself in and swiftly closing the door behind me. I held my breath, watching the guards pass me by through a small gap in the door, yelling out commands, searching for any hint of my presence.

Once I caught my breath, I ran down the dark hall, passing a grated window that looked out to the courtyard of the palace. A monstrous black horse galloped at high speed, sliding to a stop in front of the palace. I swallowed my curse when I saw Sybil covered in dirt and blood, her eyes distant and unseeing. General Darktree's movements were frantic as he pulled her off his horse, carrying her inside the palace. My soul screamed for me to follow, but guards filled the courtyard, and it was time for me to go.

I pushed down that siren's call, tugging me to Sybil, and followed the passage out of the palace. I didn't stop until I was safely in the forest, fearing that if I paused, I would lose the fight to return to Sybil.

I made it halfway into the forest when the trees to my right groaned, their branches snapping, falling to the ground with heavy thuds. I stilled, holding my breath, careful not to make any sudden movements. Sliding my gaze to the noise, my heart stopped.

Fuck. Fuck. Fuck.

I didn't pay attention to my surroundings as I should have, and now I was about to pay the price.

I called my magic to me, letting the wind shift my scent to the opposite direction. The beithir jerked, its nose raised in the air. Its massive head turned away from me, and I moved, sprinting to the largest tree I could find. I climbed as high as I could go and pressed my back into the rough bark.

The beithir hissed, its enormous body bounding in my direction, searching for me as I hid along the branches, still using the wind to mask my scent. Its forked tongue flicked in the air, still searching for my location. Calmly pulling my dagger out of its sheath, I listened as the leaves crunched beneath the beithir's body as it moved closer to the tree.

The air around me grew heavy with my magic, and I pushed it toward a tree in the distance, creating a tunnel of wind sharp enough to cut a branch in two. The beithir's head whipped at the thump of the limb hitting the forest floor, hesitating before finally slithering away.

CHAPTER 28

SYBIL

I screamed until my voice was hoarse. I stayed hunched on the ground as light and pain ripped through me, and I couldn't stop it. I couldn't keep it contained. I tried so hard to push it down, to keep it locked up. But in my panic, I couldn't move; I couldn't think. I couldn't do anything to save myself from him. It was like my magic had a mind of its own, bursting forth to protect me—protect us. But at what cost? How many this time? How many people did I hurt?

The light faded, and I felt something wet and warm run down over my lips. I brought my hand to my nose and pulled it back, finding blood smeared across my fingers. I panted, zeroing in on the crimson coating my skin when a cry turned into a mournful wail, snapping me out of the daze I was in. I looked up, my eyes locking onto Arianna. She was covered in blood, pressing her hands against the stomach of the man who had been trying to get to the girl. Arianna faced the villagers, who stood to the side, too stunned to move, calling for anyone's help. My ears began to ring, and my breathing slowed. Time felt like it had stopped as I watched her call out for help.

I felt someone grabbing me then, tugging me up, and time snapped back into place. I gasped, fighting against their hold while I tried to crawl away. Hands grabbed both sides of my face, forcing my head up. Ezra kneeled beside me; his face covered in dirt and grime. He was yelling at me, but I could only hear the ringing in my ears.

When he finally pulled me off the ground, the ringing faded enough for me to catch him frantically repeating, "We need to get you out of here. We need to go, now."

He pulled me after him, but my legs buckled, and I stumbled back to the ground, exhaustion threatening to pull me under. Cursing, Ezra put his arm around me and dragged me to his horse. I moved, but I felt listless, like I didn't wholly belong to my body. I felt numb, paralyzed to any feeling.

I glanced behind me to find that the villagers' faces were pale and stiff. A woman ran to the man who still lay on the ground. Her screams echoed past us as she sobbed into his now-still chest.

"I killed him," I said, barely breathing. "I-I killed him."

I repeated those three words over and over again. Whether they were in my head or out loud, I couldn't tell from Ezra's grim silence. Ezra threw me onto Midnight's back, climbing on behind me. He yelled out commands to a group of soldiers that stood close by, their pallid faces coming alive under the bark of his tone. Once they moved into action, Ezra forced Midnight into a frightening speed to return to the palace.

The ride was a blur. All I could think was that I had killed the man who was trying to protect the girl. My stomach roiled. Did I kill her, too? Were there others? I couldn't stop it; I couldn't control it or dampen it. I killed him. I couldn't even remember what he looked like. I couldn't remember his face or the color of his eyes. My body felt numb. My mind was blank.

At some point, we entered the courtyard of the palace, Ezra yelling out to someone before hauling me off Midnight. There was no strength left in my body. I couldn't will myself to move or stand. I heard Ezra curse and say my name, but my body felt too leaden to respond. I couldn't even force myself to look at him.

I felt him pick me up, racing me to my room, but all I could think, all I could see was the man, lying lifeless on the ground, his blood spreading around him. I heard a door slam open before being set down on a cushioned surface. Ezra snapped his fingers in front of my face, pulling me out of my trance.

"Sybil," he breathed, his face deathly pale, "can you hear me?" I gave him a small nod, and he swallowed. "I need you to stay here. Don't go anywhere; don't answer the door. Just stay here until I return, okay?" He searched my face; his eyes were panicked.

Unable to say anything, I gave him another slight nod. His hands gripped my shoulders, giving them a small, reassuring squeeze before he ran out of my room, letting the door slam shut behind him. I flinched at the sound and looked down at my hands. Blood coated them, blood from using too much of my magic. The magic that killed the villager. He was just trying to help that little girl. *I* was just trying to help her. But I failed. I failed, it was my fault, everything was my fault.

Tears started pouring down my face, hot and heavy. My body shook, and every emotion came flooding out, like a lock opening the floodgate holding back everything I had been trying to push down. I couldn't control my magic. I couldn't control it, and now someone was dead. My magic was too much for me to handle, and because of that, he was dead. All I wanted to do was help, to protect, but I wound up becoming a stain instead.

The gash on my arm burned; crimson still trickled down to my hand, but it wasn't my blood that I saw. It was his. Becoming violently ill, I rushed to the bathroom, vomiting as soon as I reached the toilet. I retched until there was nothing left, until I heaved and nothing came out. Moving to the sink, I washed the blood away, scrubbing over and over, but the red stain wouldn't disappear.

My skin was raw and burned when another pair of large, soft hands wrapped around mine. I gasped, my head jerking up. Ambrose stood behind me, and my eyes met his in the mirror. His face blanched, wariness etched across it.

"Sybil," he whispered, his voice tight with alarm. "Sybil, what happened?"

My mouth gaped open, but no words came out. Instead, my eyes burned, and more tears flowed down my face. Ambrose pulled me into a tight hug, his warmth seeping into my body. I stood there, locked in his embrace, listening to his soft murmurings, letting the minutes pass by while I wept.

Finally, Ambrose pulled me out of the bathroom, leading me back to the chaise. I tried to explain what happened then, with Arianna and the man with those children, but my words felt broken and out of order. Ambrose smoothed back the hair from my face, quietly listening. But before I could finish, my door swung open, the sudden motion making me jerk away from his touch. I stood on shaky legs, using the chaise to steady myself.

Arianna stood in the doorway, gasping for air, her lips curling in disgust. "She killed him," she choked out, pointing at me. "She killed a villager in Lowbrook. I tried to stop her, Ambrose, but she lost control of her magic and killed someone."

My stomach dropped, terror rushing through me. My body tensed, making it hard to breathe. I swallowed, taking in Arianna's bloodstained clothing. My body trembled as I narrowed in on her side, seeing her ripped uniform and a wound, her flesh still torn and bleeding because of me. I felt gutted, like someone had dug a knife inside me, twisting painfully.

My eyes shot to Ambrose, blinking through the tears burning my eyes, pleading, begging for… Help? Understanding? For him to tell me I was right about myself, that I was a monster, a stain—a curse?

Ambrose's eyes widened in alarm, or maybe even horror. "Tell me it isn't true, Sybil. Please tell me that didn't happen!"

"I'm sorry," I cried, icy talons gripping my heart, squeezing until I couldn't breathe. "I'm so sorry. I tried to stop it. I tried, but I was attacked, and it just happened."

"She's a danger to us all, Ambrose," Arianna rasped. "First me, and now one of the villagers? The girl is going to kill us all if you don't do something about this."

"No, that's not true," I replied, my hand clenching against the painful ache in my chest. "I can get it under control, please, Ambrose. I can learn to control it. Samian is helping me control it. Plea—"

"Like he has been helping you already?" Ambrose asked calmly, interrupting my pleading. "You promised your father and Liam that you wouldn't hurt anyone else. What do you expect me to do with that?"

I winced at the reminder of my promise. A promise that I had failed to keep. Hot agony ripped through me, and my stomach twisted. I fell to my knees, a broken sob escaping my lips. Misery engulfed me so strongly that I felt like I was being pulled underwater. I tried to breathe. I tried to gulp down air, but it felt impossible. My lungs—my throat—they felt too tight.

I pressed the palms of my hands into my eyes, curling myself onto the floor. Weeping, I cried out when an intense desperation coursed through me, so swift and abrupt.

I couldn't take it anymore. I couldn't do *this* anymore. They were right—my father, Liam, Arianna—they were all right.

"I'll do it," I groaned, my mind screaming, wanting all of this —my magic, this world, my life—to disappear. I wanted to go back to the life I used to have. This magic was supposed to be a chance at something new. It was supposed to be a hope, a promise of a brighter future. But it was only a wretched curse. The man lying lifeless on the ground flashed through my mind, tormenting me deep to my very core. "Please," I whispered. "Please, help me. I don't want to hurt anyone anymore."

Ambrose knelt in front of me, pulling me up and lifting my hands away from my face. "Shh, my darling Sybil," Ambrose murmured, giving me a soft kiss on my forehead. "Everything will be okay, I promise."

He pulled out a dagger, and I blinked as he cut into his palm. Taking my hand, he made a similar cut, and I hissed at the sudden burning pain. Ambrose put our hands together, giving me a soft smile. "All you have to do is repeat after me, okay?" I nodded, my mind finding its first moment of relief. Tightening his hand around mine, Ambrose began his bargain. "I, Ambrose Farra, offer you, Sybil Hart, a bargain. I will hold sway over your magic, and in exchange, you will find yourself bound to my will. Do you accept?"

Giving me a slight nod, Ambrose smiled encouragingly. Swallowing, I straightened, my heart wavering. It wasn't supposed to turn out this way. Samian's pleading from yesterday echoed across my mind. I remembered the anger on his face when he saw Ambrose's note, his exasperation at me for believing I needed this bargain.

Ambrose quietly called my name, bringing my focus back to the present, giving me another small smile, a whisper of comfort. I squeezed my eyes shut, the anguish rushing back, taking me under, and a tear softly fell down my cheek.

My voice trembled as I repeated the bargain. "I, Sybil Hart, agree to your bargain. You will hold sway over my magic, and in exchange, I will be bound to your will."

I cried out, white-hot pain lacing up my arm, moving through my body. I tried to pull my hand back, but Ambrose held firm. My blood seemed to boil, and I choked out a moan. Someone called my name, but I couldn't tell who over the roaring in my ears. As suddenly as it came, the pain was gone, leaving me gasping against the floor.

Ambrose dropped my hand, and I looked up, stunned by the new pressure surrounding my heart. His eyes were bright, and his once-soft smile turned sharp, vile, and vicious.

CHAPTER 29
SYBIL

My eyes widened, my heart dropping into my throat at the cruelty reflected on Ambrose's face. He stared at me with hideous arrogance. Triumph glinted in his sharp eyes, and he cackled, the sound so wicked and merciless. I slid my gaze to Arianna as she breathed out a laugh and looked at Ambrose with elation. The hair on my arms rose, my mind spinning, trying to piece together what happened, but something wasn't right with my body. It felt restricted, not fully my own.

I looked down, inhaling sharply at the black band that circled both of my wrists, like shackles tying me down, tying me to Ambrose.

He's not trying to help *you; he is trying to use you.*

Samian had told me—warned me.

Samian knew what would happen if I fell for Ambrose's tricks. And I didn't listen to him. I shut him out instead, and my heart ached with remorse.

Arianna moved to Ambrose, her arms wrapping around his neck, their lips crashing together in a searing kiss. My face burned at the intensity of their affection and at my foolishness for not seeing it until now.

Ambrose groaned into her mouth and pulled away, Arianna whining in protest. "Later, my love," he purred. "Don't you want to test out our newest weapon?"

Ambrose smiled down at me, and I paled.

He is trying to use you.

Samian was right, and I played right into Ambrose's hand.

Ambrose moved out of Arianna's embrace to kneel in front of me. His hand caressed my face, and I flinched at the icy touch of his fingers. A deep chuckle rumbled from his chest as he wiped the tears from my face. He moved then, so slowly, like he couldn't believe it was happening. He gripped my wrist tightly, and I hissed at the pain as he roughly yanked my arm closer to study the black band. He frowned, gripping my other wrist to study the other band. His movement felt rough and callous, so different from the soft touches of just moments ago.

Ambrose's frown deepened, his brows knitting together at the small sliver of unmarred skin where the bands did not fully link together. His cold eyes cut to mine; all the warmth he had was gone, replaced by a hardened face. He narrowed his eyes, opening his mouth to speak when Ezra rushed into the room.

Ezra stopped short, his face tight when he took in the scene around him. Noticing me on the floor, he stared at the black bands around my wrists, and his eyes flared. I could only imagine what was going through his mind.

Ezra's gaze flicked to Ambrose, noticing the raised eyebrow and the tilt of his head. He schooled his face into cool indifference and bowed low as Ambrose stood to face him.

"Arianna tells me that you sided with the rebels today," Ambrose drawled, stalking closer to Ezra. "How disappointing." The room's temperature fell quickly, ice slowly climbing the walls. I trembled, goosebumps running across my skin.

"I didn't," Ezra said, swallowing thickly. He straightened his shoulders, keeping his eyes lowered to the floor in front of him, not daring to look my way.

"Are you calling your future queen a liar?" Ambrose asked coolly. His eyes and face were utterly blank, unreadable, and my blood ran cold. Samian told me the queen was on a trip. Did this mean that the queen was dead? That Ambrose had her killed?

Ezra must have been wondering the same thing. He looked up, glancing between Ambrose and Arianna as if he were trying to decide how to play along. I followed his stare to Arianna, my heart thundering in my chest. She lifted her chin; her face glowing bright and proud. She stepped to Ambrose's side, wrapping her arms around him, placing her head on his shoulder, and giving Ezra a razor-sharp smile.

Ezra hesitated a beat before saying, "No, Ambrose. I'm not calling my future queen a liar. I'm calling *Arianna* one."

The room froze at Ezra's words. Arianna blinked once, then twice. The defiance slowly registered, and she huffed a laugh. But Ambrose just snarled at the remark.

"Then what would you say happened?" Ambrose asked, his unnaturally calm voice at odds with the tension that was building in his shoulders.

"We looked through the village and found no *hint* of rebel activity in the area. We came across a boy moving children out of our way when Arianna approached him. He came to Lowbrook earlier this year from the mountains after his parents passed away. He did nothing wrong. He was following *our* orders to move the children to a safe location. Sybil and I were trying to show Arianna that, but she and her men attacked us both. We were defending ourselves against an unwarranted attack, not helping the rebel cause." Ezra stood tall, his body stiff, meeting Ambrose's glare with one of his own.

"You know the rebels move from village to village to recruit, yes?" Ambrose hissed. A slight nod from Ezra was all he needed to continue his reprimanding. "Then what makes you think this boy isn't a part of their group, recruiting the other children?"

"Not everyone in the villages is taking part in rebel activity. You know this, and so does Arianna. If we treat everyone in the villages as part of the rebel group, then we will have an uprising that even you will not be able to stop."

Ambrose snarled, his face contorting. "You believe our army is so weak that they couldn't crush those rats?"

Instead of answering, Ezra narrowed his eyes, raising his head higher. It was an unspoken answer and dismissal, all in one. The table beside me cracked as ice splintered across it, and I shivered. This wasn't Ambrose. This was no longer the man who had helped me or cared for me.

Arianna scoffed at the challenge glowing in Ezra's eyes, and Ambrose was a predator lying in wait.

"Guards," Ambrose barked, his eyes never breaking from Ezra's. "Take Ezra to the dungeons. We will see just whose side you're on."

The guards filed into the room, grabbing Ezra by his massive arms, shoving him out the door, and into the hallway. Ezra yelled out, but his words fell on deaf ears as Ambrose turned to me, his lips curling in an unnerving smile. "Now, I think it's time for us to have a little fun with this bargain of ours, don't you think, my darling Sybil?" His low laugh grated against my ears; my throat tightened at the implication of his words.

I didn't notice Arianna until she stood beside me. Pain throbbed down my arm when she pulled me off the floor. A small noise came out of me, one made of fear. Once I was on my feet, her hand moved to the back of my neck, her nails digging into my skin, pushing me to the doorway. I stumbled and was caught by a guard who stood close to Ambrose.

I met Ezra's wild stare when the guard shoved me into the hallway. I trembled under the guard's touch, my eyes wide. It was all happening too fast. I'd been afraid before, when wolves threatened me as a girl, when my father's anger became explosive, even today, when I was attacked. But nothing, *nothing* felt like this. None of those times felt so cold or so desolate.

Ezra called out for me, grunting against his restraints as he tried to get to me. One of the guards punched him in the side, and he hissed. Looking back, he mouthed, *it's okay* over and over while they led him down the hallway.

"Ambrose, stop this," I pleaded, pushing away from the guard to hold onto his vest. "Ezra has done nothing wrong."

Ambrose didn't answer; he just stared at me with such brutality that when he stepped out of my grip, my heart shattered into a million pieces. I could only watch, frozen, as he sneered, raising his hand in the air and swiftly bringing it down across my face.

I cried out, falling to the floor, pain lacing through my face. Terror, utter terror, splintered through me.

Ezra must have seen it, must have glanced back one final time as they turned the corner. He yelled my name, fighting against the guards to get to me. I watched, my eyes blurred and burning, as the guards clashed against him, beating him until he was disoriented enough to restrain him again. They dragged him around the corner, my name still ringing from his lips.

When the last of the guards followed, Ambrose turned his piercing eyes on me. Whimpering, I pushed myself back against the wall, every fiber of my being screaming, begging for me to run, to escape this new prison.

"Grab her," Ambrose growled, not breaking his fixed stare, annoyance edging his voice. "We don't want to keep our *guest* waiting."

Ambrose continued glaring, my body too shaky and heavy to move. But then Ambrose winced. Shock flashed so quickly in those deep blue eyes that even Arianna missed it. He looked away, moving down the hall. "We don't have all day." Every word had a bite to it, an edge.

Arianna grabbed me by the neck, shoving me forward to follow Ambrose. I stumbled but found my footing before I could fall back to the ground. Hugging myself, I quietly walked behind Ambrose, my heart twisting at the sickening feeling that a far greater hell awaited me.

We made our way through the palace, turning at the door beside the dragon statue Samian had advised me to avoid just a few days ago. Passing through the entrance, the hallway changed from that once-pristine marble of the palace to the old stones that matched the outdoor corridor of the training grounds. Samian told me that parts of the old palace remained hidden within the new, but instead of the antiquated beauty of the outdoor corridor, this passage was cold and dark.

Eventually, we began to pass several empty cells of the dungeon, and pained moans filled the air. I swallowed hard, my steps faltering, my legs feeling like lead. Arianna clucked her tongue, pushing me to the door of a harshly lit cell.

I swallowed my gasp when I saw a man tied to a chair, his

body drenched and caked in blood. Some of it fresh, some old. His dark brown hair lay limp against his forehead, wet from the sweat that beaded along his face. His breathing was labored, and blood trickled down from his nose. There was a nasty cut over his eyebrow, as if he had been hit with something hard and blunted.

Ambrose opened the cell, the rusted hinges screeching, making the man open his tired green eyes. Arianna shoved me into the cold cell and stepped in with me. Ambrose entered last, closing the door behind us.

"Now, I think some introductions are in order," Ambrose said, moving behind the chair, placing his hands on the man's trembling shoulders. The man seemed to curl into himself, whimpering at Ambrose's soft touch, so at odds compared to his cold, unreadable appearance.

"Sybil, meet my good friend, Arbus. Arbus is suspected of being part of the silly little rebel uprising, isn't that right, my dear friend?" Ambrose tightened his grip on Arbus's shoulder, making him cry out in pain. My stomach churned, nausea rippling through me while Ambrose continued. "We found him spying on our soldiers with notes on our formation, where the soldiers were heading, and the types of weapons in our possession. We believe he was planning on giving this information to the leader of the rebellion so the rebels could attack our soldiers before they even made it out of the valley.

We have already deemed him guilty after squeezing out all the information he had, so we don't need to go into further interrogations. Instead, we are here to not only test out this little bargain of ours, but also to give him his punishment. Today, Sybil, your job is to deliver that punishment."

My knees quaked so much that I feared they would buckle.

"What punishment is that?" I whispered, my voice too small and weak.

"Death," Ambrose answered, his lips curling into an unfeeling grin. "Little Arbus's punishment is death. And *you* will be the one to do it."

"No."

The word rushed out of me as my stomach clenched, twisting so hard that I had to swallow down the bile that rose. Arbus started begging Ambrose to let him live. His eyes filled with desperate tears that only grew when Ambrose clucked his tongue and walked to a small table pushed against the wall, picking up a bloodied cloth. That desperation morphed into a frenzy. Arbus thrashed against his chains when Ambrose wrapped the bloodied cloth around Arbus's mouth, tying it behind his head. Arbus continued those muffled cries, looking at me with pleading despair, his face twisting with agony.

My tears fell freely, and I stumbled back, wanting nothing but to run, but Arianna's icy hands stopped me from moving.

"Come now, Sybil. We don't have all day," Ambrose murmured, a sneer curling his lips.

All I could do was shake my head. I couldn't speak; my voice was gone, my mind still unable to grasp what Ambrose was demanding of me. Ambrose sighed, displeasure leaking from every pore as he walked to me, gripping my face tightly. I gasped, meeting his cold glare, a small noise escaping my lips.

"Do as I say, and kill him." His voice was hard and flat.

"No," I recoiled, barely breathing. "I can't. I can't hurt him."

"I didn't ask you to hurt him. I asked you to kill him. Those who are found guilty of being part of the rebellion are sentenced to death." Ambrose pushed me closer to Arbus. "He has been found guilty of being a traitor, so kill him."

"Ambrose, please," I begged, my heart feeling like it was about to be ripped out of my chest. "Please don't make me do this. You were supposed to help me, help me not hurt anyone else. That's what our bargain was for, so I wouldn't hurt anyone else." The words came out so fast they tumbled into one another.

Ambrose released a frustrated breath, leveling me with a dangerous glare. Moving too fast for me to react, Ambrose wrapped his hand around my throat, lifting me off the floor and bringing me close to his face, cutting off my air. Gagging, I strained against his hold, trying to find some type of footing.

"If I remember correctly, our *bargain* was for me to have control of your magic. There was nothing said or agreed upon about not allowing you to hurt anyone. Now," Ambrose paused, shoving me against the metal bars behind me, "kill him."

Letting me go, my knees buckled, and I leaned into the cold metal bars, gulping down air. I looked at Arbus. Heavy tears were falling down his beautiful, wretched face. He continued those muffled pleas, his hands pulling against his chains. I swallowed, trembling wracked every part of my body. But I couldn't do it. I wouldn't do it. Not again.

I shook my head, whispering a silent no, unsure if anyone could hear me. A few quiet seconds passed before I cut my gaze to Ambrose, repeating my refusal, this time a bit louder.

Ambrose scowled, his jaw clenching from my rejection. His hands curled into fists, and he bared his teeth. "Sybil, I *command* you to kill him."

His words felt like they echoed through me, reverberating through my bones, through my entire being. I stood, unmoving, panting, waiting for something to happen, for some indication that his command held any sway over me. A moment passed. Then another. A small hope bloomed, a whisper telling me that the bargain did not work. That hope steeled me, and I took a step to leave the cell. "I said that I—"

Pain shot through me, up my arms, across my chest, feeling like a knife striking me in my heart. My steps faltered, and I clutched my hands against my chest, gasping for air. The pain sliced through my body again, and I groaned, my legs buckling from the hot, agonizing torture that pulsed through me. My knees hit the dirty stone floor hard, and I winced. My breathing was labored, and the agony in my body grew. Another wave of pain ripped through me, and I fell forward, barely catching myself before my face hit the stone.

Lying my head against my forearms, I cried out into the grimy, cold floor beneath me, my heart racing, my body feeling like it was slowly being torn apart.

My chest heaved, hardly able to take in air, when Ambrose knelt beside me, leaning down beside my ear. "This could all go away, my darling Sybil," he said, his voice soft and kind, as if time reversed itself, like this bargain never happened, while he moved my hair from my face. "Just listen to my command, and the pain will go away."

I lifted my head, my eyes meeting his. He looked at me warmly, reminding me of the days when I thought of him as a friend. But now? That version of him was gone. His love and friendship were nothing more than a ruse. A trick to make me trust him. But that tenderness, that affection still shone in his eyes. So I begged, hoping there was a small part of him that truly cared for me. I begged him to make it stop, to take away the pain, to rescind his command.

Ambrose gave me a soft smile, his eyes reflecting the warmth of better times as he wiped away my tears. "I can't do that, Sybil. I commanded you to kill him, and even though we may not always like it, we all must follow the commands of our masters. Now, be a good little girl and do as I say. Once you do, the pain will go away. It will be like it never even happened."

I looked away from him, unable to stand the false compassion in his eyes. The pain was spreading through my body, and I shook. I tried to take a breath, but dust from the floor caught in my throat. Coughing, the taste of iron coated my tongue while blood splattered on the floor. Warmth trickled from my nose and over my lips. My hand came up to my face, feeling the stream of blood.

Once you are in a bargain, it is bound by death. Meaning, if you don't keep up your end of the bargain, the magic of it will take your life instead.

I was dying. My *body* was dying. Unless I—

A fresh wave of pain ripped through my chest. My lungs were fighting for air. Ambrose cooed, gently lifting me off the floor and setting me on my feet. I felt weak, and the world tilted around me. My breath rasped in my lungs, but Ambrose took my hands, placing them side by side in front of me, cupping them as he had when we were in the room in the library. The memory felt spoiled, tainted by the harsh light around us.

"Remember your training from before," Ambrose murmured softly, recalling the same memory. "Feel for your magic, then picture it in the shape of a dagger."

Pushing through the pain, I moaned, feeling for my magic. The pain eased as I followed his guidance. I thought I was going to be sick right then and there. But this agony? I couldn't fight against it. I didn't want to die.

My hands trembled in his while I tried to call my magic, but nothing happened. I could feel it whirling under my skin, but it felt as though it, too, recoiled from Ambrose's command, not wanting to follow his order.

Ambrose squeezed my hands, this time commanding me to

form the dagger. A sob broke from my lips, but I pushed, coaxing my magic to listen, to help me stop this torment.

My light formed, small and pure, growing as I breathed into it, like a flame. I glanced at Arbus, still fighting his restraints, and my heart fell. My hands twitched, and my magic rushed out of me in a long, sharp spike, almost cutting Ambrose. Arianna cursed, stepping away from me.

A growl from Ambrose was my only warning before he clutched my face in his hand, the force making me whimper. I slid my gaze up, meeting the blue fire in his eyes, and I wanted to cower and hide away from him. "It's not that hard, Sybil. Picture a dagger in your mind's eye and form it. Don't think about anything else. Not your emotions, not your surroundings. Just the dagger. Form it. Now!"

Letting out a quivering breath, I focused on my magic again, letting it slowly illuminate into a sharp dagger. It felt warm and heavy in my hands, but the pain edged away. Ambrose curled his lips in a dark smile, moving my hand along the dagger until it wrapped around the hilt. Placing my other hand on top, he led me closer to Arbus, now pleading with every inch of his life. I choked on a sob; every step closer lessened the pain, replacing it with nausea and vicious self-reproach.

My heart pounded against my chest, my horror growing from the ever-closing distance between Arbus and me. Tears fell heavily down our faces, but our eyes never broke away. The way he looked at me was so full of understanding, like he knew how hard I fought against the bargain, against Ambrose, and I faltered, hating that look.

Stepping between Arbus' legs, Ambrose placed my dagger against Arbus' throat, the heat of my light reddening his skin. Arbus gave up his pleading, accepting his fate while my mind and heart thrashed against it. I wavered, but was met with another slice of pain through my heart that left me breathless.

Ambrose stepped behind me, curving his body around mine. I could feel his hot, repulsive breath along my ear and neck. With his hands still wrapped around mine, he pushed the dagger through Arbus's throat. The sickening sound, the feel of piercing skin and cartilage, echoed through my mind. I wept, apologizing to Arbus, repeating it over and over as the light faded from his eyes, yet he remained filled with quiet understanding.

But I didn't understand, not as Ambrose waited, blood pouring over our hands. Not as Arbus's body went slack against the chair, his chest no longer moving. Not even as Ambrose unwrapped his hand from mine, stepping beside me, my light dissipated along with the heat of his body.

"Good girl," Ambrose said happily, stroking his bloodied knuckle along my cheek, leaving a smear of blood behind. "That wasn't so bad, right? One rat gone, and now we can focus on ridding ourselves of the other pests."

I wept, studying every part of Arbus through blurry tears, wanting—hoping—to memorize everything about him. I didn't want to forget his beautiful face, not even for a single moment, as life left those eyes that reminded me so much of green leaves blowing in the wind.

My gaze moved further down his chest, narrowing on the glint of silver just above his shirt. I hadn't noticed the necklace earlier, but now I reached my hand out, lifting it from under his shirt. A simple silver ring rested on the delicate chain, the edges round and smooth. Grabbing the thin chain, I raised it over his head, gathering it into the center of my palm before curling my hand into a fist around it.

Ambrose came up behind me, placing his hand on my shoulder. I flinched under his touch and forced myself to turn toward him. He patted my cheek, giving me a smile that made me sick to my stomach. "That's all I need you for today, my dear girl. Evander," he waved toward the entrance of the cell, "will take you back to your room. I'll send Samian to you once he returns with your next orders."

I looked over at Evander. His skin was pale, but whether that was from what he saw or if he was always pale, I didn't know. Not as he kept his face carefully blank, his gaze focused on the wall behind me, refusing to look at any of us in the cell. Evander bowed slightly, then turned, making his way to my room. I watched him leave the cell, my legs and body feeling like they were made of stone. My heart slowed, and the room seemed to tunnel around me. The weight of what had just happened slowly pulled me inward. Ambrose let out a breath, his annoyance flaring, and pushed me toward where Evander had stood, forcing my legs to move.

I felt detached, not fully a part of this world. I silently followed Evander out of the dungeon, all the way to the door of my room, but I didn't see or feel anything.

Evander gave me another small bow, leaving me alone in the hallway. I stared blankly at my door. I wasn't even sure I was breathing until the chain of the necklace pinched my skin. I gasped at the small, sharp pain and opened my hand. My breathing came faster and faster, my heart beating wildly in my chest. I winced, the picture of Arbus slumped in the chair flashing across my mind.

I took in a shaky breath, taking step after step away from my door until my back hit the wall behind me. The cold of the marble leaked into my clothes. My breathing was too fast and shallow to get air, and my lungs burned. I grabbed my head, tucking it to my chest, whimpering as I squeezed my eyes shut.

The walls felt like they were closing in on me. I couldn't be here anymore. My feet moved before I knew it, and I ran as fast as I could down the hallway, passing guards calling for me to stop. I followed the streets I had walked on, just two weeks prior, with Ambrose, when my heart had been filled with hope and excitement for a fresh new start. I followed the path all the way through the pearly gates, leaving the city behind.

My running slowed when I reached the fields of wildflowers, gasping for air. I fell into the tall grass, weeping, mourning for what I had done.

CHAPTER 30
SYBIL

The world felt unreal to me. My mind still couldn't comprehend what had happened today. It wasn't supposed to go this way. This new world was supposed to take me away from the constant badgering of a mundane life. It was my chance to escape the never-changing cycle I had found myself stuck in, repeating every single day, more lost than the day before. This was a chance at something new, to experience the adventures that I'd read about—that I longed for in my dreams.

But this wasn't a dream; it was a nightmare. I only proved my father right. I was a monster and a curse. I was an evil that tarnished the world around me. I had taken two lives today. Two innocent lives that could never be returned.

I opened my hand, the necklace still there, though now I could see the dried blood that stained the silver. I ran my hand along the warm edges of the ring, my stomach twisting. Every breath I took made the nausea grow. Swallowing back the bile, I put the necklace around my neck, still clenching my hand tightly around the ring.

I let my hands fall to my lap, tilting my head back to stare at the pink and orange clouds littering the sky, feeling the breeze on my face. My fingers twitched, and I looked down, inhaling sharply when I saw the blood that still covered my hands. My throat tightened, and a sob tore out of me, hot tears falling down my face. I wiped the bloody flakes off my skin, my breathing turning frantic at the red stain left behind. My stomach heaved, and I vomited in the grass beside me. I held onto the sharp green blades around me, screaming into the ground until my voice turned hoarse.

Silent whispers snapped me from my hysteria. Whipping my head toward the sound, I anxiously looked around, finding nothing but the vast open field and the forest in the distance.

My eyes narrowed on the darkened forest, movement rippling from between the trees. I saw it then, a black shadow that danced along the tree line, keeping to the murky forest. My breath hitched, the silent whispers continuing their sweet melodies as I watched that shadow twist and turn. The longer I watched, the louder the whispers became.

I felt drowsy, numb. As I stood, it felt like the world fell away; only a bridge of green grass stood between me and the shadow that beckoned me to come closer.

Step after step, I ventured to the woods, my mind so quiet and calm. The song of the forest surrounded me, encouraging me to follow, to become one with it.

Stepping into the thicket between the trees, my body felt languid, like it was no longer my own. But I didn't care. I was too absorbed in wanting to be part of the song that wrapped around me.

I made my way through the dark woods, passing gnarled

trees covered in deep green moss. Small hills and caves formed, surrounding me in shadow.

A branch snapped, quieting the whispers, and I blinked once. Twice. I looked around, my heart beating heavily in my chest. The woods were quiet, the air still and heavy, as if it were hesitant to move.

I remembered looking at the forest, but the rest was a blur. I didn't know how long I had walked within the groves or how I even came to be here, surrounded by large moss-laden stones.

Leaves crunched behind me, sending an icy chill up my spine. My breathing became faster, fear keeping me as still as a statue. More leaves crunched beside me, closer this time, and I flinched, not daring to look. I reached for my side, hoping I still had Ezra's dagger, but there was nothing. I silently cursed myself for not bringing a weapon with me, but in my panic and despair, there was no room to think. I felt for my magic, but it was weak and strained from being used too much. I was completely vulnerable to the beast circling me.

I closed my eyes, trying to think of a way to escape. A twig on my right snapped, sounding closer. I forced my eyes open, slightly turning my head to the sound, breathing out as slowly as I could.

My breath wavered, my heart lodging in my throat. My mouth gaped open as a large body of a snake rose above the trees. I lifted my head high, swallowing thickly, meeting the yellow eyes of the serpent. The snake's tongue slid out of its mouth, flicking in the air, tasting my terror. Rising higher, the snake towered over me, its greenish-blue scales glimmering in the light creeping through the trees.

There was a motion to my left, something large hurtling toward me. Gasping, I quickly jumped out of the way. The sharp tail of the snake narrowly missed me, slamming into the ground where I had been standing. The tail retracted, looking like a scorpion's. My stomach dropped at the brown liquid dripping from the end of the stinger.

Noticing my hesitation, the snake struck, its gleaming teeth missing me by centimeters. I screamed, falling backward, rolling away when its tail flew at me again. Breathless, I staggered to my feet, running to the nearest path, weaving between trees, praying they would slow the snake enough for me to get away.

But the snake moved faster than I imagined, moving swiftly between the trees and quickly closing in on me. My breath rasped in my lungs, my bowels feeling watery as I jumped over fallen logs, as low-hanging branches clipped my face and arms.

A deep voice yelled from close by, and my head whipped upward to the sound, distracting me from a small tree in front of me. I struck the rough bark with my shoulder and cursed, stumbling to the ground, pain throbbing down my arm.

I surged back to my feet, ready to run, when a sharp spike pierced my skin. Pain and fire seared through me, my scream echoing through the forest as the snake withdrew its stinger from my side.

Stumbling, I placed a hand on my wound, hissing. The venom burned through my veins, making my legs feel weak. I propped against the nearest tree when a glimmer of steel flashed, flying in the air. Hitting its mark, the dagger struck the snake in one of its yellow eyes.

The tall, powerful frame of a man jumped from the treeline, landing beside me, his crimson gaze narrowing on the blood mixed with venom running down my leathers. I tensed, ready to run when he wrapped his hand tightly around my arm, pulling me after him in a sprint. The burn of the venom made my legs slow and sluggish, my vision becoming fuzzy, but the man raced along the forest floor, not allowing me to stop. The snake hissed, lunging at us while we ran. My muscles screamed, begging to stop; my breathing became labored. Dark spots formed along my vision, but the man kept running, picking up his speed.

"Take a deep breath," he yelled, slinging me forward off the edge of a rocky cliff.

I screamed, the world flying past me as I plummeted, my stomach flipping. The man jumped from the cliff behind me just as the snake snapped those sharpened teeth at him, missing by centimeters. Crashing into the freezing lake below, the frigid water took my breath away, quickly rushing into my mouth and lungs as bubbles drifted around me. I kicked my feet, fighting to break the surface of the water, but the weight of my boots pulled me down. The world was growing dark, my body too weak to swim as I sank to the bottom of the lake.

A large, callused hand reached into the darkness, grabbed me by my arm, and instantly pulled me to the surface. My lungs burned, and I coughed up water, gasping and gulping for air. I thrashed, pushing to get away from him and to stay above the water, but his hand held firmly around me, pulling me against the hard lines of his body as he swam us to the edge of the lake.

The fire in my veins and at my side cooled from the water, but the gaping wound still burned, pain slicing with every motion. Trees around the lake groaned and snapped, and I dared a glance behind us, my heart beating hard with dread. The snake was slithering between trees, disappearing into the forest's shadows on the other side of the lake. Ease washed through me when the last of its body finally vanished.

My relief didn't last long, though, not as the man pulled me from the lake, water dripping from his midnight-black hair, his golden-tanned body. Those dark crimson eyes narrowed on me, raking his gaze up and down my body. Shivers ran down my spine at his perusal. He took a step closer, and I faltered back, stepping into the water. There was an intensity in his eyes that sent electricity storming through my veins, gathering in my core.

His tall, muscular frame warned me of his strength, whispering caution that he was not someone to mess with. I swallowed, my body shaking from the cold—from his unwavering stare. I took another step back, my foot slipping on the mossy rocks of the lakeshore. Catching myself before I hit the ground, my wrists barked at the sudden impact, and Arbus' necklace slipped free from my jacket, the ring dangling above the water.

I quickly tucked the necklace back, the air around me crackling with energy. The pressure of the atmosphere grew heavy, the wind picking up speed. "Where did you get that?" he asked, his voice tight and the rigid lines of his muscles tense.

"I don't know what you're talking about," I breathed, watching him closely, careful of my movements.

We stood unmoving, the silence growing thicker. Seconds passed, and then he sprang toward me, grabbing me by the front of my leathers, twisting and pushing me into the sand and rocks along the water's edge. I yelled out, fighting against his hold, but the strength of his arms felt like boulders. I scratched, clawed, and kicked at him, every move jarring my wound.

He growled, catching my hands, forcing them above my head, and straddling me, the sudden weight of him making me gasp as I strained against his hold. I tried bucking, pulling my arms out of his hands, but his grip tightened painfully around my wrists. He moved my hands together, and I whimpered. My body was so weak compared to his, so useless. Taking his free hand, he slid it down my side until he reached my wound. He pressed down on it, sending pain through my stomach and up my sides, making me howl.

"Stop moving," he commanded gruffly. I stilled under his touch, panting, and he removed his hand to pull out the necklace from my jacket. "Where did you get this?"

Holding the necklace in front of me, I stared at it, my eyes burning. His gaze had a lethal glint in them as they bore into me. If he found out what happened, what I had done, he'd kill me. If I didn't get away from him now, it would be the last thing I ever did.

My wrists throbbed against his hold, and he leaned in close, his breath mixing with mine. "I asked you a question," he said, his voice dangerously low. "Where did you get this?"

"I-I don't know. I found it in the field," I stuttered, my mouth drying from the lie.

"I can smell your deceit," he pressed, his voice turning into a threatening growl. "Where?"

Curling my hands into fists, I pulled against his hold, using the last of my strength to lift my hips, pushing him forward. I struck, lifting my head and hitting him in the nose. Bellowing, he shifted his body enough for me to kick out, using his weight against him to roll him off me. I shot forward, hearing his growl behind me as I ran into the trees. I glanced back in time to see him hurtling closer, blood streaming down his face. His body slammed into mine, pushing me into a tree, and I yelped at his strength. The impact jarred my senses.

I whimpered, blinking to clear my eyes when I felt him press his body against my back. My breath hitched when he moved his leg between mine, caging me in. I should have been afraid. I should have been terrified of him, but I couldn't stop the heat that was curling low in my stomach. Not when his warmth and his smell seeped into my body.

"That wasn't very nice," he sniffed, his blood dripping onto my jacket.

"Get off me," I hissed, pushing against him.

"Not until you answer my question. How did you get that necklace?" His voice was softer. I could feel his breath against my neck and ear. I shivered against him.

I could feel him smile, like he knew what his presence was doing to me. Unbridled anger rushed through my veins, but a memory from my childhood popped into my head, and I smirked. I could feel his eyes narrowing, could feel the confusion and wariness tightening the muscles in his stomach. My hand twitched against the rough bark before bending behind me, pinching the skin from the side of his stomach, twisting as hard as I could. Cursing, he pushed away from me. I turned, watching him grimace as he lifted his shirt, looking for a wound that was not there.

I should have used this time to run, but I swallowed, staring at the hard lines of his stomach, pure muscle that I'd only ever seen in magazines and movies.

That moment cost me, I realized, when he whipped his head to me, growling low and deep, baring his teeth at me like a wolf. His crimson eyes turned darker, thunder clapping above us. The wind raged, the trees groaning and swaying as if they were about to topple over.

A quiet curse left me, and I crept away from the tree, keeping my eyes locked with his. Lightning flashed overhead, and I glanced at the sky, at the dark clouds gathering. When my gaze flicked back to his, my eyes widened. He closed the distance between us, and I yelped, turning to run, but I was too late. He grabbed the necklace, yanking me back, choking me. I gagged, pushing a finger under the necklace, using the force of his pull to break the silver chain. I stumbled forward, coughing, and the man took a step toward me when Samian's voice cut through the forest, calling my name. I breathed, feeling something tugging on my heart, in my very soul, but I stood still, not daring to move.

The man paused, taking a sharp breath. He narrowed those crimson eyes on me, observing me with suspicion. Samian called out my name again, and I anxiously swallowed, taking another step back, feeling for the tree behind me. My heart pounded as another clap of thunder sounded above us.

"Go," he commanded, his lips forming a thin line.

Without hesitation, I ran out of the forest, my legs burning, following that tug that would lead me to Samian.

CHAPTER 31
KIERAN

Meeting Sybil was a surprise. Even more surprising was that she carried the necklace given to Arbus by his intended as a promise, a hope for him to return safely from his mission in Volmire.

But what really caught me off guard was how fierce the need to save her from the beithir became. How my chest tightened, and my heart lodged itself in my throat. When I saw it closing in on her, I couldn't move, couldn't think. I called out to her before I could even stop myself. The worry and fear of seeing her hurt tore into me in a way I had never felt in my 346 years. It felt so visceral that my mind went blank, blinded by the need to save her.

Even after I noticed the silver ring dangling from the chained necklace, every fiber of my being screamed against hurting her, so I held back as much as I could. But, as the leader of this rebellion, I had to set my emotions aside, even if it killed me to do so.

I needed answers.

I looked down. The silver ring seemed cold and dull, as if the magic inside had faded, leaving nothing but an empty shell. I curled my hand around the ring and looked to where she had left. Part of me wondered if I should follow her, making sure she escaped safely from this dark and dangerous forest. More than a part of me, actually. It felt like a need that wouldn't be satiated until I saw her again, safe and sound, until I could hold her in my arms, feeling her warmth seeping into me.

Loosening a breath, I rolled my shoulders, willing the tension to ease. I turned my back on the path that led to her—to Sybil—only focusing on the small, worn trail leading me back to camp. As much as my heart thrashed against my chest from the distance between us, I needed to return to the others.

Traveling through the dark forest was easy enough after the beithir's attack. The forest was quiet, the fear still lingering in the air as the other creatures waited for its next attack. Fortunately, for me, with my dagger still lodged in its eye, I doubted it would attack anything for a while.

Walking up to the rusted gates, the doors slowly opened, screeching from disuse. I shut down every feeling, keeping my face blank, though dread was worming its way through me with what I had to do next.

I pushed aside my agitation and entered the camp, weaving between tents and makeshift huts until I stood in front of Arbus's red door. Laughter came from inside the hut; my stomach twisted with every sound. I clenched my jaw, considering coming back tomorrow, but Bryony couldn't wait any longer. She needed to know what had happened to Arbus before word of his disappearance spread. I'd already held off longer than I should have.

Hesitantly, I reached for the door, willing steadiness into my hand. I closed my eyes, took a deep breath, and knocked.

The laughter softened, the door swung open, and I swallowed, preparing to see her bright and smiling face. Instead, my eyes narrowed on Viv, who stood in the doorway. Her knowing gaze shifted down, slowly taking in the drenched state of my clothes, the dirt, the blood. The joy in her gray, marbled eyes faltered.

Viv frowned and stepped back, allowing me enough room to enter the hut. Although it was small, it felt warm, homey. It was one large room with the kitchen area on the right and a sitting area in the middle. There was a dark wooden partition that kept the sleeping cot hidden away. Viv closed the door softly, lingering back to give me space to face Bryony. Viv always had a way of knowing what was to come, even without using her divination magic.

Bryony was busy mixing herbs by the hearth, preparing for tonight's meal. Following Viv's example, she loved cooking meals for the group, always creating new concoctions with the herbs and game provided to her each day, though some recipes didn't always work out. More than once, the camp was laid out sick for days, but her cheery spirit and fiery soul always made up for those miserable days. She meant well, and everyone loved to see that wide smile of hers.

Finishing up her newest blend, Bryony looked up, her face paling at my grim expression. "Tell me," she sighed, setting her tools aside.

I cleared my throat, stepping closer to her and placing the necklace on the counter beside her. My hand lingered before I stepped back, though her gaze held onto mine, her golden-flecked blue eyes turning misty, as if she knew what would be lying there. My throat bobbed, and her chest began to rise quickly. Steeling herself, Bryony looked down at the ring, the silver gleaming in the soft light.

"How?" Bryony choked out, her voice low and meek. A lock of copper hair fell over her face.

"I'm still waiting for more information," I murmured. "I found the necklace in the fields outside Volmire."

My heart clenched at the lie, the words tasting like ash in my mouth. I hated seeing her face fall, hated the tears that were now flowing freely. However, if my suspicions of who Sybil was to me, to Samian, were correct, I couldn't let anyone know of her involvement. Especially not when the possibility of her needing our help in the future was so great. The rebels knew of Samian's task with Ambrose, knew how his responsibility was to stand beside him and feed us information on the court's plans against the queen and the rebellion. But Sybil? She was still too new, too fresh. They would see her participation as an affront, an obstacle that needed to be taken care of. I would not allow that to happen.

A sob broke free, and Bryony crumpled to the floor, her face buried in one hand, while the other clutched her own necklace, which held the matching ring that Arbus had worn.

Swearing, Viv rushed to Bryony's side, wrapping her arms around her friend's slender shoulders, softly whispering to her. Viv looked up, her eyes full of silent questions, but I looked away, unable to face her suspecting gaze. My face pinched as I quietly cursed myself for keeping the truth from her.

I felt Viv's piercing stare, even while she gently guided Bryony to a chair. Giving Bryony a small kiss on her forehead, Viv strode past me, pulling me into the far corner of the hut. "What really happened?" she whispered, those cool gray eyes slicing through me.

"Has Orin returned?" I asked, ignoring her narrowed eyes, her hesitation. She shook her head, sighing. "Have him come to me the moment he does. There's much we need to discuss."

Viv's lips thinned, and I stepped close to Bryony. Kneeling, I took her hands in mine, giving them a small squeeze. "I'll find out who did this."

Bryony nodded, heavy tears streaking down her face. Standing, I gave Viv a slight nod and left the hut.

I walked through the camp to the abandoned manor, its stones covered in ivy and flowering vines. I made my way to the council room, quickly changing out of my wet clothes into a fresh set Viv stored for me in the armoire. After noticing me spending most of my time here studying maps and plans, she grew tired of seeing me in the same clothes day after day, insisting I always keep fresh clothes to change into. She never had children of her own, but that never stopped her from treating every person in the camp as they were, and they loved her for it, no matter how much she nagged and harped on us.

Slipping the shirt over my head, I stopped and looked into the mirror, checking the spot on my side. I frowned at the purple welt. Samian had told me Sybil didn't know how to fight, but the truth of it surprised me. For her safety, that would need to change, but I couldn't fight against the smile curving my lips at the memory of her face brightening with the idea of pinching me.

It was something I'd never seen before, though I wouldn't say it was effective. While the shock made me hesitate, it just edged my already short temper to its breaking point.

A knock at the door pulled me out of my memory, and I grunted a clipped, *come in*. The door swung open as Orin and Viv hastily filed into the room. Viv pulled out a chair for a breathless Orin, his hair disheveled from the wind, covered head to toe in dirt. My brow knitted at the wild look in his golden eyes.

"What happened?" I asked, keeping my tone careful.

"It was a disaster, Kieran," Orin breathed heavily. "Lowbrook is in a complete uproar."

Viv's eyes flicked to mine, her face grim. I tapped a finger on the table, fighting to keep calm, but Orin hesitated when the air grew heavy. I clenched my jaw, nodding for Orin to continue when the door slammed open. I stood, tension gathering in my shoulders, when Samian froze in the doorway. His hands were clenched at his sides, his body trembling, an unsettling, crazed look gleaming in those blue-and-green eyes of his.

"Samian," I said carefully.

"I failed, Kieran," Samian breathed, his voice cracking. "I failed her."

I moved to Samian, pulling him into the room and checking the hall for any bystanders. Finding none, I closed the door behind me, locking it, throwing a shield of air around the room. This needed to be contained among the four of us.

Viv was helping Samian into a chair, her face grave. I exhaled, returning to my chair. Samian was quiet, his eyes locked on the table. I pinched the bridge of my nose, willing my magic to stay calm. I knew after seeing Sybil in the forest that something wasn't right, but nothing could prepare me for the consuming rage and fear I felt for her.

"Tell me," I said gruffly. Still fighting to keep my emotions at bay.

"I don't have all the details yet," Samian breathed. "Aster sedated her before we could learn everything. A beithir attacked her, I believe. Although I'm not sure how she survived." My jaw ticked, but I held my tongue so that Samian could continue. "They took her to Lowbrook today. I couldn't go with her, but from what I could gather, Arianna attempted to attack a newcomer in the village. Sybil tried to help them, but lost control of her magic, killing one of the villagers."

Samian leaned back in his chair, rubbing a trembling hand down his face. "My informant was with her and brought her back to the palace, but he was taken away for interrogation before I could get more answers." Samian paused, his throat bobbing. He curled his hands into fists on the table. "She agreed to his bargain, Kieran. That bastard now has control of her magic." Finally meeting my gaze, fire blazed in his eyes as he seethed.

"Actually," Orin said carefully. "She didn't kill the villager."

Everyone whipped their heads to Orin, his face darkening at our sudden attention. Grimacing, his eyes met mine, waiting for my consent to continue. I gave him a small nod, and Orin took a deep breath, bracing himself before continuing.

"I was the newcomer she was trying to protect," Orin said. "I found Silas's grandchildren trying to sneak back home after losing track of him. Commander Fenleth stopped me while I was taking them back. I told them I had just moved to the village after my parents passed. It backfired, though. Commander Fenleth thought I was a rebel, and she was going to take the children and me for questioning. Sybil got in her way, and General Darktree tried to defend her, but there was another child close by. One I didn't see in time. One of the villagers was edging toward the girl, and Sybil moved to keep the focus off him when the fight broke out. Sybil lost control of her magic, and the blast threw everyone back. No one really got hurt, though, just a few bumps and scrapes. But Silas saw Commander Fenleth kill the villager before blaming it on Sybil."

The room buzzed in the silence. I slid my gaze to Samian; his body was so still that I wasn't sure if he was even breathing. Suddenly, the table groaned as Samian's magic started bending the wood. My own magic responded, the pressure in the air around us growing thick and heavy. Viv cleared her throat, glaring at the two of us, forcing us to pull our magic back.

"I'm going to kill her," Samian whispered furiously, his lip curling. "I'm going to fucking kill her."

"Kieran," Viv interrupted, her voice too calm. "What happened in the forest?"

Samian's gaze clashed against mine, but I kept my face blank and looked back to Viv.

"Arbus went missing. I snuck into Volmire to find out what happened." Pausing, I glanced back at Samian. "I found Sybil in the forest. She was running from the beithir, and it was closing in on her. Before it struck, I called out to her, hoping she would move. She didn't, and the beithir stabbed her with its tail. She lost focus after that, so I distracted it and hauled her ass to the lake. We beat the beithir there, but once we made it to land," I breathed out, rolling my neck, careful to keep my emotions concealed. "She had Arbus's necklace and his ring. She got away before I could get more information from her."

Viv's mouth thinned. "She got away, or you *let* her get away?"

"I don't see the difference," I said through gritted teeth.

"I think you do," she pressed, her eyes narrowing. "I've never seen anyone escape from you, Kieran."

My mouth popped open, ready to fling back a retort when Samian inhaled sharply, his face and body tensing.

"It seems I have to return," Samian muttered, his lips curling in disgust. Standing, Samian's chair scraped against the floor before he disappeared in a cloud of smoke and shadow.

Sighing, I leaned back in my chair, closing my eyes, preparing myself for more of Viv's questioning.

"So," she said, annoyance coloring her tone. "Are you just

going to sit there, or are you going to explain why the hell you let someone escape?"

I slowly opened my eyes, staring at the ceiling, trying to come up with the words. I still didn't know if it was true, not spending enough time with her to be completely sure. But the way time seemed to stop when I saw her running along the forest floor being chased by the beithir, the way my magic seemed to sing when I was close to her, when I touched her—I had never felt anything like it. The rush, the pull, the *need* to touch her was overwhelming. The feel of her underneath me, the way those hazel eyes watched me, still made my blood pulse.

Viv huffed with irritation, waiting for me to answer.

"I think she's my mate," I murmured.

Orin's eyes widened, shock brightening the gold in his irises.

Viv sputtered, blinking at me. "But isn't—"

"Yes," I blurted.

"Are you sure?" she asked softly.

"I'm sure, I think. Our meeting was brief, but it was enough time to know that something was pulling me to her. Even when I watched her in the city, there was an instinctive pull to her. That's why I let her go. Just touching her made my body feel like it was on fire."

"It's not unheard of to have more than one mate. Rare, yes, but not unheard of," Viv whispered, biting her nail. "Shit! And now she's under Ambrose's control."

"What do we do now?" Orin asked cautiously, his face drained of color.

I tapped my fingers on the table, considering our options. "We need to find out the terms of her bargain. I'll send a note to Samian. We need to meet with her to get more details before we make our next move. Viv." I paused, my heart twisting at my next question. Viv was close with Arbus and Bryony after taking Bryony on as her pupil. She was smart enough to know that my finding Sybil with Arbus's necklace meant there was a connection between them—that Sybil was involved in his death, whether I said it aloud or not. "She can't control her magic. She needs someone to help her."

Viv stood and walked to the door. Hesitating in the doorway, she sighed. "I'll think about it," was all Viv said sharply, leaving Orin and me behind.

CHAPTER 32
AMBROSE

I leaned against the damp wall, watching Arianna direct the guards on how to dispose of that rat, Arbus. I kept my face blank, but I was on edge. He had infiltrated my guards so well, blending in so seamlessly, that he almost got away with it. If it weren't for his inability to shield his emotions when I passed the group of guards standing at the palace entrance three days ago, he would have gone unnoticed. Fear and paranoia came off him so strongly that I nearly choked. His face had paled as soon as our eyes met, but no matter how much I pushed on those fears, magnifying them until it was all he felt, that pest never broke. Though he may not have confessed, we both knew he was part of that infestation.

Arianna stalked back to me after finishing giving out her directions, her face glowing with pride at how the day turned out. As promised, Sybil was mine, and now I could begin my plans to become the official king of the upper realm. My blood warmed at the thought. I had been imagining this moment—imagining Cassia's reign finally coming to an end. It was just the start, though. I wouldn't stop until that vile Seelie Court fell with her.

Is she really yours, though?

That whispering voice, sounding both old and young, beautiful and terrible, had me silently snarling. The bargain had worked; the bands wrapped around Sybil's wrists were proof of that. But that sliver of unmarred skin made me wonder if she was wholly mine. Seeing her fight against my commands—that was something that shouldn't have happened.

That's because she's not truly yours to *command.*

A cold, delicate hand ran softly down my face, snapping me out of my thoughts. I snarled, my hand abruptly snatched the wrist, and pulled it away. Arianna's eyes widened in shock, gasping at the sudden, hard movement. Realizing my mistake, I softened my face, drew her against me, and gave her a devious, wicked little smile. I still had my part to play to ensure she would continue helping me.

"Shall we make our way back to my office, my queen?" I purred.

Arianna's smile matched mine as she leaned into me, pressing her soft lips against mine. Nipping my bottom lip, she laughed softly. "I thought you'd never ask," she murmured, her eyes glazing with need.

I took a step, her hands tightening on my chest, shifting through the shadows until the world snapped into place and we stood behind my desk. Our lips crashed together, and Arianna moaned into my mouth. My hands glided up her body, and I pushed her into the marbled wall behind her, swallowing her throaty laugh. My hands drifted down to her hips, all the way behind her thighs. Hoisting her up, I let her legs wrap tightly around my waist. Her uniform was still covered in dirt from

Lowbrook, but I ignored her grimy appearance, grinding my swollen length against her center.

"What will happen next, my king?" Arianna breathed as I kissed my way down her neck.

"Next," I growled, biting the soft part of her neck. She let out a little noise while I licked the pain away. "I am going to fuck you as a reward for being a good girl."

Arianna's lips curled into a smile of pure sin, humming her approval. The icy fire of her hooded eyes pierced into mine, and our lips met in a bruising kiss. Groaning, I deepened that kiss, my tongue stroking hers as I walked us to the couch. Falling into the leather seat, Arianna straddled me, gasping at my hard cock pressing against her.

"Well," I taunted, raising an eyebrow.

Breathless, Arianna leaned back, flushing while she took her sweet time undoing each button of her jacket until it fell to the floor. The silky camisole underneath left nothing to the imagination. The dark pink of her nipples showed through the dainty fabric.

Arianna arched while I leaned forward, her head falling back when I nipped the peaked bud, sucking it into my mouth. Arianna made a small, throaty noise, but before I could move to her other breast, she pushed me away. I growled, narrowing my eyes at her, but she bit her bottom lip, hooking her finger around the strap of her camisole, sliding it down her shoulder.

I chuckled softly, following her direction, letting my finger drift across her chest until I reached the other strap, pulling it down her arm. The silky chemise fell to her waist, leaving her bare. I throbbed against her, caressing the sides of her breasts while she watched. Her lust swirled around me, and I breathed it in, letting it pull me closer to her.

A knock at my door halted me. "What?" I growled, irritation

at the interruption souring my mood. Arianna rolled her eyes, lacing her hands around my neck, waiting.

"We received an urgent message," a guard squeaked.

Arianna huffed and pulled her camisole back into place. She moved off my lap, slipping back into her jacket. After straightening herself, she walked to the door, swinging it open for the guard. Sweat dripped down his blanched face, his breathing heavy. Whether it was from nerves or exertion, I couldn't tell.

I stood, my lips curling with disapproval, and walked to the bar, pouring myself a glass of whiskey. The guard rushed in, bowing low while I took a sip, hoping the burn would quell my frustration.

"Well, go ahead," I snapped. "Tell me the message—quickly."

"Ms. Hart was seen running from the palace. She's no longer in Volmire. We have our soldiers looking for her, but we haven't found her yet."

My knuckles turned white around my glass, and the guard went rigid. Taking a deep breath, I calmly set the glass down. I looked at him, angling my head. I could hear the audible swallow and feel the tangible terror wafting off him.

"W-we believe she might have gone into the dark forest," he stammered.

"Continue your search for her," I said calmly. "Tell me the moment she returns to the palace."

The guard bowed and rushed out of the office. The sound of the closing door echoed through the room, the silence ringing loudly in my ears. My body felt as if it were vibrating.

"Isn't she supposed to be bound to your will?" Arianna finally asked, keeping her voice and her face blank. But I could feel it, the curiosity, the doubt.

I gritted my teeth. "Yes," I said flatly.

She's not completely bound, though, is she?

I inhaled sharply at that fucking voice and its useless words. Picking up my glass, I hurled it against the wall, letting the glass shatter and the whiskey drip to the floor, my breathing coming too fast.

To Arianna's credit, she did not flinch at my loss of control. Instead, she closed the distance between us, capturing my face in her hands, forcing me to meet her eyes. The temperature of the room dropped as I glared at her, though my rage wasn't toward her.

I knew from the moment I saw those bands around her wrists that something wasn't right with the bargain. That fucking sliver of skin mocked me, gloating with proof that the bargain didn't fully pull her under my control. And that blasted voice taunted me at every moment with my failure. Of all the bargains I've made, none resulted in anything like this. No bargain had ever been incomplete in such a way. No bargain ever came with this haunting voice, whispering of how *she* was not wholly mine.

I heard it as soon as Sybil spoke the last words of our bargain. That ancient voice telling me Sybil wasn't completely under my control. I ignored it, pushing it to the back of my mind. But I commanded Sybil to return and stay in her room, and with her gone, it was something I could no longer ignore.

"Tell me," Arianna said softly, carefully reading the emotions reflecting in my gaze.

"Tell you what?" I growled, baring my teeth at her. The thought of having this weakness bared to her made my blood turn to ice.

"Something happened," she pressed. "You know it, and I know it. I saw you. I saw your hesitation when you finished the bargain. Something happened."

"I don't know what happened," I confessed, pulling out of

her hands, turning to face my desk. I leaned against it, my hands gripping the edge of the wood. "Sybil's bands aren't fully connected. She said everything, word for word, but both bands are disconnected."

"Which means she can fight against your command." A statement, not a question. I nodded, my shoulders shaking with rage. Arianna came behind me, wrapping her arms around my stomach. "Then we will control her in a different way."

I turned in her arms and faced her, my head cocked as I waited for her to continue. A cunning smile played on her swollen lips, and she backed away, walking to the bar and pouring out two drinks. She returned, handing me a glass while she took a sip of the brown whiskey. I watched her every move, my patience waning.

"Well, my queen," I drawled. "Are you going to keep me in suspense?"

She let out a sultry laugh. She leaned into me, placing her drink on the desk behind me. "If you can't fully control her with the bargain," Arianna purred, "control her with fear."

"With fear," I repeated quietly.

I stifled a smile. Though the bargain should have put her completely under my control, fear was always a good second choice. You could do many things under the guise of fear. Excitement bubbled in my chest, my blood heating at the thought of Sybil cowering from me while I bent her to my will, feeding on every dread, every terror.

The thought of her begging and pleading, the icy fear that I would draw from her, making it grow until all Sybil would see is the darkness, made me so hard that I ached.

I set my glass down, another laugh rumbling through me. "Control her with fear—what a beautiful idea, my love."

I slid my hand up her arm to the back of her neck, pulling

her to me, our mouths crashing together. Her lips parted, allowing my tongue to sweep in and caress hers. She moaned while I removed her jacket, pushing it off her. I caressed those full breasts of hers and walked her back to the couch until my legs hit the edge of the leather seat. She smiled against my lips, unbuttoning my pants, letting them fall, freeing my cock. Pushing me down to the leather cushions, she slipped out of her own clothes, kneading her breasts, teasing me with every move. I gripped my cock, pumping as I watched her hand glide down her stomach, all the way to her center, my breath heavy.

Unwilling to wait any longer, I grabbed her hips, pulling her to me. She straddled me, rubbing her slick folds against my cock. I groaned, breathing in her hunger. I leaned forward, eager to taste her when she shoved me back, hard. I grunted from the force, but she gripped my cock, lining me to her entrance and sinking onto me, letting me fill her so deeply. I sighed at the feel of her silky warmth clenching around me. Arianna panted, her head tilted back as she rode me fast and hard, using me to satisfy her every desire. Guiding her hips, I ground against her, pushing myself deeper, indulging her every need.

I circled a finger around Arianna's clit, pushing her closer to the edge, her mewling growing louder and wilder. Pinching her clit, she cried out as I swelled inside her, our ecstasy ripping through us. I let her ride out wave after wave of pleasure, pulling her close, our lips coming together in a bruising kiss, until she was fully sated. Leaning my forehead against hers, we breathed heavily, trying to calm our racing hearts.

"We'll start the moment she returns."

CHAPTER 33
SYBIL

I moaned, my body feeling heavy, weighed down. My eyes fluttered open, focusing on the figure sitting by the windows of my room. Swallowing, I peered up to the ceiling. I wasn't sure how I had gotten here. I remembered running through the forest until I reached Samian. I remembered falling and everything going dark. I remember feeling like I was picked up, but I don't remember anything after that.

Looking back at the figure, my vision cleared. The windows and lights were fixed; the glass cleaned up. Samian was reading a paper, his eyes skimming the page, only stopping when he heard the blankets rustling. Attempting to sit up, I hissed from a dull pain and put my hand to my side, probing my skin with my fingers. Wincing, it all came crashing back. The forest, being stabbed by the tail of that monstrous snake, and the man who saved me.

I felt the area again, but the wound was gone. My brows knitted together, and I pulled up my shirt. I had thought that being stabbed by a spike the size of my forearm would feel worse than this, that there would be a gaping wound or at least *something* to show for it. But all I found was a massive bruise, purple and blue. A shiver rippled across my body.

"It's called a beithir—the beast that attacked you," Samian said. I flicked my eyes to him in time to see his face hardening at the sight of the bruise. Concern flickered through those unusual eyes of his, each so different from the other, though they grew wary when his gaze met mine. Folding the letter in his hand, he tucked it into the pocket inside his jacket. "Care to tell me what happened?" he asked, his tone laced with skepticism.

I eyed him, unsure of what to say. I knew Samian wasn't fond of Ambrose. He had made that clear time and time again. But he created a bond with Ambrose, so there was more between them than he was letting on. After everything that happened yesterday… I swallowed, looking away from Samian and his glare. It all felt like too much.

I didn't want to believe it, but I couldn't help but wonder if he was here as a spy for Ambrose, letting him in on my whereabouts, what I was doing, perhaps even what I was thinking. If I told him what happened before I found him, before I collapsed from blood loss and exhaustion, I shuddered at the thought.

The crimson-eyed man in the forest recognized the necklace I took, which had to mean that he was part of the rebel group if Ambrose was correct about Arbus.

I closed my eyes, my heart squeezing at the loss of the necklace. Though I only had it for a short time, it was proof of my failure, of how far I'd fallen. Without it, I felt empty.

Pushing that thought aside, my hands tightened around the blanket bunched at my waist. The most important thing right now was to keep what happened in the forest to myself. If Arbus was truly part of the rebellion, I couldn't let Samian know what really happened. I needed to keep meeting that man hidden from him.

Not daring to look at Samian, I buried my skepticism deep inside, murmuring, "I don't remember much. I just remember the giant snake—the beithir—attacking me. I heard something close by, which distracted me. That's when it stabbed me. Other than hearing you call for me, that's all I remember. Everything else was a blur."

"I see," Samian whispered, though I could feel the intensity of his gaze on me. Samian stood, and I eyed him from under my lashes as he walked to a small table near the bathroom entrance and turned the page of a book left open from a few nights ago. Tension gathered in his shoulders, though his face remained indifferent. "You know, they say that once one is stabbed by the beithir, one must race it to the nearest body of water. If they beat it, the venom left behind is healed. If they don't, well," Samian closed the book with a loud thud, and I flinched. He turned to face me, and my eyes snapped back to the bed. "It's said that they will die a *miserable* death. How did you survive?"

My head whipped to Samian, an icy fear drenching my veins. I could feel the blood leech from my face. I wasn't even sure I was breathing. He knew. Samian knew I was keeping something from him, something vital.

I swallowed the lump that rose in my throat, desperately searching for an answer, any answer that would ease his suspicions, but nothing came. My mind was completely blank.

Before I could say a word, Samian leaned against the table, exhaling. "Well, no matter what happened, you're alive, and that's all I care about. I don't know if you remember, but Aster gave you a sedative before she healed you. The venom is still healing, which is why you have a bruise. Aster closed the wound, but the venom must fade on its own."

I blinked at him and nodded, not knowing what to think of the man who was now rubbing a hand against the back of his neck.

"I also heard about what happened in Lowbrook and what came after." Samian came to the bed and sat, though he looked out the window. "I'm so sorry, Sybil," he said, his gaze drifting to mine, his voice trembling. "I'm so very sorry that I wasn't there to protect you. Please hear me when I tell you that it wasn't your fault, and I will do everything in my power to help you through this."

My eyes burned, and my stomach twisted as I thought back to the villager, to the light fading from Arbus' eyes. Bile threatened to rise, and my breath quivered. "I killed them, Samian," I whispered bitterly. "First the villager, and then that person in the dungeon. *I* did that, which makes it my fault. It doesn't matter what you or anyone says. I was the one who killed them."

"I apologize," Samian murmured, his eyes finally meeting mine. Silver lined them, and he blinked it away. "I just meant that I'm here. Should you ever need anything—a friend or a light to guide you out of the darkness, I will always be here. With you. I can't convey what you have grown to mean to me, but I will spend the rest of my days fighting to show you, to protect you with everything that I have."

A tear fell down my face, and Samian wiped it away. The gentleness of his touch made my heart flutter and left me longing for more. His words meant everything to me, and as much as I wanted to believe him, to trust him, I couldn't give in to that. His bond with Ambrose made him a dangerous ally.

Everything in me cried out to believe him, to fall into his touch, but Ambrose had shattered everything good in my soul. All that was left were broken pieces. To let Samian see those pieces...

Sniffing, I cleared my throat and looked back at Samian. He was staring out of the window, so lost in his thoughts. His face was withdrawn, his jaw clenched tight. He felt like he was a world away, like a wall so tall had been built between us. The sight made my heart drop.

I was beginning to open my mouth, to say what, I wasn't sure, when a fist pounded on the front door of my room.

Samian's head whipped toward the sound, the muscle in his jaw feathering. Looking back at me, concern flashed across his eyes, and he stood and hesitated before he crossed the bedroom and into the living area. Opening the door, a guard shoved the door wider, pushing Samian to the side as he and two other guards filed in. Spotting me in my bedroom, they rushed in, ignoring Samian's shouts. Two of the guards held off Samian while a tall, lanky guard roughly pulled me out of the bed and toward the entrance. I hissed at the sharp pain in my side from the sudden movement.

Samian fought against the guards, the sound of fists meeting flesh jarring me from my shock. My body jerked, struggling against the guard's hold, and I called out Samian's name when the wood of the door frame groaned, rippling and splintering. The room turned eerily quiet, and my wide eyes snapped to Samian. His glare grew deadly as he watched the guard holding me, even though another held a dagger against Samian's throat.

Samian's gaze cut to the guard closest to him, his lips curling. "Where are you taking her?" he snarled.

"To the dungeon. Ambrose's orders," the guard sneered. "He also ordered *you* to stay in your room until you've been called for, *dog*."

The hand around my arm tightened, and I whimpered. A deep growl rumbled from Samian's chest, and the guard paled slightly. Still, he remained unmoving, while the other guard sheathed his dagger and joined him. Together, they hoisted me from the floor. Samian's burning glare never left them, marking every place they touched on my body.

"I'll be waiting for you," Samian called out while the guard pushed me out the door and into the hall.

The rest of the trip was a blur. Fear and dread consumed me while my heart raced. The guards shoved and jerked me down hallways until we reached a dark cell in the dungeon. They pushed me inside, and I tripped over the uneven stones. My knees throbbed from hitting the floor hard. Ignoring the pain, I quickly stood, twisting, lunging toward the exit. But before I could make it, the door slammed closed with a sharp sound, making my heart drop. I gripped the cold iron bars, my heart beating frantically as panic started setting in.

I shook the bars, screaming for them to let me out, but they walked away, laughing at the wavering in my voice. Goosebumps pebbled along my body as the cold seeped in through my thin nightclothes. I sank to the floor, my breathing becoming tight. My head pressed against the bars, and I whimpered. There was no way out, and no one here could help me. I was alone—completely alone.

A shiver ran down my back, and I turned, taking in the cell. It was dark and completely made of cold, wet stone. The air felt like ice, and the silence was deafening. There was a pile of dirty blankets in the corner that smelled of blood, piss, and death. I gagged at the odor and turned away, moving to the corner where the iron bars met the wall. A small hope that I would be able to see what was happening outside of the cell formed, but was quickly doused. The only things I could see were the two cells opposite of mine.

Something large moved in one of the cells, shuffling closer to the front. Gasping, I sat straighter, leaning closer to the biting cold metal.

"Hello?" I asked weakly, afraid to speak any louder.

A pained groan sounded from the cell, and a large body moved to the light. Ezra slowly came into view, his face bruised and bloody. His bottom lip was red and puffy from an angry gash, and his left eye was so swollen that it was shut.

"Ezra," I breathed, my grip tightening on the bars.

"Sybil?" Ezra whispered, confusion pinching his face. "Sybil!" His body shot up as soon as recognition hit, his voice full of panic. "Fuck, are you okay? What are you doing here?"

A small part of me was relieved by Ezra's presence, but it didn't last long. Not that the cold was already making my bones ache. "I-I don't know," I said, trembling. "I was attacked by something yesterday, and when I woke up, Ambrose had ordered the guards to bring me here."

"Attacked?" Ezra's voice was tight, and his knuckles, now holding onto the bars, were white. "Tell me, Sybil. What happened after we parted?"

Recounting what happened with Arbus and the dark forest, Ezra sat deathly still. His whole body was rigid and enraged, though his face looked grave as he stared at the stone floor. But his eyes looked almost black in the dim light. As I did with Samian, I kept spinning the story that implied I was attacked by the beithir near the lake, and how I luckily fell in as soon as it pierced my side with its venomous spiked tail.

Ezra didn't seem to question it, but a dark laugh rumbled from outside the cell.

Ambrose stepped into view, and I paled, silently thanking

whatever instinct told me to keep the crimson-eyed man a secret, but my thanks stopped there. Fear wound its sharp claws tight around my heart, squeezing until I could hardly breathe.

Walking up to the corner where I sat, Ambrose crouched down to my level, meeting my wide eyes with a dark smile curving along his lips.

CHAPTER 34
SYBIL

"My darling Sybil," Ambrose purred, his hand reaching out, gently lifting my chin. He moved a lock of hair from my face, then placed his hand on the back of my head. My body tensed under his touch, like it knew what was about to happen. His smile sharpened before he roughly pulled my face against the bars. I cried out, the pain slicing through my face. "I believe, Sybil, that I ordered you back to your room after our time together, did I not?"

Ambrose cocked his head to the side, his eyes dangerously cold, waiting for me to answer. I trembled against the bars, the icy cold of iron bleeding into my face. Ezra yelled my name, his voice cracking, but I didn't dare look away from Ambrose. I stared at him. Fear's grip was so strong that I was too afraid even to blink. A whimper escaped my lips when Ambrose drifted his hand to my throat, his lips dipping in a frown at my silence. Frustration rippled along his features while he waited for me to speak, ice climbing along the bars.

His thumb ran up and down my neck, and I shivered. Ezra

called my name again, and I glanced at him, my eyes begging him to do something, anything—though I knew there was nothing he could do.

Ambrose clucked his tongue, his hand squeezing, cutting off my air. Ambrose lazily stood, lifting me off the ground like I was nothing but a doll. My legs kicked out, and I clawed at his hand. Ezra's yells echoed through the cells, but my blood thundered in my ears.

Ambrose slammed me against the bars, his face a breath away from mine. "I asked you a question," Ambrose growled, those ocean-blue eyes colder than I've ever seen them.

"I-I'm sorry," I choked, dots swimming across my vision.

Ambrose bared his teeth at me, throwing me to the floor. I cried out, landing painfully on the bruise from my attack with the beithir. The impact was so hard that, if I weren't already struggling to gulp down the putrid air around me, I would have no breath at all.

Ezra's shouts continued echoing through the dungeon, the iron bars noisily drumming as he shook them, trying to get to me. Ambrose let out a breath of annoyance and looked back to Ezra, his pointed face severe. "If I were you," he drawled, "I would keep my mouth shut or else things will become a lot worse for her."

My bowels turned watery at the threat, and Ezra growled, low and deep, but clung to the bars in front of him, his mouth a thin line as he stilled. Ambrose returned his icy glare to me and opened the cell door. I flinched at the groan of the metal, and I shuffled to the back wall of the cell, needing to be as far from him as I could.

My heart pounded faster with every step Ambrose took as he closed the distance between us. His steps were easy, near feline, though his face was detached, so different from times before when he would hold me close. My heart wailed at who he had become, at who he *was*.

Ambrose knelt, grabbing my hair and tilting my head up. I whimpered, wanting nothing more than to curl into myself and hide away from the truth of who he turned out to be.

"One way or another," Ambrose muttered, "you will learn to follow my commands. Whether I must use our bargain to force you or use such unsavory force like this, you *will* do as I say. Have I made myself clear?" I nodded quickly, and he smirked, though it didn't reach his eyes. "Good girl. Now, let's get started with your punishment, shall we?"

"Wait," I breathed, my body feeling paralyzed. "I agreed I would listen."

"You did agree, yes. But it's easy to say one thing in a time like this and then not follow your word under different circumstances. This way, your punishment will serve as a reminder of what happens when you defy my wishes."

"What are you going to do?" I whispered, so low I could hardly hear the words over the trembling wracking of my body.

Ambrose leaned closer, his hot breath curling around my neck, making my stomach crawl. "We, my darling Sybil, are going to have some fun."

Letting me go, Ambrose stood as two guards brought in a table and a bag filled with different tools. Another guard followed, carrying a wide barrel, which he placed in the middle of the room. Ambrose walked to the table, inspecting the tools that were laid out. Finally, Arianna strode into the cell, dragging a chair behind her. Her beautiful and terrible smile sharpened when she spotted me shaking on the floor.

Placing the chair close to the barrel, Arianna walked up to Ambrose, her hands roaming up his back and down his arms while she slid off his coat. Ambrose turned to her, his face bright with excitement. My eyes widened, my breathing becoming erratic as I watched Arianna lean into him, slowly pulling his sleeves up his toned forearms, cuffing them near his elbows. After straightening the last cuff, Ambrose ran his fingers through Arianna's silky golden hair, pulling her into a deep, passionate kiss. I looked away, unable to stomach seeing them together, glancing at Ezra, his eyes nearly black with fury.

"Would you like to decide what we start with, darling Sybil?" Ambrose asked, his tone sickeningly playful. "We can play with my toys here first, or we can start with that." He pointed to the empty barrel, but I didn't look. Swallowing, I stared at him, terror taking away my ability to speak or move. Ambrose chuckled, his eyes gleaming as they turned on Arianna. "What about you, Arianna? Would you like to decide for her, my queen?"

Arianna walked to the table, humming a sweet melody, shifting through various knives and tools laid out there. Her hand stopped over a small dagger. The hilt was made of wood, with small runes carved along the sides. She picked up the dagger, smirking and waving it at me as she handed it over to Ambrose. Ambrose murmured his approval, taking it from her to study the sharpness of the blade.

Rubbing his thumb along the edge, he drew a bead of blood. "Bring her over."

Arianna knelt in front of me, cooing at the terror that painted my face. Her hand drifted along my cheek, and I edged away from her touch, pushing my back into the wall behind me, my heart beating frantically. Arianna huffed a laugh. "It would be a lot easier if you'd just cooperate," she said sweetly. Her voice was so soft and lovely.

"Don't touch me," I whispered viciously, slapping her hand away.

Arianna sneered at me, her hand snapping out, grabbing the hair along my scalp. My head burned, and I shrieked, my hands wrapping around her wrists to lessen the pain. She hauled me to the chair, forcing me into it while Ezra's shouts filled my cell, settling around me. I jerked forward, hoping to shove Arianna away when ice formed around my wrists, the frozen bite of it making me gasp. The ice froze my hands and ankles to the chair, keeping me tied down. Ambrose stepped closer, eyeing the dagger carefully, running his fingers up and down the edge of the blade. I whimpered, struggling to break free, but the frozen crystal wouldn't break.

The blood drained from my face, a cold sweat beaded along my brow and down my back at his nearness. Stepping between my legs, Ambrose let the dagger rest on my arm. My muscles tensed at the feel of its sharp edge. I eyed the dagger, keeping my arm as still as I could, my breathing coming in harsh pants. Slowly, so slowly, Ambrose moved the knife up along my arm, the razor-sharp edge slicing through my skin in a shallow cut. Burning pain followed in its wake, and I screamed, writhing and sobbing at its touch. My magic prickled underneath my skin, rising to protect me.

"We will have none of that," Ambrose tsked, somehow knowing what my power was doing. "I command you not to use your magic."

Agony pierced through me, like a chain tightening around my heart. I doubled over, my chest heaving as it spread through my whole body. My magic winked out in response, and Ambrose hummed, moving the dagger to my other arm, following the same motion as before. I cried out, hot tears blurring my vision. I begged him, pleading for him to stop.

"You haven't been punished enough, darling," he sighed. He took the blade, gliding it down my left cheek. His eyes had a wild look, and his smile grew from the sounds of my cries. "I need to know that you understand the consequences of not following my commands. This is the only way I can assure myself that you will listen to me, my darling Sybil." Ambrose put the blade under my chin, lifting my face so that my eyes met his. Leaning close, he licked the blood that trickled down my face. My eyes squeezed shut, and I whimpered at the hot feel of his tongue sweeping along the cut, swallowing down the bile that rose. "Trust me, Sybil, it hurts me deeply to do this."

Putting his mouth against my neck, Ambrose breathed in my scent as he moved the razor edge down the other side of my neck. His groan rumbled in my ear, like he took pleasure in hearing my screams, as if he delighted in them.

MY HEAD FELL FORWARD, my breathing labored. A mix of blood, sweat, and tears dripped from my face onto the stone floor below. I wasn't sure how much time had passed—minutes, hours—it all felt the same. My body was drained, my throat hoarse from all the cries and screams. I stared down at the pool of blood around my feet, unseeing and dazed. Ambrose cleaned his tools near the table, setting down the ruined dagger, his bloodlust finally quenched.

"Ambrose," Arianna whined, her honeyed voice now nauseating and foul.

Ambrose's deep chuckle rumbled, echoing in the dark cell, as he walked over to the empty barrel. My body tensed from his movement. I eyed him from under the hair that had fallen during his torment, watching while he placed his hand inside. The temperature of the cell dropped, and the sound of water filled my ears. My pulse spiked, my body quivered, and I knew that this torture was far from over.

Once the water reached the top of the barrel, the ice around my wrists and ankles melted away, but I kept still, refusing to move. Ambrose faced me, drumming his fingers against the edge of the barrel. His head was tilted to the side, eyeing me intently. Finally, Ambrose came to me, reaching out his hand for me to take. I hesitated, but when his lips twitched, I placed my shaking hand in his, letting him guide me away from the chair.

Moving my hair away from my face, Ambrose grimaced at the blood and sweat that coated my skin. "Your queen demanded her own punishment for the time in the training yard and in Lowbrook. She also thinks that you need to be cleaned up a bit."

My blood froze, my gaze drifting to Arianna. She stood, tall and proud, her eyes blazing with a blue fire that made my body quail. My hands curled into fists at my sides, and I whispered a soft *please* to her, begging for her to change her mind, to end this.

Tutting, Ambrose circled me, stopping behind me. He ran his hands across my shoulders and down my arms. I swallowed down the vomit that rose at his soft touch. "Shh," Ambrose cooed softly. "It will be over before you know it, and then we can move on from this horrible, horrible incident, darling."

Ambrose's hands stopped at my wrists, pulling them together. I whimpered at the painful stretch of the cuts along my arms and chest, and the cold bite that now circled around my hands. He pushed me forward, my body slightly resisting against his touch. My mind—my entire being—it seemed to shut down. I wasn't sure how much more of this I could take.

Ambrose let out a quick breath of frustration at my protest

to moving forward. Grabbing my hair, he jerked my head back, pain splintering across my scalp. "Move to the barrel, Sybil," Ambrose hissed. "That's an order."

He shoved my head forward, and I took one reluctant, trembling step after another until my knees bumped against the small barrel. I looked down, eyeing the water that rippled from the ice circling along the edge. Ambrose shoved me down to my knees and walked in front of me, giving Arianna a small nod.

Arianna giggled, rushing to my side, crouching. Her delicate fingers roughly clenched my hair, wrenching my head to the side so she could lean close to my ear. "I'm going to enjoy this," she whispered. "You don't know how *much* I'm going to enjoy this."

"Arianna," Ambrose sighed in warning. He slid his gaze to mine, and my throat bobbed. "Now, my darling, to make sure you have learned your lesson, I'm going to ask you a couple of questions. First, when I tell you to do something, you'll?"

"Do as you say," I croaked, my heart thumping hard against my too-tight chest.

"Good girl. And you'll do it even if I tell you to kill?"

I hesitated, my eyes widening at his question. I didn't want to hurt anyone else. Already, the deaths of Arbus and the villager weighed heavily on me. To add a third or more would break me. I didn't know if I could handle more blood on my hands, if my tarnished soul could take more.

Ambrose's lips thinned, the only warning I had before Arianna shoved my head into the icy water. The frozen chill took my breath away, and I fought against her hold. Water filled my mouth and lungs, and I screamed until dark spots danced along my vision. My body became heavy, and only then did Arianna pull my head from the water. Coughing, water spewed from my mouth.

"That was the wrong answer, Sybil," Ambrose said flatly. "Now, let me ask you again. Will you do as I say even if I tell you to kill?"

"P-please. Please don't make me do this, Ambrose," I stuttered, my eyes felt like they were on fire from the heat of tears stinging my eyes, pouring down my face.

Arianna scoffed, shoving my head back under the water. Fighting against her, I held my breath as long as I could, but the small amount of air didn't last long. My lungs screamed. My chest heaved, my body refusing to listen any longer, letting the water into my mouth and nose. Arianna pulled my head up, and I heaved up the water that burned my lungs.

As I gulped down air, Arianna threw my head back in, pushing me further down. My vision darkened; my body turned slack. I was tired, so very tired. Pulling my head up, I coughed up the water again, my head lolling to the side. Ambrose asked the question again, his tone more severe.

"I'll do it," I gasped, unable to take any more of this torture. "I'll do it. Please, please stop. I promise. I'll follow every order, even if it's to kill."

Ambrose smiled, kneeling in front of the barrel, tapping his hand against my face. "Good girl."

His gaze slid to Arianna, giving her a sharp smile. Her grip on my hair tightened, and a small laugh escaped her lips. I barely breathed out a raspy *no* before Arianna pushed my head back into the frozen water, this time, holding me under until I fell into complete darkness.

CHAPTER 35
SAMIAN

"Fuck," I whispered, my stomach dropping at the sight of Sybil lying so still on the cold stone beneath her. The moment the guards told me to take her to the medical wing, I wasted no time using my magic to sift through shadow and space to get to her. My heart raced as I quickly pulled the cell key from my pocket and unlocked the door. I shoved open the door, rushing to her side, fear gnawing at my mind.

Kneeling beside her, I felt the frigid water soak through my pants as I noted the blood and lacerations that covered her body. My magic rippled under my skin, responding to the fiery wrath that burned in my veins. Checking Sybil's pulse, relief partly cooled that flame at the feel of its steady beat, though her breathing was labored. A sheen of sweat gathered along her brow. The cold air, the dirt of the floor, and the freezing water were festering her wounds.

I moved the hair away from her face, my blood boiling at my

inability to protect her from this world. I fucking knew as soon as Ambrose found out about her, he would hurt her, just to reach his insufferable goals. But I never thought it would be to this degree.

"Samian?" Ezra's rough voice called out from a dark cell behind me.

My head whirled, and I inhaled sharply, taking in his battered face. The skin around his left eye was inflamed and puffy, though the gash along his brow was beginning to close. His eyes were tired and full of anger, but a sadness lingered behind them.

"Is she okay?" He whispered, his eyes glued to Sybil.

"She's alive," I said, feeling the heat radiating from her body. "The cold is making her sick."

Ezra cursed into the darkness, though he stood, gripping the bars of the cell. He watched me pick Sybil up from the cold, wet floor as gently as I could, sweeping my arm underneath her legs. A silent whimper came from Sybil, her brows furrowing from the sudden movement. Taking a steadying breath, I pushed down my rage so I could focus on getting her to Aster.

Stepping out of her cell, I brought her over to Ezra to let him check on her himself. I couldn't imagine what he felt, watching her suffer. I couldn't even imagine what I would have done if I were in the cell instead. I swallowed, pushing away the thought.

"I'm sorry," Ezra breathed, brushing a knuckle softly down her face. His face pinched with guilt, seeing the damage to her body. "I was supposed to protect her in your stead. I failed you, and I failed her. For that, I am tremendously sorry."

Letting his hand drop, Ezra rested his head on the iron bars, his gaze settling on the floor. His body shook, the air growing heavy. I narrowed my eyes, zeroing in on the tension in his body, how he kept his eyes from meeting mine.

"Tell me," I murmured.

Ezra's shoulders dipped. "I was found guilty of aiding a rebel by our *future* queen," Ezra spat, the muscle in his jaw feathering. "My execution is set for the day after tomorrow and," he paused, his hands tightening around the bars. "And Sybil will be the one to do it," Ezra finally said, still avoiding my stare.

"What do you mean, Sybil will be the one to do it?" I asked, struggling to keep my voice steady.

"Ambrose will be making her his personal executioner, though her official title will be something different. And with her bargain, she must do as he commands. But," Ezra's sharp gaze finally met mine, "there's something going on that doesn't make sense. He brought her here as a punishment for not following his command, but according to their bargain, she must follow his will or else she will die. It just doesn't make sense. Why bring her here for disobeying if she must follow his will?"

My blood pulsed, my magic thrumming under my skin. Ezra was right. It didn't make sense. Sybil whimpered again, pulling us both out of our thoughts. Shifting my weight, I lifted Sybil closer to me, cradling her so that her head could rest more comfortably against my shoulder.

Looking back to Ezra, I tugged on our bond. Ezra jerked at the feel of my magic as I spoke, *"Tomorrow night, I will help you escape. I'm not going to say how for your protection, but I will not allow you to die. Keep to yourself, but be ready."*

Ezra loosed a breath, his eyes gleaming with gratitude. I looked down at Sybil, my heart and mind in complete chaos. I knew Ambrose vied for the throne, but to make Sybil his own personal assassin didn't make sense. He had Arianna for that. Unless he knew more than he was letting on about Sybil, about what she was. I clenched Sybil closer. The need to protect her surged, warming my blood. I swallowed it down, allowing Ezra one last look, and then let the world fall away until I stood in Aster's office.

Aster gasped, jumping up from her chair, her hand clutching her chest at my sudden arrival, but her shock shifted into a whispered curse when she saw Sybil in my arms. Sybil groaned from the effects of transferring to the medical wing. Luckily, her bleeding had stopped, a sign that her seelie blood was continually growing, but she was still unconscious, her body turning sickly pale from her fever.

"Does she have a death wish?" Aster muttered furiously. "Didn't I just heal her last night? What did she get herself into this time?"

"Ambrose," I said, my tone flat. My mouth felt dry as I eyed Aster, noticing the way her face paled at his name.

"I see," she said, her mouth thinning. Her throat bobbed at the memories brought up by his name and by seeing Sybil in this state. "Follow me to the back room."

We made our way to the rear of the medical wing, Aster eyeing the other healers as we went, her pointed gaze warning them to keep silent. As soon as we entered the space, I gently laid Sybil on the bed in the corner of the room.

Aster closed the door behind us, locking it and looking out the small window, checking to see if anyone followed before moving a tall cabinet in front of the door.

"Looks like someone is a little paranoid," I quipped, earning an icy glare.

Ignoring me, Aster came to Sybil's side, pushing her healing magic into Sybil. A soft glow wrapped around her body, the gashes on her face and body stitching together. With the pain and fever now healed, Sybil's body relaxed, though she continued to slumber.

"What did he do to her?" Aster's voice was meek as she watched Sybil sleep. Having once been in Sybil's place, Aster knew all too well what Ambrose was capable of, though their time together was long ago and long since forgotten by Ambrose. It was what had made Aster march up to me, demanding to be included in whatever I was planning to bring Ambrose down. The memory of me spluttering like a fish while denying what I was doing, the connections I had with the rebels, flashed through my mind. She had grabbed my face, pulling me down to her level to continue her demands. She was so unruly. So different from her normal cool indifference.

"She defied his command," I admitted softly. I eyed the bands cuffing Sybil's wrists.

Aster followed my gaze, her brows bunching. "I knew something was odd about them," she said, carefully picking up Sybil's wrist. "They're not fully connected like other markings I've seen."

I wondered about that too when I noticed the unmarked sliver of skin. "Do you know what it could mean?"

Aster frowned, shaking her head. She gently set Sybil's hand back down. "I don't, but I have a feeling it's tied to her blood. Maybe it's something the queen would know about?"

I considered her words. I had been wanting to ask the queen myself, but part of me was too afraid to ask. "She may, though—"

Sybil lurched forward, gasping for air, her frantic eyes widening as she slammed herself back into the wall behind her. I stayed still, holding out my hand, gesturing for Aster to do the same. Sybil's eyes wildly searched the room as the realization slowly set in that she wasn't in the cell. Sybil's chest was rising and falling too fast, and her magic hummed. Her hands started glowing with a warm light, but she cried out, the light ebbing when she doubled over.

I cursed quietly, taking a step closer to Sybil. "You're okay," I said gently, raising my hands to show her we meant her no harm. "You're safe here. We're not going to hurt you, I promise. Aster healed your wounds." Sybil's eyes met mine, her breathing still too fast. I motioned this to Aster, and she gave Sybil a small wave.

"Where's Ezra?" Sybil asked, her voice timid and skeptical.

My heart clenched at the sound, wanting nothing more than to wrap her in my arms. But I shut that thought down. It was too soon after what she had gone through. "He is still in the dungeons," I said carefully. "But I'll make sure he is safe."

"You will?" Sybil's voice was cold, edged. Her wary eyes narrowed on me. "Don't you work for Ambrose? Have a bond with him?"

I swallowed at her tone, at what she was implying. My jaw clenched tight, my teeth feeling like they were ready to break. "No, I don't," I growled. Aster snorted, and I cut her a glare, but sighed and looked back to Sybil. "I may have formed a bond with him, but that was under the queen's orders, *not* because I wanted to. The queen needed me to keep an eye on him while she was gone, and that was the only way to gain his trust. I did it for *her*."

"Not that it stopped anything from happening," Aster muttered under her breath, looking at a spot on the wall.

I sent another glare her way, though she didn't see it. "No, it didn't. But I have a plan to get Ezra out *without* Ambrose knowing."

Sybil studied me, looking for any hint of deception, her hands curled in tight fists to keep the slight tremble in them hidden.

"I'll join you, then." Sybil's eyes were narrowed, daring me to say no. I wanted to. My body demanded it, demanded for her to stay here where it was safe.

"I'll join too," Aster added with a shrug, watching me with the same warning.

I watched them both, my eyes shifting from one to the other. Finally, I closed my eyes, pinching the bridge of my nose. "Fine," I huffed. "There's someone I want you both to meet anyway. But we have to wait until tomorrow night, so rest and replenish your magic."

Rolling her eyes, Sybil scoffed but stayed quiet, pressing her back to the wall. Her face was blank, and her eyes trailed across the room, stopping at the screens lining the wall. "You have computers here?" she asked slowly.

I sat on the edge of the bed, following her gaze to the bright screens. "There's a lot that I haven't told you about this world. This is one of them. You may not believe what I say, but please trust me when I tell you I will give you nothing but the truth." Pausing, I glanced at Sybil, who reluctantly nodded, urging me to continue.

"A few centuries ago, this world was different. We built up our technology in a way similar to humans in Mide, just less wasteful. We allowed everyone access to it, and it helped our world thrive. The farmers used it to learn more about the soil for better food growth. Healers used it to provide medicine to villages and towns without healers. We used it in schools here and elsewhere, establishing new schools to help children and adults become educated. It gave people more opportunities to grow, and it leveled the playing field between them and the nobility across Nemos.

"As you can imagine, it didn't sit well with some of the lords. However, the queen ignored their complaints. She remained steadfast in paving the way to allow commoners into her court and council room. This continued until Ambrose's father's sudden death. As his heir, Ambrose took over as the queen's advisor, though there were rumors that another was being prepared to take his place. However, Ambrose swiftly put an end to those whispers.

"Then, the queen decided to go on a trip. A trip that has lasted for over 100 years. During that time, Ambrose gathered allies among the lords in Nemos, making changes to how the realm was to be ruled. In Ambrose's terms, it was to 'return us to the time of greatness.' Ambrose rolled back the changes made by the queen that helped the towns and villages. He took away their technology, with the exception of the palace medical wing, after Aster's insistent daily protests, as it got in the way of our 'connection' to the land. He raised the taxes and tributes throughout the realm and blocked access to Volmire, unless one was invited."

"Why did he make an exception for the palace healers?" Sybil asked, still eyeing the screens.

"The official reason is so we can study the powers of the High Fae and use our research to create more powerful offspring," Aster replied. "With this information, they can force arranged marriages focused solely on the strength and magic of their future partners. But I wanted to keep it for other reasons."

I gave Aster a weak smile. The medicines she created in secret have already helped so many. Even though she knew the dangers, knew firsthand what Ambrose was capable of, she still gave everything to prevent countless deaths.

"Is that the real reason he made me do the blood tests?"

"You're quick," Aster smirked. Grimacing, Sybil looked at Aster, her face still unreadable while Aster continued. "That's partly why he wanted them done, but as far as Ambrose knows, the percentage of your fae blood and power are too low for him to waste on a marriage match."

Sybil narrowed her eyes, wariness rippling across her face. "What does that mean?"

Aster jerked her chin at me, which was my cue to continue. Swallowing down my annoyance, I sighed. "It means that your blood is different."

Hesitating, I rubbed the back of my neck, my face pinching, not knowing how much I should tell her or Aster. Though I told Ezra and Kieran of Sybil's relation to Dryden, I haven't had the chance to tell Aster of what I learned about Sybil's bloodline, and knowing Aster, she was going to give me hell for keeping it from her. I felt Aster's pointed glare, and I didn't dare meet it.

"I can't tell you everything yet, but if you give me a chance, I promise that after we get Ezra out, I will tell you then. But what I can say is that there's something particular about your blood that we have never seen before. We—"

My eyes flew to Aster, her face already blanched. I inhaled sharply, feeling the brush of power entering the medical ward. Jumping to my feet, I moved the bookcase back to its original place, unlocked the door, and rushed to Sybil. Aster still stood frozen, her memories surging. Grabbing Sybil's ankles, I pulled her down to the edge, throwing a hand over her mouth, quieting her curse as I pushed her flat against the bed.

"Pretend you're asleep. Say nothing, and whatever happens, do not move." My voice was strained, harsh. I turned to Aster, the color returning to her face, her gray eyes reminding me of hard steel. She breezed past me, taking hold of Sybil's wrist. A glow of light wrapped around Sybil when the door to the room swung open.

"Ah, here you are," Ambrose purred, his eyes gleaming with pride when he flicked a quick glance at Sybil. The small move had me silently snarling. "I believe I ordered you to return to my office once you brought her here."

"I wanted to make sure her fever came down before I left," I said, keeping my face blank though it took everything in me to push down my fury.

"Did you hear that, Aster?" Ambrose mused. Aster refused to react, keeping her eyes on Sybil, her face masked in her usual indifference. "It sounds like Samian doesn't think you can do your job." Ambrose laughed, his gaze raking down Aster's body, lingering at the curve of her breasts. I wondered if he remembered their time together, remembered what he had done to her, and if he felt an ounce of regret.

"I know what I'm doing." Aster clucked. "If you don't mind, I would like to continue with her healing. *Without* interruptions." Aster's gray eyes finally snapped to Ambrose, a cold wrath whirling in her glare.

Ambrose frowned, but he didn't respond. His eyes grew distant, and he snarled. I raised an eyebrow, throwing a confused glance at Aster before wiping the emotion from my face.

Snapping out of his thoughts, Ambrose turned to me, a quiet rage making his body tense. "My office. Now."

He disappeared in a flash of shadowy smoke, and I exhaled, letting the tension wash away from me. Sybil peeked an eye open, making sure Ambrose was gone. Aster stepped away, sliding her hands into the pockets of her coat. I tugged on Aster's bond, and her gaze slammed to mine.

"Are you okay?"

"I'm fine. Go, you're needed elsewhere."

"I'll return as soon as I can. We can make our plan for tomorrow night when I do," I said, though it was more to myself than anyone else.

Without waiting for a response, the world tilted away until I stepped into Ambrose's office.

CHAPTER 36
SYBIL

I blinked at the space where Samian once stood, picking at the edges of my shirt. It was stiff from dried blood—*my* dried blood. Nausea rose, but I swallowed it back. I was safe for the moment. Safe in this room.

I wasn't sure how much time had passed since I was taken to the dungeon, but I was relieved I didn't have to see the damage Ambrose and Arianna had done to my body. Just the thought of them, their laughs, their eyes bright from excitement, made my body lock up. A shiver ran through me, goosebumps pebbling my skin.

Pushing the memories away, I looked up, finding Aster watching me. Her face was blank, not giving away what she was thinking or feeling. I gave her a small, awkward smile and looked back at the screens, unable to stand the way she watched me, as if she could see things in me I would rather hide.

"I know what it's like," Aster murmured, breaking the silence, her voice sounding far away, "to be on the receiving end of his amusement."

My eyes met those familiar cold gray eyes, though they seemed to warm from a touch of empathy. Guilt twisted my stomach, knowing I should be glad that Aster escaped him, that she now had Samian to protect her, and I was, but envy crawled up my throat like acid. I couldn't help but wonder, though, why they acted so distant while Ambrose was in the room.

"So," I hesitated, not wanting to pry any further. "Can *you* tell me how my blood is different?"

Hesitating, Aster looked to the small, exposed window. She stood, locked the door, replaced the bookcase to cover the window, and finally pulled a chair up to the bed.

"Isn't that suspicious?" I asked quietly. "Moving the bookcase back and forth, I mean."

"My staff knows I like my privacy," Aster replied, glancing back to the now hidden door, lingering as if she was ready for someone to bust through. "I've been doing this for a while, and they understand my tics." The sadness that reflected on her face, somber understanding coiled inside of me. "Now, about your blood," Aster breathed, her brows furrowing with apprehension. "It's changing, morphing into something new. We also found some unusual cells that we've never seen before."

"What does that mean? How is it changing?"

"Your fae blood cells are slowly taking over your human ones, which means you're becoming less human. It looks like it only just started, probably when the binds on your magic were broken."

Awareness slowly prickled through me. I had been noticing that I felt stronger, that my eyes looked greener, and that my hair had darkened recently. But I shook it off, blaming the lighting of my room. "How much has it grown?" I asked, glancing back to the computers, as though they had the answer written across the bright screens.

"The official record says you're only ten percent fae, though I don't know how much that has changed. Samian and I thought it was best for no one else to know. I altered the numbers on the records that were sent to Ambrose. Samian kept the results with the correct information, but I destroyed your bloodwork so no one else could test it again."

"So, the results, could they be wrong?"

"Outdated," Aster corrected. "But yes. With what I saw, your percentage has probably doubled by now."

"Was it difficult to get rid of my bloodwork before?" I asked warily, finally looking at Aster.

She raised her eyebrow, her eyes slightly narrowing on me. "No, it wasn't."

"Right. I guess we should retest it before Samian comes back?" I said, holding out my arm.

Aster smirked, leaving her chair to gather supplies. Placing them on a cart, she rolled it to me. She wrapped a cloth tightly around my arm, just above my elbow. I grimaced when she pulled out a needle and looked away. Aster chuckled, muttering something about humans and needles under her breath, like it was something she dealt with often.

The needle went in with a pinch, but Aster made quick work of filling the vials. My shoulders relaxed once she removed the needle, and I let out a breath. She sent her healing magic into my skin, stopping the bleeding, then took the cart back to a workstation to begin analyzing my blood.

I looked back at the door.

I know what it's like to be on the receiving end of his amusement.

The air felt heavy with her words, charged by the emotions she kept hidden behind them. Though it wasn't the choice of words that I would have used, it made me feel strangely closer to her, even angry for what she had to endure from *him*. I shuddered at the thought of Ambrose, how close he had come to finding me healed and awake. What torture would he give me if he knew, if that warm glow Aster wrapped around me hadn't been there?

Both Aster and Samian's voices sounded tight and closed off in Ambrose's presence. It was like they were keeping their closeness a secret from him. As though Ambrose would see their attachment as an affront to him, as something to destroy.

Unable to stop myself, I bristled. I was supposed to be wary of Samian, to not allow him to get close, to push away the ease I feel when he is near. But I couldn't help the way my heart clenched when I saw Samian and Aster together. Even when we first met, when Samian chided her about the weather, my heart felt heavy, almost green with envy. I shoved that memory deep down, wishing it would smother.

"What was that light around me when Ambrose was here?" I asked, trying to keep Samian off my mind.

"Hmm?" Aster hummed, distracted. She was still bent over her workstation, but before I could ask again, she said, "It was my healing magic, but it acted as a shield to block Ambrose from sensing your emotions. We needed him to think you were still asleep."

"So, it's true then?" I murmured, silently cursing myself for not paying closer attention. "Ambrose can sense emotions and manipulate them." It was more a statement than a question.

"Yes," she sighed heavily. "It's a power that he usually keeps to himself, even though he uses it pretty often. I'm surprised more haven't caught on to his tricks."

"Is that something I can do? To shield, I mean."

Aster straightened, turning from her work to look at me. She studied me for a moment and shrugged. "I don't see why not. It might take some practice, but learning to shield yourself could protect you from unwanted emotions, among other things. Samian should have taught you that first. I'm not sure why he didn't."

I frowned, remembering that he had mentioned it during our first lesson. We were interrupted, and then the rest of the days became a whirlwind, leaving nothing but chaos in its wake.

I stared down at my hands, searching for my magic, but all I could feel was emptiness. It was like my magic had been extinguished, knowing that if it surfaced, agony would follow.

Aster walked over to me, taking my hand in hers. Closing her eyes, I felt her magic flow through me, its calming warmth felt like mine.

Her mouth twitched, and she opened her eyes a moment later. "Did he give you a command regarding your magic?"

I nodded, looking down to where our hands were linked. She exhaled, pulling her hand away from mine. The sudden withdrawal of her magic sent a shiver down my spine. "Did Samian explain how to feel for your magic?"

"He did, on my first day here."

"Good. While I finish up the lab work, try to feel for your magic. Don't get upset if it takes time. Just keep searching, understood?"

Her tone was stern. She had a severe look that reminded me of a mother scolding a child about to do something stupid. I didn't know if I should laugh or bristle under her steely stare, but I fought against it, knowing that she probably wouldn't find it amusing if I did either.

"Okay," I nodded, not wanting to get on her bad side.

She lifted her nose at me, narrowing her eyes to study me. I gave her a weak smile, and she huffed, returning to her work. I watched her hover over her microscope while I settled onto the bed, closing my eyes.

I took a calming breath, letting my body relax. Searching, I looked for the warmth I had found during my first lesson with Samian. That chain around my heart tightened, ready to snap tight at the first sign of magic stirring. I wavered, my stomach churning from the memory of that ache, how it felt like I was being ripped to shreds, but I pushed through. I took another deep breath, pushing further inside past the barrier that locked my magic away, until I found myself in a small, black, windowless room.

I frowned and put a hand on the blackened wall, wincing. The feel of it was so cold, so glacial, that it burned against my hand. Stepping back, I rubbed at the ache in my chest. The room felt foreign, like it wasn't a part of me. Like it was there to separate me from myself and all that I was.

I breathed in, recalling the warmth that had surrounded me the first time I reached for it, how it coated my skin and seeped into my very core. I pulled that memory closer, letting it grow and take shape.

A crack sounded, echoing through my mind. Looking to my left, a tiny fracture formed along the wall. A small light shone through, though it felt distant. I reached out, running my hand over the crack, feeling the air slipping through. I swallowed, hesitating as the ache from the chain around my heart began to throb. Bracing myself, I reached out again, pushing against that fracture.

The crack grew, the sound echoing through the room. I staggered back a step, my eyes widening as it splintered up the wall and across the ceiling. The breaking stopped, leaving nothing but silence behind. My heart thundered. Then, one final pop sounded, and the room shattered like broken glass. The walls of the room fell around me, evaporating before the pieces ever hit the ground.

Bright light stung my eyes, and I squinted, moving my hand up to shield myself from the sunlight. My eyes adjusted, and I froze, taking in the field of tall grass and wildflowers. The colors were so vivid against the deep blue sky above me. I grinned, feeling the balmy wind circling around me.

My body relaxed, and my magic came surging back, leaving me breathless. I stayed there, my eyes closed, my head tilted back, letting that warmth seep into my very bones until I felt ready to leave, to return to Aster and to Samian.

My eyes fluttered open, and I yelped, finding Samian leaning close to my face. I jerked back, my hand gripping my chest. My heart felt like it was about to beat out of my chest. I cursed, and Samian laughed, retreating to the foot of the bed. I tried to fight it, but my face burned. My soul seemed to purr at his presence, wanting nothing more than to draw him closer.

"How long have you been here?" I breathed, not wanting to dwell too long on that thought. We're skeptical of him, I told myself. Skeptical and wary, nothing more.

"Not too long," Samian grinned as Aster rolled her eyes.

"It's been two hours," Aster answered for him. "I forced him not to disturb you, but when we felt your magic, he couldn't help himself."

"So," Samian pressed, "were you able to find it?"

"If you felt my magic, why ask?" I scowled, crossing my arms, but Samian only stared until I groaned. "Fine. Yes, I was able to find it. It was like I was trapped in this black room, but I recalled the memory of when I first felt my magic. I pictured the field of wildflowers, the sun, how warm it all felt, and then the room fell away. It felt like my magic had come rushing in after that. It was exhilarating."

Aster and Samian's gaze met briefly before returning to me, but before I could ask, Aster stood, handing me a pile of papers. "These are the results of your blood work. It's just as I told you earlier. As of now, you are forty-eight percent fae, though it is steadily increasing."

I stared down at the papers, stunned by the numbers glaring back at me. "Has this ever happened before?" I asked, unease trickling down my spine.

"Yes," Samian answered sheepishly, balking when Aster's lips thinned, and her gray eyes turned to molten steel. "But that's something we will need to discuss *after* we get Ezra out of the dungeons and away from prying ears."

I scoffed, still fighting with myself over whether or not I should give him my trust, though the latter was becoming easier with his *we'll discuss this later* business.

"I agree with Samian," Aster said. Her anger remained written on her face as she eyed him, but her voice softened. "We need to make a plan. Once Ezra is out of the palace, once *we* are out of the palace, we can talk. It will be safer that way."

Samian cringed, but he sent her a look of gratitude. Aster's face remained blank, wholly unimpressed with him and his secrets. Not that I could blame her—I wanted to throttle him for it too. Their heads turned my way, waiting for some type of response. Breathing out a quick *fine*, Samian smiled, bright and wide, making my heart flutter.

Skeptical and wary, I repeated to myself. Skeptical and wary.

Crawling off the bed, I stood, just as Samian disappeared into a puff of smoke. I blinked, looking to Aster, but she stared blankly, her face the picture of boredom, until Samian returned, reappearing the same way he left.

He went straight to the table, unfurling large blueprints of…

I peered closer, narrowing my eyes. It was similar to the palace, but not.

"What, exactly, is this?"

CHAPTER 37
SYBIL

"These are maps," Samian smirked. He looked up, finding two sets of annoyed glares. Clearing his throat, he continued. "They are maps of the old palace and the hidden passageways that still remain." He sighed. "They have *long* been forgotten by most, if not all, here at the palace. I only knew about them because the queen threw me out of her office after I accidentally found these and told me to figure it out myself." Samian smiled softly at the memory, his eyes flickering with a deep sadness. "This is how we are going to get Ezra out of the dungeon unseen."

"And how are we supposed to open the cell door?" Aster asked.

"By using this," Samian said, pulling out a worn metal key from his coat pocket. "This key works on all the cells in the dungeon."

"You just magically have this key with you?" I asked skeptically, pressing my lips into a thin line.

"No, I don't just magically have this key," Samian frowned.

Aster glanced between us, watching us carefully. "It was given to me by the queen."

"The same queen that is on her 'decades-long' trip?" I couldn't help the contempt dripping from my tone. Not when Ambrose hinted the queen was no longer around, and especially not when there was one thing that had become extremely clear to me during my time here: if it sounded too good to be true, it was. Samian's frown deepened, his face hardening. He held my gaze, searching for something that I knew he would not find, not when he kept so much from me. Breaking eye contact, I looked back at the map, studying the different routes. "What are these markings?" I asked, changing the subject.

"The blue marks are entrances, red marks are the exits from the palace, the green lines are the passageways themselves, and the stars are specific areas in the palace that I've used before. This star is the library, this star here, with the dot in the middle, is the medical wing. This star with the line through it is my room."

"And the star with the double lines across from it?" I asked reluctantly.

Samian swallowed, tapping a finger against the table. "That's your room."

My mouth went dry. "You have direct access to these passageways, and no one else knows about them?" The mistrust in my voice must have been strong because Samian stood, his shoulders tensing while the muscle in his jaw feathered. His eyes were colder than I had ever seen them.

"I know the past few days have been a lot for you, Sybil," he said, his voice trembling slightly, like he was trying to control his anger. "But if you want to be a part of this, I need you to trust me. Or at least trust the fact that I'm going to get Ezra out of this palace, no matter what. However, if you can't find even just a *minuscule* amount of trust in me, then you'll sit this one out. I will not allow you to jeopardize this. Understood?"

I held his stare, my stomach churning. Shame ripped through me, but I refused to look away, refused to back down. Samian had a point. He had done so much for me, had protected me when I needed it. I knew he had, even though it made me sick to acknowledge it.

Except for when it really mattered.

I exhaled, shoving the thought aside. It wasn't his fault. Not really—not when he was forced to leave. If anything, it just showed how long Ambrose had been working on his plan to push me into this bargain. Ever since we first met, I realized. He offered me the bargain as soon as we met. Even then, Samian tried to protect me. The shame settled low, growing until it threatened to pull me under.

"Understood," I breathed. He was right. We needed to focus on getting Ezra out. We could talk about this once Ezra was free and out of the palace.

WE SPENT the rest of the night planning and resting. I stayed with Aster in the medical wing while Samian disappeared for hours. He returned with a couple of heavy bags, and then we waited for the next night to fall.

When it was time, we strapped the bags to our backs and made our way through the dark passageways from the medical wing. Sneaking out to the passageway opening was quick and easy, since most of the healers were in their rooms, sleeping.

Samian led the way while Aster followed behind me. Aster was to be the lookout once we left the passageway in the dungeon, while I focused on memorizing the routes in case there was ever a time I needed to use them again.

Once we reached the exit to the dungeon, we waited for the guards to pass. Samian stepped out first, the picture of a graceful warrior, ready for battle. He wore a set of black leathers that showed the powerful muscles hidden by his everyday clothes. It was hard not to stare while Samian peered down the dungeon hall, listening for the other guards. Signaling for me to follow, I stepped through the exit, looking back at Aster. Her face was hard as she nodded to Samian and me.

Samian and I quickly passed by the cells, careful with our steps so as not to alert the guards to our presence. We came up on Ezra's cell, and I kept my focus on Ezra, not wanting to see the cell opposite of his, not wanting to see if my blood still pooled on that stone floor.

Ezra came to the bars, leaning against the cold metal, and I gasped, rushing to him when I saw the fresh bruises and cuts along his face. Seeing me, Ezra smiled, relief washing through him.

"It's about damn time," Ezra growled, looking to Samian.

"I thought I told you to lie low," Samian frowned, inspecting his wounds.

"Eh, they just wanted to get a last good beating after I made their lives hell during training," Ezra chuckled, though he winced from the movement.

Samian unlocked the door, scoffing. The rusted hinges groaned when the door slowly opened, and we cringed at the sound. "Someone might have heard that," he said, his voice edged. "We'll need to take the long way back to the passage. Run fast, but keep watch of where you step. No need to make any unnecessary noise."

Ezra rumbled his agreement, pushing me between him and

Samian. We ran through the dungeons, the halls twisting and turning. We passed a few prisoners who pleaded for us to free them as well, but we kept going, ignoring the way they begged. Regret sliced through me at leaving them behind, but I knew we couldn't risk it. We needed to get Ezra out of here.

Somewhere in the distance, the guards yelled at the prisoners, telling them to keep quiet. Behind me, Ezra muttered something about them, but I stopped listening when I noticed a bright light in one of the cells. Brighter than any of the dimly lit cells we passed. I slowed down as we passed it, my eyes connecting with the woman inside. Her cold, blue eyes were piercing, yet they looked so similar to my father's and brother's. Ezra swore, his voice sounding shocked, but he pushed me, urging me to keep moving forward.

We returned to the entrance of the hidden passageway. Aster's grim face relaxed once she saw us with Ezra. She let out a sigh of relief, clucking her tongue at Ezra. She put a hand on his arm, sending her healing magic into him. I watched as the cuts stitched together, and the bruises faded away into nothing but unmarred skin.

Once he was healed, she removed her hand, and Ezra gave her a wide smile, hauling her into his arms, hugging her tight. Aster swatted Ezra's back, muttering all sorts of curses and the ways she was going to dispose of him if he didn't let her go. I swallowed my laugh while Ezra barked his and gently dropped Aster to her feet.

Aster straightened her ruffled clothes, still muttering those curses while Samian handed Ezra the bag Aster had carried. Ezra's face grew tight when he faced Samian, though he took the bag. I glanced between them, noting the way Samian shook his head, as if to say *not now, later*. I slid my bag onto my back and waited for Samian to put on his, though he avoided looking at me. He led us out of the passageway that brought us out into a field just outside Volmire. The field I ran to, I realized with a start, when I wanted to escape and return home.

I looked to Ezra just in time to see him drop his bag, quickly closing the distance to Samian, grabbing him by his jacket.

"What the fuck was that?" Ezra growled, baring his teeth at Samian.

"What was what, exactly?" Samian responded, keeping his face and voice calm, though tension crept through him.

"The fucking queen, Samian. What was the fucking queen doing in the dungeon?"

My eyes widened. Aster sucked in a breath, and Ezra pushed Samian away, his face pinched with anger.

Samian only sighed, his shoulders dipping. "We are still too close to the palace, still too close for prying ears to hear. We need to get into the forest quickly. Ask me again once we get to where we need to go."

Ezra only sneered, slinging his bag over his shoulder and walking past Samian to the dark forest. Aster, pale and silent, followed behind him.

Samian looked at me, his eyes filled with grief and sorrow. "Ask me again once we are in the forest," he repeated, his voice barely a whisper.

I nodded, but glanced back toward the palace, as if I could still see the woman in the cell, the queen, apparently still alive. She was beautiful, though she had an ancient look about her. I assumed the faeries here were a lot older than they looked, but she *felt* older than the other faeries I'd met. Based on the other cells in the dungeon, hers was the only one that received any light, and the couches and silks that hung along the room felt odd and out of place. It looked like a gilded cage. But the way she looked at me when our eyes met, it was like she knew me.

There was no surprise in her stare, no shock. Only a cool regard shone back at me.

Taking a steady breath, I looked back at Samian. His throat bobbed, guilt rippling along his face, but he turned to the forest, steadily walking to the front of the group. Ezra went rigid when Samian passed him, though he refused to look his way, keeping his focus solely on the trees.

We kept quiet as we walked through the field, not wanting to jinx our success in freeing Ezra. I replayed the route we took over and over in my head, filing it away so I could add it to my own map later. Something told me it was important, especially if I ever needed to return.

We stepped through the thicket into the forest, and a shiver went down my spine. I recognized the trees and rocks that surrounded us from when I ran from the crimson-eyed man. Hugging my arms around me, I kept a close watch on our surroundings. I wasn't sure what else was in the forest, but I could feel their eyes on us. I shivered, my heart pounding in my chest, and I stepped closer to Aster. Mercifully, Aster kept her eyes forward instead of casting me her cold stare and slowed her steps, letting me use her presence to calm my anxiety.

The path we took wove through the forest floor, my breathing heavy from the weight I carried and from the climb of the steep hills. The muscles in my legs were burning when the air turned colder, like a winter storm was about to sweep in on us.

We crossed through a thick wall of trees, stepping into a circular clearing. There were rocks in an odd formation in the center. I looked up, sucking in a breath as crimson eyes locked onto me.

"You," I breathed, my skin feeling too tight.

My head whipped to Samian. My mouth popped open, and

shock rolled through me. I stammered, looking back to the man, his intense stare never breaking away from me. His eyes were heated, and he smirked. Finally, his eyes flicked to Ezra, and his smile faded as he took in Ezra's tall, powerful frame. He moved his stare to Aster, swept past her, and landed on Samian.

"This is more than we agreed on," he said, his voice deep and deadly. The air around us grew heavy and still, reminding me of the moments right before a storm.

"I had no other choice," Samian said flatly. "There were some developments that occurred after I responded to your letter." Samian paused, avoiding my stare completely. "Ezra and Aster are two of my informants. Aster is the one who creates the medicine I give to you and has supported your cause for a while now. She is safe for the time being and will return with me to the palace. Ezra, however, cannot. He has been found guilty of aiding a rebel and has been sentenced to death."

Samian finally met my wide eyes. I could feel the blood draining from my face. I knew how adamant he was about getting Ezra out, but I didn't realize…

Samian looked back at the man and continued. "He was Ambrose's war general and led a unit with Commander Fenleth. His knowledge will be useful to you, if you allow him into the camp, that is."

The man narrowed his eyes, folding his arms over his powerful chest as he considered. But his eyes slid back to me, his head lifting in the air. "And Sybil?" he asked, the rasp of his voice making me gasp.

Goosebumps ran down my arms. The man knew my name. Did he know when we met earlier? He obviously knew Samian by the way they were speaking, or at least familiar enough that they knew of the other. My body grew tight, apprehension crawling down my spine.

"She stays with me," Samian growled, his voice low and threatening.

I could hardly breathe. The pressure in the air felt thin. Samian and the man stared each other down as the air grew more violent. Vines from the surrounding trees crept closer, readying to strike. Someone cleared their throat from behind the man, and two figures stepped out of the shadows. A woman with pale skin, and the man from the village that Arianna confronted. His golden eyes looked as if they glowed in the darkness. They moved to the rocks beside the man and waited. I eyed them, my stomach twisting.

The air moved then, returning to the heavy presence from moments ago, and the vines eased back. Samian still watched him, though the threat in his eyes was no longer there. The crimson-eyed man tilted his head, considering Samian's words. Minutes passed while everyone remained silent. Samian tapped a finger on the hilt of the dagger at his hip. Annoyance showed on his face when the man finally nodded and made his way to us. He stepped in front of Ezra, studying him. Ezra pulled his shoulders back, standing to his full height. He was taller than the man by several inches, but he didn't back down. Instead, his smile turned sharp, and he stretched out his arm, offering his hand to Ezra.

Ezra returned the smile and gripped the man's hand, though I could see the relief flooding through him. His tension leaked away, and the tight lines along his face eased.

The man looked at me then, his stare heating as it dipped to my lips, moving down until it landed on my wrist and the black bands wrapped around them. I swallowed, moving my hands behind my back, my face heating with guilt and shame.

"And you?" he murmured, his gaze feeling penetrating.

"And I, what?" I asked, swallowing as heat coiled inside me.

"Are you going to help us?" he said, cocking his head to the side.

I lifted my nose in the air, bracing myself. I never gave myself time to consider such a thing. I didn't even know that was a possibility, not after Arbus or the villager.

I looked at Samian, his body stiff. "This is Kieran," he said carefully. "He is the leader of the rebels and my oldest friend."

I looked back at the man, his eyes nearly glowing. A vicious smile curved along his lips at the shock rippling through me. It made sense now, the reason why Samian hated Ambrose so much, the odd way he spoke about the queen, how he seemed to know more than he was letting on. Samian was working against Ambrose, collaborating with the rebels. He was the cause of the recent failings of Ambrose's armies that I heard whispers of, the *rat* that Ambrose seemed to be searching for.

"So?" Kieran purred.

I inhaled, pulling my shoulders back. "I'll help."

His eyes grew brighter, and something like pride filled them. "Then welcome, Sybil, to the rebellion."

CITY OF SHADOW AND BONE

AN EXCLUSIVE SNEAK PEAK FOR THE NEXT INSTALLMENT OF THE MATES OF GODS AND FAE SERIES

SYBIL

"Then welcome, Sybil, to the rebellion." Kieran purred, his crimson eyes bright and filled with pride.

The rebels.

I'm now part of the rebellion that Ambrose fought to squash daily.

My lips tugged into a smile, something like pride swelling inside me so big that my heart felt light and heavy at the same time. If Ambrose caught me, no amount of torture would be enough to stop his horrible punishment.

I held Kieran's crimson stare, studying how his eyes darkened, as if he was taunting me—begging for some darker part of me to come out and play. A shiver went down my spine, and I looked away; the heat behind his gaze was too intense.

Samian caught his look and let out a low growl of warning, the sound rumbling from deep in his chest, one that Kieran readily returned. Samian stepped in front of me, blocking me from view. I could only see the braid of his silver hair, shining bright under the soft moonlight, but the muscles along his back were tense.

The pale woman beside Kieran sighed and clapped her hands. "Okay, boys, that's enough posturing for now. It seems like there is much we need to discuss, and I, for one, would like to go somewhere more comfortable to talk." She slid her dark gray eyes to Ezra, giving him an icy stare. "Are you truly asking for sanctuary?"

"Yes," Ezra said with a slight nod. "I was given the death penalty for helping you, actually." He jerked his chin at the man standing behind her.

The man gave him a small bow, though his face remained blank.

"Then we welcome you," she said, inclining her head to Ezra. "Let's leave these woods. There are creatures roaming tonight."

Each of them turned to head further into the forest. "Wait," I said, grabbing hold of Samian's shirt. "Before I blindly follow wherever they are taking us, I want to know *how* you know this man."

"Male," Kieran said, his voice deepening, his lips curving into a wicked smile.

My gaze cut to his, my brows knitting together in confusion. "What?"

"I am not a man. That word belongs to humans, not faeries. *I* am a male." His gaze bore into me, and I took a steadying breath. I could feel the pressure in my blood rising with annoyance.

"Fine," I quipped, scowling at him as I turned back to Samian. "How do you—"

"Say it," Kieran smirked.

I looked back at him, my eyes narrowing. "Say what?"

"Say what I am."

"For fuck's sake," I whispered, earning a deep laugh from the vexing brute. "Fine," I turned back to Samian. "How do you know this *male*?"

Samian's lip twitched, amusement dancing in his eyes as he fought the grin pulling at the corners of his mouth. "We met long ago, when I was a boy. His father was a farmer, and I ate some apples from one of his trees. As punishment, I had to help Kieran pick the rest of the apples."

Kieran chuckled at the memory.

"He is safe," Samian murmured softly. "I promise he will not hurt you. I would not let him, even if he tried. However, I know where they are leading us. We won't be harmed."

I looked into his blue and green eyes, studying them, and found nothing but hopeful promise, as if being here with him was something he had wanted for so long. Finally, looking over at the woman—female—I gave her a tight nod.

Bowing her head to me, they turned, leading us further into the forest.

With the moon full and high overhead, it wasn't hard for my eyes to adjust to the low light, enough to see the rocks and branches scattered across the mossy floor. We traveled along a small path that was barely noticeable unless you knew what to look out for, though after twenty minutes of walking, I still couldn't tell what they used for markers.

Samian stayed at the front of our group, keeping me close while we accompanied Kieran and the other male and female. Aster stayed a step behind me, followed by Ezra. Everyone was quiet, save for the crunching of the leaves beneath our feet.

The path led us to a rusted gate covered in vines, which groaned as the doors swung open. Huts and tents were scattered across the field beyond. Aster and I slowed our walk, our wide eyes taking in the different faeries walking around bonfires, laughing with each other.

Ezra murmured a curse, his head whipping to Samian, who only gave him a small apologetic smile. Guilt shadowed Samian's face, and his throat bobbed. Apparently, he had kept secrets from everyone.

Hearing the gate open, a wave of silence washed through the camp. The faeries tensed at Ezra's presence. To Ezra's benefit, he only followed Kieran, ignoring their cold, hardened stares. I watched him walk past us, his body rigid but standing tall. Aster and I glanced at each other, cringing. Staying in this camp would not be easy for Ezra—not when he had been working for the palace as Ambrose's war general for so long.

Placing her hand behind my back, Aster gently nudged me to follow the group toward a rundown estate that was smaller than the Marble Palace but still large enough to be fit for a king. Made from stacked gray stones, the manor was covered in purple wisteria vines that crawled along the arches and across the walls. My mouth gaped open, taking in its antiquated beauty.

We walked through large doors with flowers carved along their edges and entered a grand foyer. The vines had crept inside along the ceiling, aged with time. Dust clung to the broken furniture and the framed art along the walls, though the rest of the manor seemed partially clean—clean enough that it made me wonder how many lived within its walls now.

Samian's soft chuckle caught my attention, and I turned my head toward him. He reached out his hand and, though I hesitated, I took it, letting his smooth fingers wrap around mine. Something in my soul surged at his soft touch, and my eyes burned when he interlaced our fingers, pulling me in close and tucking me to his side. "This used to be the royal manor before the forest moved, blocking access to it."

The forest… "What do you mean, the forest moved?" I asked hesitantly.

Samian let out a breathy laugh that sent heat curling through me. "There's a reason I told you to be careful of the forest. It's alive and moves wherever it desires. It can easily ensnare anyone close enough to hear its call, though we aren't sure why. Just that most of those trapped by its song are never seen again."

I shuddered and leaned into Samian's warmth, letting his presence keep me steady. After Ambrose tricked me into the bargain, I didn't realize that when I went to the forest. I couldn't help but wonder what would have happened if the beithir hadn't snapped me out of my trance that day. My stomach churned at the thought.

Aster walked past us, her eyes going straight to where Samian and my hands were linked. I sucked in a breath and quickly stepped away from Samian, finding a painting along the wall to focus on. I silently cursed myself for allowing him that close, for feeling the way I did, especially when they were involved. Though 'involved' didn't seem like the right word. They were close, but Samian never hinted at how close.

Aster's soft footsteps moved on, following Kieran to wherever he was leading us. Samian stood still, releasing a slow breath before he moved behind me, close enough for me to feel his warmth again.

"I'm sorry," I murmured, keeping my focus on the blue and gold swirls of the painting.

"For what?" Samian said softly.

"I know you two—I didn't mean to give her the wrong impression." Guilt licked up my spine, and I closed my eyes, pushing away the image of Samian wrapping his arms around my waist. Of him pulling me in, my back flush against him.

He lied. He kept secrets from me, from everyone, I reminded myself again. And Aster—think of Aster.

"Ah, right," Samian exhaled, his voice strained. "Come, we don't want to fall behind."

The disappointment coloring his words kept me from moving. Was he upset that I'd pulled away from him? Or that Aster had seen us? I listened to his footsteps retreating as he followed the others. Tilting my head back, my shoulders sagged as I eyed the vines snaking along the ceiling. Once Samian was far enough away, I finally turned and followed, walking into a long stone hallway with several closed doors.

The others filed into a room a few doors down, while Kieran stood by the entrance, waiting. Keeping his face blank, his eyes raked down my body and back up again, taking his time until our gazes clashed. Fighting the way my blood pulsed under his perusal, I sneered at him, earning a smirk and a low laugh.

"Come now, Princess," he said, his tone playful. "You don't want to be late for your first meeting, do you?"

"Don't call me that," I grumbled, rolling my eyes as I entered the room.

A dark, sensual laugh was his only response.

The room was small, with a large circular table in the middle, covered with papers and maps. Several seats were arranged around it, with more chairs lined along the walls. Cabinets and an armoire sat in the far-left corner, while linen curtains blocked the two windows on the opposite side.

"Well, Princess?" Kieran murmured, his breath tickling my ear.

I inhaled sharply, stepping away from him with a hiss.

Chuckling, he gestured to the table—a request for me to take my seat.

Looking at the table, Samian pulled out a chair beside him, but I turned away, pretending not to notice, and sat in the empty chair next to the pale female. She arched an eyebrow as I slid into the seat, but I kept my eyes glued to the surface, picking at a scratch in the wood. Heat crept up my neck, and I could have sworn the table rippled like water under my touch.

Kieran took his place on the opposite side. Two empty chairs sat on either side of him, a clear sign he was indeed the leader of this rebellion.

"I believe introductions are in order, Samian," Kieran said pointedly, jerking his chin toward the rest of the group.

"Right," Samian said, straightening in his chair.

He began by introducing Ezra first, giving Kieran and the others a brief account of what happened, though I didn't hear a word. Instead, I used this time to study Kieran, letting my gaze trail down his tanned arms to his hands, which were covered in small white scars. I dragged my eyes to his face. His squared jaw was sharp, like it had been chiseled from marble. His midnight-black hair was shorter, the tips barely covering the delicate points of his ears. But his eyes, those dark red eyes, shone bright in the light of the room, stealing the breath from my lungs.

"Do you like what you see?" Kieran's raspy voice echoed in my head. I jerked my gaze away, my face blanching. I could hear his laughter, feel the rumble of it along my skin, though no one noticed. No one could hear.

My heart raced inside my chest, and I dared another glance.

"If you keep doing that, Samian is going to jump out of his seat."

I swallowed and looked over at Samian. His lips were

pressed thin, his eyes locked on Kieran, and shining with anger. I turned to Ezra, finally noticing he was speaking to the group.

"Good, keep your eyes on the general, though, try not to look so disappointed." Kieran purred.

A delicate hand covered my own, causing me to flinch. The female's soft ivory fingers curled around mine while she watched Aster speak. Once Aster finished, the female threw a pointed glare at Kieran, as if she knew what he was doing and was reprimanding him. She turned to me then; her round gray eyes reminded me of the glass marbles I used to keep as a child. Warm and striking, they crinkled slightly as she introduced herself.

"My name is Vivian, though you can call me Vivi," she said, her voice soft. "I'm Kieran's second-in-command." She tucked a lock of honey-blonde hair behind her ear. I watched the movement, surprise rippling through me when I saw her long, pointed ear—longer than the other faeries I've seen.

"Ah, yes." She said, noticing my stare. "I'm not a faerie. I belong to the Elven clan in the Seelie Courts."

"The Seelie Courts?"

Samian cleared his throat. "We can explain that in a moment. It will make more sense when you learn more about our history."

I looked back at Vivi to see if she agreed. Giving me a soft smile, she waved a hand to the male beside her, his golden eyes so otherworldly.

"This is Orin. I believe you met him the other day in Lowbrook."

Orin inclined his head and grinned. His hair was twisted in small locs and pulled back behind his rounded ear. "I'm Kieran's third-in-command."

"Are you…human?" I asked warily, pointing to his ear.

Orin flashed a bright, wide smile and huffed a laugh. "No, I'm not human. I'm a gryphon—a shapeshifter. I'm not faerie, nor am I part of the Seelie Court. My kind came from the deserts of Mide, but we followed the Fae and Seelie Courts to Nemos once the realms were separated."

"Ah, so gryphon…like the bird-lion animal?"

Kieran barked a laugh, and my face heated, but Orin only smiled, "Yes, something like that."

I pulled in a shaky breath, glancing at everyone around the room. Samian gave me a book on the creatures of Nemos, though I never had enough time to study it as I should have. I felt ridiculous sitting there, clueless about this world, unsure why I thought there were only different types of faeries here.

My eyes landed on Samian, who looked somber as he watched me closely. "Tell me what I'm missing."

Samian shook his head. "You have to ask me specific questions," he said, his voice tight.

"And why do we have to do that?" Ezra growled, his anger finally surfacing.

Samian held Ezra's heated glare while his thumb rubbed against the ring on his middle finger. Steeling himself, Samian took off his ring. Beautiful and intricate black lines laced around his finger—the mark of a bargain.

ACKNOWLEDGMENTS

First and foremost, thank you to everyone who has read this book! Writing has been my lifelong dream, and if my seven-year-old self could see me now, she would be running around the playground screaming with pure joy and excitement. The amount of support that I have received from everyone has been absolutely amazing, and I appreciate every single one of you!

To my editor, Hilari Cohen, thank you for your words of wisdom. You not only helped make my messy draft into something beautiful, but you also guided me through this crazy publishing world.

To my fiancé, Brian, thank you so much for being my rock. Without your support and encouragement, this book would have never happened. I love you, and I couldn't ask for a better partner in life.

To my best friend and sister, Cynthia, you are so amazing. From helping me with my cover to your never-ending support and excitement, your words and love mean so much to me. I don't know where I would be in life without you.

To my girl, Sam, words are not enough to show my appreciation for you! Thank you for being the first person to read my messy drafts and for being so patient with my nonstop texts about book ideas.

To my sweet Jackie, your support means everything to me. Thank you for reading all the messy drafts I've sent your way.

You've always hyped me up, made me feel like I could achieve anything, and I can't thank you enough.

To all my friends and family who have stayed with me through this journey, thank you. Caroline, Kyung, Johnny, Jessica, Boone, Andee, Caitlin, Allyx, Gary, Michael, Cindy, all of my ARC readers, and my TikTok/Instagram family, there are no words to express how grateful I am.

TRIGGER WARNING LIST

- Abandonment
- Body Shaming
- Discrimination
- Dubious consent
- Emotional Abuse
- Forced Imprisonment
- Manipulation
- Mental Abuse
- Murder
- Open-Door Romance
- Physical Abuse
- Torture
- Trauma
- Violence

PRONUNCIATIONS

- Amara (ah-MAH-ruh)
- Ambrose Farra (AM-brose FAR-ruh)
- Arbus (ahr-bus)
- Arianna (ah-ree-Ah-nah)
- Aster (AS-ter)
- Bryony (BRY-uh-nee)
- Cassia (CAS-see-uh)
- Dryden (DRY-duhn)
- Dubnos (DUB-no-s)
- Edris (ed-rees)
- Evander (ee-VAN-der)
- Ezra (Ehz-ruh)
- Hale (HHEY-L)
- John (j-AA-n)
- Kieran (KEE-er-in)
- Liam (LEE-um)
- Lowbrook (low-br-ook)
- Mide (ME-dae)

- Nemos (NE-moh-s)
- Orin (OR-in)
- Samian (Say-mi-un)
- Silas Tuluin (SY-les Tuh-lu-lin)
- Sybil (SIB-uhl)
- Vivi (Vee-Vee)
- Volmire (VUL-mi-ear)
- Zarina (za-ree-na)

About the Author

M.B. Atkins is a fantasy and romance indie author who lives just outside Raleigh, North Carolina. When she isn't writing and creating new worlds (or plotting scenes on colorful sticky notes), you can usually find her reading anything she can get her hands on, crocheting, spending time with her partner, or playing with her three cats—Iris, Freya, and Finn—and her melodramatic border collie, Bella.

Subscribe to her newsletter for updates on the *Mates of Gods and Fae* series!

Facebook: facebook.com/m.b.atkinsauthor
Instagram: m.b.atkinsauthor
TikTok: m.b.atkinsauthor
Website: www.mbatkins.com

www.ingramcontent.com/pod-product-compliance
Lightning Source LLC
Chambersburg PA
CBHW060814310726
48980CB00002B/303